FOLLIES, FO  S

G000090252

Follies, Fools, and Garla nd
manipulation. It is also ˰ ˰˰˰˰˰˰˰˰ ˰ove story. The central
actions of the novel take place during the Cold War of the 1960s,
and in a society where upper-class values of the gentry begin to
lose their place to the upwardly mobile *nouveau riche.*

Anthony Ashley-Chetwyne, narrator and 'son of the privileged',
joins the legal profession. Whilst a young barrister he becomes
engaged as a junior to an experienced QC in a case of espionage;
a member of the House of Commons has been selling secrets
to Czechoslovak agents in London. That involvement connects
him to behind-the-scene security and intelligence issues and a
variety of characters involved in those classified worlds. These
include 'Miss K', as she is first known, whose work with the
security service crosses Anthony's path both professionally and
personally. In that service she connects also with William, a friend
of Anthony's from Oxford days. Both she and William are posted
to Prague, William with a mission to 'turn' a senior member of
the Czech state security, hers of a very different nature.

There are surprising twists of narrative and a cast of authentic
characters to capture the reader's imagination. Told with wit and
humour, the novel as a whole explores themes of deception, lies,
secrets, and the concealments of its characters within both their
personal and public lives. Whilst probing the edges of the spy
thriller, this is a novel concerned above all with the complexities
and duplicities of relationships within the febrile nature of trust.

**"*Follies, Fools, and Garlands* is a wonderful story, an
exquisite satire, beautifully told."**

Ron Smith, author and former publisher.

E.C.Gardiner

FOLLIES, FOOLS, AND GARLANDS

To Joan,
Lute Best Wishes,
E.C. Gardiner

The lasses of Chester-le-Street,
Are bonny, and loving, and sweet.
I've heard this is so,
But of course I don't know
I've never been ~~been~~ offered that treat.

ELM VILLAGE ARTS

London

ELM VILLAGE ARTS
London
www.elmvillagearts.co.uk

First published in Great Britain 2019
Revised 2nd edition June 2019

Paperback ISBN: 978-1-9160457-2-9

Formatting and cover design by
Bhavnish Kanojia: *Digital Design*

ELM VILLAGE ARTS
Elm Village, London NW1 0BQ

ONE

Eheu fugaces...

Prague

1999

NOTES

StB: *Státní bezpečnost* (Czech), *Štátna bezpečnost* (Slovak) – Czechoslovakian state security service.

Whilst commonly referred to as the Home Office, the Home Department of Government remains its formal title and continues to be referred to as such in official, including parliamentary, reports. Similarly the Home Secretary's formally correct title is Her Majesty's Secretary of State for the Home Department. In these memoirs the narrator, of his time and as a barrister, is being formally precise rather than perversely precious.

'You haven't! Anthony, *please* tell me that we are not staying *here*.'

For a few seconds there was a look of distress, or embarrassment, and rebuke.

Finally Susan had agreed to make this journey before the twentieth century was out. Now, in the year before the new millennium was falsely ushered in throughout the world a year ahead of itself, here we were. We had arrived, thirty years after she had left this city and just over ten years since she and I had met each other again.

On the last leg of our travel we had enjoyed the late spring sunshine of May throughout the taxi trip from Ruzyně airport into the city. My companion had remained silent throughout the ride, her face turned to the side, close to the window. In her silence I sensed an increasing tenseness as we reached the outskirts of Prague. After so many years between leaving and her return I was still unsure how she would respond to being brought back here. It was at my repeated pleading, after all, that she had relented.

'For you, then. Just for you.'

I had reached for her hand which she had let rest, inert, in mine.

Outside the square, heavy block of the *Jalta* hotel, looking up to its façade of matt cream-grey slabs of marble, Susan slowly shook her head. When in the foyer of the hotel, as I attended to the checking-in, she cast her eyes around, taking in the glossy interior that could belong to any international hotel in any city.

'On the second floor, wasn't it?'

But she was distracted. I had to move close to her, holding out the key to our room.

'Second floor. The one you shared with Arnold. As near as one can tell, anyway.'

There was a delay, then a wan smile, together with a gentle elbowing at my ribs as she connected with my attempt to make humour of her stay here all those years ago.

'But you have to admit that the way Arnold tells it, even at the time it must have been really amusing.'

Susan drew herself up into a duchess-like *hauteur*.

'Of course having myself had the pleasure – if that is the word – of hearing Arnold's re-telling of events, I can assure you – '

'That nothing happened.'

'Correct.' At which Susan could no longer hold a straight face. 'Mind you, I do have to say he was a terrible actor, absolutely terrible, so, yes, much to his discredit, I had to do it for both of us. He was quite incapable – '

'Of pleasing the lady?'

At which she gave me this time a full-bloodedly sharp dig in the ribs with an elbow. 'Of acting the part. In fact he found the whole thing so absurdly funny that he started to giggle, actually *giggle* and I had to put my hand over his mouth. Too much of that silliness would have sounded rather out of place, somewhat at odds – '

'With love-making?'

'With what was *supposed* to be going on. Yes, *that.*' Said in a contrived dismissiveness of tone as if at such a distasteful subject. 'And not much of a compliment either to a lady who was doing her best under such difficult circumstances.' There was a flash of eyes intended to banish any further bantering. 'More importantly, he would have given the game away. Don't forget we already knew from Arnold's young woman about the listening device in his room, and we were very well aware of the StB listeners and their tape recorders in the basement. Which is why we had to produce that charade in the first place.' She narrowed her eyes. 'We had to leave them in no doubt of Arnold's adultery.'

'With you, night after night – '

'For as many nights as we had to keep up the charade. To ensure that Arnold and his StB lover were not connected.'

There was a finality to the tone of those words, so that I desisted from further teasing.

I knew that Susan's brief in this city tasked her to keep a watchful eye on certain persons whilst doing her best to avoid being watched herself. Among those certain persons was one of high importance who warranted special attention. I knew of this man's subsequent spiriting into England. Once installed as our guest he had proved to be, in the casual phrase used at the time, 'very useful indeed'. I was among those who had a few questions for him. He had been able to confirm a good deal of information on a case of espionage we had been preparing to take to trial. He surprised us greatly, however, with the name of a serving Minister of State who was acting as an agent for Czechoslovakia. Until then he had escaped all suspicion.

There was another man in this city for some of the period that Susan was here. William, who called me friend, was also on assignment: helping that same senior Czech security officer finally to make up his mind and defect from Czechoslovakia and the StB.

William had been selected for this task of persuasion simply *because* he was William; of how he was perceived to be. Unknowingly, it was my assumptions about the man, whom I first knew at Oxford, which had led to him being sent here many weeks ahead of Susan. Later I learned the truth of the man and knew myself to have been fooled.

Susan spoke but little of her years here. Perhaps – the breath of a hint – there had been an StB officer with whom she formed a 'liaison', one she seduced in the line of duty to keep him quiet and, as her lover, to make it more difficult for him to betray her.

I do not *know*; I did not ask. There was an unspoken accord of silence over how one had served the service. In any case, at our re-meeting I was of an age when the little green god with the flashing eyes, who formerly invaded both dreams and daylight of my youthful insecurities, had lost his potency.

As we waited by the lift in the foyer of the *Jalta* hotel Susan's look dissolved into one that might have been taken as faint puzzlement but which, with her, betokened an ineradicable and habitual sadness. I recognised that abstracted look and knew that, unbidden and suddenly, she had been taken back to some fifteen years ago when her husband had died. Just for a few seconds the widow's hands shook slightly as she part-raised them from where they hung at her sides. As she did so, her eyes glanced swiftly to each side, a customary small gesture which recalled her to the present. Then there would be a small widening of her lips in embarrassed acknowledgement that one had noticed her abstraction.

Sometimes the small parting of her lips would broaden into the most welcoming of smiles. It was a smile shaped as though meeting one for the first time. At our actual first encounter, Susan's smile of greeting had briefly hinted at a door into a possible shared future. That door had too soon slammed shut.

Eheu fugaces... Alas the fleeting years: that small fragment from an adolescent classroom repeats echo-like in the chamber of my recollections. For Susan and I had failed to enter that alternative future we might have shared in place of the separate directions which we did take. Thirty-three years ago there had been a glimpse – in the most clichéd of expressions – that 'things might have been different.' But circumstances can be our dictators. They change events, foreclose options, open others, sometimes confuse one, their nature seemingly unclear, or misunderstood, at the time.

Susan turned to me, now, with that smile – from those lost decades – which had first captivated me and tripped me over into love with her when I was presumed to be in love with another woman. Presumed by all, that is, except Susan, an expert interpreter of one's hesitations.

Once in our room, Susan lay on the bed for a rest. I bent over her and kissed her on the forehead.

'You go!' she said. 'I know – you told me, that promise you made to yourself.' Then 'Go,' more gently. She understood.

In the late afternoon soft sunshine I found what I was looking for: a token from the past – the beer that would be the first drink I would have on this visit to the Czech Republic. I sat at a small round table with a large glass and took a mouthful. Then, a longer draught of the beer, cold on tongue and back of throat, closing my eyes, savouring the taste; recalling my first glass of this brew given me by the father of the woman I was about to become engaged to be married to. But there was another reason why that door clanged shut on Susan and me with a resounding echo. And that was my failure to conceal my reaction to the revelation Susan once made to me; the secret to which she made me guardian; a secret I have guarded all the years since. Circumstances... what was it my nanny used to intone? Something about *If all the world were ifs and buts...*

Following Susan's extended stay in this city, then her marriage, the death of her husband, not until more than three years of widowhood had passed would the widow allow herself to be persuaded that it was acceptable for her to accept other male companionship. Alas...

Eheu fugaces, Postume, Postume,
Labuntur anni nec pietas moram...

Unwilled, the remaining lines of the stanza from that *Ode* of Horace suddenly also broke through and presented themselves to me as I savoured the beer again. I spoke them out in my head. *Alas the fleeting years, Postumus... piety can not delay wrinkles and old age and unconquerable death.* William, friend and traitor, would have been surprised at my recall. Even then, at an age when one should have been well beyond such petty thoughts, I wished he had been alongside me at that moment of remembering. I would have enjoyed throwing at him on the heights of his erudition this small pebble of recollected learning.

Somehow those words must have lodged inert in my mind awaiting their awakening in my advancing years, their meaning lying in wait for me to catch up with it, to age into its significance. And now to understand what the ignorance of youth failed to comprehend, because youth must have its days and old age is, whilst living one's youth, an inconceivable distance into the future. Certainly, now, I could not plead the ignorance of youth for lack of understanding. Doubtless mine was not the most poetic of translations, still a schoolboy attempt, but it prompted me to turn my hand over in that Prague bar, palm flat on the table, veins prominent, skin a parchment of creases.

Eheu fugaces... Alas the fleeting years...

~ **2** ~

Those fleeting years became decades of two separate lives. Constant partners, now, when first those two lives re-converged Susan and I became occasional companions only. Later we became lovers. The year in which we had first lain contentedly alongside each other was the same year that Czechoslovakia, as with other East European states, effectively achieved independence from its Soviet masters. Three years later, after a marriage of some seventy-four years, the country divided itself in the mutual divorce of Slovakia and the Czech Republic.

'But don't you want to go there yourself to see the changes?'

The question, repeatedly, I had put to Susan until, finally, a few weeks ago, she had relented, and agreed to this trip.

A compact she sealed with an unenthusiastic kiss. Then had added, as she pulled away: 'And to celebrate your birthday.'

Susan did see the changes.

'Of course none of this' – she waved her arm loosely to sweep both flanks of Wenceslas Square – 'I mean, you can see it's the same place, the same buildings more or less... ' She gave up on the attempt.

We both looked back, from the monument to Saint Wenceslas, along the broad, dipping enclave of the square lined on both sides with shops selling expensive tourist gifts, designer clothes and handbags, jewellery and watches, crystal glassware and the like, restaurants, all the trappings of a modern European city.

There was something else.

'It's as if, I don't know if this will make sense... it's as if the sky somehow doesn't press down on the city in the same way. So heavily.' She was shaping to say more. Lifting her hands: 'Like a blanketing of the light because one *felt* heavy here, weighed down. Oppressed.'

Indeed, today, the sky was a bright, light blue, almost cloudless and there was a suffusing warmth to the air.

Her arm in mine, guiding me, we moved on towards the National Museum, to a space a little way from the foot of one of the twin sets of steps. Susan stood at the small memorial to Jan Palach, the young philosophy student who set fire to himself in protest at the Soviet troops' occupation of the country.

'I was here at the time, of course.'

We looked down at the bronze cross of the memorial designed to appear fused into the wave of cobblestones to which it was fixed.

'And in the crowd for his funeral.' Head down, she added: 'Then just weeks later, Jan Zajíc too.'

Susan pointed to the left-hand arm of the cross. I bent down to read the simple inscriptions of names and dates.

'Such young men.' Susan tightened her grip on my arm. 'And to think, just months after this' – her eyes still downcast to the memorial bronze – 'there were men on the moon. Somehow it makes all this...' She gave up on the thought that tried to bring together two irreconcilable thoughts.

We toured the city. Susan strolled me through the tower entrance to Charles Bridge. Not far onto the bridge itself, she led me by the hand to the first of the sculptures to our left.

'This one's for you, Anthony.'

I looked up.

'Saint Ivo. Patron saint of lawyers.'

I knew the name, but not the history or how many centuries ago the man had lived and practised and been canonised.

'And of the poor.'

The saint, books held in one hand, with his other was reaching out. Below him was a group composition: an old man, a child, and a mother with an infant in her arms.

Susan made me take a few steps to view the group from another angle.

'Ah, yes. Justice, no less.' I recognised the figure.

An allegorical form, blindfolded, holding scales and a sword. Female, and facing away from all the others in the group.

At the far side of the bridge we found a place for lunch. After a small platter of cheeses and salad I ordered beers, to delay us. Somehow I hoped that our location this side of the river might suggest a detour Susan would not refuse.

'We can take our time.' I motioned vaguely to the road behind me.

Susan just shook her head, not comprehending, then suspicion overtaking her blankness.

'Perhaps we could go via Thunovská street?'

Susan turned to me, her lips compressed. Slowly she relaxed and her mouth assumed its usual lines. She nodded slightly in unenthusiastic indulgence of my wish; or whim.

'But only because it's your birthday tomorrow. And did you know, by the way, you share the date with Saint Ivo's Feast Day?' Susan narrowed her eyes and leant towards me across the table. 'It is also the day on which he died. So...' Pause. 'Be careful what else you ask for.'

We walked a small distance until, leading off from a street on another short rise of its own, we faced the entrance to the British Embassy building. We stopped in the cobblestoned street, Susan's arm through mine, leaning against me.

I disengaged my arm, unslung my camera from around my neck, and began to take it from its case.

'Susan...'

Susan turned to me, looked at the camera, looked up the slight incline to the Embassy entrance, and turned her face full on to me.

'No, Anthony, please no.'

I crumpled my face. 'Please Susan, just to please me.'

'Oh Anthony.' But said with that distinctive tone which meant that, however reluctantly, she would pander to another of my whims. 'I was very young then. And flexible. Not with this dodgy knee I have now.'

The photograph which I took that day sits in its wooden frame on the desk in my study. Each time Susan comes into the room she turns the photograph face down. For me, looking at that image of a woman approaching sixty, I can see a young woman in her twenties, stepping lightly towards the Embassy entrance. Her right hand mimes the raising of a hat, her head to the side. She is smiling brightly as if for the camera of the duty officers of the Czechoslovakian security service formerly concealed behind the small doorway of a facing building.

At dinner, aided by a strong Moravian red wine, we bandied names and exchanged impressions from our different perspectives until she fell silent. Her head slightly lowered, her eyes raised and lower lip sucked in, she was obviously formulating something.

'And William?'

Susan twisted the stem of her wine glass to and fro.

'For a long time you kept us away from him – once you and I, you know... Why *was* that?'

Ah yes, William. When Susan and I had met up again, then 'got together' – to translate Susan's 'you know' – it was perfectly true that I had tried to keep us away as much as possible from William and from Carolyne, his wife and my former fiancée-to-be. Invitations to meet for this or that event had increased once Carolyne knew that Susan and I had become more or less a couple.

Finally I ran out of reasons to keep us apart. On our first acceptance and despite turning up with another woman on my arm, Carolyne persisted in the belief that I was still in love with Carolyne. Her faith in the fidelity of my love for her was unshakeable.

When we did meet as two couples William remained remote, almost shyly withdrawn. It was unlike him and I was puzzled why he kept his distance from Susan. Susan knew, but had not told me; and would not tell me until our last evening in this city.

Susan got on well with Carolyne, however. She liked her; she liked her animation, her enthusiasms, her energy, her wholeheartedness. Despite her capacity to deceive, there was also a kind of archless innocence to Carolyne. She took to Susan because, I am convinced, she could then see for herself what she had determined herself to see: that Susan had not invaded my special sanctuary reserved, as Carolyne had to think, for Carolyne. Susan, on the other hand, could see for herself that she was neither a substitute for nor a copy of Carolyne and it was her own difference which had prompted me to love her.

Susan was still playing with her wine glass, still seeking a simple answer to her question. Why *had* I kept us away from William for so long? The fact of his betrayal had ceased to matter years ago.

'Was it perhaps because you still hadn't forgiven him?'

I made a non-committal gesture.

Susan pressed. 'I still don't know what to make of the man. His appearance is still quite... well, *striking.*'

'A sham, my dear, all a sham.' I had William's confession and his treachery – as I had thought of it at the time – as evidence. 'Believe me, William was not really...'

'Was not really what?' Susan's eyes began a mischievous crinkling at their corners.

'Was not what one took him for.'

'Precisely. That's what I'm trying to say. Susan withdrew her hand, ran a finger around the rim of her glass. 'You should know. You've known him for longer than anyone else. You and he go back together to your Oxford days.'

'Well, yes – '

'So, my dear Anthony, what exactly, *would* you say about William?'

TWO

⌒

Pupillage

Oxford and London

1957 - 1965

~ **3** ~

Susan was not the only one who could not decide what to make of William. Though I had known him from his days of sartorial pomp, the truth of the man had evaded me. Now, patrician and erect, as befits a Knight of the Realm with his accumulated honours, William is both sober and sombre. His mind, however, is undiminished – and, really, though his flamboyance instantly attracted attention in those earlier years, the one constancy throughout all the years and all the changes has been his remarkable erudition.

My first sighting of William. Forty-two years prior to my visit to Prague with Susan, William and I arrived by hazard together for our first trimester at the same Oxford college. I was just inside the gate, at the porter's lodge, when William decanted from a taxi. From the opened rear door of the cab there issued an outstretched foot wearing a two-tone brown and white semi-brogue shoe, followed by a wide-striped dark grey trouser leg. The leg was long and thin, joined with a swivelling movement by its mate, then a flowing action that pushed outwards a bowed head followed by a liquid motion of shoulders, torso, and middle parts, somehow all connecting in a current of movement. When I visualise this exit it is in slow motion, fluid. From this flow of playback memory a man emerged, standing at the pavement's edge.

The man was tall, perhaps a couple of inches over six feet. He was thin, a thinness accentuated by the cut of his trousers and jacket. He then, as subsequently, had contrived to wear clothes that bespoke his sparseness, clinging tightly to him as they did. In that first impression there was a waistcoat, a flash of bright canary yellow showing above his buttoned jacket. At his neck was a cravat of purple and carmine stripes. There was some sort of jewelled pin attached to it, a glitter where sunlight struck at his chest. As he stood to full height he placed a black fedora on his head of sleeked black hair. Then I saw his face, thin, sallow, wearing a down-drooping clipped moustache which joined with a trimmed goatee beard of the same dense blackness. Half-rimmed gold-framed spectacles perched on a long, thin nose. Beyond them there were eyes so deeply brown that they too seemed black. From one hand swung a silver-topped walking-stick.

'Hello, fellow!'

William hailed me whilst I was still staring at him from the porter's lodge. We exchanged names and learned that our rooms were on the same staircase of the same block, his to the left, mine to the right.

Our group. We were cosseted and indulged children. We had been spoiled. That may seem strange to some of my peers of the time, given that we had endured the sometimes Spartan regime, the daily vicissitudes of life, and the occasional harshness within the top four public schools in the country. But our sufferings, beginning with separation anxiety when we were sent away to prep school at the ages of seven or eight, certainly made us independent and self-assured to the point, as seen by some, of arrogance. Our development led us to *expect* things where the lesser-fortunate would *hope* for things. We were children coming from a background of wealth with the advantages of wealth. All of us in that group had 'family' behind us. At the time that term needed no qualifying typographical symbols. Family meant social status, an inheritance of shared beliefs and self-esteem; there was history, generations of *known* history to each of our families and 'good marriages' confirming or promoting one's elevated social position. Some families went back centuries, their ancestral generations documented and, in exceptional instances, celebrated nationally, or, at the least, known widely in the higher strata of society. All had attained status, power, influence, in one or other sector of society. There were also, as one would expect, in some of the families, stories of the occasional rogue or black sheep; skeletons in the cupboards which, fleshed out in the life, also had known histories. This one a cheat, or a gambler of the family fortune, that one a blackguard, or a mistress bedding her way to the nobility, or a thief, a whoring dissolute... or worse. Where the family survived setback and shame, however, its members subsequently and invariably re-claimed that fallen angel, speaking of him (and the occasional her) fondly with a sense of inverted pride. 'There you can see' – pointing to a portrait hung on the staircase – 'dear old great-great-grand-pater, bit of a lady's man, fell foul at court, don't ye know, something to do with one of the king's mistresses and some fine silverware. Wasn't his to sell, so it goes.'

William Walsh, however, was so arrestingly, colourfully and so flamboyantly present one could not question his right to be there. When he did speak, there was a powerful attraction to his speech; one might properly say speeches, given that he so frequently spoke at length, even on those many occasions when he intended, and succeeded, in dumbfounding us.

Once William had become a permanent member of our group the matter of his background simply evaporated. We had taken to William as children take to a pet dog. We became possessive of him. As to his schooling, I recall a rumour but nothing certain.

What else of William?

William carried his affectations with such aplomb and assurance that they seemed to be the measure of the man. In those undergraduate years he was never anything less than the complete dandy, fully kitted out with dress, props, and mannerisms, posturing, posing, a truly exotic creature. William never failed to attract attention; at one's first encounter with him he startled one's senses by his very appearance. And even though he went through numberless changes in clothes and colours, to our group he remained simply William; a William one thought one knew in that he had become an accustomed presence.

To go with the visual dandy, William had cultivated a *fin-de-siècle* disenchantment, an air of languid detachment from the realities of the contemporary world. He made an art-form of *ennui*. There is a photograph from those days of the man standing, in characteristic listless pose, the upper part of his long body propped against a wall, his legs crossed just below the knee, the fingers of one hand pressed into a waistcoat pocket, his other hand perched upon the silver knob of his walking-stick. The photograph itself was to be the cause of confusion (and sow hints of doubt and suspicion) in later years. It was also to be the image which, some years later, became an impetus to the defection of that important officer in the Czech secret service.

Clearly visible in the photograph was William's signet ring worn, oddly, on the forefinger of his right hand. It was a large gold ring, set with some kind of reddish-brown semi-precious stone which I think might have been a cornelian. When animated to the extent of actual movement this hand drew in the air its parabolas and curlicues of flight, the fingers of the hand spread like a wing. Very occasionally the other hand would join its flight and a pair of birds became William's most energetically expressive feature.

William's postured sensibility somehow matched perfectly his dress. In all senses, he was out of kilter, decades out-of-date. Our world, the world for the rest of us, was the last years of the nineteen-fifties. As for the young men in our group, we had deferred National Service in order to go to university. There was talk at the time of National Service about to come to an end in the near future, and some of us hoped that by the time we had done our three years at Oxford, that prospect might have been realised. In that, as it proved, we were right; but only just.

Thus, bridging the cross-over between the 'fifties and the 'sixties, we were the generation born in the year of, or the year before, the start of the Second World War. We were also the first of the 'happening' generation, as my god-son many years later once described the era of the 'sixties to his mother and me. I suppose, at the time, we were aware of freedoms, but these were mainly to do with the lack of parental restraint now that we were out of the family home. Bedding young women and getting drunk were the prime objectives of our own Oxford curriculum. As a by-product one hoped to achieve also a decent degree and perhaps even a Blue in one or other chosen sport.

However much William became what he seemed to be, it was the pretence of that persona which enabled him to do what he did. It gave him confidence and social lustre. William somehow learned to pretend so forcibly that many were deceived in many different ways.

There was no pretence to William's outstanding learning, however. Where the rest of us, for example, simply had an enforced, reluctant acquaintance with Horace, Homer, and others of the school classical canon, William was on voluntarily intimate terms. On one occasion I arrived, unexpectedly, at his room to discover him reading his Catullus, a glass of port on the side table.

'Ah, my dear fellow. Here is just the thing for you.'

Then he intoned:

'*Nulla potest mulier tantum se dicere amatam... et cetera.* And when you get to it, just substitute for Lesbia the name of the girl of the moment.'

Holding the text out to me, William pointed with bony beringed finger.

'Don't see how any girl could resist the flattery.'

I stumbled into a silent rough translation, the gist of it, resisting the pleasure it would have given William to make for me a fuller, more accurate, and certainly a much smoother version: *No woman can claim to be loved as Lesbia is loved by me, nor any lover could be truer.* Words to that sort of sentiment anyway.

'Not sure about that, William,' I replied, wanting at the least to retrieve a point or two from him. 'Don't really go for the blue-stocking type.'

And in the common belief of the men in our group William did not go for any type of girl of any hue of stocking, though he saved a good many from the boredom of aloneness. For we knew we could cheerfully entrust a girlfriend to William's care until one's return from an away match, or from training, or from those fellows-only excursions one made from time to time. He would entertain the girl in one's absence, an accommodation which worked to everyone's satisfaction throughout the years of the group. The girls seemed to enjoy well enough William's tea and music and talk.

William and I were both reading English that first shared year at Oxford. Within the tutorial group, as we moved towards the end of the year William had induced a kind of despairing resignation from the rest of us. He was, we all thought, so far ahead of us in the subject that we would not be able to catch up. He had read everything. Everything on the entire course, it seemed, not just the texts up for critical study for each term as it came along, but also background works, many of which we had not even heard of, far less had we spent a Saturday morning in the Bodleian locating arcane texts and then reading into the afternoon in the library. Because of his evident superiority we worried more about making fools of ourselves in tutorials where he was present than we were concerned about the tutor's opinion of us. We would panic as one's turn came around to lead a tutorial presenting a studied and contextualised appreciation, with critical insights, of a given literary text. There was no help for it but to turn to William for guidance, bribing him with offers of a bottle of port or a packet of cigarettes.

'*Aperçus*, my dear chap. *Cherchez les aperçus*, that's what you must do. That's what you need to give 'em. Something they haven't thought for themselves.'

William could also use his knowledge as a tease and exasperate one with it. We were on our way to hall for dinner on one such occasion. Jed, destined for a rugby Blue and a pass degree, was desperate. Not having completed his reading even of the prime text, he threatened to separate William's head from his neck if he toyed with him any further and would not give him something, *anything* to go on. His indulgence of William's whimsical way had been tested to destruction. William smiled.

'But of course, my dear chap. Bring a bottle to my room after dinner. But, by the by, if you can put in a quick cram before dinner, help you get a grip on the eighteenth-century background stuff, you might just have another quick dip into Pufendorf – '

He caught the blank looks he had intended to induce.

'Pufendorf. Samuel Pufendorf, latter part of seventeenth century, jurisprudence, natural law, the moral background, social imperatives, and all that. *De officio hominis* probably all you need as a quick summary...'

A chorus of shouts:

'Bugger off, William!'

Then, in those long, measured strides of his, with a backward wave of his free hand, he would step off towards his room, a slight limp to whichever side he was holding his cane. The redundancy of the cane we had long deduced. Given that he would shift the cane from hand to hand, sometimes in mid-stride, the limp accompanying the changeover, clearly it served no physical purpose. William, however, was quite unabashed when charged with this deception.

'Yes but don't you see, it opens doors for me. People stand aside to let me through. They *defer* to me.'

I am still not sure what William meant by this. Perhaps he simply did mean what the words literally conveyed. Except... except that I learned that nothing to do with William was literal.

Towards the end of our first year I sought out William. I shared my news with him one evening. I was giving up English.

'But why, my dear fellow?'

There were two reasons. I knew by then that I was not very good at the subject. It was not the reading *per se*, the texts themselves; but I doubted I could ever keep up with all that surrounding reading, all those contexts, all those *ideas* which somehow informed the critical appreciation and which one was supposed to know, or at least know about. Literature was turning into everything: history, sociology, linguistics, psychology, politics, philosophy, religion... it was all too much. I just was not cut out for what Literature had become at that level of study. William listened to me without interruption or comment until I had finished. Only then did he speak.

'And the *real* reason for abandoning the daughters?'

'There *is* no Muse for prose, William, as you perfectly well know. And I realise that I'm pretty much a prosaic sort of chap, really.'

William examined the nails of one hand, fingers laid against the palm of the other. Without looking up he simply asked:

'And what will you do?'

It was already fixed. Reason two: I was going to switch to Law at the start of the second year. Law was in the family, my Great-Uncle, on my father's side, had been a prominent KC, retiring some years ago into that bachelorhood which he had preserved all his life. Just before I went up to Oxford, he had shared with me a favourite brandy and the wisdom of his years.

He had questioned me as to my ambitions, my hopes and 'what you intend to make of yourself, young man.' Great-Uncle Ranulph was always jolly, though the *sotto voce* exchanges which during my boyhood years I had overheard pass between my mother and father had seemed always to elicit a tut-tutting and a shake of the head from my mother; usually, as I recall, in reference to Uncle Ranulph's changing, yet again, of his housekeeper.

In what was to prove my last meeting with the old boy, now that I had reached my own manhood, reticence had no place man-to-man as far as Great-Uncle Ranulph was concerned.

'There is not one folly which, in my devotion to women,' he said, 'I have not committed...' He twinkled his rheumy eyes upon me. 'With the exception of marriage.'

He died over the Easter period between the Hilary and Trinity terms of that first year at Oxford. Not long after I was informed that he had left a bequest to me which would be sufficient to fund the necessary years of studies and training, including the expenses of an Inn of Court, for me to pursue a career as a barrister. The bequest was conditional upon my following that route.

Carolyne became the girl I was 'with', in the shorthand of Oxford – and several years afterwards was still assumed to have fallen in love with – when the third and final year for the rest of the group came to an end. I had another year to do for my Law degree and Carolyne decided that she wanted to travel. Her father had business in Switzerland and she was going to base herself there. So we parted and did not meet up again until I had finished my time at Middle Temple Inn of Court, had been called to the Bar, and was at the end of my formal pupillage as a trainee barrister. After that, I had been fortunate in being taken into old-established chambers in Doctor Johnson's Buildings in the Temple. The influence of my Great Uncle cast a long shadow, even those several years after his death, and those many more years since he had retired. When Carolyne transferred back to London, working as a Personal Assistant to one of the directors of a company affiliated to her father's business operation, we met up again. We met as old friends, sharing a pleasant dinner at one or other restaurant or going to the cinema; the ballet once, her treat for my birthday. But it was not until after the year of my pupillage, when I had been offered a tenancy by the chambers and was beginning, little by little over the following two years to make progress into my chosen career that Carolyne and I began to take each other seriously again. After some while it became taken for granted that we would marry as soon as my fledgling career as a barrister permitted. It was then that William, in a manner of speaking, turned up again in my life.

Before that reappearance the last I had seen of William was at the Commemoration Ball at the end of his and the group's third year at Oxford. He was with one of the otherwise unpaired girls who had volunteered to accompany him. From what I can remember of the event he was *comme d'habitude,* as he himself might have said. Somehow he had managed to dandify even the white tie code of dress, most notably in the tie itself. The tie, of a wide silk and much longer than the conventional version, seemed to be arranged in an elaborate fashion that displayed in fact two sets of bows, one larger than the other, with long tails. A bright red stone glinted from a pin set into the tie. Matching that red was a red rose pinned into his lapel. A wide gold watch-chain was slung across his white waistcoat, and there was the flashing from rings which he wore on fingers of each hand. That evening William seemed to be everywhere, posing, drawing on lit and unlit cigarettes alike at the end of a gold-banded holder; an acquisition, or a prop, specially obtained for the purpose of the Ball, with which he could make even more elaborate gestures.

At parting, as for all departures of groups to their several individual lives, we promised to keep in touch with each other, to keep each other informed of our progress, to make sure that we met up again.

'And what will you do, William?'

Carelessly, as if tossed away and of no account:

'Oh, I shall teach English somewhere and work on my monograph.'

Of course, the lure having been trailed before me, I had to pursue his answer.

'My namesake. William Walsh. Minor no doubt, but not without a certain merit.'

He vouchsafed this with an air of languorous detachment as if neither the matter of his future nor that of his seventeenth century namesake really were of any significance whatever.

After that I did not see William again for several years. I did hear from him, three times in all. Once a postcard arrived at Oxford during my final year; and a couple more postcards from different European capitals were sent to my parents' address whilst

I was keeping terms at Middle Temple. From the end of that year in which I was called to the bar I heard no more from, or indeed of, William. Since there were no return addresses on the cards I could not reciprocate. I sometimes wondered what had happened to him and where, like a fallen leaf in the autumn, he had been unresistingly blown.

Then, more than five years after that Commemorative Ball, a telephone call was put through to me in chambers. The man at the other end of the line introduced himself in a voice which was, to my ear, a parody. It was a voice one might have associated with a comic haw-haw version of a military officer; baritonal, plummy, richly-accented yet clipped. It was a voice, it occurred to me, which belonged to two or three decades past.

'Colonel Jackson here. On behalf of the Home Department. Trust I haven't intruded at an inconvenient time.'

Actually it was not the most convenient time to take a call and I was on the point of prevaricating.

'Won't take up much of your time. A courtesy call really, to let you know I shall see you in chambers next Tuesday morning. Your clerk tells me you'll be free. Want to have a little chat with you about William Walsh.'

The tone allowed of no contradiction; the voice clearly belonged to a man used to being obeyed.

I was intrigued. In the event Colonel Jackson had a good deal to tell me about William – 'for your ears only, old chap', as he somewhat melodramatically put it.

If Colonel Jackson's voice was the parody of a former way of speaking, his presence seemed to have been constructed to a stereotype. Booth, our chambers clerk, known to everyone by his surname only and a man who carried his position with conscious dignity, opened the door to my room, then held it open with extended arm.

'Colonel Jackson to see you, Mister Anthony.'

Colonel Jackson almost filled the height of the doorway. He was wearing a tailored fawn double-breasted overcoat and carried in one hand a well-worn leather briefcase, whilst between the extended forefinger and thumb of the same hand he pincered the brim of a black bowler hat. In his other hand there was a furled umbrella. As he stepped into the room there was the shadow of a smile, a gesture that faded on the instant, beneath a thin white moustache. Within a long face were grey or light blue eyes, I could not be sure which, direct in their gaze, and narrowed beneath trim white eyebrows. His hair, white apart from some thin grey streaks and grown long, was swept back and covered the tops of his ears. It was this feature which confirmed that he was no longer a serving Army officer.

As I came around my desk to shake his hand, the Colonel handed to Booth his briefcase, hat, and umbrella, while he took off his coat. He then took back his briefcase and laid the coat over Booth's arm. Booth turned to me and I thought I could see the fire light in his eyes. He was not a manservant, he was a very important person to whom we all deferred, however lightly that deference appeared to be shown by the senior barristers of the chambers. To my visitor, however, Booth smiled graciously.

Divested of his coat, the Colonel appeared in a dark grey pin-stripe suit, white shirt, and what I took to be a regimental tie tightly pulled in to its collar in a small knot.

'I shall arrange for coffee, Mister Anthony.'

Booth, it was evident in the glance he gave me, let me know that this was a rare condescension and one not to be presumed subsequently.

The Colonel took the armchair, and turned it sideways on to my desk whilst I was still gesturing towards it. He laid his briefcase over some of my papers on the desk, then with hands clasped together, fingers intertwined, he rested his elbows on the arms of the chair. I sat my side of the desk and noticed the gold-embossed EIIR on the flap of the briefcase. I noticed too how Colonel Jackson seemed to colonise a lot of space, his long legs outstretched and crossed at the ankles. Just as he had filled the doorway, so now he seemed to fill my room. Granted, as the most recent and junior member of the chambers I had been allocated the smallest room, none the less the Colonel made me feel that I was his guest rather then he mine.

I waited for him to begin. I expected an explanation; why he wanted to talk with me about William. Instead, in the most casual of ways, he asked me about myself: my career to date, after Oxford, what training to be a barrister entailed. His questions seemed to be formed from a genuine interest.

Our coffees arrived, with a glare to me from Booth who had perversely, as I thought, opted to play the manservant rôle in the presence of the Colonel. He even backed out of the door, bowing slightly as he gently closed the door behind his retreating figure.

The Colonel and I sipped at our coffees as I waited for my guest finally to turn to the subject of William. Instead, he now asked me about my family, my parents, family background.

'Married?'

A *fiancée*-to-be, I explained, was as far as I had yet ventured.

The Colonel offered me his congratulations.

Carolyne. I gave her name and explained, briefly, how she and I had met, parted, met up again, and were soon to be formally engaged.

'Excellent coffee, I must say.' In making the compliment Colonel Jackson made it unmistakably clear that he wished for more coffee. I went out of the room to organise the drink. When I returned to my desk the Colonel had his briefcase, flap open, on his lap. Across the case was a foolscap-sized light brown folder.

He engaged me in some light talk about Oxford, regretting that he 'had not had the benefit of university' himself, and doubting that he would have been the right material for it anyway. I sensed that the Colonel was simply filling in time before fresh coffee arrived.

'Bit of a plodder, you know, when it comes to brain work. Would never make an academic. Couldn't do your line of work.'

Coffee arrived, on a tray held by Booth in his parodic shuffle of a humble servant.

'Sir,' he said as he placed the tray on my desk. His eyes burned with the threat of retribution. He bowed again in the doorway before leaving.

Booth's arrival with the coffee saved my further embarrassment. For by that time I had engaged in a self-effacing explanation of what I actually did do, and had babbled on for a minute or two to my visitor.

'Still sounds far too complicated to me. I just ask people a few questions. What can you tell me about William Walsh?'

The unexpectedly peremptory manner of posing the question I had been expecting threw into disarray the reply I had prepared beforehand. Of course, I said, it is a few years now since William and I... I stumbled into comments on William's undoubted intellectual abilities, the immense width and depth of his learning, his capacity for presenting a critical argument...

I floundered. The Colonel, as I spoke, opened up the brown folder lying on top of his briefcase. He turned some sheets of paper.

'Yes indeed, academic achievements exceptional. I have all his Oxford reports here, Finals results, College Principal appraisal, tutor reports and so on. A quite outstanding scholar, no doubt about that.'

'College Principal, did you say?'

The Colonel nodded.

'Old Smokey himself? Sir Patrick Dun – '

'The same.'

'But College Principals don't usually – '

'He did in the case of William.'

The Colonel lifted his eyes from the papers and locked me into their penetrating concentration.

'The question was, my dear chap, to return to the point at issue, and the question still is, What can you tell me about William Walsh?' He paused. 'The man.'

I was at a loss. In that instant I realised that really I did not know William at all in the way one knows a person one is close to. I had no ready response in that decisive way the Colonel's questioning seemed to demand. I knew the man's appearance, and throughout those years when we spent so much time together I had taken his appearance for the man. I made a lame response.

'William was always William. I mean, he didn't change, he was always considerate, always willing to listen, you know, and he was a good help to any of the students who were struggling with their studies. Altogether a good fellow, I would say.'

Colonel Jackson allowed the silence to drift, his eyes – they now seemed to me more grey than blue – were unembarrasedly full upon me, unshifting, looking through me rather than at me.

'So he was well liked?'

'Yes, I would say so. Within our group certainly.'

Another piercing look.

'And to the best of your knowledge he did not make any enemies whilst at Oxford.'

'To the best of my knowledge, no.'

'Tell me about your group.'

I outlined the history of those three years, how that group of us had come together and had somehow managed more or less to keep its core membership intact. Of course, it was a loose grouping, girlfriends came and went, we were not all together all of the time... and so on.

Without any shift of body or tone of voice the Colonel then asked me how our various girlfriends got on with William. I described the way in which William became a sort of guardian, a Dutch Uncle figure, to various of the girlfriends at various times when one of us had to be away for training or a match. They were safe with him, I said, discretion holding back the reason why the men felt able to trust their girls to the man.

'I see.'

Colonel Jackson simply maintained silence for some seconds. Then:

'Did William ever look after Carolyne for you?'

'Yes, of course,' I said, wondering where this conversation was going. 'A couple of times. You know, took her into his care while I was elsewhere and she was waiting for me to get back to college.'

There was a pause, the Colonel smoothing out his moustache with forefinger and thumb of one hand.

'And would you say *all* the girls, your girlfriends, liked him as well?'

'Yes, certainly. All the girls liked him. He was very attentive to them, as I said.'

Colonel Jackson, head down now, thankfully his gaze off me at last, shuffled through some of the papers in his folder. The fingers of one hand lightly tapped on one of the sheets.

'Did William ever express to you his sexual preference?'

I was taken aback with the bluntness of the question.

The Colonel looked at me then with a downturn of his lips at my slowness, or my reluctance. He spelled out the words of his revision.

'Did William ever tell you whether he preferred men or women? Sexually.'

I flustered out my confusion.

'Which did you *presume* was William's preference?'

To answer seemed to me at that point to be a betrayal, of William I mean, of someone whom I had called a friend.

'Let me see if I can help you here. I assume you *did* make a presumption about William's sexual preference.'

Admission. 'Well, yes.'

'And that was?'

There was no gainsaying the Colonel. 'Men. I think William preferred men, which was why the men could – you know, safely entrust one's girlfriend, without hesitation...'

'Good.' The Colonel's interruption was emphatic. It was also surprising, and puzzling. In this context it seemed to me to be such an out-of-the-way word to choose.

There was a break in the questioning, the Colonel draining the last of the coffee from the pot into his cup. He sipped at the coffee, slowly put cup and saucer down onto the desk again. I thought the 'little chat' the Colonel had invited me to have with him was concluded. I half rose from my seat.

The Colonel waved me down.

'Just a few more details, if you don't mind, *i*'s and *t*'s, dotting and crossing, then we shall be done.'

He turned again to me, his voice more relaxed, I thought, less inquisitional.

'How well, would you say, you knew William? How much did you know *about* him?'

'Well,' I began, 'know *what* about him exactly?'

Colonel Jackson surprised me with a smile.

'Well, *exactly*, for a start, which school he had attended?'

'I'm really not sure, but I heard from somewhere it was a minor public school in Cumbria.'

'Did *William* tell you that?'

'No, no, but I'm sure I heard that from someone or other during our time in Oxford.'

'You never in fact asked him?'

'No.'

Colonel Jackson leaned in towards me across my desk.

'Let's see what else you know about William Walsh, shall we? What age was he when he arrived with you at Oxford?'

'I suppose he'd have been the same age as the rest of us.'

'And where would you put that? Eighteen?'

'Yes, though one or two of us were nearer nineteen, just a matter of birthdates.'

'And you all took up your Oxford places immediately after leaving school?'

'In our group, yes, as far as I know.'

'What was the full name under which you knew William?'

'Well, William Walsh, of course.'

Colonel Jackson sat back in his chair, elbows resting on its arms, hands together, almost in an attitude of prayer, fingers interlaced.

'Family. What do you know about William's family, his background?'

A reflex forced from me a 'Well, I...' but as soon as uttered I recognised that, 'To tell the truth, I don't think we ever actually discussed that, not directly. It just was not something that came up in conversation. One simply assumed – '

'Might it be true to say that neither you nor your peers made much inquiry of William?'

The truth of the answer was shaming. 'No, I suppose we didn't. I mean, one simply took him to be one of us.'

'Ah, then you did not know your man at all.'

It was then that the Colonel told me 'for my ears only' some of what I had not known about William. Of course, as the Colonel said, as a barrister, flattering me with experience beyond the little thus far acquired, I was used to being provided with privileged information and, *of course* (carrying such weight as to be a covert threat) I knew how to honour confidences. There would be no need, *in my case*, to invoke statutory silence, the Official Secrets Act and all that, just friendly advice to keep it all to oneself, there's a good chap... given that, as a lawyer, I would know that one did not have to sign up to a state secret in order to be bound to honour that secrecy. I was incredulous.

'William, a state secret?'

'He might become so. This is by way of an advance notice, you might say. Of the possibility.'

I was at a loss. The Colonel allowed himself another of his small smiles, this time signalling the contract of a collusion between us, as he laid out facts new to me, making of them a new William, one previously unknown to me. He spoke now in a fully relaxed tone. William, he informed me, had in fact attended a State Grammar School in Leicestershire.

'So William was an imposter.' I still do not know what impelled this response from me.

The Colonel simply regarded me steadily, laying out his words like a winning hand of cards.

'William was what you had made of him.'

The Colonel was right. I could not recall William ever attempting to mislead me or feed me false information.

I learned more, though it was clear to me that the Colonel was offering an edited version of William, just enough for me to re-cast William and see him in a very different light. William, I learned, was already twenty-three years of age when he arrived at Oxford. Following school, he had opted to do immediately the then obligatory two-year National Service. After basic Army training, he had been sent to Germany. Given that he was fluent in German, he spent most of his service in listening-out posts in West Berlin. Translating intercepted radio and telephone traffic, the Colonel added, seeing my lack of understanding.

'You know, I never heard William speak German.'

'Perhaps you had no occasion to.'

Some time after this meeting, in the way that a stray recollection suddenly strikes, I recognised that there *had been* more than one occasion on which one might have perceived William's facility with the German tongue. Goethe. Something from *Faust* and something from *Werther*, William wanting, as was his way, to illustrate something, to point to a cultural assonance or something of that ilk. But the memory, vague as it was, was particular on one point: the spines of the books which William lifted down from his shelves clearly showed their gold-embossed titles in German Gothic print. Yet he had spoken out in English. He must have translated as he read. He might first have spoken the German words, as he did when reading or quoting Latin or Greek. But he did not.

The Colonel offered his own praise of William. William, he said, was very good at what he did. Exceptional in fact. A flair for languages, a natural. Put him through an intensive Russian course – 'a lot of radio traffic in Russian, of course.'

A smile for the uninitiated.

'Good deal of it in Czech, too. Started your William on a crash course in it. Would have been a rare find, someone who could have done three-way points duty for us.' The Colonel waved his arms like a policeman at a crossroads. 'We wanted to keep him. Offered him a commission.'

'We?'

The Colonel waved away my question as if back-handing a troublesome fly.

Then, as an aside, it seemed, I was informed that two years after National Service William turned up again when, of his own volition and by exercise of Deed Poll, William Wall, his name from infancy, changed his name to William Walsh.

I was stunned.

'You would have known nothing of this, of course.'

'No, nothing at all.'

For the first time the Colonel gave a pleasant soft laugh.

'Rather fortunate for us, that last change of name. Enabled us to catch up with him.'

The Colonel took out two photographs from his folder, placing them on the desk in front of me and turning them towards me. His forefinger tapped at the first photograph.

'Also known as Billy Wall to his fellow servicemen.'

He tapped then at the second photograph.

'William Walsh.' He pushed the photograph a little closer to me. 'An Unusual, wouldn't you say?'

William Walsh I recognised. In characteristic lounging pose, leaning against a wall, fedora fractionally pushed back from the forehead, walking stick negligently grounded at an angle, here was the William I knew – his hand resting on the cane's handle and displaying prominently a large signet ring on his forefinger. There was an archway and, beyond, the quadrangle of our college. Seeing the photograph actually produced a small shock of *déjà vu*. I knew not only the man but the photograph itself. It was identical with one I had taken myself. I had been pleased with it, rather proud of its composition. But that photograph was in an Oxford album I kept at my flat.

The first photograph, however, presented someone unrecognisable as William. The tall, spare figure bore a passing resemblance of build, but that was all. Beardless, dark hair cut in a short back and sides, a young man stood, arms folded, in khakis, a figure as unremarkable as he was unrecognised by me.

'I would not have known it was the same man.'

The Colonel seemed gratified.

He gathered up the photographs from my desk, closed up his folder, placed it back into his briefcase which he snapped shut. As we shook hands I said:

'I'm sorry I couldn't be more helpful to you, Colonel Jackson.'

'You have been *very* helpful Mister Ashley-Chetwyne. More than you know.' He seemed to deliberate for a moment. Then he said, matter-of-factly, lacking all accusative:

'That you appear to know so little about your friend, after all the time you spent together, assists us greatly in our thinking.'

He turned away from me, turned back to me, all in one movement.

'Ah! almost forgot.'

Reaching into an inner jacket pocket he retrieved a wallet, took from it a small card and held it out to me between the straightened forefinger and middle finger of his hand. As I took it from him I noted briefly an address in Mayfair and a telephone number.

'Should anything occur to you which you think I might be interested to know.'

With that the Colonel turned to leave. I opened the door for him. He paused, slightly stooped his head to me, a nod, an acknowledgement.

'Wouldn't be surprised if your friend William turned up to see you in the next couple of weeks.'

'Do you happen to know where William is at the moment?'

'Of course, old chap. He's in Lisbon. Working on behalf of the British Council. Gather his lectures on seventeenth century English Literature are particularly well-received.'

The Colonel forestalled my follow-up.

'We've been touring him around, learning some of the ropes. Establishing a *bona fide*. Very impressed with his apprenticeship so far.'

With that clairvoyant vision which enabled him to know everything that went on in chambers, Booth appeared at that very moment at the door holding the Colonel's coat, hat, and umbrella. His glance forewarned me of the interrogation to come.

On reflection, that day and the days following, the entire episode seemed more and more fanciful. I began to doubt the credibility of 'Colonel Jackson on behalf of the Home Department'. The more I replayed that meeting with him, the more it did not make sense. What, indeed, was it about? If, as was the clear implication, there was some kind of security issue then, surely I thought, the Colonel had been indiscreet in telling me as much as he had about William.

As a result of the meeting, however, William himself had to be completely refashioned. He was no longer the William I had known from those Oxford years. His name change, of which I had known nothing, was bewildering. Evidently, in that change of name resided an alternative, but equally concealed, history. Why had not William said anything about his past? Had we not been friends...? As soon as thought, though, I rebuked myself. One had not taken sufficient interest to ask him about his personal history, assuming he and we were all much of a muchness.

William, all the while, had been someone else. And the more time passed the more difficult it became to take the Colonel at face value. Several times I was on the point of telephoning the number on the Colonel's card just to confirm that he existed; that he was who he said he was. And several times I resisted the temptation. After all, what would I say? None the less, Colonel Jackson and the *Home* Department? The entire episode began to feel like a deception.

My week was not helped by the occasions Booth contrived to enter my room and at the same time present me with opportunities to unburden myself of whatever had passed between my visitor and me. I determined to make Booth wait; perhaps to give me time to invent a suitably anodyne version of that meeting for our chief clerk. Since my future was largely dependent upon the man, and we both understood that, it was unavoidably the case that at some point I would have to present him with a convincing story.

Whilst waiting for Carolyne to arrive on Friday evening, I searched out my album of Oxford photographs. It was an album in name only, given that just a few photographs were properly attached with legends written below in white pencil on the charcoal-coloured pages. The rest had been simply inserted between subsequent pages of the album, suggesting more or less where they belonged in the chronological order of those years.

Since William had figured largely in our group at Oxford, one might have expected to find a good many photographs of the man. In fact I found just two. In one he stood alongside me at the walled archway. In the second he stood with Carolyne, in the same setting, his arm across her shoulder, her head upturned to him. They seemed to have been taken on the same occasion. There had been a third photograph, I was convinced. But it was not there.

For someone so flamboyant, someone who was always such a visual spectacle, it was odd how few were the memorabilia of his presence from those three shared years. We had overlooked him in that regard also.

Carolyne was going to spend that weekend with me in my own small apartment. Small but cosy, as we said to each other in those days. Confined, as one might have said in aftertimes, with not enough space either to avoid, or to escape from each other.

Carolyne had had a busy week so she too wanted a quiet Friday night. I cooked a meal; it would have been steak and salad, just about the *Ultima Thule* of my culinary skills at the time.

We settled on the deep, almost worn-out sofa. I wanted to talk about William. When I had mentioned on the telephone to her earlier in the week the visit I had received from Colonel Jackson, I had elicited only an uninterested 'Oh really' from her before she had moved the conversation on to the timing and the plans for announcing our formal engagement. With her careless dismissal I realised I had never really spoken with her about her impressions of William. Prompted by that recent and unsettling visit of the Colonel, I was now curious to know if she had any special or particular observations to make.

'So tell me, Carolyne, what did *you* make of our William?'

Carolyne, and I can recall this movement minutely, gave a small flustering of her hands held in front of her, just away from her body. It was a gesture I had not noticed before. I took it, then, as a sign of uncertainty.

'Oh he was charm itself. Very different, of course, no denying that, but that was part of his appeal, wasn't it?' Carolyne took up her glass and gulped down the young claret, all I could afford in those earliest times of my legal career, and held out her glass for a refill.

'But what did you *make* of him?'

'Oh, you know, what we *all* thought of him.'

'And that was?'

A small flutter of her free hand.

'But did you never ask him about himself, his background? His family, I mean, where his family came from.'

'Did *you?*' Accusative question in answer to a question.

Not for the first time Carolyne's evasiveness irritated me and there was the beginning of something negatively charged between us. I wanted to pursue the conversation about William whilst it became clear to me that Carolyne did not. The more this realisation firmed itself, the more I pressed the issue.

'You must have *something* to say about him. I mean, after all you did spend time with him, didn't you? Being entertained by him, waiting for me to turn up.'

Carolyne very slowly lifted to her lips her wine glass, her fingers delicately holding its stem. She answered me slowly, reluctantly, carefully.

'He would offer tea, or perhaps a sherry. It did not actually occur to one to ask questions of him. Somehow, being William, things just came up in conversation. And we would talk.'

'About?'

'Well for a start, William was always interested in one, asking how one was, how one was doing in one's studies, one's ambitions... one's worries and so on.'

'And what sort of *so on* might that have been?'

'Oh, nothing in particular, you know, just things in general. But William did have a special quality of listening, one felt he was attending to you. He seemed genuinely interested, he made you feel you mattered.'

'And? Is that it, nothing more to say?'

Thinking back, I recognise in these exchanges an edge entering my voice of its own accord. I did not understand my reactions. Much later, I did. Today I would say that I was somehow aware only of something more than, or different from, what I actually knew. Perhaps sometimes we simply act out these subliminal promptings, and since we do not have positive or identifiable knowledge to justify these actions we are at a loss ourselves to explain them. Later events may make sense of earlier history.

'That was it then? Tea and sympathy?'

As it was, Carolyne irritated me further by her adoption of such a cool and patient tone of voice, refusing to rise to my provocations.

'No, more than that. Somehow he always managed to provide one with a different way of seeing things.'

Carolyne looked her challenge at me.

'Being William, of course, they could have been anything from Aristotle to Xenophon via Freud – and many more names one hadn't even heard of.'

The challenge made, Carolyne seemed to be set on furthering the contest. She put her head to one side.

'Though probably, if one thought about it, one would be able to remember some snippets.'

I held my silence. This talk of William put me even further out of sorts with Carolyne, made worse by the fact that it was entirely at my own insistence. I was angry with myself and had no-one else to blame.

'Let me see...'

Was Carolyne deliberately twisting the knife? reacting to my reactions to her?

'William had all sorts of things he could simply call up on the instant. He could always think of something which would be simply perfect for the occasion. Always had a quotation he could call upon. One time...'

Her deliberation *was* provocation, made worse by her dual pretence: that she was engaged in an ordinary, everyday exchange with me, and that she had not recognised my own loss of even-temperedness.

'Let me see... Ah yes, for example, one time William offered me something from, what was his name? strange name, Samuel something... I've got it. Samuel Pufendorf, wasn't it? though I'm afraid I couldn't now tell you anything about the man. Something along the lines of 'From man's natural state, it follows, or something like that, wonder or worship or something, blah blah, and pass one's life in a very different manner from the brutes.' Can't remember what we would have been talking about at the time.'

She looked up at me with the sweetest of contrived smiles.

'Or he would read to one. Poetry usually, such a beautiful intonation one *entered* the poem even if one did not understand it... even if it was in Latin.'

'Any Catullus, by chance?'

'Yes, I think so. On one occasion anyway.'

'*Nulla potest...*?'

I was surprised at Carolyne's response to this opening fragment.

'Ah yes!' Brightly, animatedly continuing: 'Yes, that was one of them. *Nulla potest mulier tantum...* 'fraid I can't remember how it all goes, except for *quanta in amore* somewhere, but clever you to guess!'

I think my anger must have transposed into a bit of a sulk at this point, and as I withdrew into my funk so did Carolyne become more lively, counterpoising me quite deliberately, as we both knew. *Nulla potest...* just substitute the name of the girl of the moment, he had said, don't see how any woman could resist the flattery. Just as well that William was... well, William; or one might have wondered.

'Anyway, I hope you told your Colonel Jackson that William is a lovely man, very sweet, and not to be fooled by appearances.'

'Talking of appearances,' I said, 'I looked for a particular photograph of William which I'm absolutely positive I had in my album. Can't think it could be anywhere else. It's the one that goes with these two' – and I plopped onto her lap the photographs of each of us with William. 'Same spot, but William on his own, lounging.'

Carolyne turned her body a little away from me, her back to my side, raised her glass to her lips whilst her other hand made a little fluttering of her fingers.

'Oh well, darling, not to fret. I expect it will turn up again. These things usually do.'

'I've looked everywhere.'

We survived the evening, uncomfortable with each other, closing the night with the reparation of unsatisfactory, perfunctory love-making.

Thoughts of William and Colonel Jackson kept returning. The Colonel had left me with an invitation. Anything to add about William, anything at all, he had said, however trivial or unimportant it might seem to me; not to hesitate, 'phone the number on the card.

Finally I overcame my reluctance. A female voice answered to tell me that 'Colonel Jackson is not currently at his desk' but if I were prepared to wait for a little while 'which shouldn't take long' then my call 'would be transferred.' I lost courage and said I would 'phone another time since my call was not urgent. I had nothing, after all, to say.

Colonel Jackson did exist.

In the days following our unsatisfactory weekend together, to make reparation to Carolyne and to assuage the guilt I felt for having been so unreasonably tetchy with her, I telephoned her mid-week. I offered the bait. I suggested we might talk over possible dates – early next year? – to announce formally our engagement. Of course, the formal announcement would require a formal party, so Carolyne – her good nature restored – once more informed me. But before then there would simply *have* to be that weekend with her parents, there would be so much to think about, ever so many things to be decided and... I groaned inwardly at the prospect of that unavoidable, however delayed, weekend. I foresaw, one did not need to be a prophet, the interminable discussions and plannings between Carolyne and her mother during which I would have to pretend to be involved and interested.

'Poor you!'

Even Carolyne could see what I foresaw. Once the genie was out of the bottle, the setting of a date for a formal engagement, mother and daughter would steam straight ahead to a preliminary 'talking over' of wedding arrangements – just ideas at this stage, obviously, possibilities only Anthony, so much to consider, one needs a good eighteen months to get everything in place...

Instead of just getting on with it I knew that mother and daughter would insist on sharing every tiny scrap of information with me as they proceeded. Views would be sought, opinions asked for; a *politesse* only, since whatever reservation or suggestion one might make would be discounted, over-ridden, analysed, tested to destruction, rejected.

'Poor you!'

Poor me indeed.

Carolyne ended our conversation by telling me that she intended to indulge and spoil the condemned man for the whole of next weekend and would arrive at my flat on Friday evening. Carolyne's promise to indulgently spoil me racked up my anticipation of our pleasures together, as she knew it would, and at the same time was intended to distract me from the anxieties of contemplating a marriage which would be planned and fussed over.

Carolyne insisted on taking us out to dinner on that Friday evening.

'My treat!'

When she arrived at my flat Carolyne was in high spirits, animated, playful, loving. After a quick shower and change of clothes I came back into the sitting-room to find that she had popped a bottle of champagne and was holding out a flute to me. We toasted each other and pledged, again, our love.

'We shall finish the bottle when we get back.'

When we did get back, and it was very late, Carolyne snuggled up against me on that old battered sofa whilst we drank more of the fizz. Her long, wavy brown hair was unloosed, a strand of it tickling at the side of my face. It had been a wonderful evening.

'By the way, darling, that photograph of William you were looking for – '

'It's nowhere to be found, I can tell you that.'

Photographs of William, at that moment, were not for me the most pressing of anticipations, not the *fin de nuit* I was looking forward to; though it did mildly amuse me that just thinking about William could make one adopt one of his verbal mannerisms.

'I suddenly remembered.'

Carolyne lifted herself from the sofa to stand in front of me, her legs straddling my knees. She bent towards me, her arms around my neck, my face almost buried in her breasts.

'What did you suddenly remember?' the words snuffled, my mouth so close to her flesh.

'I borrowed it – oh ages ago – to get a copy for me, and I had forgotten all about it. I was going through my own albums, when I realised I did not have *any* photograph of William. Not one. Then by accident I came across yours, your photograph of William, in one of the drawers of the bureau, you must have been in the shower or something, or late getting back, I can't remember now.' Carolyne was launched, the words tumbling in rapid succession to get her explanation done and out of the way. Frankly, inhaling the while her perfume mingled with the fleshly scent of her, I cannot say that I cared one way or another about her confession. 'I knew you wouldn't mind me borrowing it, it just slipped my mind to mention it at the time. Anyway, I was utterly convinced that I had returned it. So when you said you couldn't find it, I was equally convinced you just had not looked in the right place.'

Carolyne pulled me tightly towards her, so that my nose was buried between her breasts again, holding me there. I had to pull away. I was suffocating.

'I'm sorry, my darling. I don't know why I didn't realise it at the time.'

Her lips nibbled lightly at my neck. 'Forgive me?'

Suddenly she stood upright and went behind the sofa. I heard the drawer of the bureau opening. Seconds later Carolyne plonked herself down alongside me again, champagne flute in one hand, my photograph album resting on her lap, legs tucked to the side, her body snuggling against me again. With her free hand she began to turn the pages.

'It will be fun to see them again, anyway. I haven't seen them for such a long time.'

So she began on the early pages of photographs, all mounted, all bearing their legends, the group here, the group or some of the group there. Then she came to the first gathering of photographs not yet displayed, wedged loosely between the pages.

Carolyne handed me her glass to hold while she held up each photograph, asked the details of it if it were unfamiliar to her, passing comment on the ones she knew. We had gone through three or four such page-turnings when Carolyne shuffled another little pack of photographs for us to go through. I was only half attending by now.

'Here they are! Here's William. This is this the one you've been looking for, the one you thought was missing.'

Carolyne held out the photograph towards me. There was no doubt. It was identical to the one which the Colonel had pushed towards me on my desk in chambers. William, lounging against a wall, fedora at a slightly tilted angle, an archway and, beyond, the quadrangle of our college.

'That's that then!' Carolyne shut the album with a thud, skipped to her feet and went to the bureau to replace the album.

She returned, bending from the waist towards me, re-adopting her earlier posture, her arms straightened before her with hands resting on my shoulders, the swell of her breasts provocatively distracting. She kissed me on the lips. In the brightest of voices she said:

'Now take me to bed!'

With that she gripped each of my hands in hers and made to pull me up out of the sofa.

9

A surprise awaited me in chambers some three weeks following the recovery of the missing photograph. Booth and I had reached an uneasy truce shortly after the Colonel's appearance. I had persisted in telling Booth that 'the man from the Home Department' had called to see me on a purely personal matter. Booth, naturally, wanted the details. The chambers were his territory, as distinctly possessed as a tomcat marks out the territory of his own claim. Nothing happened in chambers, nothing was permitted to happen, without Booth either approving it or being, at the very least, apprised of it. Mystery, to him, was like a bad smell which had to be sniffed out and hunted down just as if another tom had invaded his territory.

Physically Booth was not imposing, being somewhat below average height for a man and being solidly rounded rather than athletically-built. But there was undoubtedly a physical strength to the man which showed in the short, thick fingers of his hands and the width of his wrists. Though I had never seen him exercise that power I had the definite sense that if those hands were to grip one, they would not be shaken off. And though I had never seen Booth without his jacket on, whatever the season, one sensed by the bulging at the shoulders, unconcealed by his tailors, a compact strength. Booth, at the time, was somewhere in his fifties I would have guessed – though no-one in chambers seemed to know for a certainty. In another life Booth's general appearance might have fitted him for the funeral parlour. He was always in a dark suit and of a sombre disposition, the latter accentuated perversely by his rare ventures into humour, of which he had a good sense – when initiated by himself. He was not always a ready appreciator of other persons' senses of humour. If appearance suited him for the rôle of coffin-carrier, his personality did not suit him in the least to greet or comfort the bereaved. He lacked that special kind of ingratiating, sympathising deference required for that job. His hair had retained its dark colouring, a shade or two lighter than William's jet, save for the hinted greying at the temples.

The most unnerving characteristic of the man was his way of forcing one to look directly into the deep blue of his unblinking eyes until, a wild creature facing down its enemy, one had to look away.

Looking away, I repeated my protestation.

Despite my assurances Booth clearly sensed there was very much more to this personal matter than I had divulged. He scented my equivocation.

'Personal, Mister Anthony?' He had lowered his voice to the softly accusatory. 'Not personal as will in due course and season have any deleterious effect upon these chambers, I trust, Mister Anthony.'

'No, no, no, Booth. Personal as in confidential, I'm afraid.'

Booth sniffed at that. He knew about confidences. They were the secrets everyone, from secretaries to senior partners, shared with him, and which went no further than him. Not to share such a confidence with him was, consequently, a slur upon his integrity and sense of honour. All the while I insisted on withholding something from him I was, therefore, offending him; not, I think, because he was interested so much in the contents *per se* of the secrets as in the fact that they, as a matter of principle, should be known to him. Offending Booth, given that he had the direction of the entire chambers in his hands, the distribution of briefs crucially, was a dangerous thing to do. To persist in that offence could stall my career before it properly got going.

I had not yet learned that the way to keep Booth happy, to allow him to continue to think he was guardian of all the secrets of all the persons within his chambers, was through a simple ploy of distraction. It was Philip Hathers – of whom much more anon – who let me into the secret of managing Booth.

'Just tell him something *as if* it's a secret – this is just for you, old chap, or something to that effect – and he won't worry away at the real secrets you want to keep in the dark cellar of your soul. A bit like tossing a juicy titbit or two to your pet dog to keep him busy while you prepare the joint of meat for the oven.'

Before being let into *that* secret by Philip, which was not until many months later, I still had a disgruntled Booth to deal with. He came back to my room just before lunchtime on that Monday morning. I recognised his knock. It was distinctive and announced him quite unmistakeably: a rapid two sharp raps, a pause, one sharp rap, another pause, a final fourth gentle tap. To my surprise, however, having called him in, Booth entered with a broad smile.

'*If* I may intrude upon a moment of your time, Mister Anthony.'

He came to my desk, looked down on me and, forefinger of one hand pressed to the side of his nose, he actually *winked* at me. Then he took to the armchair. He watched me carefully as he spoke.

'I wish you to know, Mister Anthony, that I have just been made *privy* – *privy* I emphasise – to some delicate matters.'

I had no alternative but to allow Booth the entire stage since he had obviously claimed it and was not to be deterred in any way.

'Yes, some most interesting matters, Mister Anthony, which give me grounds for understanding your reluctance to speak openly to me *on some other matter* of recent history.'

Forefinger alongside nose and a bowing of the head. Booth's attempt to engage me in some form of collusion was quite disconcerting, especially so since I had no idea whatsoever to what, beyond my own *other matter*, he was alluding.

'Yes indeed. A most interesting conversation.'

After a couple more such verbal manoeuvres intended, I had no doubt, to increase my curiosity to know what he was talking about and to increase my frustration at not being told, Booth explained. Magnanimity after the victory of letting me know that he knew something. His explanation, however, was guarded sufficiently – and quite deliberately – to stimulate further one's curiosity and confirm one's ignorance in equal measure

Some mornings ago a legal adviser, name withheld from me, from the Home Department of government had telephoned Booth. There was 'some particular and delicate business' which the adviser from the Home Department wished to put the way of the chambers; 'my chambers' as Booth put it, which certainly expressed Booth's sense of proprietorial ownership. The chambers were his fiefdom.

There was much to discuss, apparently, and things of some delicacy which were 'best understood rather than spoken of openly.' Booth's invitation to lunch at the club of the unnamed legal gentleman, for a discreet further exploration, clearly had much gratified Booth. He almost preened himself before me.

'Does Mister Anthony know the Savile?'

'Mister Anthony knows *of* the Savile, Mister Booth, though he is neither a member of the club nor has he ever been invited there.'

It was the first time I had addressed Booth as Mister, and the set of his eyes betrayed his annoyance at being so addressed. Booth, always and only Booth, wore that sole name within chambers as his distinctive badge of office.

'Always a pleasure to dine there, Mister Anthony.'

There were times when Booth needed no-one to buff up his sense of importance; he could do that perfectly well for himself. His little sally let me know that Booth did not view himself merely as a servant of chambers. He had importance in his own right.

'A most interesting conversation, I must say. Though, of course, some parts of our conversation are not for relaying. As you will understand, I'm sure.'

Among the few things he could say was that, in the course of a very open exchange, he had gathered that my own *visitor from the Home Department* – a dropping of the voice at these words – had suggested the meeting with Booth as a follow-up to his own visit to these chambers. With that, Booth somehow managed to insinuate that he now knew all about my visitor, the Colonel, and a very great deal more.

With that winning hand, having confounded me completely and leaving me none the wiser, Booth paused. Rising to leave, he vouchsafed a gnomic parting shot.

'Due diligence, Mister Anthony. A watching brief does not take care of itself.'

Booth left my room carrying out with him both self-satisfaction and the undivulged and unviolated privilege of his *privy* information. If it had been his intention to treat me to a tit-for-tat for my refusal to tell him my business, he succeeded fully.

Before the end of that month there were two other notable occurrences, both on the same day. The first was another visit from Booth who entered, morning cup of coffee in hand. With the merest of looks to me for assent, he made careful placement of the cup upon my desk and made himself comfortable in the armchair. Once seated he made superfluous rearrangement of his jacket and flicked away imaginary specks of dust. He took some time before speaking to me.

'You will recall, Mister Anthony, our conversation from a week or so ago. I informed you of a meeting I had with a person I am not at liberty to identify. That meeting, I can now confirm, has proved most productive and profitable.'

He waited. Too late I realised that the pause was intended as an opportunity for me to offer him my congratulations.

'There will be advantage from it for you also.'

I offered my gratitude.

'There is a brief, Mister Anthony, which though it does not exist in any *formal* appearance, is one none the less of importance enough for learnéd and authoritative and impartial advice to be sought. I have determined that brief will go to Mister Philip. It calls for someone of his seniority and experience. He will, however, require a junior counsel to work with him. In talking with the commissioning party, I have recommended you.'

I thanked Booth again. There was nothing more gratifying to Booth than to be offered thanks. He beamed approval of my gratitude.

Mister Philip. Philip Hathers QC. Though he had not been my supervisor during the year of my pupillage, he had always had a kindly word for me and, on occasion over tea or coffee, friendly chats to enquire how I was getting on. He was especially supportive during the long grind of attendance at magistrates' courts that seemed to fill the last months of pupillage. In the years since, as a fledgeling barrister, he had taken to offering me lunch on a few of those days when we were both in chambers for the day.

There might be, Booth further explained, with a knowing air, some 'particular' features of this case. Then, as he rose to leave, he looked upon me almost paternally, as if he had conferred upon me a great benefit, which indeed he had. For as things developed over the following couple of years, as a result of this engagement I was offered, earlier than one might have anticipated, some high-status work.

'More to follow, Mister Anthony.'

With that, Booth left.

Later I was to be disabused of Booth's apparent favouring of me when I learned exactly what his reference to the commissioning party meant. At his lunch with the solicitor from the Home Department – Booth's 'legal adviser' – Booth himself had been 'advised' that the commission should go to Hathers, with me as junior counsel. Some advice is dressed-up command and, if not to explicit orders, in this assignment Booth was doing as was expected of him.

Even so, the fact remained that I had indeed been offered an excellent opening to work with one of the most accomplished of lawyers, a QC who had taken the silk some ten years previously. During the preparation time for whatever trial the commission would be for, I would be able to see, at close hand, how Philip worked and to learn to my advantage from that experience. Such a reflection, however, anticipated the outcome of a meeting to which Philip Hathers and I were to be invited at a later date.

Booth's pretence to retain power over something he did not control amused me. Yet, I did come to understand Booth's stance. One could not doubt for a moment that he saw it as his duty to manage everything to the good of the chambers as a whole. To allow one to think, therefore, that there might be something he was not in charge of, was not free to manage according to his own judgement, would be a confession of the loss of his personal power. Given a chambers of individualists, one could have sympathy with Booth's point of view and practice. To keep order one must have control.

No sooner had Booth left than there was the second surprise of the day. Philip himself made a point of popping in to see me.

'Welcome aboard, Anthony. It will be good to have you with me on this one.'

Philip stretched out a hand to me.

'Now that we've got clearance for you.'

His face creased with amusement as he registered my evident bafflement.

'Ah. Perhaps we need to have a little chat. Could you free yourself up for lunch, do you think?'

Hathers and I crossed Fleet Street, his arm through mine, an uncharacteristically possessive gesture, as we dodged the taxis and buses. Within minutes we were in one of the bars of *The Cheshire Cheese,* each of us with a pint of bitter in hand.

In those days Fleet Street was still 'Fleet Street', where presses turned out miles of newsprint and reporters thronged the bars at the close of day – some of whom, in point of fact, had been there from lunchtime onwards anyway, having no remaining business, one presumes, requiring them to return to their offices. So the place was thick with the grey smoke of cigarettes and noisy with conversation and greetings, speakers raising their voices to be heard and thus increasing the general level of noise.

We left the bar to take our table in one of the upstairs dining spaces. Even here there was the constant hum of talk, of voices from the tables around us. We had arrived at the busiest part of the day, waiters bustling about, new arrivals being ushered to tables where their hosts awaited them. I commented on the level of noise.

'Yes. But very difficult to be overheard.'

We both ordered the steak and oyster pie and Philip chose a bottle of burgundy. Until our meals arrived there was only general chit-chat between us, and I had begun to wonder why he had made such an occasion of wanting to speak to me. Once served, however, head bowed over his plate, Philip did engage me.

'I gather you had a visit a few weeks back from Colonel Jackson.'

Philip's opening remark was assertive not interrogative.

'You know why he came to talk with you, Anthony?'

Of course, I replied, he wanted to talk with me about an old friend, not wishing to declare a name or any further information about William. William and those Oxford years had nothing to do with chambers, I thought, however much Booth's curiosity had been aroused by the visit of Colonel Jackson.

Philip was silent for some time, simply concentrating upon the food and appreciating his chosen wine. Then, head bowed again, his eyes upturned, those inquisitorial and accusative eyes he had turned with great effect upon unwilling witnesses, were directed towards me. I spoke up against his silent interrogation.

'Not much more than a chat really, what I knew about my friend, just general stuff about him as a person, that sort of thing, you know.'

'I do indeed know that sort of thing, Anthony.'

'Anyway, I got the impression that Colonel Jackson was interested in my friend for some sort of possible post with the Home Department or something like that. I think that's what it was about.'

With his wine glass held to the side of his mouth, Philip leaned in a little to me.

'You may well be right about that, Anthony. I have no doubt that others too will have been spoken to over the last several weeks as part of the procedure – '

'What procedure?'

'To see if one is of sound personality and sound mind – ' Philip laughed, but in a gently mocking fashion. 'That one has the right qualities. And that one uses one's mind to think in the right way, of course. What all that comes down to, in the end, is whether one can be trusted, in the opinion, of course, of the person entrusted to make that judgement. Having taken in the views of others, it goes without saying.'

He paused, watching me closely.

'Trusted to do what?'

Philip continued to regard me in that particular fashion he had developed from the start in our relationship; a disposition more paternal or avuncular than patronising.

'Principally, my dear young man, to keep one's mouth shut.'

My compressed lips of silence amused him.

'Which, I can see, you can do.'

I emptied my glass of wine, twirled its stem between my fingers. Philip, I knew, was waiting for a response from me. I reached for the burgundy to top up his glass and to pour myself more wine. Philip lifted his glass, tilting it slightly towards me as a token toast.

There was an expectation. It was still my turn to make a play.

'Philip, what is going on?'

Philip slowly replaced his glass on the tablecloth.

'I have no doubt that what you had to say to Colonel Jackson about your friend would have been most interesting to him. From what I gather, though, the decision on your friend would almost certainly have been taken already, at least in principle, some time ago – some *i*'s and *t*'s still to dot and cross, perhaps, as it might have been put to you.'

I leant back in my chair, a little light suddenly let into the gloom of my confusion.

'How well do you know Colonel Jackson, Philip?'

'A little.'

My turn to lean in, my eyes trained on Philip.

'More than a little.'

Philip was amused at the tit-for-tat of my silent interrogation of him. But I broke my own silence. 'How? How do you know him?'

'Let us just say that I too have been of service to the service. Here and there. This and that, you know.'

Of course I did *not* know, and mention of 'the service' was simply too vague for me. Philip pre-empted the questions that were contending in my head for lead position.

'Rhubarb crumble for me, I think. And for you, Anthony?'

Philip rested a hand on the menu, pointing to the options. I too chose the crumble. Somehow I sensed that as guest I must show conformity with my host.

Philip put our order to the waiter. Several times I was on the point of asking one of my questions, but he held up a hand to fend them off. Not until our desserts had been served did he allow speech. Then he was the first to speak.

'Perhaps, if I may?'

I nodded assent. Curiosity aroused, keeping silence had been difficult.

'I'm afraid your friend was largely a convenient pretence for the Colonel to see *you*, Anthony. His visit to you was a PV requirement.'

'Pee-Vee?' A moment of furrowed brow. 'What, positive vetting? *Really*?' Then an unsuppressed even more querulous '*Me*?'

'Anthony, my dear young man, I can assure you, it was you who Vernon came to see. William was just a pretext.'

'But – '

'You should feel honoured indeed that Vernon should have come along himself to have a look at you in the flesh – there's a whole branch of people dedicated to just that activity – not his limb of the tree at all. Of course, on his say-so it does somewhat speed things along.'

'But why?' Philip saw my blankness.

'All in due time. But now I'm afraid, my dear Anthony, I must confess my own portion of guilt. In choosing you to work with me on this case review – '

'But I thought Booth – '

'So does Booth.' And Philip laughed, almost a braying laughter. 'One must allow Booth his little pretensions, I'm afraid. Principally his delusion that he is in charge of everything and that he makes all the decisions.'

Philip pulled in his chair a little closer.

'So long as he thinks everything comes from him, you have the management of him. And the loyalty of the man. Never underestimate a man's sense of himself, Anthony, and never underestimate the unflinching support a man such as Booth can offer in return for the promotion of his self-esteem.'

I nodded assent. 'You mean, allow him to think – '

'Precisely.'

Philip returned us to the point.

'As I was saying. In choosing you to work with me on this particular case review, as it stands at the moment, a prosecution as it may become, I have brought upon you this, ah, prying. Inevitably. For which I apologise, this intrusion into your life.'

Philip's eyes were deep set within dark circles into which shadows the eyes themselves seemed to recede, to appear further back in his head. The thinness of his long nose also called attention to those eyes. The shadows moved, the two dark pools within them contracted.

'All to be regretted, but I'm afraid some interference is unavoidable, Anthony. One must bear in mind where the work might lead... *privy* information' – Philip laying a finger alongside his nose for my amusement – 'and some that hasn't even been classified yet, sources, matters that rarely see the light of day, and so on. Above all the need to be sensitive to these things, the way they work. And, finally, to be trusted to be discreet or, in more demotic parlance, as I said, to be able to keep your mouth shut.'

Philip looked down the length of his thin nose.

'I did, however, stand as one of your referees in a manner of speaking, put you forward if you like. After all, I have had several years now in which to keep an eye on you. And I am glad to be able to say that you, Anthony Ashley-Chetwyne, have passed with flying colours. I got the nod a couple of days ago.'

Quickly and quietly Philip filled me in with some explanations which would, he had no doubt, be of some help to me. Though, he opined, probably not of any comfort.

10

Within days of this encounter, Philip and I were invited to Whitehall for a meeting at the splendid Victorian Italianate government building. Security passed, we were shown to an office which, despite its high plasterwork ceiling, was functional rather than decorative. We were greeted by the instructing solicitor who gave us his name as Carlton. If anyone were designed to play the part of an ordinary with no distinguishing, or at least memorable characteristics, it was Carlton. Average height, average build, clean-shaven, brown hair just beginning to thin, somewhere in his late thirties, and with a generalised Home Counties speech, that was Carlton. He apologised as soon as he greeted us. We awaited someone else who was coming 'to sit in' on our meeting. A Colonel Jackson.

We were offered tea and the smallest of small talk. Within a few minutes Colonel Jackson entered the room. He smiled his unspoken greeting to us.

'Sorry to keep you. Such a pleasant day decided to stroll across from the other side. A bit blowy on Westminster Bridge. Been calling on some old friends over there. Down Lambeth way.'

I noticed Philip smiling at this, as the four of us settled around one end of the meeting-table.

'Liaison only, you understand. Left hand, right hand, that sort of thing.'

I had simply no idea what the Colonel was talking about. But with those words, the Colonel nodded to Carlton who, opening his file, took us through our instructions.

The case itself, at least in outline, may be simply stated.

A certain Member of Parliament, elected fourteen years previously to the House, had come to the attention of 'the service'. In the smallest of nutshells it was now being considered whether he would be formally charged with espionage for the passing on of State secrets to two Czechoslovakian Embassy staff. For the last five years the MP had served on the Commons Select Committee for Defence and for the last three years he had been engaged in handing over classified information. The man's clandestine activity had been confirmed by surveillance 'and other means'. What those means were I was not told. But it emerged from subsequent discussions that these means involved the creation of credible but spurious information. Such information was designed to be made available to one source only, namely the MP. He, in turn, passed that information on to his handlers at the Czechoslovakian Embassy in London. A 'friend' at the final destination of this information then had been able to detect its arrival.

In addition there was, so Philip and I were informed by Carlton, persuasive, but largely circumstantial, evidence to support an accusation of espionage. However...

That is when simple and straightforward became rather more complicated and twisted.

'It would be best, gentlemen, ahem, for reasons which I'm sure you will fully appreciate, if we were to concentrate our attention – to begin with – upon evidence which can be put into the, ahem, public domain.'

Even I could see that revealing the MPs passing of that concocted information could reveal also the friend at the receiving end. Carlton was pressing on. His way of speaking could have been applied, without alteration, to the reading out of a shopping list, punctuated with little throat-clearing coughs. To this point the solicitor, strolling around the subject, had not actually instructed us at all. It was then that the Colonel seized the proceedings.

'Perhaps, if I may? Might it not be better if we were to begin with the *objective* of this exercise? where we want to get to.'

Where that familiar first person plural, whoever they were, wished to get to was made unambiguously clear. The following outcomes would serve the nation's best interests: a guilty verdict and the shaming of the MP, who would be forced to resign from parliament; the embarrassment of certain 'diplomats' from the Czechoslovakian Embassy, their recalling to home territory without need for HM government to go through the formal procedures of expelling them – and the almost certain tit-for-tat retaliation; and the discomfiture of the Czech Communist Party and their Russian masters. More than that, the authenticity of all information provided by their erstwhile source would then have to be questioned by the receivers.

'Damaged goods, we might say.'

The Colonel allowed himself the slightest of smiles behind the fingers that stroked his thin white moustache. He resumed.

'Some may wish to argue that we might achieve these results without the need for a trial. I think not. We could, as we have in other instances, quietly make alternative arrangements. A word in the ear. Demands and conditions. In this instance we have determined such a course of action would not best serve our own interests. In this case none of our own people is at fault. Therefore, we are free to let in as much daylight as we choose. We have nothing to hide. We are the good boys and girls.'

The Colonel cast his gaze directly upon Philip and me in turn, slowly, the unspoken question asking if we had understood. What I understood was a sense that ordinary understanding was not sufficiently what was being looked for. Philip nodded a slow assent.

The Colonel resumed.

'Without going to trial, we would miss the deterrent factor. I regret to say there are just too many targets to monitor. We do not have sufficient resources to keep all of them under close observation. So that is why, in this instance' – with a small raising of the head – 'we want to make a very public show.'

The Colonel paused again at this point. Again, there was that silent searching of our understanding.

'A show trial, gentlemen. I think our enemies think we have gone soft. It's more than time we gave our enemies a sharp reminder. Heat and light, gentlemen.'

The Colonel sat back, glanced towards the solicitor and raised a hand to signal to him that he was to complete the account.

'We have prepared a portfolio of evidence, gentlemen. In the first instance, the brief you are charged with is to make an, ahem, independent review. We should like your assessment as to whether there is a substantive case, based on the information you will see on file, and the likelihood of conviction. That information, of course, if we proceed, will have to be, ahem, made known to the defence...'

Philip matter-of-factly pointed out that the review and decision to proceed or not, in any case of alleged espionage, rested with the Attorney-General's office.

'Quite so, Mister Hathers, quite so. But we have in this instance, for the moment, decided to proceed by alternative means. The portfolio to which I allude is not yet, ahem, available to the Attorney-General's office.'

'Do you mean – ?' I had involuntarily started on a question before remembering Philip's exhortation to keep one's mouth shut. The Colonel, however, interjected:

'We have taken the decision, in this case, to proceed with a certain amount of *caution*, shall we say, gentlemen. It is not impossible that the Honourable Member, by virtue of that privileged position, may have friends in other offices. Some of those offices may be close to us, here, even as we speak. Passageways and stairs, gentlemen.'

Carlton came to my rescue.

'Which lead to more, ahem, passageways and stairs which lead to offices of both the Foreign and the Commonwealth departments of government – which are, ahem, located elsewhere in these buildings.'

With a slight lifting of his eyebrows the Colonel resumed:

'So, for now, we have decided to restrict internal circulation of these materials. We would rather, at this stage, avoid even the *possibility* of contamination. We want *you*, gentlemen, to prepare for us your professional opinion. In sum, we need to ensure that the files in this case remain exclusively under our control. For some time yet.'

There passed a mute acknowledgement from Philip, accepted silently by the Colonel. Evidently they understood each other perfectly; a collusion beyond my ignorance.

Carlton then followed with the final part of his shopping-list:

'If we may presume, gentlemen, that your review concludes that there is a very, ahem, *strong* case to be answered –'

'Irrefutable, gentlemen, would be much preferred.'

Despite the Colonel's preference, Carlton persisted along his own careful tippy-toes route.

'If, as I say, you were to conclude, based on the first selection of documents which will be sent to you, that they provide the strongest, ahem, likelihood of conviction, then we shall be in a position to proceed further.'

I must say that Philip displayed not a flicker of curiosity to know more about the case at that point, not a blink of impatience. I admired his imperturbability.

'There is, however, gentlemen, a further matter which the Colonel wishes me to bring to your, ahem, attention.'

Back at chambers two days later Philip and I had our first opportunity to discuss the encounter with Carlton and Jackson. Within the clauses and subsidiary clauses to Carlton's explication of the 'further matter' were questions I had been impatient to ask. Yet he, Philip Hathers, had remained perfectly still throughout.

'My dear Anthony,' he replied, his condescension qualified by the small twinkling of those deep eyes, 'when I am being paid as handsomely as I shall be to listen to such circumlocution, given

that the extra time it takes adds proportionately to my already exaggerated fee, then I am all ears and am content to be the model
of patience.'

My concerns were raised even as Carlton had sidled up to the
last part of our briefing. If, he had said, in due course, following our own review and the case being referred 'upstairs', which
would not be for several months, the Attorney General's office
did finally conclude to proceed to trial, then – though all would
understand this could not form any part of our instructions,
which would remain unwritten, of course – perhaps one might
'Bear in mind, gentlemen, the means by which one might, ahem,
take care of the best interests of the principal witness for the
prosecution – '

'He is, after all, one of ours,' as the Colonel put a peremptory
end to the solicitor's periphrastic indicatives. 'As far as we know.'

The MP's defence team, as Carlton foresaw the eventualities, would almost certainly claim that Mister W (his sole identification, for the present, in the files) was an unreliable witness,
that *he* it was – *not* the defendant MP – who had been the source
of the information transferred to the Czechoslovakian Embassy staff; that as Eastern European correspondent for a leading
national broadsheet, an accredited reporter granted visas to
travel in 'not always the most friendly-disposed' nations, he had
the opportunity both to make and to use such contacts. Thus, if
the case reduced to the simplest of defences – one man's word
against another's – and one of those men carried formally the
honorific of an Honourable gentleman by virtue of his membership of parliament...

'We must tread carefully, Anthony. Watch where we put our
feet.'

Carlton had concluded that Whitehall briefing itself.

'Gentlemen, I shall arrange to have this portfolio sent to your,
ahem, chambers. Your man Booth has been alerted to expect

them and he understands the need to keep these papers in, ahem, close custody, as it were.'

Carlton, unpredictably, allowed himself the lightest hint of amusement at his own turn of phrase. He had also allowed me to confirm that Carlton was the legal adviser from the Home Department with whom Booth had lunched. Colonel Jackson stood, bowed to Hathers and me in turn.

'I propose we meet again in a week from now. Give you time to have a first work-through of the papers. Meet at my office, if that will be convenient to you.' Just as he was about to step away from us he stopped and half-turned back towards Philip. 'Oh and it also goes without saying that you will let us know of anything which it would be judicious to *remove* from the files.'

'But of course.'

Again that complicit understanding between the two of them.

In the taxi on the way back to our chambers, I had a question for Philip. I had not understood what the Colonel had been talking about, that 'right hand, left hand' expression when first he had arrived at the meeting, so –

Philip gave that' Ahh...' exhalation, but said nothing.

Out of the taxi in Fleet Street and when we had reached the gateway entrance to Middle Temple Lane, Philip turned to me as we walked the short distance towards our chambers.

'Our little joke, Anthony – intelligence on the one hand, security on the other. Two services. So, left hand, right hand, as the good Colonel said. But then there is the need to keep each other informed – liaison. Just to be sure that intelligence and security don't both fall over by treading on each other's toes.'

Philip clutched my arm, laughing. 'What a terrible confusion of metaphors, hands and feet.'

Still holding on to me, he walked me past our chambers. 'Of course, as you might know, neither of these services actually exists. Formally, that is. Neither of them, to date, has been ac-knowledged by HM government. *Any* HM government, of any political persuasion.' He pulled us to a stop. 'So now I'd better explain to you what Vernon meant by 'the other side', Anthony. The intelligence boys and girls are the ones housed on the other side. Of the Thames. In Lambeth. So the Colonel 'doing the Lambeth walk' is another little joke among us on this side when we consult with south of the river. And the liaison Vernon men-tioned – it might even have been to do with your friend William.' He paused, gave me a sideways glance. 'I gather there's the possi-bility of a particular job Sir John may want him to do.'

Philip smiled at my blankness.

'Sir John Holyoake. He's in charge of certain matters on the other side of the river. Lovely man, charming wife. You must meet them sometime.'

Clearly there was much, much more for me to learn.

'All in good time, Anthony, all in good time, you'll soon get the hang of things.'

Yes but... Philip wheeled us around to head back to chambers.

THREE

⌒

Plots and practices

Chambers, The Temple

Autumn 1965

11

My *Yes buts* were some time being answered for me. Philip brought the portfolio into my room two days after the Westminster meeting, and invited me to have a first look through the papers; to see what I would see, he said.

'And then to see what you make of what you see.'

I took a preliminary scan of the papers, and by late afternoon I had begun more steadily working my way through, making notes as I went, when I was interrupted by Booth on the telephone.

'Someone here to see you, Mister Anthony. I did say it would be alright for him to call in.'

'Who – ?'

But Booth had put down his receiver. A minute or so later there was the slightest of taps at my door before, very gently, it swung open. There, framed in the doorway, leaning negligently against the jamb, was William, silver-handled cane hooked and swinging gently between thumb and forefinger of one hand, the other hand dipped into waistcoat pocket, and his legs crossed at the ankles. It was more than five years since I had last seen him; and no spoken word had passed between us in that time.

He grinned hesitantly, gathered himself into slow motion and crossed the few steps to my desk where I had stood up, stunned at his sudden and unexpected appearance.

He held out his hand, gripped my hand with a surprising strength.

'Anthony, old fellow. It is so good to see you.'

William clearly enjoyed my confusion. As did Booth, who appeared holding a tray of tea things, doing again his impersonation of a very 'umble manservant. This time, however, he too was smiling broadly, and the looks that passed between him and William said that the two were in collusion. Truthfully, I did not know whether Booth's behaviour or the unannounced appearance of William was the more startling. Something, obviously, had happened in the last week or so to change completely Booth's stance towards me.

'I shall leave you, Mister Anthony, with Mister William.'

Booth stopped at the door.

'Since it is now almost four o'clock, may I ask if you will be working on those papers after your meeting with Mister William?'

I must have looked uncertain, as indeed I was, not knowing how long William would be with me.

'May I suggest, then, that I take them into safekeeping for you? for the time being.'

Permitting no gainsaying, Booth swept up the papers into their folders, tucked the bundle under his arm, glowered at me, and bowed out, backwards.

There was no time for any response, only puzzlement at Booth's untoward behaviour.

I turned to William, appraising him.

'Why didn't you – ?'

'Keep in touch?'

'Yes.'

'Well, I did manage to get off to you a few postcards – which I hope you got – '

I nodded. 'There was never an address I could reply to, only the country you'd sent them from.'

I poured teas for us.

'Ah, well, yes. Sorry. Never quite sure how long I would be at any address before moving on. But and none the less, I would have sent you more postcards from here and there, perhaps the occasional letter, old fellow, if I'd been convinced you really would have wanted to retain me in your life.' He gave the slightest of shrugs. 'I mean, life after Oxford, given that life there was somewhat contrived, artificial.'

I demurred. Of course I would have wished William to keep in touch with me, for us to have continued our friendship, I said. William did look a little askance at that. He was, in truth, the retrospective truth of things I am now trying to set down, right to do so. Friendship, as a parity of equal esteem, was a claim that could not have been sustained on the evidence of our joint years at Oxford. We had a relationship across the years there, but it was one in which I (and my peers) patronised the man.

William's dark eyes fixed me. His look also pinned down, if I may put it this way, the claim of friendship.

I offered with open hand palm up the chair at the other side of my desk. William subsided the length of his body into it, his legs stretched out.

'Had I realised that, then without doubt I would have ensured that we would have kept regular contact. Somehow.' He paused, before adding: 'Especially given the way things are turning out.'

William pulled the armchair closer to my desk and sat upright.

'But how – ?' I began.

'How did I know where to find you?'

'Yes.'

William, in a gesture which instantly diminished the gap of years, extended the immaculate, long fingers of one hand across the palm of his other hand.

'One simply had to ask someone who knows.'

Some perversity prevented me from asking the obvious question here as to *who* was this someone? I switched to asking him about his life since he had left Oxford.

'Not much to tell old fellow. Someone must have put in a good word for me with the British Council. Spent a few months' familiarisation in the office, doing a bit of this and that, some admin even to help out, earn my bread as it were. Lowly work, my friend, routine but essential, getting things organised, doing the things that have to be done so that other things may happen. Must say, I surprised myself. I actually enjoyed the work and found I was rather good at it.'

'And then?'

'And then, having served a bit of time, it was decided I should do some touring, get myself *known* as it was put to me, bring a little of English culture to the tiny minority among our overseas friends who might be interested in our heritage of literature. Spent some time working up a series of lectures and it was fixed for me to tout them around various places. Not the most demanding of work.'

'Where did you go?'

'Oh, here and there, you know. Finland, Denmark, Malta – simply had to pay respects there – Switzerland – so organised and so bland, couldn't believe the boredom; Italy, Greece – guest of the Anglo-Hellenic Association in Athens. Anywhere that would have me, really.'

'I thought you were in Lisbon.'

William turned on me his dark eyes.

'Has someone been to have a little chat with you as well?'

I pretended lack of surprise. Something Philip had said, and then this 'as well' to snag at a doubt which, fleetingly, had almost taken shape at Philip's words. Who, 'as well' as me, would have been spoken to? Keeping my mouth shut was not in itself sufficient. I had to learn how to put a complete change of behaviour alongside that silence. The best I could do was again to attempt a change of subject. I asked if he would be in London long, or whether he would be off on his travels again, the itinerant lecturer.

'Ah, well, thereby hangs a decision one might say. Right now, though, I've managed to wangle some leave to get on with my research, have rather been neglecting WW of late.'

On the point of asking it came back to me: William Walsh, his namesake. William had mentioned the coincidence somewhere in those past Oxford years.

'Shall have to put the hours in I'm afraid, so it's off to the BM for me. There's a letter-book of the old boy there, know the contents to expect of course, given that some scholar went through it some years ago. But one must be seen to be thorough in these things, to go through due process. So then, after the BM, I shall be off to the Bodleian again.'

With a small lifting of one hand he signalled the teapot, and at my negative, replenished his own cup.

'The same woman scholar, as a matter of fact, who went through the BM material also came up with an interesting finding. As we know, all the biographical references to the man give 1663 as his year of birth. Even the newer ones, they still give 1663. Yet when our sleuth of a scholar went back to the parish register for Abberley where my WW was born, she found that he had been baptised on the sixth of October of the preceding year. Fascinating, no?'

This was, exactly, an example of that arcane knowledge which had so occupied and so entertained William. Suddenly he sounded as he did in those Oxford times when, with languid enthusiasm, he displayed his knowledge, or teased one with knowledge of something rare or recondite, and took pleasure in knowing how this cast him in one's eyes. Now he was smiling to himself as if in recognition of that old reputation. But he was different from those times, or I saw him differently, no doubt as a result of what Colonel Jackson had told me about the man. He seemed to me to be just a little withdrawn from that Oxford version of himself, a little less expressive, less expansive. There were, of course, the simple facts that we were both older, each of us moving in a different environment now, and that we had not seen each other for several years.

William sipped at his tea, everything, except a cursory scrutiny of my room, now given over to those few minutes in which he savoured again the Lapsang which Booth had produced for us. The silence between us betokened the break in our relationship. Neither of us seemed sure how to close that gap, how to return to that former, much more easygoing rapport. I was still trying to work out what there was about William which had changed. I noticed that his waistcoat on this day was a dark grey, so that his whole appearance seemed more muted. I did not think this the full explanation for the difference I sensed, but it did lead me on to think that William actually appeared to me to be more deliberative, almost calculating. In those Oxford years, whilst obviously intending to make an impression, his manner and his appearance were carried with insouciance. Now it was as if William was to some degree willing himself to be that William, making himself up to be something of what he was, or what he had been.

He finished his tea, lazily reached out to the tray on my desk to return his cup and saucer.

And there was something else. William was *watching* me. By this I do not simply mean that he was looking at me, in the customary way in which one looks to and away from the other person in a conversation. Those dark eyes were searching, detectors of my every movement.

'A walk, Anthony? It is a fine sunny day. I think I would rather like to stroll around the Temple. What do you say?'

I demurred, but he insisted.

It was a calm, fine late October day. At that hour of the day there was thin sunshine still, perfect for wandering around the grounds, the courts, and the buildings of The Temple. It was quickly apparent, once we had stepped out of chambers, that William knew the place well. We wandered, seemingly at will but actually to William's direction, from Middle Temple Lane towards the Temple church. I noticed with amusement that William still transferred both walking-stick and mock limp from one side of his body to another. He punctuated our stroll with occasional brief comment, pointing to this or that historical feature or person or place.

'And how is the beautiful Carolyne?'

I was taken by surprise with the question for it presumed that he knew Carolyne and I were together once more. Since Carolyne and I had separated on her going down from Oxford, and William had known of that, one might have expected him to ask if there were *any* woman in my life. We were standing alongside the engraved stone slab, at the rear of the Temple church, raised to the memory of Oliver Goldsmith.

'Another wrong date.' William rested the end of his walking stick on the date of birth inscribed to the poet. 'Out by a couple of years, so even younger than that' – moving his stick along to the date of death – 'when he died.'

William turned his dark eyes towards me:

'Have you two set a date yet for your engagement, may I inquire?'

'I didn't know you knew.'

William just lifted the brim of his hat, a fractional acknowledgement.

'I heard you and Carolyne had got together again and were about to plight your troths to each other.'

Again I suppressed the obvious *who* or *how* questions. I haltingly explained to him my prevarication on the issue, a holding-back for no good reason which I could readily identify. It was my reluctance, I said, not yet having established myself, certainly not having achieved anywhere near a decent income... all to be considered before... you know. So, anyway, we would not announce a formal engagement until, well, sometime in the future. Carolyne and I had talked it over at some length.

'Bacherlorhood, like virginity, is a condition that cannot be restored, would you not say? Once it has been surrendered... or given away. But I must be glad for you that you are about to enter upon the state of matrimony.'

William's words brought to mind the memory of my Great-Uncle Ranulph, the cause of my being here, doing what I was doing and setting down the markers for the rest of my working life. So I asked William if he remembered me talking to him, towards the end of our first shared year at Oxford, about my Great-Uncle and his bequest.

'Of course I do, my dear fellow.'

'Well, the old boy had a few amusing words of his own to the point of marriage.' I started to quote, but had got no further than 'folly' before William took up the words and recited for me the whole text of my Great-Uncle's follies with women – 'with the exception of marriage.'

'The words are pure William Walsh, I'm afraid, old fellow. Your Great-Uncle must have purloined them. *Letters Amorous and Gallant*, no mistaking them.'

We had returned to the entrance to the church, but by raising his stick William conveyed his wish to pass by. We wandered on, mainly recalling our Oxford peers, sharing what little news of them which had come the way of either of us. Between times, William asked questions about my training, what it had entailed, and whether the law was indeed proving to be 'the right fit' for me. We were strolling back towards Fountain Court, with Middle Temple Hall to our left, when William gently laid a restraining hand upon my shoulder.

'I am sorry to drag you into all this, Anthony.'

'All this what?'

'Oh, you know, you and Carolyne having to answer all those questions from strangers.'

'No, William. Just me.'

I thought William was about to say something in response, his eyes full upon me, appearing much softer, kindlier close up than I had thought them previously. But then, I recognised, I had never stood this near to him, not full-faced to each other anyway. He turned away, head down, stepping out again so that I followed.

'Ah... ' It was a long exhalation. 'My mistake. Sorry, I just naturally presumed that... after all, the two of you were together when we were at Oxford, so you both knew me, of course.'

William quickened pace. I reached out to hold on to the sleeve of his coat, to slow him down.

'My congratulations, by the way. She is a very fine girl.'

William turned away from me, striding off again. There had been already an occasional twinge of something unresolved some days back, when I thought of Carolyne's borrowing of my photographs – distracted as I was at the time by the press of her body against me. There was something... unsatisfactory that insisted upon itself. Now there was something else which, though undefined, added another thin layer of unease to that sense of something unsatisfactory.

We walked on in silence until we entered Fountain Court. William made for one of the benches around the pool of the fountain. We sat there for some time, William just fixedly staring at the broken surface of the water where the fountain's jet fell back. Several times he seemed to be about to speak. When he did, it was a quiet reflection:

'Do you remember, Anthony, what was said of Pecksniff?'

Ah, a reference I did know: *Martin Chuzzlewhit* and the sham of an architect in the tale. Rather weakly, I replied that much was said about the man.

'But in particular: 'the more he was found out, the more hypocrisy he practised'.'

William turned to me full-face, a wan slow grimace.

'When you consider the post-war politics we are playing out, we're both caught up in it – let's at least drop pretence between us two – all that hubble-bubble toil and trouble, the games, deceiving each other and being deceived, and when we are found out, so the more do we proclaim our innocence. And that's despite the entire *table d'hôte* of inventions, lies, pretence, deceptions, secrets we do not have but must pretend to possess, secrets we steal which turn out to tell us what we already knew... this is by way of my apology for you getting dragged into *my* duplicity.'

I did not understand this final remark, but I did not take him up on it. Keeping things very general, I made in turn the lame excuse that I had not taken, still did not take, much interest in politics. After all, there had been stacks of studying to do, and now there were reams of case papers to read. One had to keep one's head down.

'Quite.'

Stiletto sharp and thin, the penetration of that single syllable was both the shortest and the most incisive rebuke I can ever recall. It was a condemnation.

Unexpectedly, there was a low chuckle from him. Then, abruptly and almost cheerily, he left me with this parting.

'Look, old fellow, I have some leave I am due. I would be delighted to meet up again at leisure, say in a couple of weeks or so from now. How about dinner on me one evening? Yes? I shall telephone you in chambers, don't want to disturb you at home.'

I started to say that I would not mind if he telephoned me at home, and offered to give him my number. But he waved it away.

'Not necessary, old fellow.'

'But – ' There were questions I wanted to put to this man who, even if he was as he seemed to be, was no longer the man I had known.

'Sorry, my dear Anthony, but I have to dash.'

With that William eased his long frame upright from the bench, stretched out a hand, gripped mine, and held it for a few seconds. He turned and walked away, his long strides easing him to the gateway of Middle Temple Lane to lead him out into Fleet Street. The ferrule of his stick tap-tapped its accompaniment to his steps, and with a long arm raised above his head, he waved his farewell as he disappeared from my sight.

William had been changed for me by Colonel Jackson. Now he had changed again by behaviour which was out of keeping with the man I once knew.

There was something else. Following his visit the seed of doubt unwittingly planted by Carolyne was beginning to take root and sprout.

12

That night, back in my flat, at one of those promptings which, however minor or lightweight, must be acted upon immediately, I looked up William's namesake. The entry in the bibliographical dictionary, a remnant from Oxford days, began:

WALSH, WILLIAM (1663 – March 18, 1708), critic and poet, born at Abberley, Worcestershire, attended Wadham College, Oxford; did not graduate. Gentleman of the Horse at court of Queen Anne from 1702 until his death...

Exactly as William had said, so was this William Walsh alleged to have been born the year following his baptism. I had no reason to doubt William's check and confirmation of the scholar's work which had first alerted him to the anomaly.

Elected four times Member of Parliament, as Protestant and Whig. Developed friendships with both Dryden and Pope. Dryden proclaimed Walsh the best critic in the nation. Dryden acknowledged Walsh's advice to him as to how to excel at verse: 'for though we had several great poets, we never had any one great poet that was correct...'

I read more to the same burden, the help Walsh had been in editing and criticising many of Pope's manuscript poems, the references to Walsh in Cibber's and Johnson's *Lives of the Poets*. I skipped to the bottom of the biographical entry where Walsh's own writings were listed to see that most of his work had not been published until several years following his death – 'aged forty-five', according to the entry. And there, published eight years after his death, was listed *Letters Amorous and Gallant*. Looking back to the preceding text I found the fuller quotation which, William had assured me, contained the original of my Great-Uncle

Ranulph's sentiment concerning the ladies in his life. From the second of Walsh's *Letter to a Friend*, I read:

> ...from this time forward, upon what Follies soever you fall, be pleased for my sake to spare those of Love; being very well satisfied, there is not one Folly of that kind (except marriage) which I have not already committed.

After *Works* of 1736, presumably the collected works, no later bibliographical entry was cited for subsequent reprintings. Apart from what appeared to be long neglect, I had not to that point seen anything which accounted for William's fascination with Walsh. The few hundreds of words of the entry did provide, however, a summation which gave me cause for reflection:

> Walsh appears to have written largely for his own amusement. His poems, amorous and elegiac, display a skilled technique, and are not without charm and elegance. Walsh was a cultivated dilettante and a dandy...

13

After William's mid-week visit I felt as if I was trying now to see my way through a fairly dense mist of elusive clue and innuendo.

My mood was not helped by Booth who did his unaccustomed best to cheer me up.

'Quite a character I would say, Mister Anthony, your visitor, Mister William.'

'Yes, quite.' My monosyllables offered no encouragement to Booth to proceed any further.

'A very interesting man, by all accounts.'

I looked up at Booth who had taken his stance at the edge of my desk, untidily covered with papers I was attempting to work my way through. Truth to tell, I was somewhat out of sorts for the work, just wanting to get the week over and done with. It was when Booth bestowed upon me that knowing smile, that unmistakable sign of knowing something that one does not know oneself, or one is presumed not to know, that my pique really set in.

'By *whose* accounts may that be, Booth?'

If Booth recognised my sarcasm he passed it by. He had his own presence. He carried himself and his responsibilities with ease and self-assurance. He had been with these chambers for the best part of twenty years and had reached that point of eminence where everyone, despite Hathers's demurral, was wholly dependent upon him. He was, in the eyes of the seniors and juniors alike, simply irreplaceable. I suppose the initial reaction Booth had taken to me was a result of me simply not knowing this magisterial position of his, not paying him proper obeisance, not acknowledging his superiority. Things were different now. Booth and I had shifted the grounds of our relationship; or rather, Booth had shifted the grounds. He was just that little bit more solicitous of me, making a point of enquiring about my weekends, what I did, where I went, how I spent my leisure. I began to relax in his forbidding presence; we began to share moments of humour. I became an individual in his eyes, rather than being just another young cub he would have to nurture and mature. But this new relationship with Booth discomfited me. Where I had been wary of him, of what I responded to as his inflated self-importance, our new relationship seemed to be founded on collusion. It was a complicity which Booth signalled and summarised with a tapping of his nose. What secrets or compacts unspoken between us were they to which he alluded by this incomprehensible behaviour?

At that moment, however, challenging Booth to reveal the sources by which William could be estimated an 'interesting man' merely added grist to the mill of his enjoyment. Like most people Booth could savour the possession of a secret only if others knew that he possessed the secret.

'Strictly on the QT, Mister Anthony, strictly on the QT.'

Booth was set on his own path, which detoured any direct answer to my question.

'Ah yes, your Mister William. I had occasion to speak with him on the telephone to arrange a convenient time for him to visit here. A most charming man.' Booth paused, reflecting how to assemble his next comment. 'His appearance in person may be, to some observations, shall we say, rather distinctive – '

I laughed aloud at Booth's circumambulation.

'That's one way to put it.'

'Though one, as always, should not judge a book by its cover.'

'Agreed.'

'As I understand matters, your friend is highly thought of, Mister Anthony, *very* highly thought of by people *we* should think very highly of.'

From Booth this sounded like an admonition. I tried to adopt a suitable face of contrition, but he was not yet done with me.

He let it be known to me that his first contact with the Home Department solicitor had led to another meeting, or meetings – Booth's nodding and winking did not make it clear. But further liaison between them I had already guessed at for myself. I thought of the nondescript Carlton whom Philip Hathers and I had met. I thought I would let Booth know that I knew his secret.

'Ah, your meetings with Mister Carlton, I presume.'

If Booth were disappointed at my little burst of knowledge, he did not show it.

'Yes indeed, Mister Anthony, the very same. An unassuming man, would you not say? one who carries his position with quiet modesty?'

From this I inferred that Carlton had shown proportionate deference to Booth in recognition of Booth's own position and importance. Booth went on to allow me to shape the impression, rather than be directly and explicitly told, that he too had been fully briefed.

'And so you see...' Booth opened his palms.

What exactly I was supposed to see tailed into its silence. Booth, however, was satisfied that I was now fully cognisant of all the information of substance he had thought owing to me. I could see his intention: since Booth now gave the impression that he knew everything, having been fully briefed, as he thought, by Carlton, there was no need for me to conceal anything from him. He expected me, therefore, to keep him in-the-know, so that he would learn everything that came my way. I did wonder if he had attempted this same persuasion with Hathers, on whom it would have had no effect whatsoever. Thus he leaned upon me, as a weaker resistance.

'I also had occasion to meet up with your Colonel Jackson, in fact he was kind enough to invite Carlton and me to lunch.' Booth looked up with triumph barely concealed. 'A most informative meeting. And one which confirms these chambers in a very favourable light. As in the past so with regard to future prospective business which we can expect to be put our way.'

Booth had played his trump. I congratulated him. He tried to conceal a certain smugness of satisfaction, barely succeeding. In all this trumpery, there was a message which he had come to deliver.

'I have spoken again with Colonel Jackson. He invites you to arrange a meeting with him, at your convenience, to keep him informed of the progress of your preparation for that *particular* case one may expect to come to trial next year.' Booth could barely suppress an accompanying wink. 'He also says, and sends his apologies, but would you mind very much going to *his* office in Mayfair. He has such a lot on at the moment. Any time will do, but Thursday or Friday afternoon of next week would *very* much be preferred.'

'I shall speak with Mister Havers.'

'I have done so already, Mister Anthony – on your behalf of course. Mister Philip would himself very much appreciate it if you would undertake that chore. As you are aware, he is committed to a case scheduled for the High Court for next Wednesday onwards. Priorities, Mister Anthony, priorities.'

This was Booth's way of putting me in my place. I had also known from the start that as Hathers's junior I would be the hack, the errand-boy, the go-between. Having been assigned the rôle I stifled any reaction to Booth's ill-disguised satisfaction in reminding me of my lowly status. But I was keen to learn, I needed to learn, I needed some high-level experience. Whatever Booth's motive might have been, the outcomes would be to my advantage.

'Of course. Understood.'

Booth locked together the fingers of his hands.

'Mister Anthony, if I may take up another moment of your time, there is one other matter.'

'And what is that, Booth?'

'There are, in these busy chambers, papers entering and leaving every working day. It has not gone unnoticed that some of our esteemed colleagues can be, shall we say, somewhat lax with regard to the security of those same papers.'

Booth searched my reaction to ensure that I had followed him thus far.

'I do not speak of those files which are boxed and properly supervised on their way to court. I refer to papers which find their way to and fro these chambers in our barristers' briefcases. *Briefcases*, Mister Anthony. Further, it has been known on at least three occasions in my time here that such a briefcase has been lost, left in the back of a taxi or left on an underground train. Fortunately, in all cases, they were recovered and no lasting harm was done.'

Booth looked again to see that I had understood the full import of what he was saying. He was going to continue, whatever one said.

'As Mister Hathers's appointed junior, you have now been made privy *to some particular papers*' – these words so quiet as to be a whispered secret – 'which we must all ensure are treated with the greatest possible security.'

I signalled assent.

'A guardedness which must extend even to one's own private chamber.' He gave time for this to sink in, though Booth's follow-up was too cryptic for me to follow. 'It simply will not do, Mister Anthony. It will not.'

'What will not do, Booth?'

He looked at me in some astonishment that I had not been clairvoyant enough to see for myself the implication of his words.

'Why, to leave on one's desk, *on display*, those same papers when one is entertaining a guest in one's chamber.'

'But – '

'There can be no *Buts*, Mister Anthony. Had I not taken swift action to remove those papers from your desk, they might have been seen by eyes not intended to see them.'

It was useless to argue. The eyes for whom they had not been intended could have been none other than those of William, for whom there had been no time even to glance at those papers, far less take any interest in them – which simply would not have been within his curiosity in any case. I suppressed my disbelief that William, the man whom only moments earlier Booth had been praising, could be regarded as a potential spy. I did what I had to do: adopt a suitably contrite air – which Booth acknowledged with an inclination of the head.

'And so I have taken additional measures to ensure the security of those files. They will be signed in and out of my guardianship, and at all times – save when required either by Mister Philip or yourself – they will remain locked in the master safe. When in your possession, it will be your responsibility to safeguard their security.'

I had a flashback to an occasion at school when the Old Beak had called me into his office for a dressing-down. There had been a minor misdemeanour which involved one of the masters' scarf, the amber ball of a belisha beacon, and the weathervane at the top of the school tower. Booth had the same capacity to intimidate.

Philip Hathers had already shared his diary with me so that we could arrange working sessions together. These sessions, given Philip's commitments, were of necessity short. But in them were displayed his surgical skill at cutting away unwanted or superfluous information. Philip, as expressed in the unbuttoned chit-chat among his peers, was known to have 'a nose.' As a person, when more fully spoken of among his peers, he had a nose like a letter-opener, long and thin, but perfect for sticking into the affairs of a case and for slitting open certain facets the opposition would prefer to keep closed.

'Get to the bare bones first, Anthony. You can put the flesh on the bones afterwards. If you have to, you can even put some clothes on the flesh for the sake of decency. But what the jury will remember will be the bare bones. You start and finish with the bare bones. They are the story. Now, let's see how far you've got with assembling the skeleton.'

Philip, I thought, had a voice that would have made a preacher, a preacher in the tradition of nineteenth century nonconformism. Somehow the dark shadows of those deep-set eyes fitted him for the pulpit. He would have preached not in any hellfire, sulphur and brimstone damnation mode, but with determined and declaratively emphatic certainty. You might not have believed what he said, but you would not have doubted that he thought it true. He was known and admired for the persuasiveness of his summings-up.

This Monday afternoon in his room was the only time Philip could donate to the exercise that week, given the pending case due to begin on Wednesday. We needed to work out what I would present to Colonel Jackson before the end of the week. I took Philip through my own 'bare bones' of a summary.

'So what's missing, Anthony? You recall Professor Godbole? 'Absences are as important as presences' – a little *aide-memoire* we do well to hold on to in our business.'

In my first and only year studying literature at Oxford we had not got on to any of the moderns in my seminars. Philip therefore presumed a knowledge I did not have, but I found out afterwards the reference to *A Passage to India*; even managed to read the book some months later.

We went on in inquisitorial fashion for another hour or so. We went through the pages of the grid, cross-checking surveillance photographs and officer observation logs, summary reports, transcripts of bugged conversations and telephone calls, copies of intercepted letters. Of all the raw materials present in the files, I think these had surprised me more than anything else, with the exception of printed bank statements belonging to the Member of Parliament in question.

'Don't look so alarmed, Anthony. I'm sure that Vernon's boys and girls have got their Warrants for everything here.'

Those authorised permissions had produced material which was certainly persuasive and might well work as an alternative stratagem, one which I suppressed at that moment.

'There is something else also, bearing in mind the good Colonel's words to us. It would seem that publicity around this case, if indeed it does go to trial, is deemed as important as the conviction. Perhaps more so.'

'Yes but why?'

'Because, Anthony – and here I speculate, of course – there might be other targets. Perhaps two or three particular targets, suspected of spying in one form or another, against whom verifiable facts either can not be obtained, or are insufficient, or are unconvincingly circumstantial only?'

This so-called speculation from Philip carried the bell-like resonance of a fine glass of lead crystal when its rim is struck. It was certain, then, that Philip must have been briefed additionally, and almost certainly before the briefing I had attended with him.

'Why just two or three?'

The numbers did not have that casual for-want-of-a-number imprecision. Not 'two or three', but two *or* three: there had been a distinct, though fractional pause between the two numerals as Philip had spoken them. I made my inferences. So: two confirmed, or pretty well confirmed on the information so far available, a third suspected, evidence insufficient or unconvincing or both. Suddenly Philip grinned, more a creasing at the sides of his eyes than a widening of his mouth. He was testing me, and it was as if he had actually watched me working things out; what I had made of what I had heard.

'Of course, I don't *know* that it's two – or – three.'

With that reply it was clear that Philip *did* know and that I was now drawn into the collusion of a pretence of ignorance.

An observation ventured. With regard to those other two – or – three, would it not be better, I asked, to continue with the surveillance and monitoring which, presumably, had been going on anyway, so that one might then be in a position to proceed against all of them and secure an even more comprehensive result?

Philip accompanied his pretence with a lifting of his eyes and, fingers splayed, pressed hands together in an attitude of prayer.

'Perhaps. Though it may be that timing is critical too, Anthony, and one must presume that those who make these decisions have a timetable of their own in mind. *When* whatever will take place here may well have a calculated effect elsewhere. Or it may have been decided that further delay would not be to our advantage? That by the time sufficient and verifiable information has been obtained on the other two – or – three persons, some other important opportunity may have been lost? Again, I speculate, of course.'

Philip's dissimulation allowed us a way of proceeding which did not oblige him to breach explicitly any knowledge to which he had been made *privy* – to use Booth's word.

I wondered aloud who these two, or three, other persons might be. Philip invited me to consider 'our man in question' and his position as an Honourable Member of Parliament. By virtue of that position, and the fourteen years in which he had been in that position, would it not be feasible to conjecture that by now the man might not only 'know his way around' the corridors of power, but also have *entrées* to some of the doors in some of those corridors? Additionally, not to forget, the man had been chosen to serve on the all-party Commons Select Defence Committee. Perhaps he had been proposed as a compensation for not having achieved either office or distinction in the considerable number of years since his election to the House. A reward then for being a good (that is, biddable) party man throughout. That too was not unknown.

'Or he was nominated simply to make up the numbers, even them out across the parties. He, as all the other committee members on that particular committee, might have been given just a cursory looking over, quite unofficially, of course, not a formal vetting. It would have been presumed that by virtue of being a Member of Parliament one is, what shall we say, *sound* in all respects – *Honourable* in person as in title.'

From an inside pocket of his jacket Philip fetched up his pipe.

'Now it is possible that there are others against whom a question mark has been entered on a file – given even such a limited going-over. Nothing definitive, you understand, a question mark, and one that could have resulted from numerous causes.'

We considered what such causes might be. We racketed them between us like a tennis ball. Drink. Over-fondness for. Loquacity when drunk. Other forms of indiscretion. The shabby and the seedy, meeting-places for the *habitués* of. Women, of course, the original sin of so many Adams, their over-fondness for. Or men. Or boys. Over-fondness for, either or both. Or women and men, *both*. Was known, yes. One of the present members of the House of Lords, no less. So it was said. But well-attested, at least attested by a goodly few. Will all come out in years to come. As it did. And loneliness. Never underestimate loneliness. All those long hours in the House. Know what to do with yourself then, your time taken care of. But what to do outside of those hours? Someone to talk with, to spend time with. If you don't have a life outside. Or that life is a long way off. Or it is dull, unsatisfying... Oh!

and disappointment. What a man will do when his genius has not been recognised...

Philip had by now got the mouthpiece of his empty pipe wedged between his teeth. The pipe waggled up and down as he spoke.

'Indiscretions make persons vulnerable to exploitation. The prospect of shame, of being shamed, of having been found out, is a powerful motivator in a man. He will go to extraordinary lengths to avoid such public humiliation.'

But there must be those, I protested, who choose to do things out of conviction, a political cause. In a way one could even argue that such men were not so much 'betraying their country' as promoting systems of government elsewhere which they considered superior. In that, they might even be regarded as men of conviction.

'Ah, indeed. There may be those who act out of belief, out of a contending and firmly-held ideology. They want to change the world to match that ideology. After long and considered reflection, however, I would say this to my junior counsel. Ideologies do not grow flowers, my dear Anthony. Ideologies, of whatever cast, promote and end in subjugation and imposition. It is of the nature of an ideology that it is held, as a moral conviction, by but a few. Unfortunately these few know what is best for the rest of us, and thereby seek to impose the practice of their ideology upon us.'

Philip looked towards the ceiling. Pipe removed, he outspread his hands, lifting them a little away from the sides of his body.

'And as none of us should need reminding: much is lost in translation from theory to practice.'

But what of these particular other two – or – three, I wanted to know.

'I imagine, my dear Anthony, they would be the two or three who have insisted on calling more concentrated attention on themselves – from a much longer list of suspected candidates:

fellow MPs, fellow travellers, Trades Union bosses, members of the GB Communist Party, high-ups and low-downs in important industries... and so on. Some, no doubt, do indeed act from principled conviction. And of *our* man there can no doubt either. *His* betrayal of country is motivated by the grubbiest of all causes, Anthony. Greed. Greed can take many forms, as we know, but greed in his case takes the form of money. Just that; impure and simple. Look here.'

Philip directed my attention to the MP's bank statements, all of which showed an undeclared and regular monthly payment into his account. Today I find that figure quite as staggering as I did then. Just one of those monthly payments was more than half the average annual income for those days. And that man's supplementary income came tax-free. Since my own income, having not long started out on my own qualified practice, was fluttering markedly below that average income line, I began to feel a sense of personal grievance towards the man. In truth, I think I felt more antagonism towards him on this count than on the prospective charges of selling whatever secrets may have come his way. More than that, the Honourable gentleman had been taking this monthly retainer for several years. By whatever route these payments found their way into his account, they had originated with the Czechoslovak State security and intelligence service. On these matters there was no doubt.

Philip stood and placed himself, back to me, at the window, stretching his arms.

'I think I need to have another word or two before we go much further. Somehow we must squeeze in another meeting. Afraid it will have to be early tomorrow morning. Say eight-thirty, no later, an hour, no more.'

With that he ushered me on my way.

Yes but, I thought, I still have other *Yes buts* that have not been answered.

14

In this period of time there was a confluence of influences which, like the meeting of several streams, created a fast current which bore me along. Even if I had held out a hand there was no branch I could have reached out to, to cling to, and pull myself to shore again. I was simply carried along to the current's destination. And that, cliché though it is, inevitably leaves one, when the current releases its grip, all at sea.

The same evening of that meeting with Hathers, back in my own flat, I could not settle to anything. So I gave in to my mood, found a bottle of port with still a couple of glassfuls in it, and stretched myself out on the sunken sofa.

I was absorbed by the case of the MP. The case papers were opening up for me a world which one vaguely knew existed, a world of shadows, of surveillance and security officers, of espionage and counter-espionage, a world which trafficked in the gold coinage of 'information'. There was an elaborate game being played, and I was standing on its sidelines, knowing nothing of the rules or conditions to which it was played. Unbidden I suddenly could not help thinking of the children's playground taunt 'I know something you don't know.' But these were Cold War years, the playground was Europe, and the players were adults. These were dangerous times with Europe split in two and most of the rest of the political world taking one side or the other. I had confessed to William my ignorance of much of contemporary political events. Even so, it was impossible not to be aware of the tensions, in the most general of terms, of those years which made very public, noisy news.

Certainly there was justice in William's one-word condemnation, that day in Fountain Court, of my lack of awareness. A good number of my peers at Oxford had engaged with the world of politics, as students and activists, as protesters. Later, some of them made careers out of politics, a few rising to prominent governmental positions over the course of the years. I preferred sport, cricket and rugby, which left little enough time for me to keep my head down over my books simply in order to attain decent marks in examinations. Politics, if I thought of them at all, meant the Conservative Party and pretty much pro everything it stood for – none of which, I confess with shame, I could have cited in any detail, all of which I took as read (never having even looked at any party manifesto), and none of which up to that point in my life I had challenged. God, in the form of the Church of England, was another unthinking acceptance, and both were self-evidently on the side of the Conservative Party. It was the Holy Alliance into which I had been born. I simply had not engaged with events in the wider world.

Just the year before I had gone up to Oxford, for example, was a momentous year. Soon after William's chivvying of my lack of awareness, I looked up what I had allowed to pass me by. Thus that pivotal series of events throughout the spring, summer, and autumn of 1956, registered by me only in passing as they were reported, were not engaged with. Czechoslovakia: the agitation by writers, intellectuals, and students for freedoms denied them by their national Communist Party and government – freedom for press and government, freedom to travel. Poland: the demonstrations in Poznan and their bloody suppression; renewed rioting and unrest later in the year. Hungary and the deaths, as later established, of thousands; Soviet troops, tanks, and air strikes to crush the rebellion, fighting in the streets, all in the name, again, of freedoms. These desires for the ordinary wants of life I had never questioned as mine by right. What I took for granted others were fighting for, and dying in the attempt to secure them. Today, I would not forget to add in other crimes and misdemeanours of that year of

1956, notably Egypt: the United Kingdom, France, and the Suez War. The point I am struggling to express is that at the time, as a youth of seventeen and approaching the end of my schooldays, I allowed these things to pass me by without any sense of personal outrage.

I confess to feeling very much more involved in the year following those events. I recall with ease the date which stirred my imagination: the 4th of October – the launch of the Russian artificial satellite *Sputnik* which, astonishingly, circled the earth in the near boundary of space in not much more than ninety minutes. I recall spending several nights with upturned binoculars hoping to get a glimpse of its track, its elevation and direction and times of passing by, as published in several newspapers. I attended to every detail, and to its follow-up satellite launched the following month by the Russians, the one carrying into space a dog by the name of Laika. That Sputnik too I tried to track through the night sky. I failed to catch a sight of either satellite, but that failure did not in the least diminish my sense of excitement and the certainty that a new technological and scientific era had been launched with those satellites. They were precursors to a future which one could see. Other happenings, the politics of suppression and the urge to be free of such restrictions within puppet states of the Russian bloc of eastern European countries simply did not resonate their significance with me. Sheltered and spoiled, because I did not know the post-war past, I had no sense of future development.

Hence William's remark, his judgement passed on me in that recent visit, was very much with me. I had brooded on his cuttingly monosyllabic 'Quite' which seemed to expand into an inclusive rebuke of all that I had allowed to pass before me. He was right. In the quiet solitariness of my flat that evening I was beginning to see my own narrowness; one's lack of engagement with the fate of others because all is right in one's own world.

But all of these thoughts were swirling and inter-mixing with quite different thoughts. There was the prospect also that this case, though it would not make my name, would nevertheless provide me with significant enhancement. Its prospect was beginning to capture my imagination. I would be junior to a QC of rare talent (and expensive talent, as Philip Hathers himself said of himself). To appear alongside him, it being known that I would have assisted with the preparation of the case, could do me nothing but good. So, yes, there was some intermittent day-dreaming too: seeing my future as a barrister take off, criminal law my chosen specialism, and the high-profile cases that would win me recognition and, so I wished, the admiration of my legal peers.

Whilst within this occluded cloud of reflection, Carolyne chose to telephone me. I must have sounded half asleep, because the first thing she asked me was whether I was OK. With that reassurance given, Carolyne was launched.

Carolyne was a dear, sweet girl. Everyone, with the sole exception of my mother, thought so. I should say, of course, that I fell in love with her. But the truth is that I fell in lust with her. I think that is true of most men with regard to most women. Women, however, fall in love with the future; and the man, the chosen one, is seen as an essential component for the translation of that woman's present to her future perfect tense. That it was lust I fell into with Carolyne I recognised even throughout the more than two years between her leaving Oxford and us meeting up again in London. Certainly I missed her presence in my bed in those stretches of time when I was its sole occupant. But girls seemed to enjoy my company and I had a good social life on the limited funds I had managed to preserve from Great-Uncle Ranulph's bequest. That and the occasional cheque father would slip my way on visits home. So the compensations of alternative company dulled any ache I might have felt for Carolyne. Did I miss everything that Carolyne was? The simple fact of the matter probably speaks for itself: Carolyne searched *me* out some time after her return to London. I had not gone looking for her.

Once having met up again, we simply stuck together, on my part by a sort of lethargy. Lack of dissent became tacit assent, at least in Carolyne's mind. Thus there had begun a new phase in our relationship when Carolyne had started to agitate to meet my parents. I had found excuse after excuse to defer that encounter between Carolyne and my parents. It was true that my parents had taken to travelling, father stepping down a rung or two at his merchant bank, so there were times when they were not at home. There were also times when mother said: 'We really would rather not, not that weekend anyway' – mother and father either having been invited by friends, or inviting friends, to dinner, or she had planned a shopping trip, or my older brother and his wife and infant would be staying with them... or there would be something else which made that proposed date equally inconvenient.

Mother, when finally I did take Carolyne to meet my parents, instantly took against her. She went quite cold on the girl. You could tell by her smile; it was late in starting and lasted longer than it should have, not quite a *rictus* but too fixed while it lasted. Mother could assume with ease that frostiness, her my-lips-are-sealed *froideur*, conveying quite clearly that there was something she might say, which should be so obvious to everyone that it did not need the telling, and in any case she would not be the one to say it. I had to wait years before mother unsealed her lips sufficiently to tell me what should have been obvious to me; so obvious that she was surprised that her younger son should even have set his cap at Carolyne. 'Men,' she said, finally unburdening herself to me, 'are easily impressed, and even more easily seduced.'

Father, on the other hand, on his first introduction to Carolyne, gave me a nudge in the ribs and made appreciative noises which he subsequently translated to me as: 'Well, my lad, I can certainly see the attraction.'

Carolyne had long dark hair that fell in loose, not altogether controlled, curls and waves to her shoulders. She was tall, three inches under six feet, just an inch shorter than me; and thus slightly taller than me when wearing high heeled shoes, which she did on virtually all public occasions and at most venues – at work or socially. She walked with a practised, but very slightly-enhanced, sway of the hips. Her eyes were a light hazel with a hint of green, usually widely-open, as if on the verge of being surprised or excited at an imminent prospect. Indeed Carolyne did like surprises, especially those which were gifts, especially gifts which she had hinted she would be pleased to receive, but which she would still contrive to look surprised to accept. Her wide lips appeared always to be fractionally turned up at the edges, as if she were about to break into a smile. Carolyne smiled a great deal, a radiant burst which somehow drew one in to her happiness. For she was a happy girl, all the while nothing happened to disturb the pleasures of her life. When she was happy she expected everyone around her to be happy too; happy, if for no other reason, than to acknowledge *her* happiness. Her generosity knew no bounds, provided it left her with a surfeit of requirements for her own purposes.

Re-reading those words I know they give a slanted view of her. Carolyne was indeed selfish, but not wholly self-absorbed. She practised her selfishness with such good humour and was so open about her wishes that one saw it as a personal moral obligation to help her to realise those wishes. There were rewards and compensations for sustaining Carolyne's good humour. She did so want to *please* one when a want or whim had been satisfied. Her appeal, to men, was like the instant recognition of a sudden scent in the immediate space around her, a scent conveying the contract, rather than a mere promise, of her sensuality. So, as I wrote: I was in lust with her. And she was not a girl who registered No. Everything had to go her way because everything always had. She had no experience of disappointment and would not have known how to cope with it.

My mind being, as one says, elsewhere, actually in several elsewheres as I have tried to explain, Carolyne's telephone-call that evening caught me unawares, my defences unorganised. Her words, to begin with, were as shapes emerging from a mist, suggesting themselves but lacking sharpness. Or, to put the matter more brutally, I was only half attending to her excited stream of words. To be even more brutal, I resented this intrusion into my reflections on William, what he had said, the dossier of materials I had been studying, Philips's taking of me to one side, that alternative world I was now, professionally, going to enter... all of these recent elements which were caught up in the same gravitational pull.

At the end of the call, Carolyne said her goodnight and left me with a scattering of toes to nose (or nose to toes) kisses. Yet as soon as she had finally ended her call, I knew I had to force myself to put order to her enthused chattering. There was something I had to act upon. I knew also that I would not be able to get back to my own thoughts and musings until I had re-assembled the best part of what she had said to me. Oh do say yes – the words were the first to insist on themselves – Mummy and Daddy are *so* looking forward to seeing you again. You know how Mummy simply *dotes* on you. If only you were older or she were younger she would have positively *fought* me for you. And other blandishments – on her own part as well as her mother's. The consequence of my abstraction and Carolyne's attrition-by-flattery was that I had agreed to go that coming weekend to her parents' place in Hertfordshire where *we* (Carolyne and her mother) would discuss the arrangements for our forthcoming engagement. In order to give us as full a time as possible to discuss matters with her parents, we were to set out early evening the next day, Friday.

Also dug out from the landslip of Carolyne's excited chatter I gathered that *we*, though not in my presence, had finally set our formal engagement for early in the following year. The engagement should take place, say mid-February, when most of the people we would want to invite, on her parents' side having already been approached – only *informally* of course – had set aside the date. And *of course* my mother would be free to invite whoever and as many as she wished. Any number could be accommodated, it really wasn't a problem, a large marquee had already all but been ordered. One could get them now, I was assured, complete with wooden floors and heating. And they could be 'dressed' (is that the word I heard?) as a luxurious dining room, and with a quick change would be transformed into a ballroom.

The deed was done. Now I had to do something. Needs must meant I had to telephone mother before the week was out and alert her. That was an obligation I was not looking forward to, though I did suspect that Carolyne's mother would be more of a target this time around than Carolyne herself. Finally, having recovered the import and more or less the detail of Carolyne's bursting information, I was able to settle back into my former flux of thoughts and determine that at my meeting with Philip the next day I would decidedly put to him my as yet unaddressed *Yes buts*.

15

The following morning, meeting early as commanded, Philip was in a breezy good mood. Almost as soon as I entered his top-floor chamber, he waved a hand towards the files laid out on his desk.

Booth was still bent at the desk. He barely registered my entrance.

'If you would just sign here, Mister Philip.'

Booth put before Philip a sheet of paper, and I realised that this was a part of Booth's newly-instituted security plan for the portfolio which Booth had brought up from the chambers' safe. Philip signed. Booth that morning, I noted, was brisk and professional; he was about his duties and exchanged only a brief good-morning with me as he left the room.

Then Philip was on his feet, putting a battered enamel coffee pot on to boil. As one of the seniors in our chambers he was permitted the privilege of his own tea- and coffee-making facilities: a small, curtained off corner with sink, two-ring gas hob, shelves above and cupboard beneath.

He came back to his desk and immediately started on the ritual – for which he was famous in our chambers – of lighting his pipe. I watched, as always, speechless and rooted in fascination. Whilst sucking vigorously on the stem of a pipe whose bowl of tobacco, clasped between thumb and forefinger of his left hand, displayed not the phantom of a glow, with his free hand he was in the process of going through all of his pockets again to locate his box of Vestas. That right hand, as I sat down at the desk opposite to him, was reaching across his body and fumblingly attempting to insert itself into his left-hand trouser pocket.

Pipe *and* coffee – this was going to be a concentrated session.

Still holding his pipe, his free hand was again patting every pocket in turn. Philip inclined his head towards the papers on his desk. His pipe jiggling up and down with every word, he said: 'Some of this material, as I am certain you will have appreciated, Anthony, is still in rather a raw state.'

Giving up his one-handed exploration, Philip then put his pipe into the breast pocket of his jacket and, now with two free hands, rummaged once more into every one of his pockets, including the back pocket of trousers and inside pockets of jacket. With a triumphant small gasp of delight he fetched up the matches. In his concentrated absorption, he ignored completely the clouds of steam streaming out of the coffee pot coming from behind him.

I made a signal, pointing over his head.

But he did not move until he had brought both matches and pipe triumphantly together in a glow of red tobacco. Puffing furiously he went off to the rear of his room to take the coffee pot from the gas ring.

By the time he brought to the desk our coffees in two chipped enamel mugs, Philip had succeeded in creating the blue fug of a cloud of smoke which, rising, flattened and spread itself outwards against the ceiling.

Philip Hathers is the one person I have ever known who could drink his coffee within seconds of it being poured into a mug. He must have had an asbestos-lined throat. Laying his pipe in the ashtray he slurped contentedly at the scalding brew.

'Ah, that's *much* better,' he muttered.

He sat back contentedly. I took from my briefcase the sheet of prompt points I would make and the questions I would ask. Philip pulled his chair closer in to the desk. He swept an arm above the papers spread out across the desk.

'So, Anthony, what have we got?

'Various documents, covering several years – surveillance logs and telephone intercept transcriptions, all recording meetings at different times of the suspect with a total of five other persons.'

'And these persons are?'

'Two of them are fellow Members of Parliament, one of whom is currently a Minister of State, two are identified as officers of the Czechoslovak intelligence service, and one is named as Eastern Europe correspondent for one of our daily broadsheets.'

'Whom it will be our business to ensure no harm comes to.'

'There are three signed statements from him, the newspaper man. Two are accounts of informal interviews conducted by him, more than three years ago, with the target MP, and a third, briefer, account of what happened on his next visit to Prague. As a result of those meetings.'

'Anything else?'

I hesitated, but Philip waved me on.

'There seems to be also another person, reading between the lines of some of these materials. There is mention of encounters with a Miss K, though there are no details of these meetings between her and the MP. There are a couple of places which hint at the existence of reports relating to several of those occasions. But none of those reports is present in this dossier.'

Philip rested his chin on the points of the fingers of his hands, elbows on the desk.

'Powder, dry, keep, but not in that order, Anthony. I think we must presume that, at the stage we have reached, it has been judged preferable not to enter into the record whatever that young woman might have had to say. We may take it, however, that if the prosecution case required the bolstering, if needs must as one says, then Miss K's testimonies would indeed be released.'

I was about to enter the correction that there was no mention, within the documentation itself, of any *testimony* from Miss K having been made, merely references to her in surveillance reports. No mention of her either as being 'a *young* woman'. I suppressed comment. Instead, I offered:

'She would also have to be made available to the court.'

Philip took off his reading glasses, twirled one of its ear-pieces around between forefinger and thumb of one hand, deliberating.

'I think, Anthony, in relation to Miss K, we should take it that if we can find a way to avoid having to use her testimony and present her in court, it would be thought an advantage. And a distinct kindness.'

I mulled over that comment as Philip left the desk to make more coffee. While waiting for the coffee, he failed again to light, with great ceremony and several matches, his pipe. Finally, with a spill of paper dug into the gas ring and the resulting flare of a flame, he got the pipe going just before the flame reached his fingers. He abandoned the charred remains of the paper to the sink where it sizzled.

Returned to his desk with the coffees, he savoured what to me was a slightly bitter drink. He was in no hurry to resume our exchanges. When he did, however, it was with his usual directness.

'How do you rate the prospect of conviction on what we have seen so far?'

Now I took my time. I had rehearsed these words, deciding upon them as a form which would make me appear decisive but neither arrogant nor presumptuous when addressed to an established and admired QC.

'Leaving aside the statements of the foreign correspondent, the rest of the material probably could be argued away by any good counsel as circumstantial, even if affirmed in person and under oath by their authors as accurate and true records. It would be *possible* for the accused to invent alternative explanations for the repeat encounters. After all, there are no *verbatim* records of the exchanges which took place between the MP and the Czechoslovak officers. Agreed that the coincidences of meetings shown in these logs, same persons, same locations, and over several years, on the face of it seem to defy chance-odds. But all in all these observations do not in themselves evidence the trading of secrets.'

'And?'

'The transcripts of telephone intercepts similarly reveal some strange and repeated exchanges which might mean something or nothing. It might strain credulity, but it is possible that they *could* be explained away. Reasons could be invented – they are not in themselves damning.'

'Indeed, yes. Sometimes words make the meaning you are looking for. So, in summary?'

'All in all, I think Carlton was right. I would say that what we have, whilst persuasive as supporting evidence, is not over-whelmingly conclusive in itself.'

'And that leaves us with?'

'The statements of the Eastern Europe correspondent – Witness W. The case hangs on those. On him, really, how convincing his testimony and how well it holds up under cross-examination.'

'Exactly. And whoever were to defend the Honourable Member would do his best to discredit the testimony of Mr W. One can readily see that we might then end up with the most unsatis-factory outcome of charge and counter-charge.'

'One man's word against another.'

'Y-e-s,' a monosyllable so drawn out that it signalled its own qualification. 'Except that our man's word must be found to be the truth whilst the other man's word must be destroyed.'

Philip tamped at the bowl of his pipe, which had gone out. He made no attempt to relight it, but merely sucked hard at its stem before laying it down in the pen holder on his desk.

'What do we lack, Anthony?' He motioned a hand to the doc-uments. 'What would transform this case from persuasive to, as the Colonel put it to us, irrefutable? Look upon these as the bare bones. What flesh would we like to hang on them?'

I offered a thought I had withheld at our earlier meeting.

'Philip, as it stands, this portfolio does not contain enough to convict. But, as an alternative, it might contain enough to squeeze an admission of guilt out of the man.'

'A confession?' Philip pursed his lips, removed his spectacles, and very slowly shook his head. 'Won't do, Anthony old chap. There will be no advantage to the gentleman in question in making confession. That will be made emphatically clear to him in interview – when the time comes for interview. There will be no offer of immunity from prosecution, no deal to be done, no offer of reduced sentencing. Nothing.'

Philip laid both hands palm down on his desk.

'There is another problem with such a confession, Anthony. It would be tendered by the guilty only on the promise of hush-hush, a quiet brushing aside, no publicity, all kept secret or known only to those few who knew. As has been such a case in recent years. But our man will not be offered the luxury of concealment. Faced with total ruination, with having everything taken away from him, his position, status, influence, lifestyle, a good life of affordable pleasures and luxuries, what options remain to him? He must defend himself, he must plead Not Guilty. He must fight. To do that he will have to engage the services of a *very* expensive legal team, led by a barrister of, shall we say, more than workmanlike repute. There can be no doubt. The Honourable Member will have to defend himself. To do that he will lie. And he will attack. He will be permitted no option. So we, my dear Anthony, must be ready to defend our man, our correspondent, Witness W, when the time comes.'

I hesitated, but went ahead: 'The statements of Mr W, as we have them, in the due process of open court, *may* be enough to warn off the two – or – three others you spoke of, but still almost certainly not enough to convict the MP in question.'

Philip adopted his pose of piety: fingertips of hands touching, hands upright in an attitude of prayer.

'There may be another motive at play here as well, Anthony. One to consider, anyway. Perhaps one might wish it to come out in court that the honourable gentleman's conduct had been known about more or less from the start, and had been monitored from shortly after his conduct came to the attention of the service. If that can be shown to have been the case, then one sows even more doubt, even more suspicion. In short, Anthony, one creates confusion where once there had been clarity. The past must then be reassessed by those who paid for it.'

There was that slow smile again.

'Doubt is a poison, Anthony.'

My final *Yes but* framed itself.

'Philip... why us at all? I mean, surely there's enough high quality legal advice available in the Home Department and the Attorney General's office to decide whether to press a charge.'

'True, and probably at a lesser charge than Booth shall submit for *our* services.'

Philip's pun clearly amused him. Then, at his own measured pace, more explaining:

'And indeed you *are* right – an opinion might have been sought from a legal adviser much closer to the Colonels' home, if I may put it that way. Had the Colonel chosen to do so. The service, after all, does have its own legal adviser available to all of its branches.'

'Then surely that makes it even more inexplicable why *we* have been asked to review the documentation.'

'Ah.'

I knew from earlier occasions that this particular long-drawn exhalation prefigured a confidence.

'Where to begin? One of Carlton's prime duties, as I am sure you will have discerned, is to act as liaison between the Home Department and the Colonel's particular sectional interests. In this instance, at Colonel Jackson's urging, Carlton has, so to speak, interposed himself. Given the nature of the Colonel's inquiries, he has intercepted the usual traffic of such matters to our political masters. Given the possibility that there may be others – '

'Those same unnamed two – or – three, for sake of argument?'

Philip made as if to doff a cap.

'Indeed, and given that one or more of those may be fellow politicians who walk the same carpeted corridors as the Honourable gentleman we have in our sights... ' Philip raised his hands as if everything else following was clear and obvious. 'An excellent man, by the way, Carlton, a first-class legal mind, would have made an outstanding barrister but for that, ahem, unfortunate mannerism. The man just can not put on a good show in public, I am afraid to say. In private, though... '

Philip allowed the rest of his speech to fade away. The explanation he had offered required a further explanation of its own.

'To put the matter at its simplest, Anthony, there are occasions when the Colonel may wish to ensure that possible leaks have been plugged in advance.'

A downward look along the length of his nose, over the top of his glasses, invited me to speak.

'Surely there could not be, and of course here I speculate' – Philip grinning broadly as I replicated something of his manner – 'that there might be some dubiety about some persons in departments and offices of state? And that is why this matter has been diverted to us?'

'Bravo, *mon brave*. Now let us proceed to speculate a little further.'

Philip's speculations certainly did not seem to me to be drawn down from the air. Of course one was not saying... none the less the more people who had access, or access to people who knew other people who did have access... including those they came across professionally for perfectly good reasons... Had the Colonel himself not hinted at this? It was *possible,* Philip surmised, that Carlton had been the first person, outside of a tight group within the Colonel's branch, to have seen the said portfolio. Carlton, whatever other merits or limitations might pertain to him, had the admirable and proven ability to keep things to himself. He could also prove a useful conduit of information, to and fro, as well as providing an early warning system. 'Sniffings,' as Philip called them, hints and possibilities. 'Always a good idea to know something of what one's masters are dreaming up.'

'But surely that means *no-one* is trusted.'

'Quite so.'

Completely unabashed, Philip made a show of consulting his watch before offering his contrived evasion.

'Anthony, my dear chap, I fear we are running out of time for today. I must get on now with tidying up some bits and pieces ready for next week. And, unfortunately, I shall be able to salvage only an hour or two here tomorrow morning. I am also obligated to be elsewhere tomorrow. And so.' Philip's hands gestured the helplessness of one caught up in events.

Tomorrow. Of course. Tomorrow would be Friday. Hathers would be off for the weekend somewhere or other, he and his wife seemingly 'known to anyone who was anyone', as the phrase is, and much in demand by those same persons for house parties, shoots in season, society do's and celebrations and receptions. As a junior, his request of me was mere *politesse* for a command.

I tried to respond with good grace.

'Fret not, Anthony, my man. We shall undoubtedly find the time early next week to put our thoughts in final order before your meeting with Vernon Jackson – '

'Ah, yes. Booth mentioned – '

'Yes, sorry old chap, having to ask you to report to the good Colonel on our behalf. Have a case scheduled for the High Court, can't be helped.'

'No, of course not.'

I rose to leave. Philip waved a hand for me to sit down again.

'Anthony, this is a rare opportunity for you – and let me say to you that this will all stand you in good stead. In *particular* good stead.' Philip's eyes twinkled their smile upon me. 'For years to come.'

I held a hand out towards the papers.

'I could do with going through them again tonight.'

'Yes, yes, of course. I shall square it with Booth. Just do be very careful, keep them under wraps to and fro. And For Your Eyes Only, as one says.'

He laughed heartily.

16

Later in the afternoon of that day, as I was preparing to leave chambers, Booth knocked his signal and entered my room. He held in his hand a single sheet of folded paper. I presumed it was a message for me, so I held out my hand to take it.

He did not offer me the paper but instead motioned to the chair beside my desk and, without waiting for any sign from me, sat down. He smiled broadly; but it was a smile of intimidation, too long held.

'Mister Anthony.' Said with a sigh of impatience.

I waited for him to go on. Booth clearly had his own sense of timing and was using it to put himself in control. I wondered again at the man's presence and his disconcerting ability to look directly into one's eyes and not waver. Holding his gaze until one looked away, he would reassert his silent domination.

He was looking at me now.

'Mister Anthony. This is most unusual. Indeed it is quite out of order.'

I did not know to what he was referring; and said so.

'Come, Mister Anthony. You have put me in a very awkward position, very awkward indeed.'

Again I protested my innocence. But as a long-serving chambers' clerk, Booth had developed the expertise of cross-questioning.

'Did you or did you not make a specific request of Mister Philip to take away with you from these chambers this evening a certain portfolio of documents?'

'Why yes. I did ask him if it would be alright. I need to go through them again tonight.'

There was a pause which Booth seemed, again, quite content to hold. In that pause, although there was no actual tut-tutting to be heard, there was an undoubted rebuke which issued from

Booth in the silence. Then he shook his head in slow movement side to side, his lips pursed.

'I'm afraid you have put both Mister Philip and my own good self into a more than somewhat embarrassing position.'

I declared my ignorance of any such thing.

'It is like this, Mister Anthony. Your insistence on taking away those papers put upon Mister Philip an obligation to seek their release. In seeking to meet your request Mister Philip has put upon me a further obligation and, in so doing, has brought into question an earlier obligation to which I had given my word. *My* word.'

I realised that Booth, having me at the disadvantage of not knowing what he was talking about, was determined to measure his own time in allowing me an understanding of the reason for this attitude of stern severity. I would just have to allow him to play me out and take his rebukes for whatever crime or misde-meanour he had assigned to me as the guilty party.

Booth ensured that his explanation was fragmented, each part of my enlightenment a little barb hooked into my conscience. Then, to ensure that I unquestionably understood my culpability, he gave me a summary:

'I gave my word to Carlton that I would be responsible at all times for that portfolio. I gave him my word face to face that it would be secured overnight, here, in our chambers' safe, and that it would be released by me and signed for by Mister Philip, as required. I further gave my word that it would be signed back during or at the end of each day it was in use, and that I would undertake to ensure that none of its contents were either copied or taken out of these chambers.'

I prised at the one weakness I could detect.

'Did Mister Hathers know of this understanding that the portfolio was not to leave the chambers?'

Booth's eyes narrowed, though still turned full on me.

'There was a clear understanding that the portfolio would be locked away overnight. And Mister Philip has been signing for these papers on each occasion he has required them – as you saw for yourself earlier today.'

'Yes, but did Philip expressly understand that they were not to leave these rooms under any circumstance?'

'I have spoken with Mister Philip – and he understands the undertaking I gave. The portfolio was entrusted to *my* safekeeping.'

It was enough, that unregarded slip into the present tense. Philip knows *now*, I thought, and *now* understands what he had not understood until he spoke with Booth sometime that afternoon when he asked for the portfolio on my behalf. Philip had presumed, had taken for granted the common practice of taking home papers to work on. Many papers not required for home-working were locked away overnight in the chambers' safe – more as a precaution against fire than a protection against theft. In fact it was not unknown for some case papers to stay in their barrister's briefcase for several weeks on end. I was drumming up a response.

Booth, however, was a very sharp man. He must have recognised his own slip and decided to switch tack rather than persist in the same accusatory direction. Being Booth he found a way of doing so without having to acknowledge any fault of his own.

'You can see how this puts us all into a very difficult situation.'

That was the closest to an acknowledgement of a sin of omission on Booth's part that one was going to get.

I assumed a posture of pondering, but in truth there was nothing I would be able to suggest. It had to reside with Booth to come up with whatever solution he could contrive. Philip was a senior member of chambers and it would go hard against Booth to go against Philip who had undertaken to 'square it' with Booth that I be allowed to take the papers with me overnight.

'Mister Philip understands that this must be the sole exception to the undertaking I have given, given on behalf of the chambers, you understand. I have just spoken with Carlton, and he has assented to the following.'

Thus, despite having chosen me as the object of his ire for the making of a difficult situation, Booth had a ready solution previously-planned and agreed. I would not be permitted to take the papers out of the office with me. They would be collected from chambers, handed over by Booth to a Home Department courier. Signed for by the courier they would then, on delivery to my home address, be signed for by me. It would be necessary for me to state a time, now, for the following morning when an appointed courier could collect the papers, together with all signatures in reverse order. It seemed to me to be an unnecessarily complicated procedure – but, evidently, it satisfied Booth's sense of protocol and lent protection to all parties. I agreed, of course, to the design and just stopped myself from congratulating Booth upon a neat way out of the dilemma.

'Thank you.'

To say more would be taken either as ironic criticism or, possibly even worse, an attempt to ingratiate myself with the man.

'It must be clearly understood this must not be repeated, that this is an exceptional arrangement, not a permanent agreement.'

I nodded assent. This was Booth's way of re-asserting his importance, that nothing to do with chambers' business could be allowed to go round him. Everything had to go *through* him, as it were. This re-affirmation of his position was quite unnecessary. Despite universal recognition of his estimable worth, either he still required the occasional buffing of his self-esteem *or* this event was seen by him as an opportunity to put a junior well and truly in his (inferior) place.

'I understand.'

With that I rose from my chair, the point of our encounter done with, and extended a hand to Booth. He remained seated, and motioned me to resume my seat.

'There is one other matter.'

With this exact phrase my House Master at school had once initiated an investigation into an alleged behaviour of mine which quickly turned into a full-scale character analysis of my traits and weaknesses. Following on from what Booth had already said, I expected something similar now.

'Mister Philip was most insistent that I should offer you his abject and fulsome apologies – his words to the letter – for the short notice which I am about to relay to you, but he finds it quite impossible himself, given his prior commitments, to respond to an invitation which has been offered. It is an invitation which bears directly upon this case.' Booth inclined his head towards the portfolio on my desk.

'Yes?' Booth had appeared reluctant to proceed any further.

'It appears, from what Mister Philip has said to me, that at some point in your deliberations he suggested to you that it might be helpful if he were to seek further advice...'

Philip had indeed said he 'would have a word.'

'Mister Philip asks me to tell you that he has been able to have that consultation, as a result of which it has been concluded that it would be most helpful if you could agree to meet a certain gentleman tomorrow evening. I apologise on his behalf for, and I quote, 'the unconscionably short notice'.'

'Who – ?'

I got no further.

'I know only what I am told. I do not pry, Mister Anthony, some things are not my business to know. Mister Philip, he asked me to emphasise the point, would not have sought to impose this meeting upon you had he been able to undertake the meeting himself. He is, as you know, previously engaged for tomorrow evening.'

This time Booth's smile was one of complicit understanding. He might just as well have winked at me, or laid a finger alongside his nose. We were both well aware of Hathers's social preoccupations.

'He will be *most* obliged therefore, but requires to know if you are willing. The meeting must be confirmed tonight, it would appear, and Mister Philip has asked that you telephone him later this evening to confirm *your* willingness. The gentleman he wishes you to meet in his unavoidable absence is one by the name of Arnold Ward.'

Booth rose from his seat.

Mr W, Mr Arnold Ward – surely it *must* be the man, the man whom we must protect as the principal witness in the case papers I would review once more tonight. I was excited at the prospect of meeting the said Arnold Ward – but determined not to show it to Booth.

'Do you intend to leave for home now, Mister Anthony?'

'Within the next few minutes, yes.'

Booth then arranged with me a time for delivery of the portfolio to my address, and its collection the following morning. Only when everything was settled did Booth hand to me a folded sheet of paper. As I took it from him, he smiled – a smile of satisfaction for having put me firmly in my place, I presumed.

When he had left the room I read the paper. In Booth's hand was written a London telephone number and the message: *Be very much obliged if you would telephone between 8.30 and 9.00 tonight. P.*

FOUR

Follies, Fools, Physics

Chambers: *The Gin Palace*: Hertfordshire

Autumn 1965

When I got back to my flat not much more than an hour later that day, a surprise awaited me. On the doormat, covered by two bills and a bank statement, was a letter from William.

William apologised for not having got in touch again sooner, following our meeting at my chambers. He had been busy. He had managed to snatch a few days in Oxford, spending much of his time in the Bodleian working on his monograph. Did I know, by the by, he asked, that since William Walsh's posthumous *Collected Works* of 1736 there appeared to have been no subsequent single volume edition of his writings? Two exclamation marks ended this observation of William, followed by the single word *Scandalous*, accentuated with a further exclamation mark. Poems reprinted in a collection 'merged' with others, occasional poems published here and there down the years in various anthologies, but not even a *Selected* exclusively of WW. Another exclamation mark. Now, he declared, he would not be able to get away for another ten days or so:

> *Am expecting to have to toddle off to the cold, cold North very soon for a few days. Left to myself I could look forward to the bracing air, long walks, and the opportunity to top up the batteries. It would seem, however, that my masters in sending me to their most frigid of outposts require me to learn a few skills other than those of literary analysis.*

As soon as possible upon his return he would telephone me one evening and arrange the dinner he had promised. Meanwhile, I was enjoined to:

> *Please give my love to the beautiful Carolyne. I expect her social diary will be bulging at present, but tell her I shall hope to see her*

*too on an occasion soon when she has nothing on and nothing better
to do. Give the dear girl a big hug from me.*

Carolyne would be pleased to be remembered by William.
She had a soft spot for the man, even though she had seemed
uncharacteristically taunting those few weeks ago when I had
told her of his visit to see me at the Temple. Truth to tell, she
had then been cross with me for not insisting on an immediate
arrangement to meet up with William again, at a time and place
when and where she could be present herself. I had to confess
that I had no contact address or telephone number for him. Carolyne looked at me in disbelief: how could I have allowed the
man to leave without getting this information from him? I knew,
she asserted, how fond she was of William. Did I know that? No,
I did not know, though I did suspect. I decided not to challenge,
since Carolyne had gone into that silent mode of rebuke which is
the adult version of a young girl's pout.

On the second thoughts that occurred to me whilst reading
William's letter, it came to me that I had given *him* neither my home
address nor my telephone number. Yet, clearly, he had them both,
the letter's arrival and contents a confirmation. Booth? That was
a possibility, I thought... but then Booth was such a stickler for
protocol and confidentiality that as soon as the thought formed I
dismissed it. I doubted whether he could be so easily persuaded to
give up such private information. Even by William.

I can not forbear, the letter continued, *to offer the following observation. The words are those of William Walsh, Esq., so runs
the title page for* Aesculapius, *or* The Hospital of Fools, *and
are assigned to Aesculapius as speaker:*

Every particular man complains of the Follies that are in
the World; and when we come hither to apply Medicines to
them, there is not one Man that offers himself to be cur'd.

From this it follows, does it not, my dear Anthony, that the whole world is sick? One knows easily enough that others are sick, but does one know one's own sickness, one's own ailments, one wonders? Perhaps we know them by other names – they are our loves, our pleasures, passions, indulgences, our vulnerabilities, even our small quirks and quiddities... And perhaps we are all happy enough with our individual inflictions and afflictions, but do not know so until we are threatened with their removal from us. What think you?

In hope of seeing you again very soon,

Fondest regards,

William

Pure William. William at his maddening most. What was I to make of the observation of William Walsh, or indeed of the observations of William himself? Whose follies? What follies? What was the man trying to say? And why Aesculapius? physician or god of medicine, human or divine, healer of the sick, depicted with a snake twirled around his staff... By some strange juxtaposition of imagination suddenly I saw William as an old man, long white beard, his walking stick with silver handle held delicately downwards between thumb and forefinger, with a snake entwined around it and all the conventional associations one makes of that creature. Another thought: *Physician heal thyself* came to mind.

I refused to be teased further. I was helped by the fact that at that very moment the doorbell to my flat rang and a crash-helmeted courier was at the door with a portfolio for me to be signed for.

I had no time to spare for William's rags and teasings. I told myself over and over that I had far more pressing things to do than muse on whatever arcane knowledge or imputation William had in mind. I had those papers to go through again and come up with sensible proposals for strengthening the case they presented. This was Philip's way of seeing if I was worthy of winning my spurs. I had to show I was something more than a junior bag-carrier.

I brewed a pot of coffee and made some toast. Then I settled down to my task, papers spread around me on the floor. For some period of time there remained continuing nagging thoughts of William and his namesake's *Hospital of Fools*. And of Carolyne'e enthusiasm to regain contact with the man. Scanning the case materials, however, drew me into my task. As I began to see more clearly how to proceed, so I became more absorbed in what I was doing.

Somehow, whilst assembling the best possible case for the prosecution of the Far-From-Honourable gentleman in question, we had to protect 'our' man, the Eastern Europe broadsheet correspondent. I looked back to my 'bare bones' summary. Suddenly, in that unaccountable way the human brain works to flash something before consciousness that one was not in the remotest way trying to call to mind, there came an echo. It was the echo of those words 'Absences are as important as presences.' Somehow their reverberation redirected my attention when I turned to the mechanical plotting of gaps in the chronology of dates. Rather than the sequence of dates themselves, it was the periods of time *between* recorded events which became important, something I had not previously spotted.

The first entries, surveillance covering two days, tracked the MP to a car park at the northern end of Richmond Park. Letting his dog out of the car, the 'target', as the observation notes referred to him, took a footpath towards the ponds, and was joined on his morning stroll by another man also walking a dog. They walked together for some minutes, then parted company. The following morning the same pattern of events was observed. Following these two days, though, there was a gap of several weeks before any further surveillance reports appeared in the record. From that point on the man with the dog appeared several more times with weeks or months between. There was a second Czech service man; again to a haphazard time-scale of meetings. The third man to appear in the records was the Eastern Europe newspaper correspondent. Never more than one of these three men had been observed in the company of the MP at any one time.

There was an intrusive sound. The ringing of the telephone broke through my concentration. I glanced at my watch. Could it really be gone half-past eight already? I had a call to make, but calling me was Carolyne. Her first words:

'Where have you been, darling, I have been waiting for *ever* for you to answer.'

I muttered something about the work I was doing, how important it was, how little time – this evening only – to get something convincing together for the next day's meeting with Hathers.

'You poor dear. And here am I at a loose end with the whole evening stretching out ahead of me with nothing to do.'

Inwardly I railed at Carolyne's intrusion, my resentment heightened by her adoption of a feigned husky seductiveness of voice. I could feel my irritability increasing. I could hear my own unencouraging tone of voice and I struggled to reassert something approaching a normal conversational mode. I tried to bring Carolyne to the point of her call and hasten its end. Fortunately, or unfortunately – and both were true – Carolyne was not a woman to be easily deflected or discouraged. In some contexts, under some conditions, this tenacity appeared as a commendable quality; under other circumstances it seemed to be the exercise of a highly-developed selfishness. My usual good humour with her had simply gone.

With 'I quite understand, darling, I won't keep you long,' Carolyne spun her words into a long thread which she wound around me. I felt their tightening, rather than heard any specific meanings. Where I would normally simply have listened through to her and then indulged her harmless – at worst, inconvenient – wishes, tonight I felt no such good will. Then there was a silence in which I was lost.

'Do *say* something, Anthony, my darling.'

I must have mumbled something to the effect of asking what she wanted me to say.

'About the weekend, silly – me picking you up tomorrow night about six. Just confirming what we had agreed.'

'Ah.'

My exhalation was not Philip Hathers's letting of breath preparatory to a lengthy explanation. Mine was the gasping of a man who has suddenly remembered something. I had failed to alert Carolyne to the fact that my Friday evening would now be spoken for. Somehow I had to undo Carolyne's plans and come up with a satisfactory explanation for not informing her. She would be hurt, I knew, whatever I said; she would feel rejected. There would be also the tricky matter of informing her parents. There would be damage-limitation or reparation, or both, to be paid for. At this stage, I had no doubt, Carolyne's mother would have made all the arrangements for Friday evening: an impressive late dinner, Carolyne's father commanded to select equally impressive wines, the tracks for the round-the-table conversations scouted and laid out.

The truth was that when Booth, at Philip's request, had come back to me that afternoon to ask if it would be possible for me to meet Arnold Ward on Friday evening I felt an instant *frisson* of excitement. Here was my invitation to meet the 'Mr W' of the portfolio that now lay strewn across my sitting-room floor.

This was someone engaged, or caught up, in that mysterious world of lies and deceptions designated by its one-word soubriquet: 'intelligence'. The prospect of this meeting had simply washed away my recollection of the prior arrangement with Carolyne. There would have been, had I acted immediately, just time enough to inform her of a change of plan, plead the necessity of important and unignorable business to attend to, and regret the inconvenience. But I was preoccupied – until this abrupt reminder from Carolyne. So, my ill humour with her on this occasion had more to do with guilt at my own forgetfulness than it had to do with her reminder of my previous commitment.

Mea culpa, reprehendo alium. When it's your own fault, blame others. Carolyne had interrupted me. Therefore she was at fault. I had work to do. Also, I had a telephone call to make. Somehow, in the lightest way I could contrive, I had to get Carolyne off the line.

I blustered an explanation which, even to my ears, sounded unconvincing. It was not straightforwardly said; there were repetitions, too many false starts, too little directness. I said too much. We, I certainly, would not be able to leave for her parents' home on Friday evening. As she knew, I was working on a brief with Philip Hathers; my big opportunity. But time was very short, Hathers could expect to be in court from the middle of the next week, so it was imperative to hold a meeting with a certain someone, a someone who could be available only tomorrow evening, for reasons I could not go into, I could not even know what time I would be finished tomorrow evening, so it would have to be Saturday morning, sorry, before we could set off, but even if we made a leisurely start on Saturday morning we could still be at Carolyne's parents mid-morning, not much traffic at that time, do it in well under two hours to their Hertfordshire place... and much else, I regret to say, to talk away my oversight.

There was a long silence at the other end of the line. Then, in measured language from Carolyne:

'When did you know about this meeting for tomorrow night?'

'Just before leaving chambers.'

'Why didn't you 'phone me straight away at the office?'

I hesitated. Then lied. It seemed the least harmful, the most persuasive thing to do.

'I was late leaving. You would already have left.'

There was another silence. I sensed Carolyne picking her way through a cram of possible questions.

'So, Anthony, when exactly *did* you intend to let me know?'

Sometimes dissimulation requires but a fractional breathing space to assemble its plausibilities.

'Just as soon as I had sorted these papers and got them in order for the meeting. I won't have time to do that tomorrow. I have to have an early morning meeting with Philip. Can't be helped, this is a really *big* case – very complicated, huge consequences.'

Pleased with my answer, especially the importance it attached to me, I hoped that the swiftness of my response would be taken for its veracity, allowing no time for Carolyne to suspect its invention. There was just enough of a pause from Carolyne to let me know that doubt persisted.

'It is now well on the way to nine o'clock Anthony, almost ten to, to be accurate.'

I resorted to the last subterfuge of a man known to be in the wrong. I grovelled. Also, I was beginning to panic. There was a telephone call to make and Carolyne was in no hurry to end this conversation. She had not punished me sufficiently for my lapse. So I made apologies to her, to her mother and father, sincere apologies, abject apologies. My apologies were effusive, but there was such an urgency about this current matter and I was so involved I had not noticed the time. Exceptional circumstances. My time really not my own on this occasion. So sorry, please forgive, *et cetera*.

Then, the guilty man having emasculated himself, one compounds the errors of one's ways by making promises. I would make it up to my darling Carolyne, when opportunity allowed we would go off for our own pre-engagement celebration – before the formal rites. And I would make it up to her mother, of course, really I would, and *of course* it would not happen again, perhaps we would be able to organise another long break with her parents, in fact I was sure that my mother was planning to invite Carolyne and her parents for a weekend sometime in the next few weeks... This was a desperate throw of the die. As far as I knew, my mother had no such plans and would not want to encourage Carolyne's mother to think that the two of them would ever be in company together for any longer than absolute need drove; I also knew, though, that nothing would please Carolyne's mother more than to be invited as house guests to my parents' place.

The wisdom of later years. A woman knows when a man has thrown himself on her mercy. It makes her powerful. Her tenderness is aroused, but she will exact conditions for one's re-habilitation. Forgiveness will be ceded little by little, inch by inch. And the errant male will be on probation for an indeterminate period of time until the woman finally decides to relent and allow normal service to be resumed. Until then, there will be little or no negotiation.

'I still don't know how I'm going to break this to Mummy, at *this* short notice.'

I was inspired to offer something which I hoped would sound impressive when relayed to Carolyne's parents, her mother particularly.

'Look, all I can tell you is that this is state business I'm working on. With Hathers. And the man I have to see tomorrow evening has a great deal to do with it. An important witness.'

'Really?'

'Yes, really. 'Fraid there's nothing more I'm allowed to say.'

Carolyne gathered this in. I knew she was deliberating, wondering how best to translate this to enhance my standing with her parents.

'But why Friday night?'

'State business doesn't shut down for the weekend, you know.'

I allowed myself the pomposity of a man made important by association.

'I have to go, Carolyne. I have to make a very important 'phone call – and I must make it in the next few minutes.'

'Really?' The note of doubt was sounding again.

'Yes, really. It really *is* important.'

There was a pause, Carolyne considering, before offering me the un-negotiable terms, a rapprochement of sorts.

'I shall come round to your place after work tomorrow, Anthony, and let myself in. That means I shall be there when you get back from your meeting. That way we can be sure of an early start Saturday morning. Try not to be late back tomorrow night.'

A command, the smallest *fiat* I could expect to get away with. She would do the best she could with her mother.

I had not escaped; but I had been allowed out under licence. There was some compensation. The sentence of spending an entire weekend at her parents' place from Friday evening until early evening on Sunday, which had filled me with considerable apprehension, had at least been reduced.

It was, by my watch, just three minutes to nine when I rang the number passed on to me by Booth. The male voice which greeted my call announced that I had connected with what was in that era still pleased to be called a Gentleman's Club in Pall Mall. I asked if I might speak to Mister Philip Hathers and was assured with a 'Certainly sir, if I may ask your name I shall inform the gentleman.' I was left to the indistinct sounds of male voices surrounded by the noises of what was evidently a lounge. I waited some time before I heard Philip Hathers greet me, followed by the click of a receiver being replaced at which the noises and other voices disappeared.

'Glad you 'phoned, Anthony. We were just on the point of giving you up. Thought I might have to resort to 'phoning you at home.'

'Yes, sorry, Philip, had a call from Carolyne and we had to alter arrangements for the weekend.'

'My turn to be sorry now. I take it from that though that you shall be able to make the appointment tomorrow evening?'

'Yes.'

'Good. The Colonel *will* be pleased, I'll let him know.'

I asked about the details – where and when to meet.

'We'll go through that in the morning, Anthony, after I've spoken with Vernon.'

Philip gave that self-amused laugh and added softly:

'Before we both give ourselves up to the pleasures of a single malt.'

We said our goodnights.

At least it was now unarguably confirmed that Hathers and Colonel Jackson were in close liaison. Now they were sharing a convivial evening, no doubt preceded by a satisfying dinner. I wondered how long the two of them had been working together to brew up their plan of action – whatever it was beyond what had been released to me. What, I wondered, were they scheming as they savoured their pleasures of a single malt?

I did my best to return to the demands of the portfolio.

18

I was late to bed that night; and even later to sleep, if one may call such that fitful dipping in and out of consciousness when one's brain refuses to give in and one tries to drill oneself into a refusal to engage with whatever thought of the moment has surfaced, or re-surfaced. Shards and splinters of recollected things, persons, conversations, insist on being attended to. The more one wills and wishes sleep, so the more remote becomes its possibility. Dancing and weaving their way through snatches of documents were names, persons unknown, and persons in the name and title of Philip Hathers and Colonel Vernon Jackson.

From a shallow respite, on the edge of sleep, I emerged to the grey light of dawn, unable to return even to the lightest of slumbers. I subjected myself to the discipline of a cold shower in an attempt to shock myself into alert consciousness. I had just dressed when the doorbell rang. It was the motorbike courier arrived to collect the portfolio. Identity confirmed, the man signed for the package and with a wave of a black leather hand was gone, roaring off to the corner of the street.

By the time I arrived at chambers, early, I was still suffering from an aching fuzziness. Booth – always the earliest of anyone to be in chambers, apart from the cleaning staff – greeted me.

'Not quite one hundred percent this morning, Mister Anthony?'

I grunted. The man's cheeriness was infuriating.

'A coffee, I think, Mister Anthony, the strongest of brews.'

To my surprise he brought a jug of the darkest coffee to my room and surprised me even further by settling himself in the armchair by my desk to share the morning awakener with me. He was in the best of spirits. Booth nodded to the portfolio which he, it could have been no other, had placed on the top of my desk, to the side.

'All intact, I trust. No accidents.'

'All present and correct,' I said.

In truth the portfolio of papers, which I had left spread across my living room carpet when, finally, I had stumbled off to bed the previous night, was in some disorder. I had merely gathered them up this morning and stuffed them into their brown manila folder seconds before the courier had arrived to collect them. I had intended to put them all back in file order once I got to the privacy of my room at chambers. Booth, however, showed no urgency to move on. Even more infuriatingly he was pleasantness itself, though his slightly changed manner towards me – as I later worked it out – resulted from that complicity, or collusion, which he presumed now existed between us.

'I shall trouble you for your signature, Mister Anthony.'

Booth poured each of us a cup of black coffee which, in the Irishism I had heard somewhere, was 'thick enough to trot a mouse on.' The heat of the brew and its intensity shocked my system into something like normal consciousness. Booth, who missed nothing, noticed its effect and smiled knowingly.

Within minutes of Booth leaving me, Philip Hathers poked his head around the door to my room. He had arrived at my office, later than promised, full of apologies, *bonhomie*, the rag of an explanation and the *politesse* of a command.

'So sorry, old chap. Unexpected delay, really sorry. My room, ten minutes?'

He pointed a forefinger towards the portfolio on my desk; another silent command. Hastily I did my best to put the papers back into file order before going up to Philip's room.

By the time I entered Philip's chamber on the top floor of the building he was sitting at his desk with a mug of scalding coffee in one hand, and in the other his pipe, which had gone out. So, before any words could be exchanged, Philip had to engage in the ceremonial lighting of its fire. The unlit pipe went into his breast pocket whilst he reached for the coffee. I had been told, by several in chambers, that in their presence Philip had put into his pocket a pipe which he presumed had gone out – and had actually set fire to himself and ruined a series of jackets. A look of faint puzzlement now crossed his face as he set down the coffee and noted that in his other hand he now held his leather tobacco pouch. I watched, trying to suppress my laughter, as Philip went through the two-handed combinations of matches and pouch, pipe and pouch, before arriving at the solution of pipe and matches; all, again, between greedy gulps of coffee.

Obviously Philip was in need of his morning awakener too. I wondered how his evening had been spent after I had spoken with him the night before. *A single malt* – the pleasure he had said he was about to give himself up to must have consisted of a good few single malts, and not in single measure either I guessed.

After some minutes, his pipe a satisfying volcano of smoke, his bodily need quenched in mugs of coffee, Philip was ready to begin our meeting.

'This shouldn't take long, old chap. In any case will have to make a dash for it at lunchtime – some travelling to do.'

I smiled at Philip's worst guarded secret. He was off again for the weekend, doubtless to fulfil yet another invitation to be a houseguest at some influential person's country retreat.

'Well, Anthony, have you managed to make any more of our case?'

Philip drew a lungful of smoke and tried, unsuccessfully, to blow rings.

'All my years of smoking,' he said, 'and I have *never* been able to make the damn things.'

'Well – '

'Let's take the prosecution case. Anything we can add, Anthony?'

I pulled out from the top of the file the summary I had made. He spent some time reviewing it. Then looked up.

'Where is the weakness, Anthony?'

'In the chronology.'

'Meaning, exactly?'

'Too many gaps. And too many large gaps between some of the observations.'

Philip made me spell out the implications 'inferred or concluded' from these. The records covered four years, but because of their intermittent nature the observed meetings showed no pattern across the whole period.

'They appear to be haphazard and occasional.'

'Or well organised by the target – our Dishonourable Member – or by some other person or persons, to appear so.'

'But easier to defend as a result. Easier to invent reasons why one was at such a place at such a time.'

'Quite so. Though he does bump into the same persons again and again. Coincidence?'

'Not beyond the bounds of an invented reason.'

'To lie?' Philip adopted the pretence of a shocked expression. 'Tut! Tut!'

'But as we know, as you've said, this man is going to be given no alternative, no lifeline, no graceful withdrawal, no option but to fight.'

Philip started to ransack his pockets again for his box of matches.

I still could not see a way out of the lack of unarguable evidence. Meanwhile Philip was still diving hands into pockets for his matches. I pushed the box towards him where he had covered it with the open flap of the portfolio. After some delay, the tobacco sufficiently alight, a small circle of red in the middle of the bowl enough for him to draw in a long breath of smoke then watch its exhalation drift upwards, he looked up to my question:

'What do *you* really think, Philip?'

A Philippian 'Ahh..'., then the response. 'Not for me to say, old chap. Though one may perhaps speculate somewhat on this point.' Puff, puff, a stream of smoke. 'Each case on its merit, of course, goes without saying, but it is possible there has been a hardening of the heart.' At which Philip smiled broadly. 'No doubt you will have followed the two rather spectacular trials of recent years. Both in the spring of 'sixty-one.'

Philip looked to see that I recollected. In truth there was only a very hazy trace of those events. At that time I would have been working solidly, day and night, revising for my finals examinations in Law at Oxford. Revision, for me, rather than its Latin 'seeing again' was in many instances an encounter with matter I had not learned in the first place. I had much work to do.

'What you will not know, however – just over two years ago now – is the case of an English gentleman which did *not* come to court. The man had worked for the other side for a good many years and had caused a great deal of damage before he was detected. In the wisdom of those in charge of such matters it was determined that his deeds would be dealt with very quietly – a signed confession and a gentleman's word that he had stopped being a naughty boy.'

Philip bowed his head to look over the rims of his spectacles, raising his eyebrows to me.

'Two years later we now know that he lied, even in that confession. Still no big fuss, the bird having flown to an Eastern sanctuary. One may suppose that to make a very public splash with *that* long-term betrayal of our nation would have been an admission, or confession on the part of the service that it had failed to spot sooner the traitor in its midst. Not exactly a resounding endorsement, would you not say?'

'I can see that.'

'None the less, at the risk of a noisy bruiting abroad, there were some at the time who did not agree with this very English *sotto voce* way of doing things. They still believe that the man should have gone to trial for his crimes against the state.'

Philip had more to offer me.

'To complicate things there were others involved from earlier years, and others suspected of being involved. The whole matter continues to rumble on in certain quarters. In fact, if my judgement is anything to go on, it's set to trundle on for a good few years yet. There are ramifications, as one says, still being looked into, still taking up valuable time which could be better deployed. So, not to repeat the error, there are those – '

'Of whom Colonel Jackson is one?'

'There are those who were, and indeed are, determined to deal *now* with any such betrayal in a different way. Even if it is to do with persons of lesser importance.' Philip raised a forefinger to signal an afterthought. 'And to *dissuade* others who might be tempted.'

He spread his hands in that 'Need I say more?' gesture of his. 'More coffee?'

A short break while Philip Hathers QC brewed up more of his black concoction.

'Let's get back to the surveillance reports. Any other comments?'

I had spent a couple of hours trying to match the transcriptions of telephone conversations against the schedule of observations. Whatever else they revealed –

'There's nothing in the telechecks to show arrangements being made for any of those meetings between the MP and the other identified principals. Nothing in the intercepted mail either.'

'Ah!' This time, one of Philip's ruminative long-drawn syllables. 'From which one may infer?'

'From which' – I measured my words – 'one may infer that there was some other means of fixing times and places for such meetings.'

'Hmm.'

I pressed on.

'A go-between. Some other person.'

Without a means of making advance arrangements for meetings it was difficult to explain how the MP could manage to meet up with either of his StB contacts at such unpredictable dates and times. Surveillance had not detected any remote means of contact – no physical `drops' where messages could be left. The lack of any discovered means of arranging these encounters was the puzzle. Weeks could go by, months even, without a meeting; then there could be two meetings within a matter of days. Those meetings had to have been arranged. They could not have happened by chance.

Once more Philip was sucking vigorously on his pipe which, as on most occasions with him, had gone out shortly after having been lit. I framed another of my *Yes buts* which had occurred to me in going through the papers the previous evening.

'It also seems a remarkable coincidence, given the haphazard timings of the observation records, that a surveillance team just happened to be in the right places at the right times to record those meetings with the Czechoslovak officers and the newspaper reporter.'

Philip, a lit match held at the bowl of his pipe, simply gazed at me for a few seconds with barely perceptible nods.

'From which you further infer? since we continue to speculate.'

'That our service knew in advance the details of each encounter.'

'Hmm. Anything more?'

'Well, yes.'

I hesitated. My guesswork could be the wildest sort of conjecturing with someone who must have had many years of connection with this world of shadowy activities.

'Could it be possible, Philip, that the source of information telling this MP where and when to meet with the Czech officers, and perhaps the foreign correspondent as well, could be the same source which informed our own security services of the times and locations for these encounters?'

At that point, a rare exception, Philip had a veritable furnace going in the bowl of his pipe. Where usually he managed thin streams of smoke there were now clouds of blue-grey rising in rapid succession.

'Interesting thought, my dear chap. Very interesting. Certainly a plausible supposition – could be the case. Wouldn't know, of course.'

But he did know. And now, instantly, I knew. There are different forms of knowledge other than the certainties supplied by verifiable fact. There is that inner, tacit knowledge – one simply *knows* that one knows, though one is hard put to it to justify that knowledge. In the years of my maturing after these times I recount, such subjective correspondences – to give them some sort of title – provided me with insights I came to trust more and more in countless interviews and interrogations.

Philip levered himself upright from his lounging position.

'I think, perhaps, Anthony, you might well have a flair for this sort of thing.'

I waited in vain for any further explanation. Philip stretched out his left arm, bent it at the elbow to study his wristwatch. By his slowness and over-concentration upon the timepiece I knew that he wanted to hustle along our business of this late morning. After all, his social engagement, whatever it was to be that weekend, would soon press upon him the need to get away.

'So, my dear young man, what is lacking? What flesh, to put the question again, do we still need to hang on these bare bones?' With the slightest of nods he turned his eyes towards the portfolio on his desk.

It was time to commit myself.

'We need the direct testimonies of Miss K.'

'Was rather afraid you were going to say that. You're quite right, of course. Gratifying to know that, I'm sure. But – '

But there were difficulties, it seemed. Doubtless there existed already reports written by the good lady herself, perhaps also transcripts of interviews conducted with the same anonymous Miss K. All duly recorded and safely filed away. And no doubt Miss K *could* testify to the matters in those files. But... even if one could guarantee the safeguarding of her identity, one could not similarly guarantee the security of what Philip referred to as her 'location'.

'Location?'

'Where she works, my dear chap, as simple as that.'

Any testimony would bring forth that information, was bound to. Would have to explain how she came by whatever information she had obtained. Could be embarrassing – Philip developed a small cough at this point in defence of the stance not to call Miss K at all – her private life would have to be divulged... And quite apart from that personal cost, it would mean the loss of a valuable source of information since she would no longer be able to operate from that 'location'. Could call in question whatever information had passed through her 'in the other direction' also. Which would be a pity, a very great pity, given how good an asset one might conjecture she had proved to be, and much else which *could* be the case, and so on to the same effect from Philip Hathers QC.

Even as he spoke on the issue of Miss K I knew that Philip was covertly telling me what he would not or could not say openly. He had a professional obligation to go as far as he could without actually making me openly privy (that word again) to anything I should not know. I recognised his dilemma.

'I understand. I think.'

'Good. Good.'

Philip's gaze was appraising.

'Things will become clearer, I have no doubt. Depending' – he gave a small laugh –'on how you learn to look at things.'

Philip was again examining his watch.

'Must press on. I suppose we might ask the good Colonel if' – pointing to a fan of papers on the desk – 'there might not be more we could have a peek at. We might just say that we are not convinced that we have here the overwhelming case he requires. It may persuade him to let us have something more that would be of service to us. Or something else if not more.'

I concurred.

Philip put the palms of both hands heavily onto his desk; end of subject.

'Meanwhile, my dear Anthony, Arnold Ward.'

Arnold Ward, the Eastern Europe correspondent whose reports I had re-read just last night.

'Sorry I can't be there myself, prior engagement and all that. Never met the man, perhaps another time – when he's over here for a little longer.'

The man, I gathered, was back in England for a very short while, a few days only, before he set off again for East Germany.

'So it's tonight or not at all on this trip, I'm afraid. Volunteered you in my unavoidable absence, am really very grateful to you.' Philip positively beamed at me, which I took as some kind of token apology for sub-contracting this obligation upon me. 'Have every confidence in you, Anthony.' This compliment also sounded to me somewhat apologetic.

'But what do you want me to do?'

Philip leaned across the desk towards me.

'Listen.'

'Just that?'

'And remember.'

'Anything else?'

'And ask the questions which occur to you depending on what he has to say to you. What he is *prepared* to say to you, bearing in mind he is not actually the Colonel's man. Free agent, you see, can be difficult to manage.'

'Is there anything else I should know about this meeting with Arnold Ward?'

Beyond ensuring that the meeting was to be kept informal, very informal, the meeting would be a casual encounter. It was not to be a meeting between junior barrister and client since, after all, no solicitor had been instructed and there was, as yet, no case either to be prosecuted or defended.

'When and where, Philip?'

'Ah yes. Do you know the Gin Palace? crossroads, Putney High Street, Upper Richmond Road end.'

'Gin Palace?'

'As known thereabouts, I gather. Simply handing on the information – just a walk away from East Putney tube. Can't miss it apparently – huge place.'

I did not know it. In fact the furthest west in London I had ever been was as far as the King's Road in Chelsea, and only then as far as *The Six Bells* – at Carolyne's insistence: 'Oh we simply must go there, it's one of the 'happening' places friends tell me. Do let's say we'll go.' When we did venture there one Saturday evening, the only things happening, as far as I could see, were a lot of drunk people about our age getting even drunker and a youngish blonde-haired woman with a slash of shiny red for lips, who had been lifted onto the bar, skirt hitched high on her thighs, being provoked to sing whilst being handed a large gin and tonic.

'Mister Ward suggests you get there early. Said he would wait for you until six-thirty or so. Don't be late. I would recommend that you have something to eat before you get there.'

'Why so early?'

Without a trace of irony, without any recognition of the circumstances *vis-à-vis* himself and me, Philip replied:

'Sometimes we have to accommodate ourselves to other persons' schedules, I regret to say. Needs drive, unfortunately.'

'Just one thing, Philip.'

'Yes?'

'How will I know him? This Arnold Ward.'

'Ah yes. Don't worry about that, Anthony. No problem at all – just go to the bar and order a drink. Mister Ward will come to you.'

'But how will *he* know *me*?'

Philip gave a small cough.

'Photograph. He has a photograph of you.'

19

I telephoned Carolyne at her office before I set off for an early meal prior to my meeting with Arnold Ward.

'I have managed to square things with mummy, you'll be pleased to know. Goodness knows why, but she still thinks you are a wonderful man – even though you have let her down very badly.'

I mumbled repeat apologies.

'Daddy was so looking forward to having some male company too.'

Now *that* I could easily believe. I had witnessed myself the ceaseless dialogue between mother and daughter. It was tiring to attend to, and yet by some miracle that defied the laws of physics, the energy they expended in talk seemed to generate even more energy, especially when they were talking at or to each other simultaneously. Carolyne's father must have had years of it.

'Well, we shall still be there at a good time tomorrow morning. So not all is lost.'

'You do realise, my darling, how I have had to puff you up, make you sound indispensable to the national interest, in order to excuse you from this evening?'

I felt some embarrassment at this inflation of my importance, more so because I myself had hinted at something along these lines to Carolyne the previous evening.

'Really, though, it is *such* a disappointment, especially to Mummy.'

'Yes, I do know that. You have already twisted that knife.'

There was a silence. I was the one to break it.

'I mean, it just can't be helped on this occasion. But I shall be able to make up for it another time. And this *is* important, it really is.'

There was another silence, more exactly an almost-silence in which I began to suspect something wrong with the connection when she spoke a little more forcefully, I thought, than in her accustomed voice.

'By the way, darling, I have had a call from William.'

'Really? When?'

'Earlier this afternoon.'

'And?'

'He wanted to know if we would be free to have dinner with him tonight.'

I was taken aback, for more than one reason. The first formed as a simple, instant question: how on earth did William get to know the number for Carolyne's office? But then, how had he obtained my home address? And what a coincidence, and what bad luck, that he should ask us out to dinner on the very night I would be otherwise engaged.

'I thought William had to go away for a few days.'

'What on earth makes you think that?'

'I had a letter from him, came yesterday. I thought I'd mentioned it to you, but perhaps not.'

'Most definitely not.'

It was the Carolyne tone of voice which advanced upon one, threatening to attack, putting one on the defensive.

I mumbled further apologies.

'Sorry, meant to, of course. But with this present business going on... Anyway, you will have told him that we cannot make dinner tonight.'

The pause was fractional, the tone decisive.

'I told him that *you* would not be able to make dinner tonight.'

'And?'

'Well, since you will be otherwise engaged and since I would otherwise be doomed to a long and boring evening all on my own...'

'Yes – ?'

'I said yes, I would be delighted to accept.'

The pause was of my making now. William's wish to see Carolyne, it seemed, was to be fulfilled on the very heels of his letter to me. William's own plans, I learned, had been changed and now he found himself with a free evening and at a loose end and did not know what to do with it. He was, after all, an old friend to both of us, and his invitation to Carolyne was actually opportune. It would get me off the hook and send me off, guilt-free, on my own evening's entertainment. Even so... But after all, William was, well, William; and as we all knew... *et cetera.* What rankled was that trace of eagerness in Carolyne's voice to spend time with William.

'Well, why not?'

The lilt of a chuckle was back in Carolyne's voice.

'That's exactly what *I* said. Why not? You are going to be busy, and now he and I need not be bored. He can babysit me as in the old days. It will be a wonderful opportunity for us to catch up with each other.'

I had a passing image and an inward chuckle as I thought of poor William subjected to the barrage of words from Carolyne in her interrogation of him as they 'caught up with each other.'

'Where are you going?'

'Anthony, my darling, I was in such a flutter when he telephoned, I just wasn't expecting a call from him of all people, so I can't actually remember. I think he might have said something or other about a Soho restaurant. Oh, wait a moment, Dean Street, perhaps. Could that be right?'

If she could not tell me then I, of course, could not know where William intended to take Carolyne. The irony was simply not recognised by her in her excitement as she immediately proceeded to offload more of what she simply *must* say to me.

'Anyway, the thing is, my darling, a change of plans. I shall not be at your place when you get back later tonight. Obviously. William's not calling for me until eight, so by the time we get to this place he has chosen, wherever it is, and then the meal and getting back and... and in any case you might be late back yourself, mightn't you? '

'Quite understand. Give William my regards, tell him I'm sorry to miss him and so on.'

'Of course. I'll even give him a big kiss from you.'

'*That*, my lovely Carolyne, is something you will *not* do. I positively forbid it.'

She was laughing, obviously back in good spirits, and me back in her good books again. God bless William.

'Oh well, he will just have to make do with a big kiss from me then.'

A girlish giggle.

'I shall be at your place first thing in the morning, Anthony. Make sure you're up and ready to fly off.'

I assured Carolyne that I would be ready and waiting.

'Enjoy your evening with William.'

'I'm sure I shall. And you enjoy your evening with your mystery man.'

There was the smacking noise of lips sending a big kiss down the line.

Temple to East Putney was a direct connection on the London Underground. The Gin Palace, as referred to, was unmissable, as promised. Why so-called, whatever its actual name, was immediately evident on entering its cavernous interior. It was a drinking house, sited in a huge Victorian building, its long bars already crowded with early evening drinkers, most of them men, and most of them probably having stopped off on their way home at the end of the working week. Some of them, having formed small groups and now relaxing into their own free time, doubtless would soon forget that they had called in only 'for a swift drink or two'.

I managed to press myself towards the nearest bar, the whole length of which was taken up with men standing, in places two or three deep, in their groups. Eventually one of the barmen came to take my order, one ear turned towards me, his body leaning across the bar itself. I ordered a pint of bitter with which I withdrew, trying to find for myself an unoccupied space. Between sips of beer I regarded the crowded space before me, trying to guess – if he were there – which of the scores of men could be the Arnold Ward for whom I waited.

And waited.

I had finished my pint. This was not a place where one stood with an empty glass in hand. To get to the bar I had to make a passage through the middle of a group of men standing just away from the bar itself. After a wait I managed to order another pint.

I turned away from the bar and suddenly my tankard was knocked upwards in my hand, only my grip on the handle preventing the entire contents being shipped. But there was a patch of wet on my jacket, the rest of the ale slopping onto the bottoms of my trousers and onto my shoes.

'So sorry, very clumsy of me. Let me buy you another pint.'

I looked up from the front of my jacket to see one of the men from the group I had passed through to get to the bar and was now trying to pass back through to get to my table again.

'Here, let me.'

The man took from me my glass and in the same moment handed me a large, folded white handkerchief.

'Thanks.'

The man grinned at me. I was thanking the cause of my accident in the instant before the delayed reaction of anger began to set in. He thrust out a hand.

'Arnold.' He held my look for a fraction of a second. 'Arnold Ward.'

Automatically I took his hand.

'Anthony.'

'Pleased to meet you, Anthony.'

He swept a hand loosely around the group of men.

'Why don't you join us?'

The three other men shuffled to make space for me to stand among them. Each introduced himself in turn with outstretched arm. Sam, David, Reg. They were men all in their late thirties or early forties, I guessed. But Arnold himself looked younger than his companions, not more than middle thirties, I'd have said. And tall.

A full pint of ale was thrust into my hand.

'Cheers!' all round.

Some casual conversation, voices raised against the surrounding noise. Arnold did some character assassinations, masquerading as biographies, of the other men as he introduced each of them in turn. All were newspapermen. Reg, the oldest by far, twenty years older than showed on his passport, Arnold alleged, had a column in one of the popular dailies. 'Not that he's got two ideas to strike together to make a spark – but always willing to plagiarise.' Sam was a sports writer – wrote the same report on the football matches he covered, just changed the names and scoreline to fit. David (I noticed he was never Dave) was a political reporter – Westminster his usual turf – who turned politics into gossip courtesy of his public school contacts in parliament. Arnold spoke of himself simply as a foreign correspondent.

'And you, Anthony? What's your line of roguery?'

I glanced at Arnold. He just noticeably half-closed one eye. I explained, as briefly as I could.

'I'm not sure we should be keeping this kind of company...'

'Now I could tell you a few things about Sam...'

It very quickly appeared that each of them could tell a few things about the other three.

Arnold wrapped it up, in a semi-serious tone, by asserting that I could be useful to any one of them, one day, you never knew what accidents might befall in the future. 'We could run to a bottle of scotch as a retainer...'

'Another?'

I reached into my jacket pocket for my wallet. The company would not hear of it.

'My round, I think.'

I have no idea whose round it was in the order in which that and other rounds followed. I know that I passed from alert defensiveness at the start of my absorption into their company, through a loosened relaxation, to a careless freedom on my way to drunkenness. My socks were now a comforting wet warmth.

After two hours the group began to disperse.

'Promised I would be back by nine.'

'Duty calls. Caretaking tonight, manning the desk.'

Among the leavings, Arnold turned to me to make his farewell also.

'But – '

He leaned towards me, tapped me familiarly on the cheek and bent his head closely towards me to whisper 'Toilet, then give it a good twenty minutes' as I felt his fingers push something into the breast pocket of my jacket.

Noisy farewells and promises to meet up again sometime soon. I waved to them as they left.

I took time to finish my pint. Despite all the noise around me suddenly I felt isolated. And visible, no longer absorbed into a group. I felt I had been drawn into some strange reversal of reality, where the ordinary assumed something out-of-the-way, the smallest actions betokening something other. Trying not to be obviously looking around, I looked around. Was there a watcher there, watching me? Why else Arnold's extreme caution? There was a flurry of thoughts which seemed to shuffle together like a melded pack of cards where no card carried its face value only. I tried to shake away such thoughts. They were inventions of a drunken brain, I told myself. I was at that stage of intoxication where one is still aware of oneself and one's actions, onwards from which one is talking silently to oneself and laughing at the little idiocies one is perpetrating. As if in instant confirmation that such a point had been reached, my foot slipped from the brass footrest which ran around the bar. The pint mug I was holding hit the bar with a solid, loud thump as I lost balance, throwing a wave of beer over its side onto the bar, spray from its landing then spattering my shirt and tie. Remarkably, three thoughts simultaneously occurred to me. One was a sort of Oops! drunker than I thought I was; one was the recall of something one of my tutors had said to me – 'We know so little of human consciousness, Anthony, except that it is highly soluble in alcohol'; and one was the observation that if I was trying to make myself inconspicuous, blend in with the setting, I had just called express attention to myself. Heads had jerked in my direction at the crash of glass on wood.

I held out at the bar until the pressing urgency of an overfull bladder sent me to the Gents at the rear of the building. I had enough wit, or imagination, left to lock myself into one of the cubicles whilst simultaneously tearing desperately at the zip of my trousers. The relief of a swollen bladder must be one of life's distinct, albeit minor, pleasures. But to the point: I found in my breast pocket a scrap of paper. Pencilled thereon was the simple message: *Spotted Horse, High Street.*

I have to say that I felt a momentary thrill of excitement as I pulled the flush and watched the screwed up ball of paper wash away around the bend of the WC. It was like a little rite of initiation into an alternative world of secrets and deceptions.

The Spotted Horse, to return its definite article, was easily found. The few minutes' walk in the cool air and the drizzling rain actually cleared my head somewhat; enough to function rather more wittingly, less amusedly at my own condition.

When I entered the bar I did not see Arnold. The lighting here was subdued compared with the brightness I had left a few hundred yards away. There were still spaces at a couple of tables along the side wall and, although the place was busy, it lacked the

crush of the previous pub, and was distinctly less noisy. Having no
other instruction I went straight to the bar, then hesitated. I needed
to reduce my consumption of alcohol. I ordered a small glass of
red wine and took it to the furthest of the two empty tables, then
sat, looking back into the room. Instantly and immediately, just two
feet away from me, Arnold's tall figure passed in front of me in the
act of lowering himself into the chair opposite.

'Mind if I join you?'

'Do by all means,' my reply addressed to the already-seated
figure.

I noticed, placed before him, a tumbler of what I took to be
a double Scotch.

'Just to be sure to be sure.' Arnold waved a hand in the direction of the entrance. I took his gesture to refer to the manner
of his leaving the first pub and the means of getting us here
together.

'Sorry about that cloak and dagger stuff earlier. It's that
bloody AA course they make you do – for your own safety they
say.'

He had been talking down to the table, but looking up he saw
my lack of comprehension.

'Don't tell me you've got away without doing it.'

Another glance told him all.

'It will come your way. AA, Awareness and Avoidance – seeing without appearing to look, seeing without been seen. Makes
you bloody paranoid.'

Then Arnold uttered what sounded to me like a strange-
ly-pronounced obscenity. He repeated, with a slight change of
pronunciation.

'Fuchs.'

I could make no connection. Arnold laughed.

'Fuchs. Klaus Fuchs. Dear powers-that-be, they've sent me a
virgin.'

I was still none the wiser.

'Gave atomic bomb secrets to the Russians. Came back to England from Los Alamos.'

Not even a very distant bell rang.

'Met here at times, in this pub, 'forty-six onwards, with his KGB handler.'

My look of surprise must have told Arnold everything about my innocence.

'Don't worry. It's not a tradition that's been kept up here.' His eyes crinkled with amusement. 'So far as we know, that is.'

It would have been so easy for Arnold to have adopted a superior, patronising manner towards me. But evidently he accepted my credentials, such as they were, whatever he had been told, as my *bona fides*.

In fact we fell to talking with each other easily enough, he with less reserve than me. We exchanged some basic personal stuff.

'Always like to know who I'm dealing with.'

I agreed, and yet the additional years Arnold had on me gave him in my eyes a far more extensive knowledge of people, a greater knowingness. He was, in the cliché, worldly-wise, at least he made me feel greatly inferior in my lack of experience – simply by his presence. Certainly he was well over six feet, broad-shouldered, made for the second-row of a rugby scrum, his thick, dark wavy hair pushed back from the temples. His eyes were of a rich mahogany colour, unusually uniform, no flecks of another or lighter colour appearing. They looked directly at one as he spoke – and yet there was wariness to them. So I thought then; or was such a thought fashioned out of what I knew of the man? That he was a foreign correspondent for a leading broadsheet, covering Eastern Europe within the Soviet bloc – and at the same time 'being of service to the service.' Was that not how Philip Hathers had expressed such a loyalty?

'You first.'

So I recounted my own progress to this point; briefly because in truth there was not much to tell. But Arnold probed. I had withheld the naming of my school. When, in the face of a direct question, I told him, Arnold pursed his lips and nodded lightly several times.

'Thought so.' A pause. 'Public school boy.'

Was that the hint of a criticism? Or was I, not for the first time, becoming sensitive to the issue of my background?

'Grammar school lad myself. One of those that thought it was a public school, acted like one – school song, school shout, play up, play up, and all that rousing King and country doctrine, do and die, ours not to question why. Even had our own Cadet Corps.'

He laughed, and with a small flicking of the fingers of one hand, urged me to drink up.

'Which I joined, of course. Liked the idea of being allowed to wear my hobnails and stomp around the quad. Didn't get in the way of a scholarship to Cambridge, let us say – though not sure it helped much once I got there, not with all those super-size donnish brains in the place.'

He lifted my glass and stood.

'No, no, let me.' At which, actions to words, I took a five-pound note from my wallet and offered it up to him.

'Mine next then. A word of advice, though. Get off the red wine. Whisky – they all drink whisky. Make it last as long as you like, splash of water, another splash of water while you refill theirs with the neat stuff.'

He turned away to go to the bar. Who 'they' were and what he thought he was preparing me for escaped my comprehension, though it was obvious enough he spoke from actual experience of some kind.

He returned with two glasses of large measures. I spluttered on the first sip of the unadulterated whisky, much to Arnold's amusement.

Then, spoken as an abrupt start, a change of tenor. 'What do you know? And what do you want to know?'

I relayed what I knew.

'How does it look? Have we got enough to nail the bastard?'

Two men leaning across the table towards each other, heads bent, Arnold with a pad and pencil sketching what looked to me like construction diagrams of some sort – beams and joints and infills taking shape as I talked.

I explained as best I could, my lips beginning to feel somewhat anaesthetised. I explained how circumstantial much of the observation and intercept materials could be made to appear. I explained that, if prosecution proceeded, his direct testimony in the witness box would be essential. He seemed unconcerned.

'Of course, of course.' A window took shape. 'Goes without saying.'

But, I wanted to know, would this not damage him? – giving evidence in open court in his own name without the protection of a screen and the cover of an assigned letter of the alphabet?

At this he laughed aloud, then chinked together our two empty tumblers. He lifted them up to take to the bar for a refill. When he returned to our table Arnold turned over a page of his notepad. A couple of verticals and a crosspiece looked like the beginning of an OXO matrix.

'You appear not to have been fully briefed, Anthony.'

I listened in some amazement as Arnold told me that standing up in court and being known, his profession made public, was something which would actually do him good. It would in fact 'help the cause'.

How could that be?

'You have to know that I'm in good odour with the StB.' In what I noticed was an habitual action, he ran both hands through his hair, taking it back and away from his temples.

Arnold, head down again, was designing an external doorway complete with double doors.

'*Státní bezpečnost* – in the Czech version. *Štátna* in the Slovak. You might even say I'm good friends with some of the boys of the state security – one of them quite high up.' He looked up quickly, his eyes narrowing. 'And one of the girls. You might as well know this now, because you will need to know it at some point in the future.'

Arnold pushed his notepad across the table towards me.

'What do you think?'

I started to mutter something about not knowing all of the implications, so far as I understood matters from the papers I had been allowed to see.

'No, no. *This*!' He stabbed a forefinger at his drawing. 'Want to knock out the entrance and put this in instead.'

I saw two doors which together made a pointed arch.

'Thought I'd try to get some reclaimed stained glass for these panels.' He pointed to the segments at the top of each door. 'Was originally a Victorian manse, thought a bit of gothic would not be out of place. Bought the property a couple of years ago, surplus to church requirements, the local vicar these days has to cover three of the village churches. Very rural, you see. Do you know Herefordshire?'

For the next indeterminate period of time Arnold animatedly enthused about the house and its location. Clearly he was in love with both.

And with an unnamed woman.

20

I recall the treacherous state of the wet pavements as I stepped out of the pub at the end of that evening's drinking. They were moving beneath my feet. As a result I was making sideways movements as I pursued a forward direction. A straight line was out of the question, and the simple fact of the matter was that I did not know where I was going, which direction – other than forwards – to follow. I was lost, I was in an area of west London which was wholly unfamiliar to me. Finding my way 'back' to my starting-point for the evening was not possible when 'back' had no meaning and forwards only, onwards, onwards, ever onwards, held out the likelihood of coming by chance upon a place from which 'home' would become a possibility. I was drunker even than on those mad, extended drinking sessions at Oxford, in which the foolhardiness of youth was required to assert one's manliness.

It was drizzling still, and against the lights in the street, as I made the mistake of looking upwards, the thin rain created the effect of a diaphanous, shimmering material.

A drunk man should not look up, never mind stare fascinatedly at what he is seeing. What little of his balance mechanism is left to him deserts him instantly. What does not leave him or, rather, what invades him or arises from him in this condition, is a drunken humour in which no minutiae are too small to warrant one's attention and everything amuses one. *Ebrius risus*, amusing in itself that I sought in Latin that drunken silly smile which accompanies the laughter in one's head at one's own foolish actions. And in particular actions which fail to imitate those easy, taken-for-granted motions one makes when sober. Everything takes long unhurried time. Even raising one's hand to one's eyes becomes a slow-motion deliberation to deflect the beating rain, and the empty space around one is populated with invisible presences to whom one addresses the most inane remarks.

Looking up which, as I say, a drunken man should never do, suddenly I was looking down. Now on my knees on the wet of the pavement, I found humour in humour itself – and for the first time in my life contemplated the deeply ironic realisation that humour, the word, comes from the moisture brought forth from the earth. Every man, drunken to this level of dissolution of the mind, experiences revelatory eurekas, some of which he may even remember later: for no good reasons since invariably they will have lost their shine in the light of the day, dross for gloss. In my own case, for a period – duration can not be quantified by a man gone so far down into his drunken consciousness – I tried to improvise one of those *facetiae,* those brilliant witticisms in which consciousness, humour, and laughter are brought to a sparkling and unifying verbal radiance of phrase. I know, as my old-fashioned fountain pen scores these words onto superannuated writing paper, that my ambition then, on all fours as I was, makes no sense whatsoever. What is even less comprehensible to me, however, is the fact that I remember (still) with perfect clarity every minute detail of this episode in Putney High Street.

Finally, having got up, I gave up. I looked for a taxi. Even that is not true. I waited for a taxi to appear; in the certain knowledge, emboldened by alcohol, that one would appear for my service. One did and, by stepping into its path, I brought it to a halt.

Arrived at my flat, I negotiated a fare with the driver by the simple expedient of handing over to him my wallet and asking him to take from it what was due. He took some notes, I neither knew nor cared how many of what colour from my wallet and pushed it back into my jacket pocket as he allowed me to lean against him in our climb up the steps of the entrance to the apartment building. I asked the man if he would mind, please, be very much obliged, so kind, if he would unlock the door for me. He did, and I fell into the passageway.

Somehow, though the memory of how, is completely obliterated, I must have managed to raise myself up, climb the stairs, unlock the door to my flat and manage to throw myself onto the bed.

The next apparition of consciousness jumbled a network of impressions which all seemed to be going on at the same time.

There was a vein at each side of my forehead which, in synchronised collusion, were hammering out their insistent, loud, percussions on the tympani of my eardrums. There was an empty space in my head where other noises reverberated; and there was one sound in particular which was outside my head but a very long way off, so very distant. The sound became a breath upon my face, the breath became a voice, and the voice was Carolyne. And it was an angry voice.

It was also, sounding within that raised voice, the first assembling of anything that could be called understanding.

'Late,' was the only part of speech which I was able to separate from its surrounding vocal noises, the string section imposing itself on the percussion, as it were. The voice was coming now just inches away from my face whilst in the far distance physical force was being applied to my body.

Carolyne was tugging at the belt of my trousers, then waistband and zip. Jacket and shoes had already gone.

'Don't you help, Anthony.' Not for the first (or last) time did I interpret Carolyne's heavy irony for an unaccented statement of face value, gladly giving up my middle region to her activities.

My smile must have been inane. It is surprising how quickly a young man, emerging from the stupor of an alcohol-induced coma, can be brought to a very local level of responsiveness whilst remaining insensitive and deadened throughout the rest of his body.

Carolyne slapped me. She actually *slapped* me, *there* on the one part of my body showing any signs of interest in recovery; and slapped me hard enough to make my body jack-knife into a sudden U-shape. She used my momentum somehow to haul on my shoulders, my hands now firmly clamped between my thighs, and get me into a sitting, though somewhat swaying, position on the edge of the bed. My gasping for breath had given way to a low moaning.

'Stay there!'

Even at that moment, feeling the weakness of my body and contemplating my nakedness, her command amused me. After a few experimental attempts I knew that I simply could not move and there was, in any case, nowhere for this naked man to attempt to go. I was still smiling broadly when Carolyne re-entered the bedroom.

'This is *not* funny, Anthony Ashley-Chetwyne.'

Addressing me thus by my hyphenated surname meant that 'this', whatever the extent of 'this' was, was serious. Very serious. I recall, in my fuddled state, that I could get no further with the thought of something serious other than by adopting what, doubtless, was a ludicrous version of a serious face.

I was hauled and pushed into a scaldingly hot shower. Carolyne's bare arm reached through the curtain and I was saved from being seriously injured as the water went from hot through tepid to freezingly cold.

'You *stay* there until you're sober.' The order was imperious and commanded in a voice I had never previously heard from Carolyne.

Finally, every part of my body shrunken and shrivelled, I was allowed to step out of the shower and into a large towel which Carolyne held open for me. She rubbed me down not as a mother tenderly dries her child, nor lingeringly as a lover, but with harsh brusqueness which turned blue skin once more red.

'Shave.'

An arm pointed to the basin of hot water.

With grim, set face, Carolyne dressed me, and then we were on our way in her car, my window wound down so that I could gasp in mouthfuls of fresh air. Silence between people is not simply an absence of sound. It is a personality, it is a third party; it has its own character and a very specific identity – and is one of many such possible silences. And each one is filled, if not overflowing, with its own especial emotions and thoughts, as well as endless replays of the history which preceded and precipitated the silence in the first place. This silence between us, as Carolyne drove us north to escape London, was bursting with tight-lipped anger. I said nothing: there was nothing which occurred to my dulled sensibility which would in any way excuse or ameliorate the condition in which Carolyne had found me when she had let herself into my flat that morning. Even the thought of speaking made my eyelids droop.

Not until we were into the reaches of Hertfordshire did I find anything to say. Glancing down I noted, with some bemusement, that my wristwatch appeared to be missing,

'What time is it now?'

Several things seemed to happen in such rapid succession that time concertina'd upon itself. There was a sudden squeal of brakes, something between a scream and a roar pitched into my ear, a fierce swing of the car into a layby, and a violent heave of the handbrake followed instantly by Carolyne turning in upon me and flailing her bunched hands against my chest. I was shocked. So shocked that I did not try to avoid or evade her flailings. Eventually she stopped, the wrists of her hands resting on me, her head lowered onto my neck. She was sobbing. I put my arms around her, somewhat awkwardly, as we were half-turned to each other in our seats. The sobbing went on for some time, slowly subsiding.

Carolyne sniffled something to me. I did not ask her to repeat herself for fear of starting off once more her anger. Finally she raised her head away from the damp patch on my shirt, looking directly at me from wet, red eyes smudged around with the black of her mascara.

'Why did you have to go last night.'

Not a question, but a rebuke to put me in the wrong again. I mumbled soothing sounds.

'None of this should have happened. None of this *would* have happened. Oh, Anthony, why, why, *why* did you have to go?'

I tried to rub away the question by smoothing the palm of a hand across her back.

'I'm sorry, I'm really sorry. Afraid I did have rather too much to drink.'

She lifted away from me, sat back in her seat, head bowed, hair falling forwards, hands clasped together in her lap. Her body shifted as she inhaled in short bursts, staccato, suppressing the sobs. Then she lifted her hands to her face, the sobs bursting out once more. Very slowly she lowered the fingers of her hands just as far as her cheeks, pulling down fractionally the lower lids of her eyes. She made a half turn towards me, simply shaking her head to and fro.

'Oh if only you hadn't... None of this would have happened, Anthony, none of it.'

'None of what?'

All of it made perfect sense to me. I had gone out the night before and got stupefyingly drunk. I had been apprentice to a master. Arnold Ward had drunk copiously all evening, from early evening, before my first drink, to chucking-out time; pints of bitter then unnumbered doubles of whisky. Unthinkingly I had joined him as round succeeded round of drinks.

Idiot!!! Such an idiot that several exclamation marks would not suffice to indicate my sudden realisation. Water. And the man had even told me in advance – in advance of the whiskies anyway – water, the secret to salving the spirit, dilution followed by more dilution... Going to the bar when it had been his round, bidding me stay where I was when mine – he would get the drinks, taking my offered notes of money – had he refilled his own glass with water only? What was it he had said? Water for yourself, whisky neat for them – whoever 'they' were – and for me too I now very strongly suspected. I was repeating to myself the threnody of why? why? why? why me? why would he do that to me? when Carolyne threw herself against me, arms once more around my neck.

'Oh Anthony, Anthony.'

We sat there like that for some time, calmness returning. I ventured a question.

'So are we running a bit late?'

Carolyne pulled herself away from me, her glare withering.

'Late? *Late?* I had already 'phoned mummy to tell her we would be late, so she said she would put lunch back a bit. *Now* we shall be *too* late even for *late* lunch.'

Somewhere between a prayer and a confession I repeated several times over 'I'm sorry, I'm sorry.' I could think of nothing else to say.

Carolyne reached across into the back seat, retrieved a hand-bag and started rummaging through its contents. With handker-chief and spit she set about tidying her face, then started applying fresh cosmetics. Just as she was about to put on her lipstick, a thought:

'Then what time was it when you got to my place?'

The lipstick remained poised.

'A bit later than I had intended.'

'I thought you were going to come round early.'

'Woke up sleepy, couldn't tear myself out of bed.'

'Ah.'

This too was not the pondering character of Philip Hathers's long-drawn exhalation. This was Anthony's small sop of satisfac-tion, a little of his guilt transferring back to Carolyne, and glad of it as a stop to hostilities. Carolyne, make-up repaired, seemed to accept that portion, for she turned to practical matters.

'I shall pull in at the next pub we come to and 'phone mummy to say we have had a breakdown.'

Chilly, a single word though in fact an epithet dense with its own *gravitas*, perhaps best describes our reception when, at last, we made it to her parents' house. There was no hug for me from Carolyne's mother, just an outstretched arm and the briefest of handshakes. Carolyne's father, looking at his wife and looking ill-at-ease at the same time, managed to avoid a handshake altogether.

'You've finally made it, then.'

In acting on his wife's orders – it was so obviously the case – he had contrived to adopt a manner of greeting which he must have thought conveyed the right degree of disapproval. Actually it was all I could do to stop myself laughing; the existential absurdity of his remark just happened to tingle my sense of the ridiculous. Were we not manifestly, in the flesh, present? And therefore must have arrived? Carolyne, in contrast, was held close by each of her parents in turn, and fondly kissed. Whatever Carolyne had said in that last telephone call had cast me as the villain. There were distances to be closed. I would have to work on the mother, charm her out of her punitive state of mind. Oddly enough I had confidence in my ability to do that: as a boy and then as a young man I had never had any difficulty in bringing round older women. My mother, however angry with me over something, would soon forgive me. Aunts on both sides of the family and other women, friends of my mother, thought me charming and obliging. I grew up liking and being liked by mature women. I found them interesting – they had tales to tell – where girls and, later, young women more or less of my own age often seemed to me somewhat shallow. I continued to lust after them, of course, the girls, despite their frivolousness.

I'm wandering from the point. I set Carolyne's mother as my target, and set about ingratiating myself with her in the most direct fashion. I asked if I might have a few words with her, apart from Carolyne and her father who had preceded us into the house. I made confession. Women love *mea culpas*.

'I am so sorry we are so late getting here. It's entirely my fault, nothing to do with Carolyne. My fault entirely.'

Having relieved her daughter of any attachment of blame, I then explained, briefly, the circumstances of the previous evening. In a tone of what I hoped would be taken for sincere regret, I lightly insinuated the phrase 'government business', can't say more, sorry, absolutely imperative. There followed other stepping-stones: unavoidable meeting, went on far too long, could not walk away, insulting to the host, and so on and so on, ending with what I hoped would catch her curiosity. When curiosity is hooked, the barriers begin to come down.

'Truth of the matter is, I forgot the water.'

She could not prevent herself. She had to ask.

I explained.

The set of her mouth loosened, just a little. A smile began to form.

'Men!'

Women have a way of saying that word with a unique intonation; part exasperation, the male creature being beyond comprehension, daft but endearing, bent at times on self-destruction – a foolhardy creature who knows he is entering a danger zone and yet insists on going in. But, and this is another *Yes but*: it enables them to patronise us in their own special way, treating us as boys never fully grown-up, as from a woman who never outgrows her motherhood.

Carolyne's mother put her arm through mine to lead me indoors, gently shaking her head to and fro. No longer condemned, I was then on probation for a little while longer, not to be given in to too quickly. Mrs Walker became Jane again, and her husband, as relieved as I was to see that I was out of the dock, immediately reverted to Peter. They were fond of me because their daughter loved me. Jane needed at least my nominal consent to the preparations she had already put in place for the formal announcement of Carolyne's engagement to me.

And then there would be the bustling busyness over goodness knows how many months to plan for a wedding – for which no date had as then been set, but the pressure to nominate one would surely continue with renewed vigour. Because, 'After all,' as Jane had said previously, 'it takes a year to eighteen months to plan a wedding' – a fact, if it were a fact, which did not altogether displease me.

My mother, who took against Carolyne when we had spent a weekend with my parents, was virtually obligated to take against the parents too. It was, I believe, at father's instigation that my parents subsequently – and my mother unwillingly – had met the Walkers just once (on the neutral territory of a London restaurant for lunch). My mother objected to them because they so evidently lacked what she called, in the privacy of her own home, 'class'. By the term my mother meant the accumulated passage of a family, the successive acquisition of a cultured and cultivated way of behaving – and of developing 'taste'. And this term, as far as I could see it manifested in my mother, meant an ability to avoid the vulgar and the cheap. It was, for her, a refinement of sensibility by which people classified themselves, not at all an expression of prejudice on her own part. Once I ventured to ask her how she could tell this difference in persons.

'It speaks for itself, my dear. It could not be more obvious.' And that was the beginning and end of the matter.

My mother really did believe, it was a fervent article of faith with her, that families which traced themselves and their wealth and possessions back through the generations somehow also bespoke the permanence of things as they should be. She did not enquire how such families acquired their wealth in the first place. She waved away suggestions that any family's status could begin with murder, cheating, robbery, malfeasances of any description.

'I am talking about *now*, Anthony,' she had responded tetchily on the few occasions, before going up to Oxford, I had ventured on the subject. 'We provide the reference points for society. We supply *stability*.'

Stability, for my mother, meant I think the preservation of the *status quo* and her position and that of her family within it. Having uttered the touchstone word, however, she had closed the exchange on the matter as far as she was concerned. That was it, *finis*, nothing more to be said, nothing more that could be said on something so unquestionably right.

Dear mother, these prejudices aside – however unlikely it is that this will persuade those who did not know her in a better light – was a wonderful woman, tender-hearted and generous in all other respects. With privilege went duty was her creed, and she was known locally in our manor for her charitable works, for her support of local events and institutions – drawing the line only at anything located in *The Red Lion*, it not being seemly for any lady to be seen inside that particular building.

Yet, at the time of which I now write, half-way through the decade of the nineteen-sixties, even mother could see that things were changing. To her mind the Walkers represented a good many of the changes with which she found fault as not being within her conception of the natural order of things. For a start she resented the fact that the Walkers had money, quantities of it to be disposed freely according to their choice or whim. Jane Walker, I now think out of embarrassment on her first meeting with my mother who had adopted an aloof coldness, managed to touch on a list of their acquisitions and indulgences: a large purpose-built modern house, made to their own design, with driveway and twin wrought iron gateway, a swimming pool, tennis court, cars, holidays in foreign countries, always a winter getaway included... and much else to the same burden. Oh and Peter was thinking about investing in a villa, only a modest one of course, perhaps in Spain, perhaps all going well, who knows, possibly even on one of the Greek islands. The simple truth is that the Walkers had much more money than my family. Most money coming in to our home was spoken for before it arrived. There had been the school fees for my brother and me, from which father had just about recovered; there were the sub-, stantial upkeep costs of the manor house and its estate, always some part of it needing work done; there were the gardeners to be paid and the general handyman; mother could not do without a housekeeper and a housemaid, a general help to her for all manner of things; and there were also the costs of retaining the small London *pied à terre* father had kindly allowed me to occupy from the start of my time at Middle Temple. The privileges my mother claimed for our family came at the cost of keeping up appearances, including those substantial donations to charities which mother supported and, in the region, represented.

Mother was very precise about her use of the word money; money was what the Walkers had. Status, by which mother meant all that was implied in the term *position*, including all the social advantages which came with *family*, its longevity particularly, the Walkers lacked. Money in itself was rather vulgar, and its ostentatious display worthy of the most withering ostracism. Like all of us, to differing degrees, she was a victim of her upbringing. She was the daughter of a Lord-Lieutenant, after all, and before her marriage had met with various members of the royal family on their visits to the county, her father receiving and accompanying them in his official role.

All of these submerged and largely unacknowledged predispositions of my mother had virtually guaranteed that Jane and Peter Walker would fail to make the right impression with mother. Carolyne's parents, in sum, were *arrivistes*.

'What does the father *do?*'

The day before the Walkers met my parents for this first occasion, I had no certain answer to this question of mother's.

'Something to do with import/export, I believe.'

'Hmm.'

Father, like most long-married men, took his cue from mother, and so was rather restrained; perfectly polite, but lacking his usual openness, his habitual *bonhomie*. Yet I liked the Walkers. There was something very straightforward about them, where my home life had been ringed around with various taboos, things one should avoid talking about, subjects and persons it was not in good taste to discuss. Not that there was any prudishness at home. Mother was not in the least embarrassed by anything of a sexual nature. In fact it was she, not father, who had delivered, first to my older brother and then to me, the 'facts-of-life' lecture. Much after this meeting with mother, I learned that she had relieved father of the responsibility because 'he was sure to have made a mess of it.'

'And do remember, Anthony, when your time comes, that making love with a young woman is an expression of mutual consideration, not at all the same thing as rutting.'

Living in the country one had been brought up with the experience of seeing animals of all kinds, including deer, on the estate. Mother's homily included the mechanics of sex, but was much more concerned with respecting a loving relationship; not the perspective, one must say, of a young man still awaiting his initiation. Love could wait. Let the rutting commence.

Once Carolyne's mother had thawed towards me, everything eased. Carolyne took the longest to forgive me; she held her sulky look for a couple of hours after our arrival.

David – an embargo on golf for that weekend imposed by his wife – took me for a walk around the property. He wanted to show me the area where he was planning to build a walled garden, and wanted to share this enthusiasm with me. I knew then, and know now, nothing to do with gardening, but I appreciated the ploy that got me separated from Carolyne so that, as was later confirmed by David, her mother could give Carolyne 'a good talking to.' It must have worked, because by the time we returned to the house Carolyne was in a much better mood, and the rest of the weekend passed off well.

Before I could see the results of Jane's therapy of Carolyne, David had detoured me to the old stable, one end of which he had set up as a bar. He opened a couple of bottles of beer, poured each into a glass. He raised his.

'*Nar zdravi!* or something like that. Cheers!'

A few minutes later David asked:

'What do you think of it? The beer.'

'Good. Very good.'

David lifted up one of the bottles, turning the label towards me.

'A Czechoslovak beer. Make some bloody good beers there. Thinking of buying some in if I can whip up enough interest to make it worthwhile. And provided there's not too much damn paperwork involved in getting it into the country.' He tapped the label of the bottle with two fingers. 'There must be clubs and restaurants where something different like this' – taking an appreciative mouthful – 'adds a bit to your name. Niche value, curiosity value, if nothing else.'

One seizes on coincidence, translates it into something of significance. Most coincidence, however, is just that: conjunction without connection, two things unrelated. But by this mention of Czechoslovakia, David Walker had jolted me into recognition of the fact that I had a lot of memory to retrieve from the previous evening. By Monday I would have to have in order all that I had learned from Arnold Ward throughout our extended drinking session.

The Czech beer did, however, allow me to ask if that was David's line of business – beers, wines, spirits.

'Anthony, my line of business is called opportunity. Anything I can buy and sell on for a profit, preferably a large profit. The bigger the profit, the better the business.'

By the end of our visit late afternoon on Sunday, everyone was jolly with everyone else. Carolyne and I set out for the drive back to London. For the first half-hour Carolyne chattered away to me. There was *so* much to talk over, *so* many ideas for the wedding to discuss, and wasn't it just *so* exciting! Finally a date had been set, and agreed, for the formal engagement of Carolyne Jane Walker to Anthony Ranulph George Ashley-Chetwyne.

'By the way darling, I forgot to ask you how you got on with William on Friday night.'

'Fine.'

There is an assertive way of saying this monosyllable which is intended to put a stop to further conversation. But there may be also the listener's bloody-mindedness which pretends not to have heard the command.

'He was in good form, was he, William?'

'Of course.'

'So what did you two find to talk about?'

'Oh, this and that.'

'Such as?'

'The old times. Oxford.'

'What else?'

'What do you *think* we talked about, Anthony?' Each word as if snapped between her teeth. 'We talked about *everything*, everything of interest to us, to William. You know William, you know his world of learning and how entertaining he can be. He was just... He was the William we both knew and loved.'

I pressed no further.

Carolyne became thin-lipped, her hands tightly gripping the wheel of the car, her knuckles white. I attempted some light talk, a little bantering about the engagement, making an honest man of me. I saw silent tears slowly run down her face. I went to wipe them away with my handkerchief, but she shrugged me away. I tried to put my arm around her, but she twisted her shoulders as if shaking off a wrap or stole. Of course I asked:

'What's wrong? What's the matter?'

The look, from her half-turned head, was withering. With that look I knew that, no matter the jolly features put upon things at her mother's insistence, I had not been fully forgiven by Carolyne. It was clear that I had to undergo the penance of a more prolonged suffering in order to be absolved of my drunken crime.

'No, I won't come in.'

Carolyne dropped me outside my flat.

'I shan't see you tomorrow, Anthony. I shall be busy. I'm going out.'

Allowing the merest peck of a kiss on her cheek, she drove off, over-revving each gear before changing up.

21

'I trust you had a very pleasant weekend Anthony.'

Thankfully, it was not far short of lunchtime before Philip Hathers popped his head around the door to my room in chambers on the Monday morning.

'So sorry, got a bit delayed.'

Why Philip Hathers persisted with this vacuous explanation for being missing on a Monday morning following a weekend house party somewhere or other no-one could tell. One wondered if Philip himself did not expect to be believed. The charade carried an implied suggestion, borne by a shrug of the shoulders and an apologetic smile, that it simply would not do to take leave early from influential persons, people who 'counted' in some way, who had had the good grace to invite one and one's wife for a full schedule of entertainment and wished to extend that invitation to stay on for the Sunday evening. It was an almost invariable habit of Philip, these Monday morning absences. The only exceptions were those occasions on which he had Monday morning court appearances. As a lawyer in our chambers, as with all of us, he was self-employed. Unlike some of us, and me particularly as a junior barrister, Philip had some years ago reached the apogee of his profession; he charged large fees, was much in demand, could pick and choose his cases, and finance a good measure of leisure time. He could also afford now and again to take a case which took his fancy, lowering, or even forfeiting his usual fees. The 'interest' of a case was of more motivation than the money, he had declared to me. From his heightened position, and blessed with financial security, of course he could afford such high-mindedness. Though envied, he remained well-liked.

'Change of plan, if you don't mind. Won't meet with you now – one or two bits to see to, case scheduled, as you know, court number two, final meeting with solicitor at three. How about just after lunch, then? Say, two o'clock? My room?' He put up to his mouth an invisible pipe, by which he let me know that we would meet in his room out of his consideration for me. There would be a blue fug of tobacco smoke. This advance notice meant that Philip expected there to be a report back from me requiring some concentrated thought.

And with that Philip's head withdrew and he was gone.

Post-lunch, as requested, I made my way up the several flights of stairs. Philip waved me into his room. He had begun already the conjuring of matches, tobacco pouch, and pipe from various pockets. As I stepped into his room he had arrived at the combination of matches and tobacco pouch, the matches being put back into a pocket while he then, one-handedly, rummaged through his pockets in search of the pipe.

'Help yourself.'

He nodded to the enamelled pot of coffee on his desk. 'Mugs over there.'

I took a fiercesomely black coffee to the sink to dilute with water. Philip was looking in some puzzlement at his new combination of tobacco pouch and already-filled bowl of pipe. Finally, though, a suitable conflagration was underway, and a satisfactory stream of blue cloud spread outwards from its point of arrival against the ceiling.

'Well, Anthony, what did our Mister Ward have to say for himself?' Philip sat back in his chair. 'Hope you survived the encounter with dignity intact. Those newspaper chaps can drink a bit, you know.' He smiled contentedly. 'All passed off smoothly did it?'

I forewent all comment. Instead I relayed what I had learned; what, with much effort, I had compelled my brain to recollect. The first point stressed by Arnold was that the Czechs had reached a point at which they were getting fed up with our delinquent MP. He had received, as I had seen from his bank statements, extremely large amounts of money from them; regular monthly transfers had gone into his account for years now, and he had enjoyed all sorts of additional benefits including sponsored holidays and invited 'fact-finding' trips, together with a range of expensive gifts both for himself and members of his family. At the start of his betrayal of country the information supplied by the MP had been seen by the Czechoslovakian service as very promising. He had handed on information which, so said Arnold's source, had undoubted value.

At this Philip leaned across to me. 'Didn't mention a name, I suppose?'

"Dušan', so he said.' Hesitantly, I added: 'Though I think there should be inverted commas around that name.'

'Go on.'

Among other things he, the MP, had knowledge of defence contracts which included funding for radar development projects, jet engine development, and missile navigation systems, together with some procurement details for arms and armaments, all mixed in with large amounts of unrestricted information. He had been able also to provide information, usefully confirmative, to the StB and to Moscow via the StB, on army and naval deployments and on spending estimates.

'This we know.'

At the beginning, for close on two years of his hire, his Czech paymasters had been satisfied with the returns from their investment in the MP. A point was reached, however, at which they had become increasingly disillusioned with the low grade of information supplied. The MP had expended his usefulness, it seemed, and the StB's interest in him was waning rapidly. On his trips at that time to Czechoslovakia to take advantage of the hospitality of a free holiday for himself and family, the MP had been visited by a senior StB officer – the same Dušan. In effect the MP was told that his continuing service was being reappraised, that it was possible all payments in cash and kind would be stopped, unless –

The ultimatum seemed to work. Something over a year ago, the MP had passed on some very interesting information concerning a certain Cabinet Minister. That Minister, after much questing and gentle testing, then more pointed persuading by our faithless MP, had now agreed 'to play for the other side', as Arnold had put it – though as yet had not handed on anything of substance. He was, it seemed, still feeling his way in and seemed not fully convinced that the StB measures designed for him would keep him secure from detection. The StB, therefore, was trying to tailor-make an alternative reporting system for the Minister since, in their eyes, he could become a much more important asset than his 'fat bastard' colleague MP.

Philip raised a hand to stop my narrative. He drew on his pipe several times, exhaling imaginary smoke, the fire having gone out. He seemed to be considering something. After a few seconds he waved me on to continue.

At present, I said, the few items of unrestricted information that had come from that Minister, in order that he could avoid personal contact with any Czech officer, had issued through the conduit of our target MP. Arnold Ward's view, from the whispers that had come his way, was that the Czech StB would like to separate the two, dispense with our dishonourable MP, and deal directly with the Minister. The MP was clinging on for dear life and using his recruitment of the Minister to protect his value; and to protect his continuing additional income. As soon as it became convenient, though, the StB would ditch him. Dušan, who continued to insist on meetings with the MP whenever the latter visited the country, had already made that decision.

'Was a name put to this Minister?'

It was, and I gave it.

'Ahh.' This was a Philippian pause of extensive proportions. 'Then there is no question but that we have the right man. Confirmed at both ends. There is a problem, though. We do have records of the two of them, the Minister and the MP, meeting up

– rather more frequently than one would expect, outside of locations one would ordinarily expect – but... we do not actually *know* what has passed between them. Not *recorded* as firm evidence. At best we have some hearsay, some parts of some of their conversations overheard. But with the two of them now, it would be so much easier for either one of them to deny any wrongdoing...'

I waited.

'Therefore, this way is the only way that makes sense.'

I waited again – for an explanation. Philip looked at me down the long length of his nose, glasses perched on its tip.

'Go for the master's dog, not the master.'

Philip added, with anticipatory satisfaction I thought, an expanded explanation. Go for what you can get which, in this case, was the MP. Go hard, go public, expose and show no clemency – and in so doing scare the Minister witless, stop him in his tracks, put an end to his betrayal before it had got very far, together with those others who would then heed the warning. So very difficult, and inevitably messy, to go direct for someone as high-ranking as a Minister of State.

'What else?'

I named another MP whose special interest was international trade and who, according to Arnold's account, had also been a willing recruit – from the other side of the House. It seemed, though, that this third MP reported directly to yet another StB officer based in the Czechoslovakian Embassy in London.

'Now that *is* interesting. We had rather presumed that both he and the Minister used our prime suspect as a go-between. I suppose the Colonel has this information?'

Arnold had said that he had reported on arrival, so presumably –

'Good, good... What else did Mister Ward have to say?'

According to the correspondent our suspect MP, as I had said, had become little more than a prime source for the sniffing out of gossip. This he recounted to his Czech handlers in London

– suddenly I saw the canine reference! – with gusto and relish; so much so that the MP seemed to believe that this relaying of tittle-tattle was the prime task required of him by the StB and was worth all the gold of his betrayal. Some of that gossip related to prominent government ministers and senior politicians.

'Do we know any of these pillars of society, Anthony?'

I named the four names I could remember. Philip's vigorous nodding to each name confirmed that the gossip which the MP passed on had already reached other ears. But in the main, as Arnold had said to me, what was passed on was predictable enough gossip: sexual proclivities and away-from-home activities, excessive drinking, the financial irregularities of additional incomes. Some of such gossip might lead to blackmailing possibilities for the StB in the future, but uncorroborated gossip had, for the most part, mere embarrassment potential, and was not worth the large sums of money paid over.

'We don't know our good man's source for all this, I suppose?'

I hesitated. Arnold had not actually *said*, had not stated as such.

'I see,' said Philip. 'Perhaps, though, you might share what you think – whether inference or deduction.'

I stitched together as best able the fragments of Arnold's conversation. Since his appointment as Eastern Europe correspondent some seven years ago, Arnold Ward had travelled regularly into and out of Czechoslovakia from his base in East Berlin. The territory of his assignment also covered Poland. It was a curious, and in some way, an ambivalent if not contradictory, relationship which his job entailed with the Czechoslovak Communist authorities. On the one hand, and especially so at the start of his time in Prague, he was viewed with suspicion. Plainly, coming from Western Europe, he could not be trusted. On the other hand, those same authorities wanted him to make himself available at Hradčany Palace for their press briefings and conferences because they wanted *their* version of news to go into the wider world. To that end and for that purpose only he was a welcome guest. Thus the Czech StB, as with all newspaper correspondents on its soil from western Europe, attached a security service watch on him. If he drove across the border from East Germany, then he would be followed from that crossing onwards. If he flew into Ruzyně airport, then he would be followed to his allocated hotel in Wenceslas Square. He was subject to twenty-four hours a day surveillance. Over time, he had got used to two officers following him around wherever he went. Though the watch changed personnel across days and times, Arnold had learned to recognise the team from which his watchers were drawn. They were, to give them their due, as Arnold had put it, less oppressive than their Stasi counterparts in East Germany.

'So it is said, Anthony. He is not alone in that observation.'

Since handing on to a Czech contact there the name of the would-be informant Minister of State, Arnold's surveillance had become noticeably less burdensome, and he and his watchers now shared a *modus vivendi* between them which had become much more relaxed.

I stopped at that point in my re-telling of Arnold's story.

'Good, good.' At which Philip too paused, looking up at me above his glasses at the end of his nose. 'But there's something else, is there not? – unless I mistake you.'

Well, there was something that had changed.

'Go on.'

'There is a Czech StB officer... '

'Yes, yes.'

'A female Czech StB officer...'

'Oh dear. I fear a complication coming on. This *is* unexpected. Out with it.'

On one of his visits to Prague, the team that followed Arnold from the airport included a woman. A young woman –

'And? in the proverbial nutshell – '

'She and Arnold are lovers.'

The Ahh! From Philip was accompanied this time by several sideways shakes of the head.

'Now let me guess. This young lady, this doubtless very attractive young lady, decided that the best way to keep a watchful eye on our Mister Ward during the night shift was to share the darkness with him? And doubtless the same bed?'

'Well, yes. At some point.'

I had wanted to tell the story with all its incidental detail which, in Arnold's version had prevented me tipping over into irremediable insensibility in *The Spotted Horse*. For the duration of the telling. His story done, I more than tipped over – I plunged. Never the less, at the time of telling it had seemed important to Arnold that I understood how his love affair had come about: the woman's good nature in letting her married male co-watcher leave early to spend unexpected time with wife and children; her quiet words with the old man at the reception desk of the hotel while Arnold smoked a cigarette outside the entrance; then her going swiftly upstairs to his bedroom, returning a few minutes later to keep the old receptionist engaged whilst Arnold slipped upstairs to his room. When he entered, he knew that the listening bug concealed there had been de-activated; there he waited for her arrival; she the first to leave in the morning, having reconnected the bug, to hand over her watch to the morning assignment.

As for the woman herself, to Arnold, she was simply wonderful. They shared stolen times, she was constant in the care she took of him, her concern for his well-being, the small gestures that made his time in Prague so much more bearable, the contrivances they had to engineer simply to get their messages to each other when she was allocated elsewhere, to other duties. They were in love with each other and had declared their love to each other. Arnold had looked so sad at the impossibility of a future together, unless... Perhaps my state at the time, softened by alcohol, *had* disposed me to be sympathetic to their cause; perhaps this sympathy led me to accept Arnold's request that I act as go-between on his behalf. Yet I did not doubt for one moment, neither during our encounter in *The Spotted Horse* nor later, Arnold's sincerity or the truthfulness of his narration.

'Spare me the details, Anthony. Just let me ask you this.'

'Yes?'

'Does this young lady, this doubtless very attractive young lady, now wish to *leave* the country of her birth?'

Philip could see the answer in my reaction.

'And does she, by any chance, wish to come to England?'

Philip sat back in his chair, hands across his stomach, the fingers of one hand drumming against the back of his other hand.

'And do I take it that Mister Ward has asked you to plead his cause in this? I take it that he has not yet reported this through his usual channels? And that this change in things has not yet reached the Colonel's ears?'

I flushed. 'He asked me to relay this. He thought it might be better coming from someone who would let Colonel Jackson know.'

There was at this point an *entr'acte* in which Philip got up to make another pot of coffee, simply by spooning more grounds into the enamel pot and putting it once more on the gas ring. Back at his desk he started his habitual routine that always prefaced the actual lighting of his pipe.

'This does put a different coloration on things.' He watched appreciatively as the zig-zag of smoke he contrived to exhale by turning his head a little from side to side dispersed. 'Tell me, Anthony, from your reading of the man – is this his idea or does it come from the very attractive lady in question?'

'I think Arnold is very much in love with her.'

That was unquestionably so. There were his drawings, redesigning a property he had acquired or planned to acquire, in which it was quite clear he intended to locate a future for himself and his lady.

Philip wrinkled his face. 'Didn't by any chance let slip a name for this very attractive young security officer, I suppose?'

'No, 'fraid not.'

Philip sucked noisily on his pipe which, within seconds of becoming a glowing point of red, he had failed, as almost always, to keep going. Hands dipped in and out of pockets as he continued to speak.

'Ah well, we can't stress to someone how essential it is to keep one's mouth shut, and then expect him to break the rule for our benefit, can we?'

And Philip positively chortled.

'Obviously, we shall push it along the line, though I don't think this is going to make anyone jump up and down for joy. Not seeing Arnold again any time in the near future?' – taking in the negative from a look towards me – 'no, thought not. But you two *have* said that you *will* meet again, haven't you?'

Arnold had hoped to be back for a few days before and over the Christmas period, but would have to be back in East Germany before the New Year. We had made a loose promise to meet up and Arnold had taken my contact address and telephone number.

'There is an alternative way.'

'To do what?'

'To get the young lady out of there. Mind, it would be very much down to her, to her own resourcefulness.'

In between igniting several matches before managing to re-light his pipe, Philip recounted matter-of-factly this surer way. That was for the young lady to work her way to a transfer to the Czechoslovakian Embassy in London – 'Speaks excellent English I imagine?' – where her special skills might be useful to those colleagues already employed there in the same line of work. Then, once re-assigned –

'She could simply walk out into Kensington Palace Gardens, find her way to the nearest police station and ask for political asylum.'

Philip allowed himself a small, slow smile.

'An unlikely event, of course.'

He tried, and failed as he always did, to blow some smoke rings. The coffee pot was rattling on the gas hob. Philip rose with his mug in hand to pour himself more coffee. He returned to his seat.

'And even if this very attractive young woman did find her way into a west London police station to ask for asylum, she would have to be able to bring something with her. In order to succeed in her request.'

'But isn't everyone entitled to ask – '

'Indeed so. All may ask, but not all will be admitted. And in her case she would have to bring something valuable. Valuable to us. Things we did not know, or things we wanted to confirm. There would be that price, tit for tat. And as a simple matter of fact, even if she did succeed in working her passage for a transfer it would take many months probably for such a re-assignment.'

He raised his eyebrows, and looked curiously at me.

'Not a solution that would appeal to either of our young lovers, I imagine. I mean, given the fact that lovers are not very patient. Waiting, for lovers, is an agony and torment of its own very peculiar nature. Is that not so, Anthony?'

But he pre-empted my possible response with a grin. Then, in a snap of movement, Philip suddenly sat upright, his tone changed.

'Right. Enough of this stirring of sentimental sediments. That little business of Mister Ward we shall put aside.' He looked at his wristwatch. 'Time's getting on and I have another meeting at three, as I warned. So, tell me, what else did you learn from Ward about our naughty MP?'

My hesitation was that of the messenger who fears he is to be shot for the message. In the meeting with Arnold I had felt out of depth anyway – one who knew very little of what was 'going on', as was the phrase that seemed to come my way so frequently.

Philip sensed immediately that we had arrived at the nub of things. Now he waited, in his most encouragingly avuncular fashion, waving circles with his pipe in a take-your-time movement.

'He has a couple of tapes.'

'Does he indeed?' Philip pulled his chair tight into his desk, leant forwards, elbows on the desk, looking closely at me. 'Do tell.'

In none of his written statements had Arnold mentioned any recordings, as Philip instantly recognised.

'Arnold tells me there are some interesting things said on tape which he must have overlooked when writing his accounts of those meetings.'

'And did he tell you what those missing bits amounted to?'

'If what he told me was correct, then I would say that they provide useful additional evidence, very useful. One can not be more positive, of course, not having heard the tapes themselves.'

Philip sat back, head tilted upwards, considering.

'That's the problem with irregulars, Anthony. They don't stick to the rules.'

FIVE

⌒

Garlands and lovers

London and Buckinghamshire

Winter 1965

22

I had to prepare for the lesser cases which fall to the lot of a junior barrister. Despite Booth's 'redistribution' of case-load in recognition of my working with Philip, there seemed more than enough to do. Among those cases I was scheduled to defend at the time were one serial burglar, two cases of malicious damage, one of uncomplicated fraud, and one ex-boxer accused of assault for beating up a man he suspected of having an affair with his wife. In all these cases the best I could do would be to plead for the minimum sentence, laying before the court whatever in the way of extenuating circumstances could be advanced. It amused me somewhat to think that in my chosen profession one had to be able to produce the arts of begging, beseeching, imploring. In some cases actually to plead forgiveness for the unforgiveable. Barristers, in this sense, were supplicants – and junior barristers especially so.

I left chambers early. I needed to prepare notes for my next meeting with Colonel Jackson.

At my flat a plain white envelope, marked 'Anthony' sat on the hallway carpet. A glance confirmed the handwriting of William. Lacking any address, the envelope must have been delivered by hand by William himself. So, not only did he know my address, he had been here in person. I poured myself a glass of wine and plonked down on the settee to open the envelope.

My Dear Anthony,

I am so sorry we were not able to meet for dinner though it was, of course, a great pleasure to be able to entertain Carolyne in your absence. I regret we shall not be able to meet in the immediate future either. My masters will not allow me to defer any further my travel to the North. I am inescapably to be trained to do something or other, it seems. Oh, taedium dierum! *It is a bore and a nuisance, but it is also a duty which one must neither resist nor refuse. I set off soon. I do not yet know how long I shall be away though I fear it may be weeks. Now that we have re-connected, however, I promise faithfully to stay in touch with you and Carolyne. I shall not fail to contact you again on my return.*

Thought the enclosed might entertain. The work on W.W. goes on, news of which soon, I trust.

My sincere best wishes to you and Carolyne — do give the dear girl a big kiss from me,

William

That was authentic William, his adopted posture to life – *Oh, the boredom of days*, no matter that he was about to be prepared for adventure. A thought insisted on itself, though: in all the sidestepping of that weekend with Carolyne's parents, I had put off any repeat questioning of her evening with William. When I had opened the topic on our return to London, she had not been in the best of communicative moods and her responses had come unwillingly. Truth to tell, she just did not want to talk to me at all. Silence is, after all, one of the weapons women seem to be particularly adept at wielding to punish a man. On the other hand, if I forbore asking again, no doubt my failure to ask would be additional confirmation to Carolyne that I did not care about her *really* and was not interested in what *she* was doing, being so taken up with my own selfish pursuits. And after all, I could almost hear her say this to me, he is *your* friend as well.

I was distracted from any more self-accusative thoughts when I found inside the letter's envelope a plain filing card, inscribed in William's hand:

Rivals

Of all the torments, all the cares,
With which our lives are curst;
Of all the plagues a lover bears,
Sure rivals are the worst!
By partners, in each other kind
Afflictions easier grow;
In love alone we hate to find
Companions of our woe.

Of all companions we are wont
As direst rival see,
Is one, best known, who bears the brunt;
Both friend and enemy.
Lover or friend, how to forswear
The one, or both, and cope;
I can endure my own despair,
But not another's hope.

W.W.

I read the poem through several times. What was I meant to make of it? It puzzled me; it seemed to contain some knowledge, private to the poet, a covert reference of some kind withheld from the reader. Here was a teasing enclosure from William Walsh by another William Walsh. How like William. It was also a reminder why I had unprotestingly given up literature at Oxford; all that close reading and interpretative analysis one had to go through in order to suck the juice from the fruit.

None the less, something of that poem nagged away at me. I made a duty telephone call to Carolyne. We had not spoken since returning from the weekend with her parents. She needed to know that William was going away. If I left this news until later, Carolyne would condemn me for not letting her know as soon as I knew myself. Her number rang for a long time before she answered.

'Oh Anthony, I'm trying to get ready to go out. I did tell you.'

Did she? Mumbled apologies from me.

'What is it?'

I started to relay the news from William – though got no distance.

'Anthony, I do know that. Unless you have forgotten, I had dinner with the man that Friday night while you were drinking yourself insensible in some den or other in the company of some other reprobate.'

Carolyne's forgiveness of me was still fragile; and conditional, that much was obvious, upon my continuing good behaviour.

'Unless there is anything else, Anthony? I don't have much time.'

It was an unsatisfactory and very brief conversation which left me still not knowing what was so urgent Carolyne could not spare her soon-to-be-formally-engaged suitor more than a minute or two of her time. But I chose not to press: the delicate peace which we had managed to broker between us would not yet stand any testing. To ask what she was about to do, where she was going, would be to confess that I had forgotten what, presumably, she had already told me. So I took the wise man's option of cowardly restraint. Doubtless, whatever she had said to me previously about this evening had also dissolved in alcohol. In any case, I needed the temporary peace to last with me through the evening. There was thinking I wanted to do.

We made a loose arrangement to meet up later in the week.

Arnold Ward. An irregular, as Philip had put it, recruited by the service. The service: such a handy portmanteau term which I had learned to use. Using it seemed to suggest a familiarity with what the term represented and its workings which I had not then acquired. I did recognise, however, that I too in some way had become an irregular, though one of much more limited and specific use, my recruitment nodded through for the particular present purpose. Other than acting as Philip's junior, I presumed the service would have no further interest in me. Arnold's recruitment, however irregular, was different. By virtue of his professional standing, of his appointment as Eastern Europe correspondent for a leading opinion-making broadsheet, he had access to places and persons not available to others. Indeed, by virtue of his position, he was actually invited to such places to meet such persons the service could not otherwise easily get close to.

In preparing notes for another meeting with the Colonel, I was reconstructing the history of events from Arnold's own written statements. He had first come across our salesman MP in the early days of his present appointment. He had been preparing a general feature on the defence of western Europe from the threat of the Communist bloc. In the course of that preparation, among a dozen or so Ministers and MPs he had spoken with, one MP from the all-party Commons Select Committee on Defence had stepped forward. It was evident from Arnold's summary document prepared for the dossier that the MP had claimed to be much more important than his parliamentary record or his position indicated. By 'nudge-nudge' language and 'wink-wink' gesture he had claimed to be 'connected' to higher, as well as 'other', movers and shakers of national policy and its implementation – and, thereby a well-informed insider of the international context of policy and cooperation. In talking to me of the man, Arnold had said that, from the whole encounter, he had gained a definite impression that he wanted Arnold, by virtue of his journalistic *entrée* to political circles in Prague, to effect an introduction on his behalf. There were no actual words to say so as such, and yet – as Arnold insisted – he was in no doubt. The

MPs own insistence that they should meet again soon added to this impression.

The manner and tone of the man had made Arnold wary. He did some journalistic digging and could find no support for the man's claims of connections higher or more powerful than those which would be consonant with his membership of a parliamentary Select Committee. Several of his parliamentary colleagues in fact regarded him as no more than a time-server; some said openly that it was his fidelity to the party line which had earned him his selection to the Committee. It was his turn to be fed a sop to his ego, to keep him quiet; it was how things worked. It was not unusual for Honourable Members, of neither great distinction nor intelligence, to be rewarded in such fashion.

Arnold had arranged a follow-up meeting. Untrusting of the man but nevertheless curious, he arranged a lunch-time meeting at *The Marquis*, just a few minutes' stroll away from the House. It was a popular place with MPs and it was not at all unusual for an MP to lunch there in the company of a reporter. Arnold had calculated that, because the pub would provide his man with a sense of familiarity and security, he would be more likely to be indiscreet; at the least, more direct, he hoped.

Arnold had arrived before his guest. In this second meeting, after pre-lunch whiskies, but during the second of two bottles of claret with their leisurely meal, the MP, in language now barely disguising his intent, had put himself forward as an 'unofficial ambassador for the promotion of east-west understanding.' He claimed tacit approval of Her Majesty's Government as his impulse in volunteering himself in this way. Though, of course, since HMG could not officially endorse such a move, it was down to him, using his own initiative, to find the means to effect exchanges of information. After some parrying, the MP asked Arnold to put him in touch – 'at the

Prague end' – with someone from the Czechoslovak security service with whom he could 'begin to trade' to the mutual benefit of both countries. Arnold had responded, testing the man, by saying that contact could be more easily effected simply through either a formal or informal approach to the Czech Embassy in London. No, no, that simply would not serve either nation's 'need to arrive at an understanding which will reduce security tensions between us', in the words recalled by Arnold.

Arnold had concluded their meeting by saying that he would see what he could do on his next visit to Prague. The MP then insisted on cognacs with their coffees 'to seal their understanding' – on the further, silent understanding, that Arnold would be paying the bill on behalf of his newspaper, the MP having graciously agreed to the interview at the request of the reporter.

So far, this narrative was easily and openly retrievable. I now knew, however, following my drunken evening with Arnold, that there were two substantial matters which could not be retrieved from the files. The first was that Arnold, after lunch with the MP when they were into their second cognac, had returned to the question of 'trade'. What did the MP have which he thought could form the basis for mutual trading between him and the Czech security police?

'Now that would be telling, wouldn't it?' With which, suiting action to words, in Arnold's re-telling to me of this part of the meeting, the MP had lain forefinger vertically across his lips.

'Secrets, dear boy. Secrets.'

'And in return for these unmentionables?' Arnold had asked.

'Considerations, dear boy.'

The second omission from the portfolio was the fact that Arnold, at that second meeting, had managed to tape all the exchanges between him and the MP from the second bottle of claret onwards.

'Under the table,' Arnold had said. 'Fits into a briefcase, handy device. Borrowed it from a colleague who's into gadgets and gizmos.'

Apart from this crucial omission from Arnold's written reports, the rest of the narrative was known. On returning to his office Arnold had spoken with his Editor. Without delay the Editor had arranged one of those informal and unminuted meetings to which a senior government departmental adviser is invited; and which are subsequently denied to have taken place. As a result of that meeting which did not take place, Arnold had been contacted by someone from Colonel Jackson's sectional interest. The upshot was Arnold's speedy clearance to act as an irregular and on his next assignment to Czechoslovakia to make contact, through one of his watchers, with someone at another level in the StB. And that had duly come to pass. Arnold had met Dušan and walked across the Charles Bridge with him to a small bar, made cosy and comfortable by an open fire. Arnold had passed on his information.

A further statement of Arnold covered this episode and also, on his next return to London, a brief meeting insisted upon by the MP who was eager to know that Arnold had done as he wished and passed on his willingness 'to exchange friendly talk' with someone in the Czech system who would appreciate 'the mutual benefit of such exchange.' There was no mention in this statement of the additional matters I had learned direct from Arnold, including that Arnold had contrived to make a tape recording of this meeting.

On his next visit to Prague some weeks later Arnold had noticed the surveillance conducted on him now pretended no concealment. His watchers were quite ready to be known, openly present, not trying to conceal their presence. They would acknowledge him with a half-wave, even going so far as to share a drink with him on discreet out-of-the-way occasions. It was within this greater relaxation he had been afforded that the young and very attractive female officer (whose name Arnold had kept to himself) had been able to allow her male companion officer to finish his duty early and go home.

As time went on Arnold had become treated as a favoured guest. Privileges were extended to him. Instead of his usual allocation to the somewhat bleak and austere brutalist building of the *Jalta* hotel, a room at the *Grand* was reserved for him. He refused the offer on the grounds that such special treatment would make him an object of suspicion to his journalistic colleagues – and any others who might be keeping a watchful eye on him. Dušan, with some reluctance, finally agreed. On each journey to Prague after that Arnold found the drinks cabinet in his room was amply stocked. No charges were made for his consumption of any of its contents. Visiting outside of the capital became rather easier and a taxi when requested always arrived promptly. Tickets to cultural events in the city were offered, together with various other 'entertainments' (one could almost hear the inverted commas in the tenor of the word as Arnold spoke it); and Dušan started to arrange well-camouflaged occasions for lengthy casual chats with him. Arnold, having introduced the MP to the StB, himself became viewed as a friend of the Czechoslovak state. He presumed that, Czech contact having been made with the MP, what the Honourable Member had had to say must have held some actual or potential value to the StB, so that as a reward for this good deed Arnold had became a welcome guest in Prague. Within a year he was given information to take back with him to London. Arnold had found himself cast as a courier, a both-ways conduit between Prague and London. Reporting back on his returns to London he would be given information from the Colonel's section to pass on to Dušan.

His London contact, on behalf of the service, was a Miss K.

What Arnold had impressed upon me was how, over the months passing into years, he had felt increasingly insecure with this status which he had not sought but which had been – force of circumstances – imposed on him. Though acting for both sides, as it were, Arnold had stressed that this did *not* make him a double-agent. He was, he insisted, merely a two-way trafficker of other people's goods.

From the start, though, he had felt uneasy. Something about his first meeting with the MP had triggered an alarm. The feeling that he had to take action to protect himself had been very strong. Hence his recording of their subsequent second and third meetings.

So far only I and Philip, whom I had informed, knew of the existence of these two recordings. I had no doubt that they existed, and I had no doubt that their substance extended to detail missing from his submitted written reports. As such, they could be powerful evidence which would support Arnold's testimony when matters came to court. He had made those recordings and withheld them, in the first place, for his own protection. Now he wanted them to service a different need. They had become, bluntly expressed, Arnold's weapons of blackmail. His price for handing over those tape-recordings was the extraction from Czechoslovakia of a young and very attractive female StB security officer.

At the time of my meeting with Arnold, a question.

'Have you said all this, about the tapes, to whoever Miss K is?'

'No.'

'Why not?'

'Because...' Arnold had stopped, and looked at me inquiringly. 'I take it then that you don't know who Miss K is.'

'Correct.'

'Well in that case I'll give you the following reasons. First of all it would bind me even more closely to the service – and I want to keep my distance. I didn't ask to do what I've been asked to do. And now' – he looked at me somewhat plaintively – 'I don't want to do it any more. I've had enough. I'm thirty-six, I've found the woman I want to be with, and I want to get out, and I want her to be able to get out with me.'

With forefinger he stabbed at the table.

'I don't want to do all this travelling any more. I just want to settle down, move in with her and switch to the home front.'

My unchosen rôle as courier, to-ing and fro-ing between Arnold and Philip Hathers, was about to be extended when, later in the week, I would carry the news to Colonel Jackson. I was fairly certain he would not much like what, on Philip's as well as Arnold's say-so, I would have to say.

23

The night before my scheduled meeting with the Colonel that week I nerved myself to telephone my parents. I was hoping father would answer the call, and then act as broker with my mother.

Father answered.

'Well, my boy, have you done the deed?'

The deed was done; a date set provisionally in mid-February of the coming year for the formal engagement to Carolyne.

'Congratulations! To both of you.'

'Father, I wonder, would you mind – '

'No, of course not. I'll get her for you now. You'll want to tell her your good news yourself.'

I cursed silently that father would not be the bearer of my news to mother, and thus avoid, or at least postpone, the antici-pated ear-bending. But he was off and away. Then voices in the hallway, father's low pitch of words brief but unclear, mother's some way off but sharply clear: 'I suppose the silly boy has now actually committed himself?'

A silence of several seconds: mother composing herself. Then the sound of a receiver being picked up from a hall table.

'I have to offer you my congratulations, Anthony.'

It was mother's social-necessity voice. Convention required such an affirmation. Her tone confirmed reproof.

'And has she' – almost always my mother referred to Carolyne as *she* – 'or, rather, has her mother set a date for that ridiculous party she insists on throwing for your formal engagement?'

Mother was launched.

'Why we have to have such an ostentatious frippery as that I really have no idea. Really, it is not at all a required thing. It will impress only the impressionable who, in the scheme of things, one is not required to impress. I suppose there will be there all her tennis housewives and every market trader *he*' – Carolyne's father was ascribed a similarly impersonal pronoun – 'has ever had dealings with. All the money but none of the style, I'm afraid, no understanding of the etiquette. A simple announcement in *The Times* is all that is needed...'

I left it until fairly late in the evening, but I felt duty bound to call Carolyne as well. Usually she telephoned me every night that we did not actually meet up, and our brief conversation of the previous evening had left me in no doubt that I still had ground to make up. It felt to me that Carolyne had stirred into flame again the embers of her resentment of my drunkenness that had delayed the start of our previous weekend. There was nothing for it. I would simply have to throw myself on her mercy.

I tried to do so as soon as she answered. More apologies. She was upset, certainly, but I did not hear the rasp of pique in her voice this time. She seemed subdued.

'What is it, Carolyne?'

'It's nothing. Nothing for you to worry about and nothing you can do anything about.'

'Yes, but – '

'Anthony, it's nothing. Bit down, that's all. Time of the month I suppose.'

We settled to meet, as usual, on Friday evening. A meal out. Yes, that would be nice – but unenthusiastically endorsed.

The next day I arrived at the corner block of red and grey in Mayfair where, as arranged by Booth, I went to my meeting with Colonel Jackson. I had to show identification and wait some while before I was allowed in to meet him. He was fulsome in his apologies for keeping me waiting. Unasked, a tray of tea and biscuits arrived.

'Ginger nuts. Made for dunking. Do go ahead.'

Setting the example, the Colonel dunked successively several ginger nuts in his tea and sucked away appreciatively their sodden portions, with almost closed eyes, before he began our business.

'I understand that you and our Mister Ward hit it off rather well.'

Yes, I had enjoyed his company, though I deleted the details.

'So.'

With that one word, shaped as imperative, I summarised for the Colonel all I had learned from Arnold about the MP. The Colonel nodded occasionally, but was otherwise silent. I came to Arnold's other matter of the young woman StB officer; and hesitated.

'Go on.'

I went on. Colonel Jackson was impassive, simply holding his head fixedly across the room beyond me. When I had finished pleading Arnold's case, the exchange of audiotapes for the extraction from Czechoslovakia of his young lady, without shifting his posture in any way the Colonel spoke to the angle of wall and ceiling.

'No, no, no. Not our territory in any case. Would have to hand it on to John' – the Colonel caught my look as I tried to complete the reference from somewhere in memory – 'John, Sir John Holyoake. This sort of thing is his playground, not ours – and his boys and girls are rather busy at the moment.'

Memory then clicked – because Philip had also mentioned the man to me. If an infallible memory was a vocational requirement for service to the service, then, I thought, I was clearly unsuited to the engagement.

The Colonel swivelled towards me.

'So now, where does that leave us? – leaving to one side, of course, that offer to trade with us. Where have you and Philip got to in your deliberations?'

As firmly and succinctly as possible I gave the considered resumé which Philip and I had agreed on.

'Mmm. So you are both agreed. We need something more.'

The Colonel slowly turned to face me.

'Then, reluctantly, I think we are left with no option but to produce Miss K. We shall need to have a little chat about this. Then we shall need to organise a meeting with the young lady in question – *after* I've had a few words with her.'

With that he signalled that our meeting was at an end.

'But what about – '

'Arnold Ward?' The Colonel tutted between parted lips. 'No, no, no, I'm afraid it simply won't do. We are just not very good at responding to ultimata. Of which your friend has just issued one.'

'But – '

'No, no. We shall leave things as they stand. Which you may tell your new friend when next you see him.'

Meeting closed: Anthony Ashley-Chetwyne dismissed.

Carolyne telephoned me that evening, early, shortly after I got back to my flat.

'I have something to tell you, Anthony.'

I waited for her to go on. For a moment I thought we had been disconnected, but the line clicked back in. There was a sort of snuffling sound at the other end, but no going on from Carolyne. I thought perhaps she had caught a winter cold.

'No, I don't have a cold.' Pause. Snuffle. 'I've been crying.'

I immediately set about reassuring her; it was really not such an important matter, missing those few hours from our visit to her parents, things had turned out alright, we had set a date, perhaps we could set another weekend very soon to see her parents again. How about next weekend?

Just a very light sniffing then. Something indistinctly said, but broken, as if the words rapidly clicked on and off.

'Say again, my love.'

'Anthony, I have to go away.'

Questions: where? when? for how long?

Carolyne's voice sounded a plain, unenlivened speech, as if reading back to me a memo. She was not well, had not felt 'her usual self' for some time. I would not have noticed, of course (I did notice this accusative, however). She had spoken with her mother and they had decided that she needed to get away for a while (of unspecified duration) for some rest and recuperation. As it so happened Daddy would have to travel out at the weekend to Switzerland; there was a crisis in his Berne office – some sort of contractual thing, and there was a shortage of staff. Quite opportune. And Daddy had arranged it with her employer; they did a lot of business together, it appeared, they were old friends. She would go out to Berne with her father and would certainly be away for the whole of next week and probably into the following week as well, if not the whole of that second week. It would be the simplest solution all round; she was familiar with the Berne office, of course, having spent a whole year in the past working there. It would be such a help and a relief to Daddy, and the change of scenery, the lightness of the air, and so on, could not fail to help recover her spirits.

Yes, she supposed it was some kind of depression, Mummy certainly thought so. Had just been feeling down for some weeks, in fact, though of course one does not notice it oneself at the time, it is so gradual, an accumulation.

Sorry. But knew I would understand. But of course we would still have our meal together tomorrow evening, early if I would not mind. Really sorry about it all.

Then she would set out first thing on Saturday to her parents' place.

So, so sorry.

I treated her news lightly, so that Carolyne would not be further upset. Even as I spoke reassuringly to her – a week, or two weeks if that length of time was needed, was not very long, I did understand, I would be fine, not to worry about it at all, she could 'phone me – I thought her sudden absence would set things right between us: a tit-for-tat, her absence, my misdemeanour, all square now. Perhaps a little too brightly I gave her my love and said how much I was looking forward to seeing her.

'Oh, Anthony.' The syllables were drawn out, almost in the way mothers have of tiredly rebuking a child for repeating something it knew it should not do. I waited for the admonition.

There was an intake of breath. Then she put down the receiver. There was another click on the line.

In the middle of that same evening, there was a second telephone call.

'Anthony, my dear chap. So sorry to disturb you at your place of rest. Do you have a moment or two?'

It was Philip and, from the background noises, I guessed he was speaking from his club. He immediately confirmed my guess.

'Vernon – Colonel Jackson – and I have just been having a chinwag, filling me in on things. Wants you to know he was impressed with the way you did things today. Very thorough.'

I muttered some expression of gratitude for the compliment.

'Upshot is, old chap, the Colonel would like another chat with you on a matter arising. Would do it myself but, as you know, I have a case on at the moment taking up all of my time...'

So much of your time, I thought, you still have enough of it left over for dinner and drinks with Colonel Jackson. Philip seemed to sense my thought for he added –

'Apart from a little essential rest and recreation, as it were.' Said to a gentle chuckle. 'Anyway, point is, the Colonel would like you to call on him again. Next week. Booth will fix the day and time for you. Be very much obliged.' A small hesitation, before: 'Both of us.'

I was just bidding my goodbye and was on the point of putting down the receiver when Philip said:

'Oh, by the by, Anthony. I don't suppose you will be at a loose end over the weekend, will you? Elizabeth and I are having a few people to stay, spur of the moment thing, come up Saturday morning, whenever would be convenient, you stay over too, of course. Would love to see you if you could possibly make it. What do you think?'

I replied that, as it happened, I had just heard from Carolyne... *et cetera.*

'Wonderful. Now that *is* a most fortunate coincidence.'

24

That Friday Carolyne came to my flat direct from work and was waiting for me when I arrived. She did indeed look unwell. She was pale, fidgety, and seemed to lack both energy and enthusiasm. I did my best to offer commiserations but she seemed to be dismissive of my sympathy.

Dinner was a somewhat tedious affair. Nothing seemed to animate Carolyne, despite the fact that I had decided on a Chinese restaurant for our meal, Chinese being Carolyne's latest favourite food. She poked at the dishes as they were presented, picked at small amounts of the food, and left me to try to inject some talk into the silences.

'Oh, I meant to ask you again about your evening with William – '

'Not now, Anthony.'

'Yes but – '

'I've told you all there is to say.'

I fared equally badly with every attempt to break into her sullen withdrawal.

Back at my flat Carolyne apologised. I deserved better, but...

This *But* assumed various forms: listlessness, lack of interest in anything I offered up for conversation and a shying away from me when I tried to take her in my arms –

'No, Anthony, not tonight, I couldn't ...'

'I only meant to offer comfort.' My rejection took on the injured hurt of an honourable intention denied. 'I wasn't going to, you know...'

Of course I was going to, you know. Of course I wanted to; but the final *But* meant we slept a fitful night together apart – a third person would have had comfortable space between us.

Carolyne was up and dressed in the morning as I dozed away some of my sleeplessness. When I peered up at her she gave me a grim-faced smile, leant down to me, put her hands to my face and kissed me on the forehead.

'I'm sorry, Anthony. I'm so, so sorry. I've been horrid to you.'

So saying she buried her face into my neck.

'I have to go.'

So saying, Carolyne left.

25

When I arrived at Philip's family home in the Buckinghamshire countryside at mid-day that same Saturday, a tall, middle-aged woman came to the head of the steps as my taxi from the station pulled up at the end of the driveway. She waved, then held both hands outstretched to me. No sooner had I paid off the taxi and turned towards the house, than she clasped me to her, planted a kiss on my cheek and exclaimed:

'You must be Anthony! I'm Elizabeth. Philip's told me all about his protégé. You are most welcome, I am so glad you were able to make it. Come in and meet everybody.'

She put an arm through mine and led me up the steps into a large hall with a reception room off to the side. Elizabeth Hathers took me into the room, still holding on to me, and with her other arm swept around the room, alighting on the other guests seated in deep sofas or armchairs.

'Colonel Jackson, Vernon, you know, and this is his wife Jennifer' – who smiled and bowed her head towards me – 'Simon Carlton you also know, and this is Sarah' – pointing to a young and very (actually, *very*) attractive young woman seated alongside him. Each in turn extended an arm to shake my hand. 'And here' – tugging me towards a couple who rose to greet me – 'we have Sir John and Lady Geraldine Holyoake.' Sir John shook my hand.

'No, please. John and Geraldine.'

They were a distinctive couple: the woman, short and a little plump, but with a gracious smile, the man towering over me, thin grey hair smoothed and flattened to his head, thick white eyebrows and a severe look.

Introductions done, there was here, as always on such occasions, that embarrassed moment when a newcomer has stepped into a grouping that had already convened, and no-one quite knows what to say. Philip, however, broke the hiatus.

'A little pre-prandial, Anthony. What will you have?'

As Philip moved away to get my whisky his wife, now seated, patted the settee cushion alongside her. I sat beside her and, as the perfect hostess, she reanimated the discussion.

After a cold luncheon the entire party set off for a walk. There was a general bustling in the hallway when Philip appeared, holding above his head a silver flask.

'Do fill up, folks, before we go. Choose your poison. It's going to get cold very quickly this afternoon. Some small screwtop bottles in the kitchen if you haven't got one of these' – pointing to his own flask.

Led by Elizabeth, the walk assumed the character of an expeditionary march of several miles. We walked across open land, along a low ridge, then down to the bank of a fast stream, following its pathway, then over a footbridge, and into woodland belonging to a neighbouring farmer. At different times I found myself walking with the Holyoakes, or teamed with Simon Carlton and Philip, or paired with Elizabeth and, last of all and bringing up the rear of the column, I found myself alongside Sarah, the young lady who had caught my eye.

She asked my full name. 'Because,' she said, 'I was only told to expect an Anthony, and Anthony is all you've been introduced as.'

I gave my name, which she received with raised eyebrows.

'And I was not told at all to expect a Sarah, which is also all you have been introduced to me as – Missus Sarah Carlton, I presume.'

She laughed. Her laughter, in that clichéd but in this instance accurate description, tinkled.

'What on earth makes you think that?'

'Well, when I arrived, you and Carlton were sitting together – '

We were scuffing our way through piles of fallen leaves, those ahead kicking them into the air much as children delight to do, when Sarah put a restraining hand on my arm. We stopped to face each other.

'Sarah Hill, as was. You probably know *of* me as Miss K.'

Her eyes were a striking light blue.

The chill of late afternoon soon set in and the sky began to darken over. Red-cheeked we returned to the Hathers' place. The object of the walk, more than anything else it seemed, was for the party to work up a collective appetite for dinner. On our return all were free to do as they pleased; take a rest in their bedrooms, bathe or shower themselves warm, or simply relax with the day's newspapers in the large sitting-room. Elizabeth showed me to my room in the rambling former large Victorian country house to which various additions had been made. I decided on a quick bath and a change of clothes; after which I went down to the hallway where Philip intercepted me and guided me into a book-lined study.

When I entered the study Colonel Jackson, Sir John Holyoake, and Philip Hathers were already present. John Holyoake beckoned me. I noticed that Elizabeth Havers had put out tea and cakes on one of the side tables.

'Come in, come in, come and join us.'

Philip Hathers took over.

'You recall, my dear Anthony, one of Vernon's – the Colonel's – expressions?' Philip glanced towards the man. 'Left hand, right hand?'

'Yes.'

'Well, John Holyoake here is the right hand. Or are you the left hand, John?'

'Oh left hand I would say, the sinister side, quite definitely.'

The exchange sounded almost rehearsed.

John Holyoake, I learned, headed a section in the 'other' state service which was also 'an organisation which does not theoretically exist.' I read those words, several decades later, ascribed by his biographer to a Prime Minister of that era as he faced embarrassing disclosures. At that moment, however, the flesh and blood contradiction of those words once more had a huge hand clasping mine.

Sir John had a mordant sense of humour and a manner whose ease and relaxation contrasted with the Colonel's briskness. But it was also evident that the three men before me now had known each other for some time, years probably, as one sensed the taken-for-granted between them. They had all 'come through' the war that had ended twenty years ago. John Holyoake himself, I learned, had served in the Royal Navy, mainly on minesweeper duties before 'ending up', as he put it, in Naval Intelligence.

'Thought we should have a little chat before the others arrive. Tea?'

Somehow it seemed incongruous that John Holyoake, a large man rising to his full height, should be pouring tea into delicate, floral-patterned, china cups.

We settled, each balancing a cup. The three men exchanged glances among themselves.

'I'll begin, then, shall I?' Both Philip Hathers and Vernon Jackson inclined their heads towards the ex-naval man. He continued.

'We want you to know, Anthony. Things are getting to a most interesting stage when we assess what is currently on the books with regard to Czechoslovakia. We both' – a glance towards the Colonel – 'have matters of importance to attend to. And we both have to ensure that things do not become so complicated that we shall no longer be able to manage them.' Pause. 'Or get in each other's way.'

Explanations followed. Of course it was important, essential even, that our deviant and conscienceless MP should be brought into the full light of punitive justice. As well as receiving his own desserts, it would be a powerful warning to others. And there *were* others, suspected by Vernon's people for some time now, and lately confirmed to their joint satisfaction. They had no doubt; but the legal eradication of 'doubt' in a case of law required a higher level of proof. To which there was now a report of hitherto unknown audiotape recordings –

'We have no doubt,' the Colonel interjected, 'these recordings actually do exist. Nor do we doubt that they contain what its owner alleges of our MP. That they are somewhat self-incriminating. Whether conclusively so or not we can not say. At some point in the future we may need to address more forcefully the matter of separating owner from owned. To get our hands on those tapes. Meanwhile...'

Meanwhile there had been talks with Miss K –

'Whom you have now met, Anthony. An utterly charming girl, as I'm sure you will agree, who has confirmed that if need be it will be her duty to testify in court to her, um, dealings with the MP the Colonel has in his sights.'

John Holyoake paused, inviting Philip and the Colonel to add anything he might have missed. What he had omitted, the Colonel supplied. Missing from the portfolio of reports and statements as supplied were the testimonies of Miss K; withheld intentionally by the Colonel because he had hoped to win the day without the need to drag her into it and disclose her part in the MP's prospective downfall and disgrace. There was the fact also, offered in a tone almost of confession, that he did not want to lose such a valuable asset as Miss K – Sarah. Exposing her to what would be a messy and drawn-out High Court case inevitably risked her exposure; however carefully one tried to guard against it. The Colonel had rather hoped to be able to keep her where she was.

A deliberate tract of silence was then laid out before me in which I was meant to consider Sir John's and the Colonel's little speeches. There were several *Yes buts* left dangling in the air. I reached up for one of them.

'Have you seen them, Philip? Miss K's statements?'

Colonel Jackson answered for him. 'No, he has not. There is a *caveat* to those statements, necessarily and unavoidably.' At this I *was* able to guess ahead. 'They record only the formal de-briefings.'

I took the point. Questions and answers. I was familiar with witness statements. They were, after all, post-event recollections, tidied versions of circumstance. Events, their perception and construction, can change over time – how one sees differently what happened and the meaning one attaches. Putting them into any form of words is what gives events their shape. However well or poorly written, that fashioning of the event shapes its reality. And if you stood those reports alone, detaching them from their context, they would be a form of fiction and, as in a fiction...

'Godbole?' An interjection from Philip, as if he sensed the direction of my thoughts.

I replied: '"Absences are as important as presences".'

'Omissions, deletions, concealments – deliberate or intentional – matters forgotten or overlooked or ignored *et cetera, et cetera*. As important as what is *in* any report.'

'Just so.' This from the Colonel in confirmation of Philip's offering. I found it difficult to think of Colonel Jackson as Vernon, then or since. His rank and surname somehow seemed to me to be at odds with his first name. 'Which is another reason why I am still holding on to those statements which our Miss K – Sarah as you now know her – made at different times. I think it would be better if you were first to have an informal chat with the good lady before reading them. Might be easier that way to get an understanding. Find out what's missing, as it were.'

I turned the Colonel's words towards Philip. 'Do *you* intend to talk with her this weekend?'

'No, my dear chap, I do not. She might feel rather awkward with me, constrained – might be like talking to one's father, someone of another generation, too old to understand. It might be easier for you to talk with her first, someone her age, she might feel more comfortable.'

I knew then why I had been invited to this weekend gathering. 'When?'

'As the opportunity presents itself. Sooner the better, but not with unseemly haste. Would help to establish a relationship with her, we think. She knows you have been OK'd.'

At that the Colonel, with a lift of his eyebrows, added: 'Actually, I've puffed you up a bit with her. Made you more important to us, can't say what of course, she understands that. But should get you off to a good start with her.' So saying, there was the half lowering of an eyelid.

'More tea?' John Holyoake levered himself out of the armchair.

Philip Hathers then went through his ceremony of pipe-filling and eventual lighting, whilst John Holyoake opened a cigar case, offering it to both the Colonel and to me. We both declined. But when pipe and cigar were satisfactorily emitting their red glows, John Holyoake turned to me.

'Now, as to your wayward MP. Vernon and I have consulted and, in the light of other matters, we are agreed. Though it saddens me to say, your MP must wait for his come-uppance. As I said before, we don't want things getting in the way of each other. So, first things first.'

There was also clearly no rush to tell me what first things were to be first. John Holyoake drew contentedly on his cigar, the Colonel lunged for another cake, and Philip once more hunted for matches to put to a pipe that had gone out.

'When you met Arnold, Arnold Ward, he mentioned the name Dušan to you, I believe.'

'He did.'

'Well...' John Holyoake's 'Well' had the same ruminative character as Philip's 'Ahh' and was equally drawn out. 'We too have an interest in this man. Have had for some time. All thanks to Arnold in the first place.'

Arnold, the go-between for messages to and from Dušan.

'Things have now reached an interesting stage with this Dušan. It has become a question of priorities. Agreed, the man could be very helpful to you in confirming that your reprobate MP has indeed been passing on naughties. In the light of recent developments, however, he could prove to be even more important to *us*.'

The irony struck me instantly. We were all 'us' when it came to 'them', the outsiders, the enemy; but there were actually two sets of 'us', and each 'us' had a 'you and yours', 'them' – the other 'us'. Left hand, right hand.

'And so that we don't trip over each other's feet, Vernon has kindly agreed to hold off for the moment and let us manage Dušan instead.'

Clearly John Holyoake's 'us' party had taken precedent over the Colonel's 'us.' There was the tinkling of tea cups and saucers.

'Now, however, there is the matter of Arnold Ward and his threat to withdraw his services. Unless he can be persuaded to change his mind. Which is where you come in once more, Anthony.'

'I don't see – '

John Holyoake raised a hand. 'It is very simple. It seems that Arnold Ward trusts you. He trusts you because he confided in you something we did not know from our, let us call them, regular means – '

'Miss K'.

'Indeed. Now, as far as Arnold Ward is concerned, you are only connected in a remote way to the games we are compelled to play. You are a lawyer who is going to act in *his* best interests should certain matters materialise. Prepare him for the eventualities that may ensue during a trial. Yes?'

'With Philip, as Philip's junior.' Not one of the three men responded to my qualifying statement.

'You have arranged to meet up again with Arnold when he returns to the UK for a few days over the Christmas period. Well, we would be very much obliged to you if you would be sure not to miss this opportunity. We would ask that you make yourself available for that meeting, whenever suits him – which we would hope would not be *in*convenient to you. And add your voice to our request that when he bumps into Dušan on his next visit there he puts to the man some observations – concerns which we shall put to you to put to Arnold. We might then see how the service could be of service to resolve his own affair of the heart.'

I must have looked doubtful.

'This would not be, *could* not be a promise, not as such – but put in a way that gave the man optimism. Hope.'

'Well – '

But John Holyoake drove on.

'We think it very likely that when Mister Ward does return to the UK he might be rather difficult and not want to co-operate with us. If we do not fall over ourselves to give him what he wants, he may very well not want to play the game. I rather suspect that he *will* refuse, so that he can make his point, and we can't very well torture him into compliance, can we? Anything more you can glean from him would be most welcome to us.'

John Holyoake turned his palms outwards where they rested on the arms of the chair.

'We are looking to you to use your powers of persuasion, Anthony, to employ your advocacy on our behalf. You, as I say, are in a position to offer the man a future by offering him hope. From us he will want a copper-bottomed promise. And that we can not, will not, offer. At present.'

'You want me to lie to the man?'

'Anthony, Anthony.' Holyoake raised his large head, his thick white eyebrows lifted in a look of deep offence. 'How could you think such a thing? No, no, no. Exactly as I have said is exactly what we are looking to you to deliver. To keep our man on board and prevent him doing anything precipitately – for a few weeks at least. A few months should see it through, we would hope. You will be our temporary measure, Anthony, until we can get our own man in place and get close to Dušan.'

This much clear: the first things to be put first were Arnold Ward and Dušan, not the MP. John Holyoake was not done with me. He leaned forward. 'The man we have in mind to get close to Dušan is your friend William.'

Mouth shut. I recalled Philip's prime requirement. A surprise can be so forceful it is a bodily shock, so I am not wholly convinced I managed to conceal my reaction.

Sir John smiled, a smile that grew wider. 'A singular man, your William – an Unusual, as Vernon says. But fiercely intelligent, cultured to his fingertips, and just the man to appeal to our Mister Dušan who has, we understand, some highly developed and somewhat exotic tastes of his own.'

The cargo of his final words carried a weight of implication.

'We have, as a courtesy gesture, forwarded a photograph of your William as advance notice of someone Dušan may expect to be joining the UK Embassy staff there. Not something we would ordinarily do, not this far ahead anyway, but in this instance we wanted to know the reaction. We wanted to induce his anticipation. Whet the appetite, one might say.'

A photograph of William. Could it possibly be the same photograph, which I had taken at Oxford, the same which Colonel Jackson had pushed across my desk towards me, the same which Carolyne forgot she had borrowed and had forgotten to return? Certainly, if so, in it there was displayed an exotic creature in his full pomp, lethargically posing, strangely dark, distinctive and remarkable.

'And I am pleased to say' – Sir John opened his arms as he so said – 'that our man Dušan appeared to be very favourably impressed, was in fact very eager to meet him. Things there can be very colourless and dull, Anthony, whereas your William...'

My William?

'But I thought William was one of the Colonel's men.'

'Mine to begin with, Anthony. Yes, we did have plans for him. But first we needed to establish his *bona fide*. So we sent him on the rounds, as you know – the itinerant academic. Then, however' – a shrug of the shoulders at the waywardness of fate – 'just as we were about to make some use of him, John discovered a very special and pressing need. Only he did not have any candidate of the right credentials. Of *appearance* most notably, and' – the Colonel's eyes flicked upwards and aside as one might do when searching for a word – 'and *disposition*. So we passed William on to him.'

'Given that in the usual course of events we both look for people who fade into the wallpaper, it was fortunate that Vernon just happened to have someone of more *flamboyant* looks. He just needed a few special tutorials – to provide him with a wider perspective.'

It was mildly amusing to listen to these two men of the world tip-toe around their descriptions of William, of what they took them to mean and him to be.

'Is William there now, in Czechoslovakia?'

'No, no. Slowly, slowly. We have to keep him on the roundabout for a little longer.' Sir John looked briefly upwards, to the ceiling. 'Anticipation is the greater part of love. Now who said that?'

We all looked around at each other, none recognising the source.

Sir John had something else to add which might have stirred a little even William's imperturbability.

'As a matter of fact, Anthony, we are going to promote him, well, *endow* him with a title. Honorary Cultural Attaché – sounds good but means nothing. Except that it gives him open doors to our own embassies and consulates, and gets him on foreign guest lists.'

Dinner with the Hathers that evening was a wonderfully relaxed event. The four women, to judge by the laughter issuing from the kitchen, were having a jolly time in each other's company as they got ready the food which Elizabeth Hathers cheerfully admitted had been 'bought in' partly-prepared. The two bottles of chilled white wine which Elizabeth had taken into the kitchen may have contributed to the chatter. Dinner, when it was served, was late – and the women entered the dining room with flushed faces.

Simon Carlton sat alongside me, a generous schooner of chilled *Amontillado* held in one hand.

'I trust you had a, ahem, useful exchange all round.'

In the same quiet voice, and tapping me on the arm, he explained his absence. 'None of my business. When I go to watch a play, I do not, ahem, want to know what's happening in the dressing room.'

Something remarkable happened as the evening progressed. I noticed that Simon's ahem-ing diminished in frequency in proportion to the volume of alcohol he consumed until finally it seemed to have vanished completely, overwhelmed by his unhesitating fluency.

At the dinner table, amid much laughter, conversation flowed easily, lubricated by the diverse bottles of wine Philip produced to accompany each course. When pudding was served, with a dessert wine, Philip tapped on his glass.

'No, no, do not fret, my friends. I am not about to make a speech. But I am about to make an announcement.'

He stood, a hand holding each lapel of his jacket, the barrister hanging on to his absent gown.

'As some of you know, two years ago, in the somewhat arcane euphemism of my trade, I received a tap on the shoulder.' Philip stopped, a broad smile on his face scanning each of us in turn to search for comprehension or puzzlement. 'In plainer terms, I was invited to join the judiciary. I turned down that invitation. One is usually invited only the once. To be invited twice is rare. To be asked three times is unheard of. And so, dear guests' – he raised his glass – 'I have decided not to refuse at the second time of asking.'

We drank to his good news. I tried not to show my shock.

After dinner Philip asked us all to select our personal favourites from his collection of records. I had not come to terms with Philip's surprise announcement. I had had no inkling of it. Nor did he say anything more to me about it that evening, but rested a hand on my shoulder as he stood behind me, talking with Simon. At some point the Colonel and his wife together with John Holyoake and his wife made up a foursome at bridge – a game I have never played, never understood even. Philip and Simon made their apologies and made their way to Philip's study – 'a couple of things we want to clear up' – together with a bottle of single malt.

Elizabeth Hathers sat with Sarah and me. Clearly, to me, and I think to Sarah, she was acting as a go-between, to ease our conversation, to help Sarah and me to get to know each other. We would have taken to each other without her guiding hand. Of that I am sure.

The company did not break up until something like 1.30 in the morning. Breakfast, Elizabeth Havers announced, would be late.

In the event, breakfast turned out to be an impromptu affair. Cereals and toast appeared on the table, while several of us were in the kitchen at the same time cooking up eggs, bacon, mushrooms, whatever one wanted for oneself or for someone else who wanted it.

Breakfast was followed by an hour or so of idle chat or a skimming of the Sunday newspapers, followed by another of Elizabeth's brisk walks before a light lunch and departure. The Colonel and his wife Jennifer, then John Holyoake and his wife Geraldine, left within minutes of each other. A black limousine arrived for each couple to spirit them away.

Simon Carlton came up to me where I stood on the steps of the house alongside Sarah.

'My apologies, Anthony. I would love to offer you a lift back but I'm afraid I can only, ahem, fit one of you in.'

On the gravel stood a two-seater red MG sports car with wire wheels. Simon and *that* car. Another incongruity.

To my surprise Sarah made reply before I could. 'If you don't mind, Simon, I shall just go back on the train. Anthony's going back to London too, so we shall be company for each other.'

~ **26** ~

The train back to London, as a Sunday service, took longer than its weekday equivalent, the journey made even longer this day because of 'Works on the Line' as the notice at the station declared. I minded not at all. Miss K and I sat opposite each other in an empty carriage.

'Well, Miss K – or should I now call you Miss Hill?'

'*Missus W*, if you must be formal. Though I would much prefer Sarah, since that is the name I go by.'

I had to delve. '*Missus* W?'

Sarah's laughter was bright, teasing.

'Did they not tell you?'

'Tell me what?'

'Who I am – but only for the purpose of being so.'

'Sarah, you are a sphinx speaking to me in riddles.'

She leant forward, so that she was close to me, a hand gently patting my knee, resting it there long enough for me to note for the first time the rings that she wore on the second finger of that left hand.

'I am Missus Sarah Ward.'

As Philip might have said: wind, my, out, sails, of, taken – but not in that order. Followed by a dead calm. On the part of Sarah anyway. She half-turned away from me, and when she looked back at me her eyes were twinkling with a mixture of amusement and challenge. The brightness of those light blue eyes captivated me. So much so that I had to look away. I tried to reassert the appearance of composure.

'Very well, then, *Missus* Sarah Ward – '

'Wife to Mister Arnold Ward, whom I believe you have met.'

The surname had not registered with me when first spoken by her. Sarah had so completely filled our encounter with her presence and so absorbed me within it that I simply had not thought of her having a life, a living history, outside of her being there. Probably I would have ignored any surname she had given. But now, suddenly, Sarah was someone else, as it were. My instant reaction was one of bewildering confusion. Just days ago Arnold had talked of being in love with and wanting to settle down with a woman StB officer. The shock of knowing that Arnold was already married to the woman who sat opposite me now was mixed with even greater disappointment.

I stammered out a reply.

'Arnold didn't, when we met, I mean he said nothing about... didn't mention that – '

She was calmness itself.

'Why would he? But so that you do know now, you know that Missus Ward, formerly Miss Sarah Hill, is my name for the purpose of one of my tasks at Whitehall.' She turned that teasing smile upon me again. 'Where I am employed.'

I was being played with. I was also being challenged to work things out. 'Am I permitted to know – ?'

'Perhaps you do not need to know my legal name until, if need be, you need to know. You may take it, however, that Missus Sarah Ward, to put a name to your Miss K, is known to be married to Mister Ward. Arnold. It is a marriage which one might say, my dear sir, has certain advantages.'

She spoke to me *de haut en bas*, sounding as might an elderly duchess to a serving-man. She held the pose long enough for me to begin to revise my impression of her. Then she burst into unrestrained laughter, a stream released. She reached across to pat me on the knee again. Now I noted the large sapphire within a surround of diamonds on her engagement ring. It suggested great expense.

'He must love you very much.'

Sarah withdrew her hand.

'You must not assume that everything is as it seems, Anthony.'

She held up the back of her hand to me, waggling her ring finger.

'Fake. A good fake, but fake.'

She enjoyed watching me consider the implications.

'Ah, then what you have told me is not true?'

'Oh no. Everything I've said is true. In a manner of speaking, that is. What I am known as is what matters for the present.'

Sarah looked up to ensure that I had taken the point. She seemed so assured, much more secure than I felt in this one-to-one exchange. She discomfited me, not altogether unintentionally, by her poised presence, her control of the situation. Yet she was about my age, perhaps even a year or two younger I guessed, but with a maturity and certainty that impressed. There was something else. She was a very accomplished actress.

'Anthony, you look so serious. Am I making things difficult for you? Have I been teasing you?'

I was absorbed again.

'You need to know that a woman will only tease a man she likes and one, she thinks, who will take it in good part.'

'Then I shall take that as a compliment.'

'Good. Because I believe I am meant to tell you all, Anthony.'

Facing me, the woman whose husband was in love with another woman, smiled encouragingly.

Sarah telling me all began on that return train trip to London, and continued over several early evening meetings in the following couple of weeks around Charing Cross station, conveniently located between our respective places of work. Over coffee or tea we chatted our way into her story. There were times, I admit, when Sarah looked directly at me, her bright eyes wide upon me, that I drowned in their pools. There was nothing wary in her regard. It was as if, having decided to trust me, she trusted me wholly and implicitly, nothing withheld. That trust I did take as a compliment.

I learned that Miss Sarah Hill, as she had been known, was first employed – 'placed' might be a more apposite term – in Whitehall to act as eyes and ears for the Colonel's section. There had been rumours, nothing definite, but rumours that had been whispered for some time in offices and corridors. Names may be whispered in calumny, or for spite, revenge, or jealousy; but sometimes the nature of the whisper and the manner of its repetition call attention to themselves. Whether credent or not, several names had been given air.

Amid this whispering, Arnold Ward tipped off the service about the possibility of one particular MP putting himself out for hire to the Czechoslovak authorities. He was found to be an established and frequent visitor to certain of the Whitehall corridors, authorised by virtue of his membership of the Commons committee on whose behalf, he claimed, to be seeking informal 'guidance'. The regularity of his appearances, however, suggested more than due diligence in the performance of his position. More than a year passed, at which point it was decided that a closer eye must be kept on the MP.

That closer eye would be kept by Miss K, already in place and employed as Miss Sarah Hill in one of the offices of what was then the Ministry of Defence –

'Now merged just last year, I expect you know, with the other Ministries – Admiralty, War Office, and so on. To be truthful, we're still finding our way around the new organisation.'

'And Arnold?'

Following his tip-off to the service Arnold Ward, recruited as an irregular, had been asked to report back, through Miss K, anything picked up on his travels through countries in the east European communist bloc which he thought might be of interest to Her Majesty's Government.

'We knew that Arnold was being monitored wherever he went on his assignments – Poland, East Germany, Czechoslovakia. And in particular it seemed that the StB was keeping him closer company than usual. And we knew, of course, that they would also want to keep an eye on him when he was over here between tours.'

Knowing that Arnold would be monitored by 'them' when on home territory, there was a choice. Miss K could meet him clandestinely; in which case Arnold would go missing for durations of unaccounted time. His absences, noted as they would be, might be the very thing to confirm StB suspicion about him.

'Professor Godbole.' I could not prevent myself interjecting. 'Absences are as important as presences.'

I was disappointed that Sarah knew instantly the reference.

'Which is why it was determined that we would meet openly, with no attempt at concealment. That way we would be able to meet much more frequently than we would need to for the mere purpose of reporting back and forth. It would keep Arnold clean at this end, as far as his watchers were concerned. But, of course, we would need a reason that justified so many open meetings between us. So – ' Sarah laid her hand onto the table, her thumb beneath her fingers, twisting the engagement ring to and fro – 'we decided to get married. Engaged, at least. Married a couple of months later on his next leave back here.'

'But – '

'An arranged marriage. Registry office in Marylebone, with invited guests, photographs on the steps.' Sarah broke off for a moment. 'Just no signatures actually put to any paper.'

Sarah, with that smile which simultaneously disarmed and enticed, rested her chin on the splayed fingers of her hand so that the mock engagement ring flashed once more at me.

'And no, Anthony. Though for the sake of appearances we did, and do still share an address. We come and go from the same rented flat.' She narrowed her eyes. 'Two-bedroomed.'

Sarah spoke easily and openly about Arnold. They had become 'bosom pals' – an expression which today would carry innuendo it then lacked those decades past.

'He is such fun. We share the same sense of humour, and it amused both of us to be taken as a married couple. It made that part of my job so much easier.'

I could see an objection to this arrangement.

'But didn't being with Arnold, and being seen with Arnold, also bring *you* to notice? I mean, I presume that the StB watchers were then able to keep a track on both of you. They only had to follow you to find out that you worked at the Ministry of Defence.'

One should suppress any triumphalism at the first detection of what one takes to be a flaw in the opposition's argument.

'Exactly. And just what we were hoping would happen.'

I have learned in later years since to practise not only Philip's counsel to keep my mouth shut, but also to employ the art of tactical silence. It can be a powerful way of learning.

'Knowing where I worked would make Arnold even more interesting to them, don't you see? Being in bed with me, thinking us husband and wife – and knowing where I worked – made him more credible as the source of information. Information which we wanted him, inadvertently of course, to reveal on his visits. He became potentially very valuable to them – so they began to look after him, not just watch him as they would any other western visitor.'

Sarah's taking in of her bottom lip told me there was something more.

'And it all worked just as planned. Until...' She bit on her lip again. 'Then he fell in love.'

'When did he tell you this?'

'As soon as he felt able – months ago.'

'Did you – ?'

'No. I did not report this on.'

'Why not?'

'We were, and still are, good friends.'

'Yes, but – '

'I know, I know.' Sarah backhanded away my objection. 'Can you think of any better reason to give a man some time to work things out?'

Sarah was more withdrawn in speaking of the MP. She was more considered, deliberative, and, at the beginning, there was much biting of her bottom lip. At the end of her account, when pieced together, I was to understand her reluctance.

Working in the Ministry of Defence as a personal assistant to one of the most senior of civil servants there, Sarah's task of making contact with the MP was easily contrived. She simply had to make her presence known to the man. Looks and personality – though unsaid by Sarah herself – did the rest.

'Strange, really. He viewed me as a potential source of information, and I looked on him in the same way – listening for him to tell me things which would condemn him by his own words.'

But at first the MP had been wary, guarded. He had approached Sarah with due circumspection, but kept returning to her even so.

'Somehow I had to get him to trust me. Being a married woman, at least as far as he was concerned, certainly helped. To win his trust I had to get him closer to me.'

'How?'

'Oh, by the usual means a woman signals to a man that she is interested in him.'

'No, no. I meant, how did being a married woman help you to get close to him?'

Sarah was clearly puzzled at my lack of perception, my failure to understand.

'Because I too had something to lose.' Patiently, spelling it out for me. 'A marriage. Just as he had a marriage to lose, and with it his family, respectability, position, privilege... Everything.'

'Yes, but I mean it's not as if you were... ' My objection tailed away. I knew the words in advance of saying them. But Sarah challenged, looking at me directly.

'Yes?'

'Or perhaps you were, I don't know. Not my business.'

'Attracted to him? Only because there was a need for it to appear so, Anthony, only that.' She cast her eyes down, hands in her lap. 'To begin with.'

Was this an admission? A confession? I maintained as impassive a face as possible, suppressing the inward shock. Such a beautiful woman, such a bloated man.

'He needed time to work out if there was the prospect of an affair with me – and whether it would be safe to go ahead. Of course, I had to make it appear to him that he was making all the moves. Whilst at the same time he had to think that I was holding back.'

'Because?'

'So that he would not be suspicious. I imagine it was not every day that a young lady would have thrown herself at him. He had to win me.'

The MP had acted perfectly the part of a charmer, a lady's man, towards Sarah.

'He thought that if he persisted, showed perseverance, the way ladykillers do, I would be bound to yield. I would not be able to resist, and he would be able to seduce out of me everything he wanted.'

'Did he?' As soon as said regretted, breaking the rule to shut up. Just listen. 'Sorry.'

'He seduced out of me unique scraps which the Colonel's section briefed me to feed him. When those feeds started to come back to us from a contact whom Arnold had nurtured then we could be certain that he was the source.'

I recall a long silence, Sarah sipping at her coffee, fidgeting with the rings on her finger.

'In the end it was his own insecurity which undid him.'

'Meaning?'

'He is not the stuff of which spies are made. Not even informers.'

Sarah pursed her lips, then drew in her underlip. At this point in her accumulated narrative – our second or third meeting? – she deliberated for some time. Finally, decisively, she put her question to me.

'Is there anyone, any *one* person, one can trust, without reserve, without hesitation, finally and completely with everything that one is?'

I could only take a deep breath at such a large, such a consuming question. Sarah reached a hand across the table, rested it on the back of one of my hands to the side of my coffee cup. She made me hold her gaze until I was drowning again.

'We became lovers, Anthony. And I became his lover in order to betray him. Should the need arise.'

I was startled not because Sarah, Miss K, had taken a lover, but that 'Mrs Sarah Ward' would choose to go to bed with *that* man, that balding, spreading, middle-aged, self-important, grasping betrayer of his country.

A slow sad smile shaped itself on Sarah's lips.

'I know what you are thinking, I can see it on your face. You're right. A most unlikely lothario. But he was very *kind* to me, he wanted me to have presents, expensive pieces of jewellery – his way of impressing me. And flowers. Always flowers. I *liked* being with him, Anthony, he was different from the way he appears when you do not know the man' – a small hesitation – '*closely*. I enjoyed his company, we complemented each other.' She paused, then with a small shake of the head, she said: 'He was not the same man as he appeared to others.' Another small sideways movement of the head. 'I don't suppose you, as a man, can understand what on earth I'm going on about.'

She was right. A man does not see what a woman sees in another man, particularly a man whom one has decided to despise. Sarah interpreted:

'I thought not.'

Head down, I turned my cup to and fro in its saucer.

'Inside the man, Anthony, there was another man. A man interested in me, *concerned* about me, worried about how our liaison might hurt *me*. He showed me consideration I had never known before.'

Then, as I thought, the final confession.

'I became fond of him. A little in love with him, I suppose... there *were* attractive things about the man.'

There is another confession which belongs to that same moment. But this one was unvoiced, suppressed. I, already, was a little in love with 'Miss K.' More than a little. Yet, unthinkingly, the impulse expressed itself none the less in an alternative, perhaps sublimated, fashion. I blurted out an invitation to Sarah to join me for dinner on Friday evening. Then, as so often happens with something impetuously offered, one immediately withdraws the offer. Of course, I said, I would quite understand, after all she was a married woman – at which she laughed – and I... I was still clearing the ground for her to make an easy refusal when her gaze stilled me.

'I would like that.'

During that dinner we talked even more easily as the evening progressed, and as a bottle of good claret eased away any remnant embarrassment. Sarah wanted me to understand her reactions, her behaviour, as Miss K. It had not been her set purpose to become that MP's mistress, nor was it any part of the brief given her by the Colonel's section. Yet some things were 'understood', as she put it, things which would neither be asked nor expected of her, but...

That *but* hung in the air between us.

Within that monosyllable resided the unspoken, unrecorded substance that fleshed the bones of the 'facts of the matter' which, presumably, were withheld from those written statements which the Colonel was reluctant to release. His instinct for so doing was about to be given weight at this dinner with Sarah.

First, though, I learned that, from 'Mrs Sarah Ward's' point of view, the MP's vanity was an assumed affectation: 'He really was not like that at all.' He lacked confidence in his own self, she said, which was why he assumed the contrary, bragging persona.

'All an act, Anthony, just a mask. A modest man at heart – and that was his real charm.'

I was not prepared for Sarah's defence of the man. I did not want to hear of his humble background, the poverty of his childhood in a family of seven children, leaving school at fourteen to earn a shilling to put into the family purse, the gift from heaven of a junior clerk's office job in one of the local mills, his autodidactic attempts to become an educated man, his passionate engagement in local politics, the good work he had done there, his passionless marriage, two children grown up and away from him, his disappointments as a long-serving MP who had been passed over for higher office, the sop of the committee membership he had been given, and the wealth, the comparative wealth at least, of many of those he mixed with... and so on. And so on again, in the familiar style of a cheap poor-boy-makes-good romantic fiction; except that in his case having made good, he turned to the bad.

Yes but, I thought, at each stage of Sarah's retelling to me of the saga; and at one stage actually voicing the challenge that the man's version of his own story might not be, well, in all respects accurate.

'Yes but it's all true, Anthony. In his case it *is* all true. I mean, I checked, of course I checked. He's not a bad man – a weak man, yes.'

Yes but –

'*Was* not a bad man. He is a good man who has done a bad thing, a silly thing.'

Sarah knew what I had still to learn. If one gets close to a person the more one learns of that person then the more one begins to understand that someone in ways that explain him and what he has become. The problem then is that the understanding pleads for forgiveness for things wrongly or badly done – as if that person, in the grip now of the explanation one has conceived for him, is no longer responsible for what he has done. And that, something else which I began to appreciate even more forcefully in Sarah's unburdening to me, is a temptation which a prosecutor must nerve himself against.

'As I said to you before, in the end it was his lack of faith in himself which undid him. He wanted so very much to impress me. He could not believe that a young and beautiful woman – his words, Anthony – could ever allow herself to share a pillow with him, as he put it. Given that he was middle-aged, with spreading middle, balding, and of no consequence, which was how he saw himself. In fact, he is quite presentable. But he really was insecure and had a low opinion of himself.'

Sharing her pillow, he shared also a version of his secret. The pillow-talk account he gave was an attempt to compensate for his physical deficiencies by creating an alternative, more romantic image of himself. He admitted to his rôle as an informer for the Czechoslovakian authorities. He claimed to be a double-agent, passing information 'from here to there' in order to get even more valuable information 'from there to here.'

Did the man, I did momentarily wonder, actually believe, or come to believe, in this other justification for his self-elected mission?

To me, as I listened, all self-explanation seemed simply inflation of the man's self. As, for example, his claim that what he was doing was not without its own element of danger, but he ran the risks for the common good of this nation. Yet in all that I heard of the man from Sarah, there was no admission that this selfless, self-appointed task had involved his receipt of large amounts of money and payments in kind for his release of information 'from here to there'.

Sarah impressed me with her self-control and her precision of language. I had no doubt that she could be the missing link we needed in order to have the man convicted. Her testimony in court would be convincing. It would be calmly stated. Given that she could tell me so matter-of-factly of her intimate relationship with the man, I was absolutely convinced she would be robust under any cross-examination. There would be the matter of Sarah's appearance in court – albeit behind a screen – to be managed, but her full testimony, the digest of which I had just heard, would prove conclusive where the written portfolio reports were unconvincing. We *would* be able to get our man. Something else, though, had been nudging me off this train of thought.

'When you said he *is* quite presentable – '

'Yes, Anthony, I do still see him from time to time, not as before, not as a mistress. Our paths do still cross, I am still earning much of my crust at the Ministry, and still keeping my eyes and ears open. Where there's one, there may be more than one.'

When coffee arrived Sarah ordered a port to go with it, a somewhat unusual drink for a woman, as I commented. Her look was amused, but her slight shake of the head dismissed my patronising. Seeking amends, I joined her in her choice.

'Anyway,' Sarah began, and halted just long enough for me to know we were about to change subject. 'What about you?'

Sarah was a gentle, though ruthless, questioner. She did not permit answers which evaded the point of a question; vagueness had to be refined, mere gesturings of words were challenged. So I was constrained by successive questioning to tell my story, my background, family, school, university, choice of career to bring us to my involvement with her former lover, that errant MP, and this table in this restaurant on this night.

More coffee, more port.

'And what about *your* young woman, Anthony? You must have one.'

I know I reddened, the question taking me utterly by surprise. I did my best to cover, to recover, and somewhat reluctantly told Sarah briefly about Carolyne, how she had come back into my life after we had drifted our separate ways when she left Oxford.

'Do you intend to marry the girl?'

I felt uncomfortable with Sarah's directness. But I told her of my status, a soon-to-be-engaged man. Sarah touched the rim of her glass to mine, offering silent congratulations. With deliberation, and very quietly, Sarah asked:

'Do you love the girl?'

The reflex of an answer. Yes, of course. Of course I do. Naturally. And after those protestations, other words unintendedly added:

'So, yes, I suppose I do.'

Sarah's was the slow, indulgent smile of one who has hit upon another's vulnerability.

'Then, Anthony, I suppose you do not.'

Somehow I managed to shake myself free. It discomfited me to be the object of Sarah's inquisition. She raised too many questions. But we finished up somehow in a shared self-mocking laughter. We were at the end of our evening, waiting for the bill. Sarah reached across the table, put the palm of one hand over the back of one of my hands, as if to detain me.

'There is something else, Anthony.'

I leant towards her.

'You do know that the quality of information passed on by him declined, don't you?' Him, the you-know-who MP of our subject for the night. 'Some time ago now. And what he handed on became more and more low grade stuff.' Her hand tapped upon the back of my own. 'I am told that all he had to say to his masters over the best part of a year has been nothing more than low-grade gossip, really.'

I knew this, from Arnold, but I knew also, from Sarah's poise at that moment, that there was something more. She made me look steadily at her. She withdrew her hand. She bit on her underlip, as if deciding something.

'Someone tipped him off, Anthony.'

Her eyelids blinked several times. She looked down into her lap, then again directly at me in a steady gaze.

Aah! A Philippian moment.

'You don't mean...' I stopped myself.

I remembered that long look Sarah had given me in the moment of her admission: 'Someone tipped him off, Anthony.' That steady gaze was challenging rather than pleading, looking to see if I had indeed understood. I had. But it was something which I was determined I would keep to myself. I realised that keeping silence made me complicit; I had elected myself Sarah's guardian. It also made it impossible, given her revelation, to see how she could be the principal witness for the prosecution. She must have known that. She must have been relying on me somehow to find a means of protecting her, of removing her as a prospective witness. I could not see how to do that and still proceed with the case. We were back to where we had been, but one, fortunately, for the present put on hold. Sir John's more urgent business now took precedence.

During the first of those weeks in which I saw Sarah, I had received two telephone calls from Carolyne. The first was mid-week, to alert me to the fact that she would definitely not return for that weekend. She could not say with certainty when she would be back. Things were taking longer than expected, it was all very complicated, there was so much to do. As things looked, however, it was very likely she would have to see out the best part of the following week. There was some good news, though: she was already beginning to feel stronger now, less distressed, change of air, of environment, and so on, knew I would be pleased. It was a brief exchange in which she sounded distant; I do not mean geographically, from Berne to London, but cool, detached from me. Her manner was clearly part of the penance which had not been lifted from me. But it rankled. Enough was enough, I thought. That thought itself was precipitated from another and wholly unbidden thought which insisted on itself the moment I heard her voice. I had not missed her. Not really. That is, to add to the degree of qualification: not *really,* as in an ache that absence engenders and magnifies. Not for the first time I had not missed her.

Carolyne's second call to me was on the Friday afternoon. She telephoned me at chambers, the very first time she had done so. I was surprised, therefore, to hear her voice. Yes, she would now definitely have to stay on for the following week. She knew I would understand – a phrase which was becoming one of her favourite addresses to me.

'Do you miss me, Anthony?'

Of course can be as swift as any physiological reflex action.

Carolyne's absence to that point had been little of a trial, certainly less than it might otherwise have been. My early evenings had been taken up by those meetings with Sarah and I had had three days in court, so the week had passed quickly. So quickly also, I knew, I was being absorbed by Sarah, Miss K, Sarah Hill, *Missus* Arnold Ward. It was an infatuation. Unreciprocated. Sarah had not shown the slightest sign of interest in me to that point, nor did she even by the time we got to our final evening and our farewell parting. She had been friendly, had smiled, talked – given what she had spoken about with some hesitation at times, but without any withholding from me, even of the most embarrassing matters. Yet I had not seen any of those 'usual means', as she had put it, by which a woman signals to a man that she is interested in him.

In some senses I felt at a disadvantage with her. She seemed so much more mature than me, even though – as I had now found out by the simple expedient of asking her – she was a year younger. Her presence carried a romance with her, the nature of what she did, her involvement in that grey world where sunlight and shadows were monochrome. She had – how best to express this? – not so much an outright beauty such as staggers a man on first sighting, but looks betokening the presence of a deeply sensual nature within a quick and developed intelligence. One simply could not be bored in her presence. In her absence I felt abandoned. We had made no arrangement to meet up again.

Now I had a weekend to get through on my own. For reasons I was loath to admit, I issued a challenge to myself: to see if I could so occupy my time that Carolyne's absence remained a light acknowledgement rather than something pressing heavily upon me.

In this I succeeded rather well. I did miss Sarah though.

On Saturday I took myself off to Charing Cross Road mid-morning to rummage through the second-hand bookshops in search of William Walsh. Unsurprisingly, I found no editions of his work. One of the booksellers, however, insisted on consulting his catalogues. Bent over his desk, a border of white hair springing sideways from his bald head, he muttered to himself as he turned the pages. Triumphantly he looked up, gold-rimmed spectacles perched beneath the bridge of his nose.

'*The Works* was it you wanted, sir?'

'The *Collected*, yes.'

'Mmm... of 1736 would that be?' Head bent down again.

'Yes, I believe so.'

'*The Works of William Walsh Esquire in Prose and Verse*, to give the volume its full and accurate title, sir. Ah!' Head up, the eyes of a man bright with enthusiasm. 'Published by that scoundrel Edmund Curll. You know of him, of course?'

I confessed ignorance.

'The shop from which he published the volume you wish to trace is just a few minutes' stroll away' – he raised an arm, pointing a direction – 'in Rose Street beneath the sign of the Pope's Head – not the primate of the Catholic church, sir, but Alexander, the poet of the *Dunciad*. Now *there's* a tale that might be told, Alexander Pope and Edmund Curll and the twenty-year war between them.'

Having nothing more pressing to do, I was prepared to listen to the tale, but the bookseller caught himself up.

'My apologies. I digress. I regret to say that I can not find a copy of the work in any of my current listings. Would you wish me to make inquiries, sir, to see if I can locate a copy that might be for sale?' There was an amused tittering. 'Though I must tell you immediately, sir, that if I were to be successful in tracking down a copy, it would cost you very considerably more than the four shillings of its original price.'

I declined the offer.

Instead I took the narrow stairs to the rooms on the next floor. There I browsed through several guides to literature of the period, all of which omitted William Walsh from their critical pages. I found one anthology of seventeenth-century verse which reprinted two of his poems, and repeated scant biographical details, including the mis-assigned birthdate. I did then find the entry on W.W. in a volume of the original issue of the *Dictionary of National Biography*. Yet again I read that W.W. was born the year following his baptism. Written by one Adolphus William Ward, the account asserted that W.W. was 'ostentatiously splendid in his dress', and I wondered if William's adoption of William Walsh as the model for his own sartorial *alter ego* had been prompted by his reading of this very source. I also wondered at the coincidence of names in the *Dictionary's* biographer, Adolphus William Ward. I had collected a William from Oxford days, and a Ward in the last few weeks. I mused somewhat quirkily that I needed only to encounter an Adolphus to have a full set. From then until now, several decades later, I have still not met a living Adolphus.

Downstairs again I bought the copy of the anthology.

The shopkeeper was animated. 'If I may, sir, I think it possible to locate an alternative source for your William Walsh.' His eyes twinkled over the lenses of his glasses slipped further down his nose. 'It will not contain his complete works, regrettably, but it will contain his poetry. And it would be far less expensive. There would be no obligation to buy, but I think this would be a very pleasing volume for you. Would you be interested?'

I was.

'It may take some time, sir. I wonder if I might take some contact details from you?'

I handed him my card. He studied it for a moment.

'You shall hear from me Mister Ashley-Chetwyne when I have news for you.'

That afternoon I settled down to do something which I had not done for a long while. I read some poetry. It was also, in another sense, something I had never done before. My readings in English poetry, such as they had been, had always been within the set texts of set authors – the canon of big names. Now I found myself being drawn into *Minor Poets of the Seventeenth Century*. I found it quite fascinating. Soon I was absorbed, breaking only for a mug of tea and some biscuits. Much of the collection was love poetry, expected of the poet in his time, many addressed to an ideal, or idealised lover. Her name was variously: Chloris, popular with several of the poets, Caelia or Celia, Phillis, also quite popular, Biancha, Lucia, Anthea, Lydia, Althea, Amanda, Cynthia, Flavia, and Julia... among others, including a name with lovely softly-sounding vowels: Fidelia. The subjects repeated, but one of the principal themes which emerged, as I read haphazardly through the volume flipping from page to page, was that of the lover whose love for the woman could never be surpassed by any other man. I read also of a contrary, the man steeled against

Each flatt'ring kiss, each tempting smile

bestowed on him in vain, which

Some other lovers may beguile!
Who not thy falsehood know.

The man, deceived once by the woman, is immune now to her seductive arts:

But I am proof against all art!
No vows shall e'er persuade me
Twice to present a wounded heart
To her that hath betrayed me!

It is possible, of course, to judge by the little literary knowledge of the period I had, that this poem, as, presumably, many others, was composed as an 'exercise' – the sort of verse which an educated man would pen. Yet I wondered... several poems on the same theme of love betrayed did somewhat mark out Thomas Stanley from the surrounding voices singing paeans of praise to the beauty of woman.

What did arrest me, however, was an ingenious verse by an unknown poet, a Mister I presumed, certainly Anonymous, called simply *A Question*. I was intrigued. 'Between two suitors', ran the opening, 'sat a Lady fair.' She wore a garland on her head, but only one of the two suitors wore a garland like hers. So

> *From her own head, She took the wreath She wore;*
> *And on him placed it, that had none before.*

Now that both men were garlanded, they were 'decked with equal pride'. Her own head then bare, the Lady took the garland from the first of the suitors and placed it on her own head so that she and the second suitor were then 'With garlands decked.' There followed the Question:

> *Now, which did She love best? Of him, to whom*
> *She gave the wreath? Or him, she took it from?*

I ignored *The Answer* and read the sixteen line question several times over but could find within them no giveaway whatever, no clue to the anticipated response. There was nothing hidden away; the lines did no more than describe the lady's actions before posing the question. I tried to argue the answer both ways, but one of them repeatedly insisted on itself. I simply could not make the alternative answer credible to myself. Who *would* the woman love most? – the man to whom she had given or the man from whom she had taken?

To one lover she had given her crown, from one lover she had taken his crown, as I put it to myself, placed it on her own head, and then given that garland to the second suitor. Clearly, therefore, the second suitor must be the winner. King and Queen, as it were, sitting alongside each other, the bare-headed chap the loser. It was obvious.

It was now late afternoon and dark outside. I had been reading by the light of a single table lamp. I got up to draw the curtains, switch more lights on and make another mug of tea, via a visit to the bathroom.

I was just resettling to find out what *Answer* Mister Anonymous would give to his own *Question*, when the telephone rang. Carolyne.

She appeared to be in much better spirits. What was I doing, she wanted to know.

'Really?' She accented the word to sound both doubt and a denial.

'Yes really. Actually there is something you might have a view on.'

I picked up the book and read to her *The Question*, said I had been pondering what would be the correct answer. So, which would *she* say was the favoured of the two suitors.

'I'm not sure I understand.'

In my own words I retold the situation of the poem. So, which of the two men did the lady choose as her lover – the one from whom she had taken the garland, or the one to whom she had given the garland?

'It all depends, doesn't it?'

'On what?'

'Well, I can't really say – I mean, whatever it is we don't know about.'

I tried again. More than once again in fact.

'She might just have felt sorry for the fellow who didn't have a garland, you know... him being without...'

I gave up.

'Anyway, I have some news for you.' She did sound more animated than in her previous calls. She waited, though, for me to ask.

'You'll never guess.'

I waited.

'I saw William.'

Now I did have questions.

'He's here, in Berne, a guest of the English Department of the university. Giving some lectures. We just happened to bump into each other. What a coincidence! Isn't that amazing?'

'I thought he was going to be sent somewhere for some training.'

'Yes, he did say something about that. Anyway...'

Carolyne's excitement spilled words at a pace. Anyway, it seemed, William was at a loose end, being there on his own, Daddy having gone on to Czechoslovakia of all places, for goodness' sake, something about a beer, wanted to import some to the UK, did I remember? Daddy had said he'd said something to you about it, the thing was he had gone out there earlier in the week, and then had had to get back to London, some urgent business to attend to, so it would be some time before he could come out to Berne again, couldn't actually say when, which meant that she would be left to hold the fort for yet another week, staff shortage, but I knew that, she had already said, hadn't she? so she had found herself at a bit of a loose end, but anyway, the thing was she and William – what a surprise to see him here, *so* unexpected! – had decided to do a bit of touristy sight-seeing together, which they had done today, a little trip to Neuchâtel, the lake, so beautiful, I would have loved it, and now she would have to get ready, they were going out to dinner somewhere, but I wasn't to worry about her because she had William to look after her, now wasn't that lucky? So what was I going to do with myself tonight?

'Nothing.'

'Oh you poor dear, don't be miserable. Love and kisses, have to dash.'

I returned to *A Question*. Then tried to make sense of *The Answer*. The answer to another empty week I knew without thinking. Sarah.

∼ **28** ∼

In retrospect those last months of 1965, starting with the Colonel's autumnal visit to me in chambers, composed in themselves a compact season of surprises – events and persons which took me away from my hitherto taken-for-granted reality. It was a short season which none the less, or because of, its compression into such a short space of time, made me test the security of my life, its predictability, its settled nature. Things that were so soon became no longer so. The Sunday of that weekend was its own season of telephone calls.

Mother telephoned me late morning – after returning home from church I guessed.

'I did try to 'phone you yesterday, Anthony. Where were you?'

Mother had then, and retained to her death, the utter conviction that I should be present to her, in person or by telephone, on any occasion and time of her choosing. She took my absence as the dereliction of a son's obeisance.

I explained.

'But wasn't Carolyne with you?'

I explained.

'She is *where*?' Mother managed to sound both incredulous and critical. 'And *what*, may one ask, is she doing there?'

I tried to explain, but mother had something to say.

'Do you know, Anthony, I have had a letter from *that woman*.' Mother's more acerbic declarations often began in the shape, though not the intention, of a question.

'Which woman, mother?' I knew, but it is also a son's duty to tease his mother, especially when she is so evidently out of humour.

'Which woman? *That* woman, of course, who else?'

Silence.

'*Well?*'

'Well what, mother?'

'Well *what?* What do you have to say about it?'

'Mother, until I know what is in the letter I have nothing to say about it.'

There was an intake of breath, mother calming herself. 'You mean to tell me, Anthony, that you do not know *what* that woman has written to me?'

'No, I do not.'

There was a prolonged 'oh' sound as I visualised my mother shaking her head from side to side in disbelief.

That woman, it could be no other, was Carolyne's mother who, as my own mother sharply stated, had sent a letter proposing a specified date in February of the new year when Carolyne and I would formally announce our engagement to be married. There would be a party, hosted at the Walkers' home which it would be their pleasure to fund, and would mother kindly let her know which of the Ashley-Chetwynes' family, relatives, and friends mother would wish to be present, together with their addresses, so that *she* (Carolyne's mother) could send them formal invitations.

'I trust you did not agree to this date, Anthony.'

'Well, no. I don't think, well, that is – '

'Did you discuss this? Did you not say that you would talk first with your parents?'

'Well, no. Not as such, no, we haven't actually talked *directly* about a particular day, though we did talk – '

'*We*, Anthony?'

'Carolyne and her mother, really...' Frankly the two of them on that occasion had been so excited, their chatter so unstoppered, that I had been glad when Carolyne's father gestured me out of the room to share a beer with him.

'It is outrageous. Has the woman no sense of the proper way of *anything?*'

Mother berated me with the failings of my prospective mother-in-law. Without a by-your-leave, with no consideration, without even the pretence of consultation it seemed that *that* woman had simply gone ahead and –

'Well it is *not* convenient, Anthony, it is simply *not* convenient. We shall be otherwise engaged' – mother recognised no irony in her words – 'on that date.'

I was tempted to ask mother what would be her alternative and prior commitment for that day. I suppressed the impulse. The only acceptable date for my mother, I knew full well, would be the one that she herself proposed and Carolyne's mother agreed to.

'I shall write to her, at my convenience, and suggest an alternative date.'

There was a pause; one of those pauses in which one is so obviously expected to say something. I missed the cue.

'That is if you still insist on going ahead with this matrimonial match with the daughter of a, a *trader* and with *that* woman as a mother-in-law.'

Dear mother, whose sense of *form* – the word she selected to denote every aspect of social interaction – determined her prejudices. Provided the right form was adhered to, she was prepared to think well of any person, and she would go to endless lengths and trouble to support those of whom she thought well. To men she extended the courtesy of more than one encounter to prove their fitness to form. To women she offered the first few seconds of their first meeting to persuade her of their acceptability. Carolyne's mother had failed my mother's test. She had new-made wealth to envy; but she had not form.

Having said what she wanted to say mother left me holding the receiver in my hand. There was that annoying little click sound again that had become a feature of my calls. I rebuked myself again for the umpteenth time for forgetting to report the fault and have it fixed.

Carolyne telephoned mid-afternoon to tell me that William sent his best wishes. They had had a lovely time at the lake, really I would have loved it, we must go there together some time. Oh, and William will be back in London soon. Something about a briefing before having to off again to somewhere else, and...

Uncharacteristically, Carolyne subsided into silence, where usually she would unroll all her news to me 'so that you know' as she was wont to say. Prompted by some obscure impulse I inserted a question into the gap of silence.

'Where are you, Carolyne?'

I heard in Carolyne's voice a small quaver before resuming its usual tone.

'Actually we decided to stay over, it seemed silly to have to travel back on the same day and waste the day in travel, so we're just about to set off now, William has a guest lecture or a post-graduate seminar tomorrow, can't remember which, perhaps it's both, and I have to be back at work anyway...'

'Let me speak to William.'

There was a confusion of sounds, the sharp noise of a receiver being put down, then:

'Anthony, old fellow. What a delight to speak with you.'

'I thought you were going to be away somewhere. That note you left me. I thought you said you would be for some time.'

'Ah yes. A little in-service training, as one might say. I do believe it *would* have been some time, a number of weeks in fact to do the whole thing, from what I gather. Actually, to be completely truthful my dear fellow, a great deal of it, if not the entirety of it, would have been wasted on me – given my, let us say, rather limited needs. So I pleaded my case and when I get back they are going to cut it short – keep it to the few bits and pieces that might come in handy.'

It was the voice of cultivated urbanity, the familiar languid voice; William *comme d'habitude*, as he might himself have said, unchanged, unperturbed.

'Rather fortunate all round. Given the standing invitation from Berne it meant I could accept sooner than anticipated *and* go out the week before, have a few days to myself. And then... *O ridenti faciem fati*, for here was Carolyne. In the flesh, in Berne.'

I did wonder whether William's smiling face of fate smiled also on less happy occurrences – whether it was the same fixed smile, a rictus, irrespective of good or bad outcomes.

'I must also offer up a *mea culpa*. It is my fault entirely that we are still here. I did rather bully Carolyne into staying over – for purely selfish reasons, of course. One could not know whether one would ever pass this way again.' A hesitation. 'I say, old fellow, I hope you don't mind me looking after your darling for you, I have seen to it that no harm has come to her. She has been splendid company. I do envy you.'

I muttered something about being sure he would have taken good care of Carolyne.

'Rather like the old days, looking after your girls for you while you sporty types went off and bloodied each other's noses or threw a hard leather ball at each other.'

It was the old William. Despite my ill humour of the moment, I laughed.

'Ah, but I have a little news for you, Anthony. We shall celebrate when we meet up – but you may congratulate me now.'

William would not proceed until I showed curiosity.

'Old Smokey has come up trumps for me.' William sustained the pause to stir my curiosity. 'A fellowship at our old college. Visiting for, well, however long, until I shall be able to take it up as a permanent position.'

I offered my congratulations.

'I shall put Carolyne back on now, so that you two lovebirds can have the last words with each other.'

Carolyne was *so* looking forward to seeing me again. Her brightened spirits were evident even in her speaking on the telephone. She tried to reassure me. 'I do feel,' she had said, 'almost back to my old self.' The Carolyne I knew for her animation, for the joy she could be when one was with her, for those qualities of sparkle and exuberance were returning. Unsaid, there would be fun at our reunion. And yet... and yet... was there something contrived in all this, something held back, something unvoiced? Ah, but who was holding back what?

There is a doubt that niggles and which is like a small but insistent draught under the door. Unless you block the door, the draught will not go away.

I tried to replay in my head not Carolyne's words so much as their tone and manner, their way of being said. I tried to detect a difference. Truth to tell Carolyne had sounded, well... just like Carolyne. Almost. That small draught persisted in intruding its cold breath. What a coincidence, coincidence, coincidence... the word a rolling echo in my head. Unable to block *this* draught I took up a dictionary.

I found a subsidiary, more expansive definition.

Coincidence: event or circumstance occurring in conjunction, or synchronously, with another event or circumstance and in such a manner as to suggest a connection of cause and effect, where no apparent connection of the kind exists.

Yes but this was Carolyne and *William!* And William, as one very well knew... *et cetera.*

At that moment, the relief of distraction. The telephone rang again.

'Good evening, sir.' A strange, strangulated voice I did not recognise. 'A message from Reg and Dave and Sam. They would very much like to see you again. Tonight, same place, about eight o'clock if that's ok with you. Hope you might be at a bit of a loose end and can join us. Sorry about the short notice.'

'Who –?'

But the receiver had been put down at the other end. Click.

I was left to ponder. Reg, David, Sam? I mulled over the names. Then Ah! Arnold's colleagues, those reporters, the Gin Palace.

29

The draught of doubt persisted as I made my way to the Gin
Palace. I recalled something Arnold had said to me about the
AA course he had done – Awareness and Avoidance. I played
over those two terms; and I wondered how long I had avoided
an awareness which now no longer seemed beyond countenance.
Trust and doubt: was I was being played for a fool? I lurched
against the seat with the movement of the carriage on the Underground tracks.

There was no Reg, there was no David, no Sam. But Arnold
Ward was there, at the populated bar, his upraised arm signalling
his whereabouts as I pushed through the door.

'Sorry about that, Anthony. Didn't want to use my name.' His
first words to me; in that strained voice I had not recognised
earlier on the telephone.

'Isn't this all rather paranoid, Arnold?'

Resuming then in his usual voice: 'Perhaps. Told you it
made you paranoid, once you've signed up to all this' – a loose
backhand motion – 'once you've learned the imperative of
not taking chances. So, just in case. You know how it is. Ears.'
And he tugged with thumb and forefinger at the lobe of one
ear.

'You surely don't think – '

'Anthony, I don't know whether *you* are being bugged or not.
Probably not, but I didn't want to advertise the fact that I was
back here. Slipped in on the sly this time. Drink?'

We managed to find a spot away from the bar where we could
lean against one of the wooden divides topped with a scrolled
glass panel.

'I gather you've met the missus.' Arnold grinned.

'Sarah? Yes.' A little dubiously, watching his reaction, I added:
'Lovely girl.'

'Oh yes, first-rate. We get along really well, a real Darby and Joan in the making.' He looked at me over the rim of his pint glass. 'She took to you, you know. Quite taken.'

I took Arnold to be winding me up.

'No, seriously, I can tell. Known her long enough after all, seeing that she's my unlawfully wedded wife.'

'What did she – ?'

'She didn't say anything. That's how I know. She did tell me that she had met up with you a few times, though.'

Arnold started to ask me a good deal about those meetings with Sarah.

I became suspicious.

'No, no, Anthony, I'm not in the least jealous. I assure you. In the hackneyed phrase, We are just good friends. And we *are* good friends. But just that – good friends. Despite being married. And despite her being my handler – makes reporting back so much easier.'

That was something unexpected. I was about to put a question. Arnold, however, answered a question I was not about to voice:

'And no, we don't talk extra-maritals.'

That tracked me into asking, 'Does that mean Sarah does not know about – '

'It does, Anthony, it does. And I've no intention of telling her, at least not yet.'

We drank up our pints. Arnold gripped me by the elbow.

'Come on!'

Arnold picked up a duffel bag at his feet against the bar. We left the Gin Palace and headed along the street to *The Spotted Horse* where we were able to sit with our drinks, the Sunday night quieter here, conversations and occasional laughter not loud enough for us to have to raise our own voices. We talked about and around a number of things, and I was keen to know more of his correspondent role. Arnold was very good company: amusing, clearly both very intelligent and perceptive, with a droll sense of humour and with a breadth of experience which made him an interesting object of regard.

I learned that he had been back to the flat shared with 'the missus' – 'Miss Sarah Hill as was. Gone one in the morning by the time I got back.' She had briefed him about me, and explained that our meetings had been to share what information she could add to my knowledge of the MP on whom she had been keeping a close eye.

'Shameless bastard,' was Arnold's comment. 'Not a bloke's bloke – too shifty, sidling around everything, everything by suggestion and a hint of this and that. Came out with it in the end, though – unmistakable, he had to if he was ever going to get his hands on the money. Which was all the grasping bugger was after. But I tell you this' – Arnold put a large hand on my forearm – 'he's not the bigwig he made himself out to be. Not really that important.'

'I take it you did not much care for him, then.'

We both exploded into laughter.

'How do things stand now with regard to him? If you can say, that is. Sarah says she doesn't know how it will go. Up to you mainly, she says.'

I was flattered that anyone could think that in my junior position I would have much of a say in the matter. Sir John Holyoake's 'puffing up' of me to Sarah must have had its effect. I was learning, however, to be guarded, and especially in company, even in company I enjoyed, such as that of Sarah's and Arnold's. I could not tell Arnold that Sir John's 'left hand' service was about to take precedence over the MP's case – something clearly also unknown to Sarah – and that it was very likely that the question of proceeding against the MP would be held in abeyance. For this, frankly, I was grateful. For there was also Sarah's confession which could well be dragged into any court proceedings entered against the man. Frankly I did not know what to do with her secret.

I prevaricated. 'I think the assessment of his case will go on for a time yet.'

Arnold nodded.

I wanted to change the subject. Given that we were meeting so openly, he must have been fairly sure that there were no watchers.

'Told you. Slipped in this time. You and Sarah are the only two who know I'm here. Came the back way – via the long route.'

The long route turned out to be the slow train journey to Cologne, and from Cologne to Brussels with some suburban backtracking on the way, all on slow trains halting at every stop, and from Brussels on the last flight out to London the previous night. All this, he explained, took up an extended day's travel, instead of his more usual pattern of flight to London from Tempelhof, West Berlin.

'Besides, if anyone from the other lot *is* actually watching, there's now good reason why we *should* be seen together. It's not unknown for Sarah to be watched, and you and she have been together quite a few times recently, so...' Arnold held up the backs of his hands to me, fingers splayed, as if to sign something very obvious. He gave a small laugh when it was clear to him, by my lack of reaction, that it was not obvious to me. 'Best that you *are* seen with me – assuming you've been seen with Sarah. So, that makes you my friend, as well as Sarah's friend. Removes a possible complication, don't you see?'

Shrugging a 'suppose so', I went to the bar get more drinks for us. I returned to the table, Arnold making a small circular movement with the forefinger of one hand.

'There's another 'besides'.'

'And that, Arnold, is?'

'It's not them I don't want to be seen by at the moment. It's our own lot.'

I was puzzled. 'Why?'

'I don't trust them.'

I took a large draught of beer; really because I could not think of anything to say. But Arnold went on to have his say. They, 'our own lot', wanted everything from him without giving anything to him. All he wanted was a particular young lady to be 'enabled' (his word) to come to England. For that he would willingly testify against 'that grubby bastard of an MP.'

'So, I need to know. That's why I'm here. Will they or won't they agree?' He leant forward to bring his eyes closer and level to my own. 'I think you already have their answer, Anthony.'

I had to blink at his prolonged stare.

'It's No, isn't it?'

I said nothing. His lips pressed into a grim, straight line. Then he nodded, several times, rapidly.

'Thought so. Now let's see if we can change their minds on this. And you can be the messenger.'

He stood to leave, swinging onto his shoulder the strings of the duffel bag lifted out from under the table.

'Drink up. Let's go.'

'Where are we going?'

'Your place.'

Arnold insisted we part outside the pub. 'Just in case any of our lot...' – at which he raised a forefinger to the underneath of an eye. To give him a headstart to get to Regent's Park he would cross the river to Putney Bridge underground station and I would backtrack to East Putney and take my time about doing it. I thought Arnold's arrangements both unnecessary and rather absurd.

'I've told you. I don't trust them, our lot. The meeting at your place has to be private.'

Something like twenty minutes after getting to my apartment, leaving the latch up on the front door as instructed, Arnold pushed open the door to my sitting-room at the top of the flight of stairs.

'Glasses?'

His first word as he pulled from his duffel bag a bottle of single malt whisky. Glasses, whisky, and a jug of water on the coffee table, we settled down to each other's company.

'So?'

Arnold lifted onto the settee beside him his duffel bag. From it he took a small portable tape recorder and a spool of tape which he proceeded to thread into the machine and play back to me.

The tape recorded a good part of the second conversation Arnold had had with our 'greedy bastard MP' in *The Marquis* in Westminster.

'May I make notes?'

'For you to report on, Anthony. None of this goes via Sarah.'

The gist was that the tape comprised mostly a humming and hawing towards, with circlings around, the MP's true target. Whilst his intention was clear by inference, there was no actual, unambiguous commitment of intent stated in plain words. I was impressed though with Arnold's dexterity in drawing him on. I was impressed also with the way Arnold had contrived to insert the date of this meeting into the recording by negotiating the date of their next meeting: 'Now let's see... the seventeenth today' – 'Eighteenth' (in the MP's voice) – 'Sorry, lost track, been travelling the last two days. OK, eighteenth of February, and I'm due to go out again next Tuesday and scheduled to be back here on the twenty-third of next month. So, diaries out, let's see if we can pencil in a date after that.'

Arnold produced a second tape – this one of the third and brief meeting between Arnold and the MP. This tape, in which Arnold was able to relay to the MP the potential interest of the StB, was more incriminating. There was much self-aggrandising on the part of the politician, his access to the corridors of power, his influence, his close relationships with various Ministers, and so on. Even though within the context of the exchanges as a whole, of both tapes taken together, there was a decided direction and purpose, there remained an ambiguity that could be exploited.

'Devious little bastard.'

It was mention of money, the amounts they, the Czech service, might be willing to pay that brought the MP closest to a confession of intent. Even so, however, intent is not accomplishment. Talk of 'the exchange of beneficial information' with a view to 'enhancing mutual understanding, reducing suspicion, and developing a framework for future cooperation between our states' made it clear, in the context of the rest of the conversation, what he was prepared to do as his own contribution to those ends.

'What do you think?'

'I need to consult.'

'You do that, my friend. Then report back. Make them understand, Anthony, the deal. Tapes and testimony for the lady.'

30

I was early getting to chambers on Monday morning. But not as early as Booth. Booth's room directly faced the entrance door and his habit was to leave the door to his room open. On that ground floor, to one side of Booth's office, was a meeting-room which could hold a dozen or so partners, and on the other side was a secretarial office.

'Good morning, Mister Anthony.'

Booth spun his chair around, a squat figure in his striped dark suit and sleeked back dark hair reminding me of the words of Philip: 'Our dear Booth is the spider of these chambers. He holds all the threads to all parts of these chambers and detects the slightest vibration of what is going on even before anything is actually said or done.' Philip intended his words not as a criticism but as an acclamation of the man's peculiar power.

'Coffee, Mister Anthony?' Booth waved me towards him. 'To warm you on a cold winter day?'

Where Anthony served his coffee in old enamel mugs, Booth served his in china cups from a silver service on a silver tray.

'Standards,' was his explanation. 'Think of our clients.'

He poured me a cup of beautifully-balanced coffee. He saw my appreciation.

'A special blend for the morning. Go to Kensington to have it made up.'

I sensed there was something Booth wanted to say to me.

'I am sorry Mister Philip's news must have come as a bit of a shock to you.'

'His elevation?'

'Yes indeed. Of course I have known for some time, but you will understand...' He waved a backwards hand as explanation. 'No-one more deserving, we can all agree.'

I had not seen Philip for a whole week; not since his weekend house party.

'The High Court case continues, Mister Anthony, and is due to do so for three or perhaps even four more weeks. We shall see Mister Philip only fleetingly between times. He is engaged in a complex case, you know that, very complex, but we can not have extortion and gang warfare on our streets and fear and trembling among innocent folk.'

With a small movement towards the coffee pot he invited me to a refill.

'So, Mister Anthony, it is opportune timing to talk about you and your, ah, future with us here. Mister Philip has entrusted me to talk over some things with you in his unavoidable absence. You have a few minutes?'

I nodded.

'The first thing, and the most important confirmation of Mister Philip's regard for you, is that – when the time comes – he intends to bequeath his chamber to you.'

I thought of that room, its slightly battered appearance, the smell of pipe tobacco smoke impregnating its very walls, the special concession of a curtained-off gas-ring for tea and coffee making, the bowing shelves weighted down with reference tomes, the overall slight idiosyncrasy of a chamber – and was moved that Philip should think of it as my inheritance.

'Besides, Mister Anthony, you are the youngest barrister in chambers and none of the seniors is willing, or possibly even able, to negotiate so many flights of stairs in order to reach the top.' Booth laughed at his own humour. 'And to have to do so sometimes several times a day. They are comfortable where they are.'

'Well, I shall be – '

'Of course you will, Mister Anthony, of course you will. There is another matter.'

'Yes?'

'When at some point next year Mister Philip leaves us to take up his new role, it is evident that he must cease the work which he has practised for these many years with such distinction. Within that work there is something of a, shall we say, delicate nature, in which you are concerned with him.'

Booth paused with an enquiring look to confirm that I was following him.

'Yes, quite. It is also a matter which has been concerning Mister Simon – '

'Simon Carlton?'

'Whom it has been my pleasure to meet on friendly terms on several occasions over the years, most recently this weekend, in fact. He is disposed, he wishes you to know – and he has consulted – to accept Mister Philip's recommendation that, upon his departure, you step forward in his place.'

Booth mistook my silence for lack of comprehension.

'To provide a discreet service, Mister Anthony. As the need arises.'

'But – ' and I went on to explain. I was still a junior, only now beginning to take on cases just about middling in the scale of things, I did not have the years of experience which, surely, were what was required and, most important of all, I did not feel confident enough in myself to –

'Nonsense! if I may say so, Mister Anthony. We must all begin from somewhere before we move on. It is not a question only of the starting-point, it is a question of how easily and well one can move on to where one is going.'

Booth leant back in his chair, appraising me with a steady gaze. And yet, where once that gaze would have challenged me, now it was approving of me. Then Booth smiled.

'Not to accept, Mister Anthony, would be to call in question the judgement of three wise men.'

Philip, Carlton, and himself? Or Philip, the Colonel, and one of the other two?

'Then I suppose, in that case – '

'By the by, I have not long since, just a few minutes before your arrival in fact, spoken with one of the wise men who would *very* much appreciate it if you would allow me to make an appointment on your behalf to meet up with him – at your *earliest* possible convenience. Say Tuesday afternoon at two o'clock? Curzon Street, as before. From your diary that would appear to be possible.'

Colonel Jackson. I agreed, and was rising from my chair. Booth reached out a hand, placed it on my forearm.

'On another by the by, Mister Anthony, did you know that your Great-Uncle Ranulph was himself of great service to the service in the post-war decades of – what is the shorthand? – the 'red menace'? Post-First World War we speak of, of course.'

I had not known that.

'And so you see, Mister Anthony, it is in the bloodline. You must take confidence from that.'

I was taken with an altogether different, and rather sideways thought. Mother would have approved of this man and I could see the two of them, an incongruous pairing, sharing with each other their prejudices on family and 'form', breeding and bloodline.

One of the three wise men bestowed on me a smile and a wave of departure as I left his room to ascend to my chamber.

On my desk had been placed a brief, red-ribboned and tied in a bow. It was not a new brief. It was a defence brief originally assigned to Philip Hathers but now sub-contracted, I suppose would be the term, to me. It was part of his clearing-out exercise prior to entering the judiciary. Inside I found, in his own neat, black handwriting, both summary and directive notes as to how to proceed, together with a suggestion that I meet with the defendant's solicitor in the next day or two. A case of considerable money owed for a long time, refusal to pay, a confrontation, words then fists, then one of those fists grasped around a heavy glass ashtray, blows, actual bodily harm. Defend the indefensible, unless one could show the accused was defending himself from physical assault by the injured party.

Tuesday afternoon I arrived at the box-like structure of offices in Curzon Street some minutes before two o'clock and was made to wait. Identity check completed, some minutes later I was taken up to the Colonel's office. The door to his office was open and he signalled me in. As I stepped into the room I saw Simon Carlton seated in an armchair pulled up to the edge of the Colonel's desk.

'Come in, come in!'

The Colonel pointed to another chair drawn up to the front of the desk.

'Glad you could join us, Anthony. Simon and I have just been having a bit of a prelim.'

Simon rose to shake my hand.

Greetings completed, the Colonel, elbows on desk, palms of hands together in an attitude of prayer, chin resting on the tips of his fingers, narrowed his eyes. For some time he did not speak while I, becoming somewhat uneasy at this delay, did not feel it my place to start. The meeting was, after all, at the invitation (or insistence) of the Colonel.

'Well, gentlemen, action deferred, as you know. But, as soon as Sir John's little bit of business is over with, you should know that we still intend to pursue our sinful MP. We may now be getting a little closer to him.'

Colonel Jackson beamed to each of us in turn. There was no doubting that there would be personal pleasure for him to succeed in the chase.

'Well?' The word was brusquely interrogative in tone and directed to me. 'What did our Mister Ward have to say to you on Sunday evening? Especially in the meeting adjourned to your apartment.'

I was stunned. How did – ? There was that familiar hint of a smile at the corners of the Colonel's lips.

'We weren't expecting him. Luckily, our Brussels office picked him up as he was sneaking in the back way. Simon here will make notes as you go along.'

I recovered as best I could and recounted the facts of the meeting, the Colonel looking blankly to one side of me as I proceeded. He interrupted me only once.

'Does the second tape also identify the date of that meeting?'

'Yes.'

At the end of my account the Colonel picked out of its cradle the handpiece from one of the three telephones on his desk.

'Tea now please. And some ginger nuts. We have some news to chew over.'

The merest hint of a wink intentionally betrayed him to me. But we sat on in silence for some minutes until a very smartly-dressed young woman pushed in a trolley loaded with tea things and a plate, decorated around its rim with yellow and red roses, piled with biscuits.

The Colonel himself poured tea for us and motioned to Simon and me to help ourselves to biscuits while he plunged the first of his into his cup, dipping it two or three times before taking the sodden half of the biscuit into his mouth.

'It's all in the timing, you know. If you're not to lose the thing into your drink. Awkward fishing about for the bits.'

There was some social chitchat while we drank tea and ate the biscuits – the weather, the sharpness of the last few days, the drudgery of having to start one's Christmas shopping soon. Then:

'Can we get this into court? Simon?'

'Transcripts, ahem, authenticated by expert technical confirmation that each tape is unadulterated, has not been, ahem, tampered with or edited in any way...'

Colonel Jackson drummed his fingers on the desk for a few seconds.

'But without hearing these tapes we can not even be certain whether the speech is indistinct... or where it simply fades into any background noise.' The Colonel looked from Simon to me.

'All I can say is that the parts of each recording played back to me were distinct enough. One could follow what each man said.'

'Which brings us, gentlemen, back to our Mister Arnold Ward.' The Colonel fingered his moustache. Looking again to me, he asked: 'Don't suppose there has been any change in his requirements, his demands?'

I shook my head.

'Pity we can't just get him to fall madly in love with some other pretty girl.' Pause. 'Sarah, for example. Now that would be *most* convenient.' Another pause, but fractional. 'Given that he's already married to her.'

Simon was clearly amused at the Colonel's alternative solution to the dilemma we faced if the crime of our targeted MP was to be brought into the public domain. It was not a solution I enjoyed contemplating. I did not want Sarah to be in love with Arnold, even if he were her husband in that marriage of deception. I wanted her to stay *out* of love until... The Colonel jerked me back from the start of a daydream.

'Then, gentlemen, we must leave things as they currently are. We have more time on our hands. As you know, I've agreed with Sir John that we will hold off. Until he has been able to execute his own plan for another of our Czechoslovakian friends. All I can say is that he's had this man in his sights for close on two years now. And if John can land him that will be a very significant achievement. Therefore, we don't want to get in each other's way, trip over each other in the same playground.'

He looked to each of us to see if either Simon or I had anything more to say.

'Very well, then. But as soon as possible, once we get the All Clear from Sir John, I want to be able to swing into action against our money-grubbing MP. Get him, and we shall frighten off the others.'

Simon and I both rose to leave. Colonel Jackson waved a palm downwards. Obedient as schoolboys we sat down again.

'And Anthony, a word to you. It is even more important now that you keep contact with our Mister Ward. You can tell him you have made a very full report. Which will take some time to evaluate. But tell him this new information does indeed significantly alter things.'

'Does that mean you *will* agree – '

'No, it does not. It means that he must *think* we are likely to. And after all, how do we know that this new love of his life is not an StB *femme fatale* who has been put his way by the opposition? The sweeter the girl the more one must suspect a honey trap. No? We shall find means of looking into that. For now, though, it is imperative, Anthony, that somehow you charm those tape-recordings out of Mister Arnold Ward's possession.'

I was about to object.

'We can not bow to blackmail. It is the man's *duty* to cooperate, as he has done in the past. Now it is *your* duty, Anthony, to keep him on board. On board, Anthony.'

That same evening, a call from Carolyne. I tried to stay in good humour. Good news: she was booked on a flight to return to London on Saturday. Daddy had already returned home, as I knew, but would be going out to Prague again later this week, before joining her in Berne, and once they had cleared the import and export papers they would both be free to leave the Berne office. I was puzzled.

'Oh Anthony, what do you know about business? If everything works out we shall be buying that beer from here, the one you and he seem to have taken to, and then we shall export it from here to England.'

'Seems a roundabout way of getting the stuff here. Two journeys.'

Carolyne laughed. 'Oh no, it will go direct from Prague to London.'

'Then why – ?'

'As I said to you, Anthony: what do you know about business?'

Anyway, the thing was, she was worried about me, all on my own for so long, so she had asked William to be sure to call on me when he got back to London.

'He will be on his way back tomorrow, early flight. Then, the poor dear, he will only have a couple of days before he has to set off to somewhere else.'

'Am I allowed to know where he's going?'

'I should really let him tell you himself. But if you promise to look ignorant when he does tell you – it's Prague. Some lectures there at Charles University before the end of term, you know, organised by the British Council.'

'Really?' The next best thing to saying nothing. I thought Sir John had said that William was to 'go the rounds' for some time yet before being sent out to Czechoslovakia in pursuit of that Dušan of the refined tastes. Perhaps there had been a decision to hasten things along. I wondered if Carolyne knew anything of the purpose of William's posting to Prague.

'The thing is, we shan't see him for some time, when he goes. I gather he will be staying over for the Christmas period at least – indefinitely, in fact, is the word he used. So he can't say when next we shall see him once he's gone.'

There was a pause which I was not quick enough to fill.

'Oh Anthony, I shall miss him. Won't you?'

'Well, yes, I suppose I shall.'

'So make the most of him when you do see him.'

'Do you know when that will be?'

'It's meant to be a surprise. Can't say more, sworn to secrecy.' There was the merest hint of a pause before Carolyne whispered, 'I do hope you haven't made any plans for tomorrow night.'

So much for Carolyne's ability to keep a secret. Carolyne herself simply *loved* surprises – as I've said, provided she knew in advance what they would be. But, I had to admit, Carolyne sounded more cheerful, more spirited, than for some time. The therapy had worked. And I almost forgot the draught of Doubt beneath the door. Almost.

'He does *so* want to see you, Anthony. Can I say that I've spoken to you and you will be free tomorrow night?'

Barely agreed to before verbal launch re-commenced. She would be back on Saturday. We would be able to have Sunday afternoon together – a boat trip! suggested with more enthusiasm than my acceptance of the proposal. Westminster to Greenwich for a late lunch, then back to my place, and a lazy evening, the two of us, and... an early night. This last offered in a tone of soft seductiveness clinched the arrangement.

'I shall be saying my goodbye to William tonight, and you can say farewell tomorrow night. Love and kisses.'

There was a whispered something else from Carolyne which I could not hear clearly, then the click of a receiver ending the call.

No, the door might have been closed and intimacy offered, but the draught beneath now blew stronger and chillier.

I saw Philip briefly just after lunch on the following day, Wednesday. He popped up to my room, head around the door, hand waving to me.

'Can't stop long, old chap. Managed to wangle a recess, question of new evidence. Admissibility. Judge has to have a look at it.' He sighed. 'Just hope the old duffer doesn't take too long at it, hoping to get away for the weekend, you know.'

He grinned at me as he leaned across my desk, resting a hand on my shoulder.

'Couldn't tell you earlier about, you know... was only confirmed that week – before you arrived. Sorry. Then out of chambers since, a couple of odd occasions only have managed to pop in. But you have been in and out too.'

His house party, his news, his translation sometime next year to the bench. All was understood. Philip pulled an armchair close to the side of my desk, simply raising his eyebrows as token request. He then reached into the breast pocket of his jacket, pulled out his pipe, laid it on the desk before him, and started – unusually for him – a two-handed rummage through other pockets for tobacco pouch and matches. To my surprise, and to my disappointment too I confess, he managed to lay out all three items.

'Sure you don't mind?'

'Of course not.'

We sat on until Philip had filled and lighted his pipe and it was glowing satisfactorily, plumes of grey-blue smoke making moving swirls against the ceiling.

'Gather Booth has spoken to you about your inheritance?'

'Your room, you mean?'

Philip nodded, contentedly exhaling a thin trickle of smoke from the corner of his mouth.

'Best chamber in the building.'

'Yes but shouldn't it be offered – ?'

'Has been. Too many stairs to climb.'

As Booth had said. I laughed at Philip's comical gesture, shoulders hunched, hands in front of him, fingers pointing downwards, miming the slow and painful climbing of the stairs.

'And in your case, old chap, it comes with something very special, a little treasure.'

'And that is?'

Philip grinned widely, just catching his pipe as it fell out of the corner of his mouth.

'The coffee pot. I intend to bequest it to you with the room.'

I was about to say, 'What, that old – ' when Philip held up a hand.

'It is, of course, not just any old enamel coffee pot.' Philip made one of those dramatic pauses he employed to such good effect in court. 'It is the very same enamelled pot your Great-Uncle Ranulph took through the trenches of the First World War. In fact he came by it in France.'

'Really?'

'He shouldn't have been there at all – didn't have to be, volunteered, but...' Philip spread his hands. 'Found it in a shelled-out kitchen of a house outside Arras.'

When I thought of that enamel pot in Philip's room I could believe easily its origin: once white, with blue banding, a domed lid with a decided dent in it, the porcelain chipped from various parts of the body, the base browned from innumerable hours of flames beneath it. There was silent history in that pot.

'It should come to you, Anthony. Makes the best coffee this side of Temple Bar.'

The bequest raised questions.

'I had not realised that you knew my Great-Uncle Ranulph.'

'Oh indeed. Last thing he did here was to see me through my pupillage.' Philip saw my look of surprise but contrived to suppress his smile. 'Ahh... did I forget to mention that to you?'

I shook my head in disbelief. 'Philip, you have forgotten to mention it to me every year since I first arrived in these chambers.'

'So I have. Guilty as charged.'

Philip slapped the top of my desk in sheer delight as he swayed with laughter. Then he explained, or excused, himself.

'It's very important, especially when one is just starting out, that your achievements are your own, that you have the opportunity to show your own mettle. It might be that family connections predisposed one to want to think well of you.' He had that serious, asseverative look. 'But a family name alone is not proof of quality, though, only of pedigree. You still have to do your own barking.'

Slowly, almost ceremonially, Philip rose and held out his hand to me. I responded in like fashion.

'And that, Anthony, you have done. I am delighted – not least because I can hand on to safe hands. Some things don't go well with being a judge.' He pulled a face, mock-solemn, jaw dropped, head tilted downwards a little.

Philip moved away towards the door.

'Philip, just now you said 'family connections', plural. But as far as I know there's only ever been Great-Uncle Ranulph in the legal – '

Philip raised a hand and stopped at the door. Turning about, he left his parting shot.

'I meant your father who, if you didn't know, also spent some of *his* wartime in Military Intelligence.'

Father, beyond muttering 'Oh, you know, this and that, as we all did' when asked about his war years, had certainly not mentioned anything of the kind to me.

This brief encounter with Philip unsettled me. I wanted to believe that so far as I had achieved anything, a qualified barrister now of some growing experience, with a promising future – about which I was beginning to feel more sure – I had succeeded through my own efforts, application, and qualities of personality and temperament which suited me to this career. Thus Philip's words discomfited me. There was a family name, after all, and an uncommon one. Within that family of Ashley-Chetwynes there had been Great-Uncle Ranulph, his career, his achievements, and his bequest that had put me in a direct line to my present occupancy within his own former chambers. Here was his former pupil, Philip, who had then taken me under his wing... And now, there was some sort of unwitting and unspoken commendation coming from my father's past. Was it this conjunction of circumstances which had put me in line to inherit a position where I could be of service to the service? In however minor a fashion.

31

When I left chambers at the end of that day it was a dark, wet, cold, mid-November early evening. Upon unlocking the door to my flat, I found on the doormat a small white envelope. A glance at my name inscribed on the envelope told me that this was the posting of William I had been half-expecting, following Carolyne's alert.

I poured myself a small port and opened the envelope. Inside, on a long thin card, shaped as a bookmark, and written in William's own hand was a title and an inscription:

The Cruelty of Ladies

...a man must be
imprudent indeed
to let his Passion
take very deep root,
when he has no Reason
to expect any sort
of Return to it.
W.W. 1692

There was also a note.

My Dear Anthony,

How sadly true. Given such words as are found as Preface, what can follow? It forbids a future. Without ado and further expla-nation, I would very much welcome your company this evening. I shall telephone you at seven tonight and, should you have kept the evening free, I shall welcome your company in helping an old friend to drown his sorrows. If further persuasion is required, I do still owe you that promised dinner.

Yours,

William

Was I meant to be teased again? The announced call duly came, William affecting his habitual *ennui*. I was determined to preserve calmness when we would meet later, neither to reveal nor challenge – but to *powder, keep, one's, dry*, but not in that order.

A couple of hours later we met up where he waited for me at the Underground exit of Leicester Square. After a brief and vigorous handshake, William strode us on for the minutes it took to arrive at his chosen hostelry hidden away on a corner of Dean Street. There was, I noted to my quiet amusement, no sign of a limp – in either of William's legs. The walking stick flailed its movements even faster than usual, barely touching the pavement to William's stride. Arrived, William headed for the small downstairs bar.

'Whisky.'

Neither question nor command, whisky was a statement of fact which duly arrived at the bar for us.

I raised my glass. 'Congratulations, William. It is wonderful news, your fellowship.'

William pulled a face, shrugging his shoulders at the same time. 'There is worse, my friend.'

'And that is?'

'The monograph, due early next year, that will faintly amuse and entertain the two-score persons whom one might expect to take a professional interest in the thing.' Now William raised his glass. 'In all its splendour, I give you *The Cultivation of Refinement in Minor English Poetry of the Late Seventeenth and Early Eighteenth Centuries.*'

At which he drained his whisky, turned away from me, and signalled at the bar.

'And again.'

With the second of our whiskies we found a table in the corner of the small bar.

'But congratulations, William. That's wonderful. I am so pleased for you.'

William acknowledged with a small sideways tilt of his head. 'Carolyne sends her love.'

To my instant satisfaction I found the dissimulation came easily. 'How is she? Is she better for that stay in Switzerland, would you say? I mean, she *sounds* better on the 'phone now.'

William smiled, his dark eyes half lowered.

'She was in the pink when I left her, old chap.'

When he looked up, the dark pools of his eyes were expressionless.

'But you will see for yourself at the weekend.'

'Thank you for looking after her, William. I'm sure bumping into you out there was a real fillip for her. She was very down when she went out there, you know.' Shamefully, I found the pretence of naïvety easier and easier to sustain.

'I know. I do know. Carolyne and I talked.'

The familiar languor, the effete affectation that was William was somewhat toned, not missing, but a little subdued.

William lifted his head, a gesture to the upstairs restaurant.

'I have taken leave to book us in here for dinner. My treat. I did promise.'

The sommelier's presentation of the *Châteauneuf* to our dining table suggested that William did not intend to economise on this treat, though the burgundy seemed to empty rather speedily. William appeared to be in a rush at everything this night, something at odds with his habitual languid air. A small circular movement of an upraised forefinger produced another bottle of the wine before even our main course had been served.

'You are certainly setting about drowning your sorrows in some style, my friend. And while I am perfectly willing to lend you assistance in this task, the principle of *quid pro quo* suggests that it might be of assistance to *me* in this task if you could define, or, at a minimum, point in the direction of those sorrows whose burden we are to alleviate by casting ourselves adrift in a sea of alcohol.'

My pomposity of mock-William address to William produced the slightest of smiles. He ran his spread fingers down his goatee beard.

'Anthony...' There was more stroking of his beard. 'You deserve to know. You are entitled to know.'

I waited for the explanation. And was kept waiting by the arrival of our dishes, by distractions as to the quality of the meal – William was insistent that I enjoyed the food and find it first-rate – and by trivial comment and question on all manner of inconsequentialities. I began to think that William was regretting the offer to take me into his confidence.

He waited until our empty plates had been taken away. Abruptly, he clinked his glass against mine.

'I am in love.'

William could not have made a more unexpected confession. William's dandyism, since first meeting him those years ago in the street outside our college in Oxford, had always suggested to me that he was far too absorbed with himself – with how he looked to himself, with how he thought of himself – to submit himself in love with someone else.

I gestured helplessly, and began on several different sounds, none of which made recognisable words. William simply laughed, but it was a grim, tight-lipped laugh.

'I know, I know, old friend. It's simply unimaginable, wouldn't you say? *Me.*'

There was something accusative in his tone as if he knew exactly what I had thought and was challenging me to make denial.

'Am I to offer you my congratulations?'

William rested the side of his head along the extended index finger of the hand that cupped his chin.

'That would be imprudent indeed.'

I caught the echo of W.W's words.

'Am I to take it then that this love is one of unrequited passion?'

With thumb and forefinger he drew to each side of his finely clipped moustache and downward until they met again at the point of his black goatee beard. He lifted his hands, palms up, as if in supplication. Very quietly, and slowly, he responded.

'The passion, my dear friend *is* requited, *has been* requited, but the love – ah, the love – must be refused. It is futureless.'

William lifted his head to stare at me until I was a little uncomfortable with that prolonged attention. His eyes appeared once more black, bottomless pools, where light was absorbed, sucked down without reflection. More than those dark eyes, however, I was struck by William's countenance: the whole of the man bespoke a great unhappiness. I was moved at this apprehension; and, to be truthful, a little unnerved that he was so uncharacteristically changed. This was not the William I knew, had known.

With a physical effort he drew himself together, sat upright, lifted his glass once more, and forced a grimace.

'Enough! or too much.' William raised an interrogative eyebrow. 'Another William. Blake, this time. One defines the other – one can not know the limit of enough without venturing too far.' He paused. 'And so, since I have not yet had enough, let us venture more.'

The subject of William's love, requited or unrequited, simply dissolved away. I had never known William consume such quantities of alcohol and be so seemingly unaffected by it. More than an hour later, memories of my drinking session with Arnold Ward flashing warning lights to me, William appeared to be stone cold sober. At least, in my mellowing state, he seemed to be fully in control of himself.

'Ah!' I remember the moment with clarity when this gasp of a monosyllable came to my rescue, enabling me to get a grip on the rest of that evening. 'I learned an interesting thing about you, William. Actually more than one.' At which point I paused. 'Billy. Billy Wall.'

I had not thought ahead to what William's reaction might be to me knowing this fraction of his past from before we first knew each other. I was surprised though that he showed no surprise.

'The Colonel?'

I nodded.

'Well, my dear fellow, I suppose he had to know what you knew, or did not know, about me, and there is no reason now why you should not know what he knew. We are, after all, both on the same side.'

I stammered something to the effect that learning this about him, where previously one had not known, somehow put him in a rather different light. He became someone else, someone whom one did not know.

William held up a hand.

'You had only to ask. We were together for three years at Oxford, Anthony, and I counted you – still do count you – a friend. Had you asked, I would have told you. But you did not ask.'

It was true. Flushed with whiskies and red wine perhaps neither my embarrassment nor shame actually showed.

'I would have told you, Anthony. It was by then immaterial in any case. Billy Wall had served his turn.'

I uttered some kind of feeble defence: I mean, naturally, I, we, well, we had simply assumed, being there all together, that –

'That I was the same? That I came from the same background of wealth and privilege?'

I could not argue both *pro* and *contra*. My defence had already admitted William's charge. I nodded.

'Only, of course, not a status so elevated as that which you and your group occupied. Hence you were able to patronise me by adopting me as your very own performing pet creature.'

Remarkably, there was neither anger nor rancour in his tone; though there was additional embarrassment in the facts that he had so clearly seen our own unacknowledged motivations. But something had been cleared away between us. William was open in a way I had not seen him before, his language less expansive.

'Well, my dear friend, I permitted myself to be petted, and submitted to the patronage.' His long, bony fingers ran over his trimmed beard. 'There were some good times. There were some very good times.'

I made one attempt to suggest that his manner, his appearance, his whole presentation had called out for attention, and that was what had attracted us to him in the first place.

'It was my two-finger salute to the world.'

There was a silence. A challenge of some kind had been tossed onto the table.

'You were going to explain Billy Wall to me.'

'Was I?' William's eyes glinted momentarily. 'Billy Wall, my dear fellow, is going to take another bottle of *Châteauneuf* to explain.'

'I am in no hurry, and the wine is splendid.'

William waited until the wine arrived and we had chinked glasses together.

'I am a Westphalian Jew, Anthony. You know the history of Westphalia?'

I shook my head.

'A kingdom, a short-lived kingdom, just a few years, *but* in 1808 a law was passed there granting Jewish males equal rights with other males.'

William tuned those dark, absorbent eyes upon me.

'Imagine that, Anthony. A kingdom where Jews were equal and treated equally.'

There was both irony and great sadness in his voice.

'Of course it did not last long, things had reverted many scores of years before I came along. I was named Wilhelm, my family name Wallzenstein, and the place of my birth is Telgte, on the river Ems. The map tells me that the town is some seven or eight miles east of Münster, but I have no memory of my birthplace and no desire to see it.'

I was about to say that I would have thought that naturally one would want to visit –

'There is nothing there for me, Anthony. There is no-one.'

A small silence again, but now I felt no compunction to think of anything to say. As William's narrative progressed, these silences marked the divisions between sections – the shortened versions of several chapters of his life.

'My family migrated there from Beckum, where there had been a settlement of Jews, never large in numbers, since the early part of the nineteenth century. By no means a long migration for Jews – it can be no more than twenty or so miles from Beckum to Telgte. My grandfather made the move with his family. He was a pharmacist, as my father, his eldest son, became. And there they lived peacefully and, according to my mother, were respected in their neighbourhood. So much so, that a good many residents in that quarter of town would consult my father before consulting their doctor. Of course' – William allowed himself an ironic smile – 'my father was cheaper than the doctors.'

William sat back in his seat, deliberating with himself how to begin a new phase of his story.

'You know of *Kristallnacht*, of course?'

I nodded. Even I knew of the events of *Kristallnacht:* the state-inspired smashing of Jewish homes, shops, businesses, synagogues, throughout Germany by brownshirts and civilians; the looting and burning; the thousands of Jewish men arrested and sent off to concentration camps...

William must have thought I was struggling for the facts of the matter.

'Ninth of November, 1938.'

As soon as said, I realised. 'Twenty-seven years ago this night.'

With a mere flick of a wrist William acknowledged.

'Well, that terror of November 1938 did not begin that night, or that year. The persecution of the Jews is an ancient pastime for many nations, but for the Germany of that decade it began again with *Die Juden sind unser Unglück.*'

William looked up, saw my lack of comprehension.

'The Jews are our bad luck. Misfortune. Calamity. Disaster. *Unglück* can be all of those.'

From their home in Telgte William's mother and father kept their weather-eye on Beckum where they still maintained friends of the family. The terror campaign against the Jews had started early at Beckum, it seemed, several years before comparable out-rages against the Jews in most other parts of Germany. William's father began to have nightmarish forebodings of events to come. These woke him and kept him awake for nights on end. By the time William was eighteen months old, his father had decided: 'We must leave. We must move. We can not stay here.'

William's father put his plans into action. There were distant re-lations of the family in Holland. He would send his wife and son to them, in Amsterdam. They would be two of the tens of thousands of German Jews who made their way into the Netherlands in the decade that ended with the start of World War II. From Amsterdam mother and son would arrange a crossing to England – at which point of arrival, apparently, the plans became more vague. Once ar-rived, the mother was to make contact with any Jewish organisations which would organise, or enable her to seek, a settlement, wherever that would prove to be. Notified of the place, William's father would later follow when he judged it best. The father's own parents and his wife's widowed mother, however, absolutely refused to make the journey. 'We are too old,' they said, 'for anybody to trouble us. We are not a threat to anyone. They will leave us alone.'

William's father had another reason for delaying his own de-parture. What funds he had been able to raise had been forward-ed to Amsterdam, for transfer when his wife had settled on ac-commodation in England. With her went also a volume of cash sufficient for immediate needs. He needed time, however, quietly to convert to cash his remaining goods and assets, and to do this little by little while his wife, to neighbours' inquiries, was 'visiting relatives in Holland.'

'So, in nineteen thirty-seven, mother and infant son arrived in England. In the year after that sums of money arrived in Amsterdam and were duly transferred to my mother's account here. Then, the year after that, came *Kristallnacht.*'

I had never before seen William look distressed.

'So, you see, my father was right. His nightmares came true.'

William bowed forward, forehead held in the palm of a hand, elbow propped on the table. There were little sideways movements of his body. I was at a loss. After a time, half a minute perhaps, he raised his head and dabbed a handkerchief to his eyes.

'Sorry about that, old fellow. Not used to talking about these things.'

'I am privileged that you feel able to tell me.' Fortunately, William was able to take the sentiment, which was genuine, from the stiffness of the language.

'Then, nothing.'

From that night of smashed glass and broken bodies his mother had heard no more from her husband, from their remaining parents, from their relatives. Complete silence. Unbearable silence, unbroached absence. No trace of any of them then or since. Gone. Nobody knew. Or nobody told.

'Mother tried, of course. For years she tried, she tried every avenue one could think of. And when I was old enough I tried too. Many times.'

In my life until then I had had no access into personal grief of this order; nor, indeed, had I ever been so close to anyone who had suffered any kind of comparable tragedy. I had escaped such suffering. To fill the absence of anything worthwhile occurring to me to say I poured out the last of the wine into our glasses. I managed also to catch the eye of one of the waiters.

'Coffees, please. And cognac.'

I wanted to know anything else William wanted me to know. For the first time I really wanted to *know* William.

'So, my dear Anthony, there you have it. Mother with three year-old son, newly-arrived in this country and trying to make a life for us. She did well, she did remarkably well. Our one consolation was that we had money, enough money, not to live lavishly, but to live sufficiently.'

William brusquely added a few more facts to his story.

His mother had taken the step of anglicizing his name: William for Wilhelm, and Wall as a contraction of Wallzenstein. His mother, Analise, from the moment of arrival to these shores, had simply adopted Anna as the name by which she would be known. She was desperate to make them appear less conspicuous – in order to merge into another life.

'Though of course Mother's English was very limited and heavily accented. Mine, to begin with, of course, was non-existent. But the people from the association were very kind, and we settled, perhaps reluctantly accepted in the community, but more willingly accepted as our story became known and as the events on mainland Europe unfolded into war.'

At the end of the war the mother applied for and was given British naturalisation: she became officially Mrs Anna Wall, and he became officially William Wall.

A pensive silence.

I drained my wine, seeing the waiter approach with coffee and cognac.

'And Walsh? Where did that come from?'

William set his lips in a straight line.

'It came from me. After mother died, after I had finished my National Service.' William looked up at me. 'She died because of the sheer pointlessness of it all. Of life. Of living when one is denied one's life.' He gathered himself, sat straighter in his chair. 'But, she saw me through to manhood.'

William took a careful sip of coffee followed by one of cognac.

'I had no choice, as I saw it. To live, I had to get a life. I had to have an identity, a change of name – and then begin to live *into* that name. Create a life to go with it. *Verstehst du?*'

'William, I am so sorry. And so ashamed that I did not show a proper interest in you those years ago – '

William backhanded away my apology.

'It is of no matter. I had your company, the company of you all.' Suddenly, leaning back in his chair, he gave a curt laugh. 'Does one play with one's pet? or does one's pet, in asking to be played with, control its masters? What think you, Anthony?'

During that evening, prolonged with more coffees and more co-gnacs, I developed a very real affection for William. Among all the truths, the half-truths, the theories, the beliefs and prejudices we hold of human consciousness – and at the risk of repeating myself – this is certain: it is indeed highly soluble in alcohol. I did remember, though, to prompt him with a repeat of an earlier question.

'Ah, Walsh. Yes, I shall explain.'

After his mother's death William came into possession of a small terraced house, and sufficient income for him to finance an extended period of leisure. In the event he devoted three years to study – 'to catch up on what I had missed' – as he modestly put it, and in the final of those years applying for and obtaining, against his expectation, an Oxford scholarship. That made him unique among the rest of us, the group, though we had not known it. And he was way ahead of all of us as individuals, and probably collectively too. He decided, for the imbroglio of reasons he had already given me, that he would go to Oxford as a new man, with a new name. He decided to take Walz from the family name Wallzenstein which, anglicising the pronunciation of its first let-ter (from its German 'v' sound to 'w') Walz became something very close to Walsh. So that was a possibility. It became an im-perative of choice when, in his studies, he came across the seven-teenth-century William Walsh.

'A cultivated dilettante, my dear Anthony. I had my name and my identity in one. It was irresistible.'

Thus William, impelled by a conviction of fate in this discovery, had set about creating his own W.W..

'It fitted, you see, like slipping on a well-made suit.'

He described an elaborate curlicue in the air with a raised hand and forearm, a characteristic gesture of his invented dandy I had seen on innumerable occasions in our Oxford past.

'And now, it seems, for the common weal I am obliged to continue to wear it for some time to come.'

He laid a forefinger across his lips.

'Can't say more.'

'I know. You are a state secret.'

William and I convulsed into unrestrained laughter.

'Seriously though – '

There had been something else which I wanted to move on to, but I simply set us both off again. It was that character of laughter which, having detached itself from its prime cause, can then be set off by any prompt, however irrelevant. A bit like the way skin sensitised by tickling responds to all touch.

But the something which had puzzled me from those Oxford days still nagged away. As we recovered composure, so the topic came back to me. I asked William about all those times when he seemed to be missing; unseen by anyone, and then, out of the blue, he would be back among us.

'Old Smokey.'

William had to unroll that one for me. Our College Principal, a former war-time member of the service – so I then learned – and now rendering the function of spotting likely recruits, had been tipped off by the Colonel's section about William. Observe closely, make independent evaluation, and if judged sound, repeat the invitation already tendered to William during his Billy Wall days – within a nutshell that, or something similar, must have been the watching brief given to our Principal.

By the time Old Smokey himself had got around to invit-ing William to throw in his lot, William was set against the idea. William Walsh was to be a scholar and set to seek an academic position in pursuit of his sole ambition. His reluctance was met by a succession of invitations to informal meetings with the old fag himself.

'He took to me, as one might say.'

Gradually William's defence was worn away – 'bored away' were William's own words to describe our Principal's unceasing determination to seduce William into making the right decision. To his great amusement, William told me that as one of his in-ducements, the old boy had actually offered himself to William –

'As if that would have been the clincher. I mean, how could one possibly refuse?' William's laughter was curt, dismissive.

Appeals to nationalism also meant nothing to William. The actual clincher, Sir Patrick offering himself this time only as an example, and what persuaded William to reconsider, was the simple argument that the academic pursuit and a limited period of service, several years at most, were not incompatible. What persuaded him to accept was the assurance, a 'promise' as near as could be given, that recruitment to the one would actually ad-vance his progress in the other. If only William committed him-self, options could be explored. Things – that ubiquitously useful but indefinite word – could be arranged.

'So here I am, my dear, an itinerant salesman of English lit-erature on behalf of the nation. Keeping eyes and ears open, of course, wherever I may be sent to impress the locals.'

William, brightly and carelessly, told me he would be off the very next day to be briefed; and then, within a day or two, he would be leaving for Prague – as I knew from Carolyne. We would keep in touch of course. I could expect the odd postcard or two.

We shook hands on leaving the restaurant while we each awaited a taxi for our separate homeward trips. That November night seemed particularly cold after the warmth of the restaurant. It was also one of those nights when there is wetness hanging in the air, changing the quality of the lighting around, diffusing and refracting its various glares. I was filled with a sadness for William – 'if only I had known' ran through my head as a threnody; it was a remorse heavy with guilt and self-reproach. It was my own fault entirely that I had not known at all the man. I suppose it was a plea to the injured to assuage the guilty, to provide some assurance, some forgiveness that made me say what I did to William as we parted:

'But there *were* good times, William? I mean, we *did* all get on well together, didn't we?'

'Indeed.'

'And the girls took to you as well, so...' The thought died in its own breath. I did not know how to make recompense for the man's wounds.

In a reverse of my first sighting of him, fluidly rising out of the taxi at the gate of our Oxford college, he now entered the back of a cab, a wave of motion, of legs and body following. With one hand on the inside handle of the door, holding it open, his other hand held that familiar black fedora which he levelled onto his head as soon as seated. As he was closing the door, he called out to me.

'Yes indeed. Lovely girls. Jollied every one of them.'

He pulled the cab door shut and the taxi made off towards the traffic of Shaftesbury. In the back seat he half-turned towards me, lifting his hat in a goodnight salute.

SIX

Ravellings

London and Buckinghamshire

End 1965 – Summer 1966

32

Questions. My trade, to ask questions. My talent, if talent it may be called, was to become an expert practitioner of the art of questioning; for which the service in the years succeeding to now found occasional employment. There were persons to be questioned; persons to be cross-questioned. I learned to use silence; I learned to detect lies when someone talked too much in an attempt to persuade me; I learned that knowing something of persons, howsoever small a fact which they thought unknown, when revealed at the right moment, tricked them into suspecting I knew much more that was secret; I learned to imply, not state; I learned that the order of questions could be more important than each question on its own; I learned the forms of hesitation; I recognised changes in the tone of voice, or its pace; I saw small tremors thought concealed; I learned to watch a person's hands; I learned to be devious and patient, to follow the by-ways of a roundabout route... but the questions in my head which I had taken to that meeting with William were of a different, and entirely personal, order. They had arisen, unbidden, lacking distinct form. They took the sensation – the nearest analogy I can think of – of an anxiety that was bodily. After that telephone call from Carolyne, and after my last sight of William disappearing into the late-night traffic of Shaftesbury Avenue's theatreland, the anxiety settled to an irritating, permanent sensation. Then his final words: *Jollied every one of them.*

No more questions, your Honour.

Even so, the absurdity of it all began to spin its own traceries as soon as I turned away from that disappearing taxi to await my own carriage. Not *every* one of those girls, surely not – a refusal to believe tinged with its own jealousy. I mean, *William*, the William of those Oxford years who had no interest in girls in that way. It was ridiculous. That, however, was the William we took him for, entrusting our girls to him... and that included Carolyne. Now William was in love. And Carolyne had woven me improbable excuses and taken absences from me.

Truth may be known, but there can still be resistance to accepting it. I had encountered that night a very different William. He had acquired a different identity and he had also a real, not presumed, history. He was to me now someone else. It would take time to reconstitute him in that new likeness. William had become a lothario, *unless* – the sliver of an unconvincing alternative – he had lied.

For and against, to and fro, the more I told myself to forget all these stirrings, the more disquieting became my confusion. By the time I got home well past midnight I was wide awake and sobering by the minute. A shaming admission, but seeping through all the tangled thoughts of those Oxford years past and another past starting just a few weeks ago, was the beginnings of a relieving consolation. I had reached the end of the beginning with Carolyne. Perhaps. Love was not unconditional.

Even as I threw myself onto the bed, I knew that the possibility of sleep had retreated to a remote corner of my brain, my mind being otherwise engaged. Then, and in aftertimes, I have sometimes thought that there are thoughts which have their independence of the thinker; they attain a life of their own and are no longer possessed by the thinker. They go their own sweet or sour way, making their own connections, colliding with other thoughts. Thoughts that trigger memories.

Memories that trigger memories, discovering the myriad of them unattended to that had passed by in their own past times. Memories that change the nature of past occasions to make them other than as one had lived them in their time. Even memories can adopt new identities.

After several hours attempting sleep I got up. One of those unbidden thoughts would not be dismissed. On an undeniable impulse I riffled through the untidy wedges of papers on my desk. Somewhere were those letters from William. There were words which, re-read, were stripped now of their innocence. There they were, in their naked duplicity. They were there in the first of his letters to me after we had met up again at my chambers, hoping to see Carolyne soon *when she has nothing on and nothing to do.* The second, following the evening when I had first met with Arnold Ward: *it was, of course, a great pleasure to entertain Carolyne in your absence.* In that set of mind, as I was by then, the merest commonplace of language became an imputation. More – a condemnation. William's own words as he spoke with me from Berne where he found Carolyne *in the flesh.* And just last night, when I had asked him how Carolyne was: *She was in the pink when I left her, old chap.*

Fool! It was all there. Wasn't it? Yet, perversely, my mind still insisted on putting the case for the defence.

Were not those also pure William? Was it not possible that they were no more than the curlicues of those elaborate hand gestures of his? Airy nothings?

Were they?

What was it that defined coincidence?

> *... an event or circumstance occurring in conjunction, or synchro-nously, with another event or circumstance....*

And what was it that had impelled me to look up the word on that earlier occasion? Something acted on, though imperfectly understood; not even that, something vaguer, the lingering af-ter-effect of a scent, a smell, a few molecules changing the char-acter of the air one breathed. Was that the moment when some-thing swept in with the draught under the door? The whiff of something, to give it its ordinary name, of Doubt.

> *...in such a manner as to suggest a connection of cause and effect...*

No, no, not coincidence; consider Carolyne's and William's appearance at the same time in the same location. Contrivance. That dinner they had shared when I had my first meeting with Arnold; her late arrival the following morning to rouse me from my drunken stupor; her head in her hands, the tears, on our drive to her parents; William's fortuitous 'turning-up' in Berne where Carolyne had gone for the clear air and the refreshment of her spirits. And, and, and... The draught that whistled under the door turned to a roar that threatened to crash in the door itself. And other events, so many of them, in the retrospective of Doubt could be viewed alternatively, even as far back as...

As when?

Fool! Had not William already made admission, revealing this other self?

Ah! My own long-drawn inbreath. William and Carolyne had deceived me. Nothing else matched the circumstances. Doubt hardened to unquestionable certainly as the light of dawn broke through the partly-drawn curtains of my room.

William was in love. He had said so just a few hours ago.

He was in love with the woman I was presumed to be in love with.

Doubt, at last, had blown away any lingering misgivings.

Booth greeted me at chambers a few hours later that morning.

'Good morning, Mister Anthony. I shall not ask how you are. I can see you are looking a little peaky.'

I grunted.

'Would Mister Anthony like a coffee? Perhaps if I may make you one of Mister Philip's brew? – as black as the inside of a coal scuttle.'

'Thank you Booth.'

The purpose behind Booth's waylaying of me that morning soon became clear. He had arranged an afternoon meeting for me with Carlton –

'The purpose of which?'

'I could not possibly say, Mister Anthony. I do not enquire to know more than is needful for me to act in my rôle as go-between and manager of diaries.'

Booth doing his pompous best, tempered with evident amusement at his own pretence. Yet somehow there persisted in his words the implication that he knew very much more than was absolutely needful. I was struck with a sudden realisation; or, rather, a realisation which I had suppressed for weeks suddenly surfaced.

'Booth, may I ask: were you ever – as the expression is – of service to the service?'

The man tilted his head downwards and sideways. There was a suppressed smile and a look of indulgence.

'Only in a manner of speaking did I have that honour. At the end of the war years for just short of two years. Clearing up operations as one might say. Army Intelligence. Germany, Berlin. A very great deal of filing, checking and cross-checking, tracking down, confirming identities, that sort of thing.'

'Ahh.' An understanding filled out. 'And did you, by any chance, work at any time with Colonel Jackson?'

'I had that honour too, Mister Anthony.'

At that Booth's face creased into such a broad smile that he showed his top teeth.

'I was wondering when you would ask.'

I looked him directly in the eyes, trying to embarrass an explanation from him. He simply held my gaze.

'But when Colonel Jackson called here, all those months ago, why the pretence? – acting as though you didn't know him.'

'That simply wouldn't have done, Mister Anthony, now would it? – if you had known that the Colonel and I were acquainted.' The tone was of the schoolmaster rebuking the errant child who had failed to see what was immediately and blatantly in front of his eyes. 'It might have made for difficulties – Colonel Jackson had to be free to make his own first impression of you, and you might later have suspected me of relaying matters about you to him. You do see that, of course?'

'Well, yes, but why all that play-acting when you served the tea to us? – all that 'umble servant routine, and glaring daggers at me.'

Booth broke into unrestrained and loud laughter. His words still punctuated by the last of his mirth, he added:

'For your eyes only, Mister Anthony. I could not let you know that the Colonel and I knew each other, but on the other hand I wanted the Colonel to know that, as at all times in the past, it was an honour to be of service to him – in however a 'umble way, taking his coat, serving him tea. I have the highest regard for him as a soldier and as a man.'

With a raising of his eyebrows and a glance at my empty cup, Booth inquired if I wanted more coffee. Not quite as ferocious as Philip's concoction in what I now knew was once my Great-Uncle Ranulph's coffee pot, even so Booth's brew that morning was powerfully strong.

As he poured, Booth spoke quietly.

'You may say these are favoured chambers, Mister Anthony. Here *particular* services may be requested and confidences honoured. You meet Simon Carlton at three. His place.'

Dutifully then I arrived at the Home Department that afternoon where, the formality of an identity check done, I was led up to Simon Carlton's office. We exchanged greetings. Simon telephoned for tea and cake to be brought to his room.

'Must admit to a weakness for cake. Much prefer it to, ahem, biscuits. Fruit cake alright with you?'

There was some small talk between us.

'And how is, ahem, your fiancée – Carolyne, isn't it?'

I was taken aback that he knew. Simon registered my reaction.

'Someone must have mentioned her when we were, ahem, guests of the Hathers.'

Carolyne was now an out-of-bounds topic with me. I diverted. I asked about him, and he surprised me with his answer. His wife and three children were well.

'Three girls. Eleven, nine, and, ahem, five.'

Yes, they were all happily settled in Ewell. No, they both – he and his wife – had agreed that he should not mix business with his family; hence his wife – Grace by name, grace by, ahem, nature – did not appear at the occasional gatherings such as the one at the Hathers' place.

Tea and slices of fruit cake arrived.

Simon made dumb show that we would talk after we had eaten the cake. After appreciatively running his tongue over his lips, Simon began.

'I thought it might be helpful, Anthony, if we were to have this informal get-together just to ensure that we, ahem, share the same view of things.' An afterthought: 'And the same understanding, given Philip's impending, ahem, withdrawal, leaving you holding the brief, as it were.'

The first of these understandings, unconfirmed of course, but seemingly issuing from Sir John Holyoake's 'side of things', was that, all going well and with a fair wind, 'they' hoped to have brought their task to the point where, sometime into next year, 'we' would be able to proceed against our deviant MP.

'Right hand, left hand.'

'Indeed.' Simon nodded. 'They have their own, ahem, quarry to pursue – and it is all a question of timing. Who goes first. You know all that.' Even so the Colonel was still definitely decided on proceeding against the MP – 'Still absolutely in his sights. Even more determined, if that were possible. And there's a new report, coming from, ahem, inside the Ministry itself, suggesting that the Cabinet Minister mentioned in the files 'is getting in deeper' and, without intervention, serious and irremediable damage might ensue – '

From *inside* the Ministry. I fastened onto that phrase and for a moment was seeing once more Sarah's drowning pools of light blue eyes.

' – and so to that end, Sir John has agreed to try a rather shorter game than he had originally planned in order to, ahem, 'clear the field', as it were, so that we might proceed with our action at home.'

Simon spread his hands wide, inviting response.

'This new report. Does it contain actual *evidence*, or is it more in the nature of an impression?'

'Impression – at present, perhaps evidenced later. Ahem, perhaps. Meanwhile we have Arnold Ward's tapes as potential prime evidence. They are authentic, you have no doubt?'

'None whatsoever.'

'Then let us assume that they meet all, ahem, technical requirements.'

In the silence which ensued, Simon tilted his head backwards, his neck stretched and his eyes gazing at the ceiling.

'We need both the tapes and Mister Ward himself. I think we are both, ahem, decided on that?'

I confirmed.

Elbows propped on his desk, the fingers of his hands laced together, Simon quietly summarised.

'Simple enough. We must have the tapes and Mister Ward must have his, ahem, damsel.'

But the Colonel was not easily persuaded out of a decision once made. Additionally he clearly did not take kindly to pressure of any sort being applied to him, least of all anything that might attempt to hold him to ransom or to blackmail him. Simon, however, believed that Colonel Jackson would, *eventually*, agree to Arnold's ultimatum – tapes for the lady – since there could arise other 'considerations,' as he put it; the emergence of a 'subtle but unignorable pressure' from 'elsewhere.' So saying Simon rolled his eyes upwards to suggest 'elsewhere' was somewhere 'above' –

presumably within the Home Department itself, and presumably also, a higher region in which he had full confidence and trust.

Sadly, it was his experience that the whiff of things kept secret for too long inevitably, somehow, seeped out; and would be inhaled by others frequenting or inhabiting the corridors of power.

'Politicians are, ahem, very insecure persons, Anthony. They trade in gossip and, ahem, believe far too much of it.'

In any case there was, he asserted, an inherent life-span to every secret. None better than the Colonel, a most astute man, would know that he could defer action for a limited time only – for how long was a matter of judgement – before the possibility of acting would begin to decay, for the simple reason that things, inevitably, would change, would have changed.

The Colonel's objection, Simon believed, was a matter of principle, not practicalities.

'He will, ahem, come round. And we should be ready when he does.'

In the event Simon had no doubt that the extraction of Arnold Ward's young lady from Czechoslovakia *could* be achieved –

'Once appropriate, ahem, confirmation as to her authenticity has been thoroughly established. Going ahead might involve us in having to do some, ahem, damage limitation, perhaps. But I'll start the ball rolling here. There will be, at some point, the matter of a, ahem, a passport anyway.' Simon brushed a forefinger across an eyebrow. 'Or two. Depending on how one decides to set about it.'

But here was the rub, as Simon put it: the man, meaning Arnold, now refused to have anything more to do with the Colonel's boys and girls. He had cut himself adrift.

'But what about Sarah?'

'He refuses to report to her, so she has reported. Therefore only you, Anthony, are now, ahem, favoured with his presence.' Simon was by now playing with the small silver sword of a letter-opener. 'May one ask, have you, ahem, made an arrangement to meet again?'

Arnold had said at an earlier meeting that he expected to be home for a few days before Christmas. I could not know if he had subsequently changed his plans.

'How, ahem, how *exactly* did you leave things at your last meeting?'

'"Tapes and testimony for the lady", his exact final words.'

'Then he will be back to learn the, ahem, decision. Therefore.'

Therefore, as Simon went on to say, when next I met up with Arnold would I ask him to let me have some details about his young lady. Not her name; Arnold Ward would not agree to that, one could be certain of that, but physical details. Height, weight, 'upper, middle, and lower body measurements' – Simon's circumlocutions – skin tone, colour of eyes, any distinctive feature of note, and photographs of course, to include a head-and-shoulders shot, if at all possible. Unsmiling, of course. Oh and crucially, a shot of each side of her face. It is easier to look like someone else head-on, Simon said, than from the side.

'And do tell him that if the young woman has, ahem, short hair, please to ask her to let it grow.' He patted his own shoulder. 'It is always easier to, ahem, cut and shape than to add to.'

A few parting words:

'Oh and of course, it goes without saying that this stays between the two of us, ahem, for now.'

As I emerged into the swirling, cold wind of Whitehall, another question posed itself. Was I now in collusion with Simon Carlton independently of my collusion with Colonel Jackson, whilst I was also colluding with Arnold Ward? An intake of breath set off a nerve in a back tooth. And in all of this, there was Sarah Somebody, whatever her name truly was, and what she had confided in me which I had promised to keep in the dark if at all possible.

By the following morning I was trapped within *two* entangle-ments. There was the matter of Carolyne and William which became more ravelled the more hints and clues to my decep-tion, if so it was, sprang to mind. I see-sawed between believing I had discovered the irrefutable truth and thinking the whole thing still too incredible to consider. The more time passed, and the more I was tipped towards this sense of the incredible, the more the whole business seemed unreal. A similar sense of unreality also now attached itself to my worrying over the ques-tions of collusion with which I had left Whitehall yesterday.

Distraction came in the form of a telephone call.

'I hope this is not an inconvenient moment, Mister Ash-ley-Chetwyne. Robin Pendine here, *Mundus Librorum,* bookshop off the Charing Cross Road?'

'Ah, yes.' Then I recognised the rather high, slightly querulous voice.

'I have here for your inspection a copy of volume V of *Cooke's Pocket Edition of the original and complete works of select British Poets,* to give you its short title. May I tell you about the volume? If you have a few minutes.'

'Fire away.'

'Are you familiar with this production? No?' The voice pro-ceeded more animatedly. 'This particular example is, I would say, in very good condition throughout, bearing in mind the publi-cation date of 1797. There is some loss to the boards, but the spine is uncracked, the binding solid. I would describe it as bright throughout, with only some very light spotting here and there on some pages. The engraved plates show particularly well. Would Mister Ashley-Chetwyne be interested?'

He was, and I said so.

'A very good example, if I may say. And, of course, within this volume you not only get the poems of William Walsh, but you get a bonus too.'

I put the question.

'The bonus is that within this same volume you also get the poetry of Richard Glover, William Somerville, and Isaac Watts – names likely to be familiar to you, sir, but, perhaps less familiar to you, in addition you get a collection of the poems of John Pomfret *and* Thomas Tickell.'

If I had been in any doubt, the last two names mentioned decided the matter. Just for those hitherto unknown names, the sounds of those names, I had to have that book. With that decision came also the thought that I might even be able to impress William with some arcane knowledge of pieces composed by names known only to a few. As soon as that thought presented itself, I railed at my own ingenuousness. William was now the enemy, was he not? Why should I in any way set out to humour or amuse him? If I was right.

If...

The smallest of all conditionals in the English language, but limitless in extent.

I arranged to call in at Robin Pendine's world of books the next morning, Saturday; the day Carolyne would be returning from Prague; the day before we were due to take our pleasure cruise on the Thames from Westminster to Greenwich.

Carolyne telephoned me within an hour or so of my arriving back at my flat. She wanted to confirm what I knew already: that she and her father would be on a late flight Saturday night into Heathrow and Daddy would be staying overnight at her place ('Well, really it's Daddy's place anyway, as you know') rather than drive home at such an hour. Her insistence on telling me again was not for my reassurance. It was for hers, to gauge my receptiveness to her, to know I was unchanged. So I thought.

But anyway, I, poor dear, would have to suffer without her until Sunday, though we did have that day to look forward to, and it would be lovely, a leisurely day, a boat trip on the Thames, lunch together... really it seemed *such* a long time since we had been together... and there was so much to catch up on...

'So whatever you are planning to do tonight and Saturday night *without* me, please be sure to be up and about by the time I get to your place on Sunday morning.'

Carolyne took her stream of chatter to be a conversation. It was not the moment to ask questions or make challenges of her. Sunday was the day appointed for that.

I was up and lively early on Saturday. I made my leisurely way to the bookshop off the Charing Cross Road. Robin Pendine, his horseshoe of white hair sticking out even more horizontally than I remembered, looked up instantly from his counter as I stepped into the shop.

'Mister Ashley-Chetwyne.'

He waved busily to me with both arms, hands reverse-flapping. He had much to say as he seated me at a bench which acted as an extension to his counter. From under that counter he retrieved the Cooke volume, insisting on taking me through its pages and pointing to the various 'embellishments', as the title-page announced them. 'And here we have...' punctuated his own enthusiasm in sharing the book with me.

I made a duty call that afternoon to mother. It could not be postponed any further.

'I was wondering when you might find a moment or two to call in your busy schedule.' Seamlessly mother went on. 'You have Carolyne with you, I presume, and have a weekend of pleasurable activities to attend? something doubtless to keep you away from us, from your *family*. You know, Anthony, it really is more than time that you came home for a weekend, just *one* weekend, that is not so much to ask, and it is *such* a long time since we have seen you. Of course you may bring your fiancée-to-be with you. Have you bought a ring?'

I did not know where to begin, and the fractional pause was all mother allowed me.

'Then don't. I have my mother's solitaire which might as well go to Carolyne and be of some use *and* keep it in the family. So what are the two of you up to tonight? '

I took an intake of breath, ready to speak.

'*And*, Anthony, we must make our arrangements for Christmas, it is not at all too soon. I assume you will want to bring Carolyne here for the Eve, Day, and Boxing? I thought I would invite my sister and hers with your father's brothers and theirs – plus both sets of children, of course – for Boxing Day, have a family celebration of your engagement, just the family, before *that* woman puts on her excessive display next year. I have let her know, by the way, that the date she suggested is completely out of the question. Some of the family simply won't be able to attend, and if she is determined to go ahead with this vulgar show then I must insist on dragging in all our relatives and their attenuations on both sides of the family. I have written to say I shall offer an alternative day when I can confirm a date on which all forty-two of us can be present.'

There was a satisfied Hmm! sound.

Eventually I managed to disabuse mother of some of her presumptions, explain what had happened, where Carolyne had been, and so on. I could not tell her that the door of Doubt was now pinned wide open by blasts of a cold east wind. I simply as yet had no idea how I was going to negotiate the pending separation from Carolyne. Nor could I shake mother from the fixed idea that Carolyne should have my grandmother's ring as her engagement ring.

'Don't be silly, Anthony, it's a perfectly good ring, actually it's a very good ring, a Tsarina, best part of three-quarters of a carat of diamond, more than good enough. A little ostentatious in fact, so it would be perfect. And no, I don't feel in the least that mother would object to it being handed on, probably quite pleased in fact. No need to get sentimental about these things.

I'm sure the girl will be delighted with it. If it doesn't fit you could always have it altered.'

It was understood by Carolyne that we would set special time aside – *some*time – to shop together for one. There was also an understanding of sorts that we would do this by Christmas or, possibly, early into the new year. She would not be pleased to accept an old handed-down ring. I knew because I knew that Carolyne would want her *own* ring, one chosen by herself. She was hankering after us going away for a few days – Paris, Madrid, Rome – and purchasing the ring together in one of those cities. She had mentioned this wish several times. 'So romantic,' she had claimed.

This prince, however, now realised that there had been no wooing; the princess had simply claimed him before starting on a new romance. Or renewing an old one.

33

I was pleased with my purchase of the Cooke's pocket volume. I idled my way haphazardly from one page to another, taking more care of that book than of any other I had ever handled.

The light faded.

In the early evening I took up the volume again and started to read with more deliberation the poems of W.W. I came upon something which was both familiar but somehow different too. Something caught on the branches of a memory. At that I took up from my desk all the sheets of paper in William's hand and put them on the settee beside me.

I compared William's handwritten version of *Rivals* with the printed version on the page before me. The Cooke's version, confusingly, was called simply *Song*. William's was a faithful copy of the first stanza of the William Walsh poem. The second stanza, however, did not correspond, except for the identical two closing lines:

> *I can endure my own despair,*
> *But not another's hope.*

The preceding six lines in Walsh's poem were addressed to Sylvia – I supposed W.W's idealised lover. William's version was addressed to a 'companion' who was 'both friend and enemy.'

> *Of all companions we are wont*
> *As direst rival see,*
> *Is one, best known, who bears the brunt;*
> *Both friend and enemy.*
> *Lover or friend, how to forswear*
> *The one, or both, and cope;*
> *I can endure my own despair*
> *But not another's hope.*

So. I was 'the direst rival.' So. I was 'Both enemy and friend.' There was no other way to read this re-writing by William of William Walsh's poem. Why had I not seen this artifice before? This had been William's way of sounding both a declaration and a warning note.

Fool not to have seen all this, all the contrivances.

There scrambled into mind again, slipping and sliding over each other like scree dislodged on a slope one is climbing, fragments from letters, from poems, from words spoken. Once one *knows,* all those things that had been present already for some time fall into place. None of those things have changed in themselves. They are what they were. What has changed is a different way of looking at those same things.

A fool and his follies.

I shuffled other pieces of paper from William. William being noble; William renouncing his love – that bookmark he had made for me, written in his small, neat hand. William and Carolyne. How had one missed this? and for how long had one not been looking? Could it really be as long ago as William's and Carolyne's final year at Oxford that he had 'jollied' her? With William Walsh in one hand and William Walsh's version of William Walsh in the other, what had been absurd became translucently clear. Left hand, right hand. Right hand: authentic William Walsh. Left hand: the sinister, William's fabrication. There are moments which, charged with their own being, are of their nature ironic, requiring no working over, no translation.

I threw the papers to one side and stalked to the cabinet to get myself a drink. Damn! No port, no beers, no alcohol at all. Not bothering to put on a coat I dashed out of the front door, slamming it behind me, and headed for the nearest Off-Licence.

That evening, after a couple of beers and then into a glass of port, I turned back to some poetry – not the just-acquired Cooke volume, but the *Minor Poets of the Seventeenth Century* bought weeks ago. The pages fell open where a roughly-torn fillet of paper acted as a bookmark. And there was Thomas Stanley's lines of adamantine resolve set against the seduction of love.

Very carefully, in fact with exaggerated precision, I copied out two of the stanzas from the Stanley poem, folded the paper with geometric precision and put it into my wallet.

How can one bookmark the future?

34

I woke to a shaking of my shoulder. I turned onto my back, leaving part of the inside of my head where it had been lopsided on the pillow. When, to a dull ache, it reunited with its vertical part, I opened my eyes. Slowly, and to the thinnest parting of their lids.

Somewhere in the distance there was a female voice.

The voice repeated something. Words started to assemble in my head.

'Come on, my love. You've done it again, *despite* my warning.' But the voice was not harsh, aggressive, but gentle, coaxing.

A hand softly stroked the side of my face.

'Shower and shave, while I look out some clothes for you.'

Carolyne's face focussed above me.

'What time is it?' Why, in such a condition, body awash with the after-effects of alcohol and that deep unconsciousness, that unstirring sleep, why, I ask, is this almost invariably the first question asked by the male just beginning to emerge from hangover into wakefulness?

I let the cold water of the shower shock me into the semblance of awareness. I shaved as thoughts began to assemble themselves. They were the same thoughts I had taken to bed with me when I had thrown myself onto the eiderdown after having fallen over myself several times in the attempt to undress.

Carolyne had tidied the bed and laid out a complete change of clothes for me. She planted little pecking kisses upon my body, helped me to dress, fussed around me.

'That's better. We still have time for all we planned to do. Just as well I got here early, though.' Said with soft indulgence. 'Ready, Sir Knight?'

Carolyne, clearly, appeared in the best of playful moods, lively and light.

We made our way to Westminster Embankment, then to the steps to board the boat that would ply downstream to Greenwich Pier and bring us back later in the day.

Carolyne went into the saloon. I went up to the uncovered deck. I wanted to feel the cold wind against my face. After ten minutes or so I joined Carolyne. There had been hardly need for me to speak, Carolyne filling the spaces with her own spirited chatter. I caught some snippets. Most passed me by. She pressed her body against me, her arm looped through mine, holding me tightly close, as we listened to the loudspeaker commentary informing us of the places and history we were passing by.

Disembarked at Greenwich we walked ourselves around *The Cutty Sark* in her dry dock, admiring the lines of the old tea clipper, before heading for a pub and lunch. We sat at a plain wooden table, Carolyne all the while holding on her lap one of my hands between the palms of her two hands, leaning in to me to kiss me on the cheek from time to time, and telling me how much she had missed me.

I waited until after lunch, after I had ordered and been served more drinks. I took from my wallet the neatly-folded paper of the Stanley verses prepared the previous evening and placed it before her. Carolyne looked with curiosity, excited. She began to unfold the paper as I watched for her reaction. Unfolded, she smoothed the paper with the flat of a hand.

> *Each flatt'ring kiss, each tempting smile,*
> *Thou dost in vain bestow,*
> *Some other Lovers might beguile!*
> *Who not thy falsehood know.*
> *But I am proof against all art!*
> *No vows shall e'er persuade me*
> *Twice to present a wounded heart*
> *To her that hath betrayed me.*

There was a time-delay, Carolyne head down, her eyes following the lines for a second time. Then I saw her cheeks begin to colour, her bottom lip begin to tremble so that she caught it between her teeth.

Quietly, 'Tell me about William,' I said.

After she had buried her head between her hands, after the first staccato gasping intakes of breath, after the *diminuendo* of sobbing, she did tell me. What she told me was disjointed, made up of half-started sentences, isolated phrases, syntactic dislocations, repetitions, switches from one time-setting to another, and variations of 'Sorry.' Reassembled, there was a narrative.

Yes, at the very last of the Oxford days, William and she had... you know.

'Jollied?' I suggested might be the word.

She did not know why it had happened, but it had. It was just something that, you know... Then, when she had gone off to Switzerland, where Daddy had offices, you remember, as a base for a year's travelling, William had managed to make contact. Yes, she must have left details. Obviously, how else? He had come out to spend some time with her. Over several weeks, in fact. But they had separated, neither wanting at that point a permanent commitment. No, she could not explain the attraction, it was... and their, well, getting-together, was something she had not *consciously* decided on, it was... Oh! I would *not* be able to understand – but it wasn't as if she had *decided* to go to bed with him... Again I would not understand, but it was as if she had *found* herself in bed with him, somehow mesmerised, not herself, or another part of her, a part of her which was new, and strange to her somehow had been brought to life in her... Oh, it was *impossible* to account for it all, how could she explain what she herself did not understand? And William? He had been decisive for both of them and, yes, she had agreed, the pattern of his emerging life would not suit her. She could not be rootless, itinerant. She could be away and enjoy elsewhere, provided there was home to go back to. So, they had parted, and it was over and then we – Carolyne and me – had met up again and, and she knew that she wanted me for her husband through life, to marry me, bear my children, she knew that, there was no doubt and everything was fine, she was happy and she thought I was happy. Then...

Then a young man, in his early thirties she guessed, wanting to speak with her about William. Or so he said. But actually, on reflection, she realised that they had spent most of their time talking about me. One of Philip's Ahhs! from me at this point – a nice young man sent from the service's vetting branch: obviously. Carolyne *of course* would have been involved in the process of *my* pee-veeing, however cursory, as well as seeking confirmatory details of William from her. In talking to the nice young man about me, who wanted to know 'how close' a friendship there was between William and me, he had casually asked if she happened to have a photograph of us together. After a quick search through her own Oxford photographs Carolyne realised that she did not possess any photograph of William, with or without me in the frame. Thus she had borrowed that photograph of William she could clearly recall having seen in my album. She had two copies made: one for herself, one for the nice young man who called a second time after she had contacted the number he had left with her. Looking at that photograph had brought William back to mind in a more tangible way, made him real again, just thinking about him, just wondering about him really, and then...

Why the pretence, why the subterfuge? Why not just say so at the time? Immediate thoughts, but no time for me to put the questions, Carolyne rushing on, wanting to get her say over and done with, like a stream washing away all the detritus caught up on its banks.

Then, recently, when William had re-emerged into their lives, hers and mine, it just happened again that he was left to look after

her on that occasion when I was 'otherwise engaged' (the irony leapt from the common phrase), getting drunk that night we
were due to go to her parents' place. Yes, yes, she would not lie,
they had again...you know – but no, they had not just 'bumped
into each other' even more recently in Berne, they had met up by
arrangement. She could not say what it was about William, it was
just... So what *was* it about William? It was a fascination, one that
robbed her of self-will, she just felt... Whatever the 'just' was, she
could not say (*would* not, I substituted), but there it was. William
did love her, he had declared himself, the poor man was desperate, he *wanted* her but was terribly torn between wanting her and
his loyalty to an old friend. Me. After all (after all *what?*) she and
I had recently become engaged – or at least very soon would
be – everyone knew, both our families, and, and oh! it would be
so, so cruel now to think of disappointing me... because I loved
her – I *did* love her, didn't I? Besides... William had given her
a good talking to. While his prospects had not been propitious
when they had left Oxford, the future was even more uncertain
for him now. And if a man has no future to offer to a woman...
the *et cetera* of that conditional was left hanging. In any case he,
William, was going away soon, for how long he did not know. But
what he did know, what he believed, was that the man who would
return would not be the same man who would have gone away.
His words to her. I saw it as an escape-mechanism on his part.

But oh! she had been so silly, so very, very silly, she knew that,
but she knew now that the thing with William was more like, well,
more like an infatuation, almost a schoolgirl thing, it was like a
fantasy, not real, it was...

'Passion?' I offered.

Carolyne glanced away quickly at the word. She regathered
herself. No, it was not serious love, not as she loved me, but
something that had, it was... She and William had talked, he had
talked sense into her, she knew it was oh so stupid, and he, well
he could not be more for her than a *divertissement* (that, certainly,

was authentic William), really he was quite unsuited, she deserved better, a more stable living, marriage, children, and besides... I must please, *please* forgive her, she really did love me, it was me she wanted for a husband, me to share her life with... *ainsi de suite, und so weiter, et cetera,* and so on.

'*Please* don't leave me alone, Anthony, *please, please* don't leave me on my own. Not tonight!'

The victor and his spoils of tarnished goods. We agreed, that is *I* agreed, not to act in haste. Soon, very soon, Carolyne pleaded, we would settle back into our true selves. William was not... William was a fantasy.

'It is *you* I want Anthony.'

The look and sound of distress appeared very real.

Despite Carolyne's self-abasing submission of herself, the look of pain she carried, her attendance to any matter that would in any degree, slight or large, contribute to my well-being, her care of me in the weeks that followed, I knew that things inevitably would fall apart between us. Lacking all other explanation, I was left with Carolyne's passion for William, a passion that had simply overwhelmed her. She could not explain it. I could not understand it, though it suddenly struck me at one moment that passion came from the Latin root of suffering, and the Latin of suffering was to endure, to submit to. I abandoned the Latin snake with its tail in its etymological mouth: such circular ironies were more William's habit of thinking than mine.

Mine told me that I loved Carolyne, *had* loved Carolyne – not in any overwhelming way, as Carolyne had been overwhelmed with William – but this crisis confirmed to me that I did not love her unreservedly, forgivingly of any injury or hurt. I had fallen in lust with her and that lust had run its course. It had been overtaken by *William.* Whatever it was that William possessed, which was invisible to men (men attracted to women, I mean), was clearly evident to women. The green-eyed god looked down with flashing eyes. That undefined, that rare attraction of William's must have been both concentrated and overpowering and – to my male ego – clearly and inescapably sexual. One could not compete with what must have been such an intensity of high excitement and fulfilment as Carolyne saw in and experienced with William. Why else would Carolyne have put all in jeopardy? Such reflections, in all their variations, corroded my self-esteem and confidence. Our love-life, caught in the little god's beams of light, faded away, like an over-exposed photograph.

35

Arnold Ward telephoned chambers at the end of the following week.

'A Mister Ward to speak with you, Mister Anthony.' At that instant of Booth's voice, I was hit with a wave of paranoia (despite having accused Arnold of the self-same condition), followed instantly by a wave of absurdity at the thought that Booth (or anyone else) could be listening in on my conversations.

'Anthony, glad you're there. Calling you from the office, just got back in. Any news?'

However fantastical that paranoia of being overheard, I still forestalled Arnold. 'Tonight, Arnold, usual time, usual place. If you're free.'

At which I then felt ridiculous, playing at a game in which I did not belong.

The Gin Palace that Friday night, as every Friday night, was crammed with drinkers and a high volume of noise. I manoeuvred my way to the bar and ordered a drink. Arnold appeared at my side and put an arm around my shoulders. We greeted each other.

'How's the missus?'

He laughed. 'Haven't been home yet, haven't eaten. Came straight here from the office. Had some copy to file.' He leant in close to me. 'So, do you have something to tell me?'

'I do.'

'Not here. I know this great Indian restaurant in the Fulham Road.'

A taxi ride later, Arnold and I sat opposite each other at a table in his chosen restaurant, a candle burning between us, and the spicy aroma of joss sticks in the air.

I told Arnold what I knew, what I had learned from Simon Carlton, but without saying from whom the information had come.

'Just that?'

I confirmed.

'No *when* mentioned?'

I shook my head.

Not until later, after a huge meal, both of us discovering we were far hungrier than we had thought, did Arnold again address the issue.

'Tell them – ' he waved away my objection as I was about to make it – 'tell them that everything is getting trickier there. The Czechs' Russian masters are beginning to lose patience, there's corruption everywhere and things are slacker than they would like. There's a lot of agitation, protests of different kinds, some of it escapes public censure, some of it results in some quiet spiriting away of so-called dissidents. There's a lot of opposition to the official party line. Word is, unless matters improve to their way of thinking, might not be long before the Kremlin overlords exercise a really firm hand and slap things down. Greater repression, greater direct control. Things are moving out there, Anthony, things are brewing up. Everybody's watching everybody. Things are tense.'

Arnold raised his glass of cheap brandy, *gratis* of the house.

'Tell them, whoever they are you speak with, that they really don't have the leisure of time on their hands. For me, as well as them.'

Not knowing who of *them* to report this to, I none the less agreed to do so.

'And I shall see you the week after next. Let's say Thursday week. Can't do it by 'phone from anywhere over there. So, Spotted Horse, same time?'

As we got to the door, to leave, Arnold slipped a package into the pocket of my coat.

'And you can hand these on. Let's say they're an earnest of intent—freely and voluntarily offered up.' He stopped, raising an index finger. 'Oh and by the way. You can tell them that everything they wanted passed on to their Dušan *has* been passed on. So I think I've more than earned a little favour in return.'

Carolyne and I now spent the weekend together apart, as one might say. She carried her suffering in her quietness, I carried my hurt in the set of my mouth. We were over-civil to each other, the playfulness between us gone. We could not help each other, and yet neither of us would enforce the final wrench away from each other. For Carolyne there was the hope that in time, Time the great healer would work the magic of its amnesia upon me.

I decided that Simon Carlton would be the recipient of Arnold's information.

'Pop over any time, just, ahem, call ahead.'

An essential day's work in chambers followed by a day in court took me to the middle of the week before I could see Simon. I told him Arnold had stressed the need for action, things were worsening there.

'I think we can be sure that they, ahem, know that.'

I handed over the package from Arnold. Simon's eyes widened as he opened the envelope and saw the reels of audiotape.

"An earnest of intent,' as the man said, 'freely and voluntarily offered up."

'Indeed so, ahem, it shall be reported to the Colonel.'

Simon was elated. The technical boys, he said, could do their work on them, and then they would be able to make transcriptions. The Colonel, he was sure, would be very pleased – 'Well, shall we say, ahem, softened? More inclined.'

Now that Philip had declared himself unavailable for new briefs, and was easing himself out of existing commitments where he could 'sub-let' them, as he put it, more work was being offered to me. He was apologetic about it when he called in on me at the end of the High Court case for which he was prosecution QC; the one which had largely kept him away from chambers.

'I am sorry, Anthony, to be leaving you to pick up the bits and pieces.' He pulled out his pipe from the breast pocket of his jacket, followed by the usual rummaging around with both hands in the various other pockets for matches and tobacco. 'But wouldn't do for me to stay involved, simply wouldn't do for a bewigged member of the bench. Rather afraid you were elected in my place.'

'Elected, Philip?'

He pressed tobacco down into the bowl of his pipe with crooked forefinger. 'Nominated, then. And found acceptable, as of course I knew you would be.' He struck a match, holding it above the bowl of his pipe.

'So it *was* you? But what if one had not wanted to – '

'Some invitations one is not at liberty to refuse, Anthony. We must all be prepared to do our little bit of national service – even if it is *out* of uniform. Particularly in times when the, ah, official service is understaffed and under-resourced.'

I watched the blackened curl of match flare alongside Philip's finger and thumb. He must have felt the heat at the last instant, shaking the match out.

'By the way, very glad to hear you and Simon appear to have hit it off' – sucking noisily on the stem of his unlit pipe – 'Very important that, to have a good working relationship. Makes for understandings. Thereby, good decisions.'

'I am not sure if one is expected to thank you or not, Philip.'

His burst of laughter was unrestrained. 'Can't advise you on that one, my dear Anthony. State secret. But I do wish you well.'

Finally, several spent matches later, having at last contrived to set fire to the tobacco in his pipe, he left my room, a haze of smoke following him up the stairs as he went to his own chamber two floors above.

'Bits and pieces' fairly summarises also my time over the remaining period before the Christmas break that year.

I saw Arnold again, as we had agreed. Beers in *The Spotted Horse*. He entertained me with tales from his furloughs, as he called his periods of time within eastern European communist states.

'At least we are free to complain here, do the grumpy old bugger routine about anything and anybody. In fact it's a national sport here, but very different there, Anthony. You never know who's listening to you and what's going to be done about you if your words reach the wrong ears. You don't breathe in air so much as an atmosphere. Suspicion and distrust. *And* there's no such thing as irony over there, you know – simply no understanding of it.'

Eventually we turned to the business of the evening. He pushed an envelope towards me over the table.

'All in there. Don't mind if you want to look.'

I did. There were five 127-film-size colour prints and their negatives: one each of a full-face shot and of each side of the woman's face; one full-length from the front, one full-length from behind.

'Wasn't really sure what was wanted. These should do, they can blow them up as they wish.'

It was strange. Looking at the full-front close-up created a small shock of recognition. There were features that reminded me of Arnold's unlawfully wedded wife. The resemblance diminished, but did not disappear, the harder I looked at the photograph. Arnold tipped up the envelope in front of me. With the negatives a lock of light auburn hair, held with an elastic band, fell out.

'Thought that might help.' Arnold responded to my look. 'Yes, quite right. Wasn't my idea.'

There were handwritten notes too: height, weight, and Simon's requested 'upper, middle, and lower body measurements.'

I gathered up the photographs. 'Lovely,' I said. 'A lovely woman.'

'She is to me, Anthony. She is to me.'

I raised my glass of ale. 'Then here's to you and' – but Arnold would not be drawn – 'and your lady.'

'And you?

'Fine.' With full stiff-upper-lip restraint I held back from telling Arnold what I very much wanted to share with someone, another man who would understand that I was struggling to forgive Carolyne's inconstancy. It would be folly not to end things with Carolyne. I knew that, yet was held back from the cruelty of it – that agonised, beseeching look of Carolyne.

Thus we limped on together towards Christmas. A card arrived at my address from William to hope that Carolyne and I would enjoy 'the festive season', to say that he was very sorry not to be able to see us but his new job prevented him from returning to England. He could not tell when he would return. It was a most un-William-like message; prosaic, dull, matter-of fact. I could not tell whether it was so because William now understood that I knew about him and Carolyne; or whether it showed that, to the contrary, he did not know. At the foot of the back of the card he had given the address for the British Embassy in Prague, to which I might write to him. I tore the card into small rectangles and threw them into the rubbish bin.

In these weeks Carolyne herself did everything she could both to distract and to please me. Attempts to re-engender my love for her mixed with occasions when her face showed both suffering and silent contrition – a condition signalled by a tremor of her lower lip. Despite all, it pained me to see her unhappy in these between-times. Innocent party as I was, by not acting decisively, the longer I delayed the longer I punished her; and felt guilty for so doing. Time passed to the point of an expectation that we would continue with each other. Caught in this dithering uncertainty, I extended to her my mother's invitation to spend 'Eve, Day, and Boxing' with my family. Carolyne, eager to please, to atone, readily agreed; much to my surprise and not altogether to my wish.

'But won't your mother and father...?'

It was settled.

In the event, Carolyne determinedly set out to charm my mother. Father was a pushover. The combination of food, drinks, striding walks through the countryside, the company of others of my family, worked their relaxing tonic. When we left, my mother held me back as father and Carolyne went towards the door.

'A charming girl, utterly charming. It is such a shame about the mother.'

Carolyne and I shuffled together into the new year, greeting its arrival with her parents. There was a big, boozy party at their home, crammed with guests, many of them Peter Walker's business associates and their wives. Everybody seemed at ease with everybody and determined to have a good time. The Walkers had even arranged for musicians to play and had organised a marquee to be attached to the back of the house. 'A dummy run,' Carolyne's father said in passing – the venue for the reception of my formal engagement to his daughter, itself a dummy-run for the marriage a year or so later. Complete with its own temporary wooden floor and electric heaters, it became more and more densely populated as the evening wore on. It was impossible to resist joining in, often ending up within a group of people all dancing together. I imagined my mother condemning the evening as an ostentatious show and rather vulgar, whilst father would have found himself in a small gathering of like-minded sixty-something men, their laughter louder as their consumption increased. Two concentric rings of all present, holding hands with the neighbour on each side of one, arms crossed over chests, swung up and down to *Auld Lang Syne*. Soon after, the drift away to the arrival of taxis and hire cars.

Carolyne and I made our way to an annexe in which Carolyne's mother had thoughtfully assigned us the bedroom. We fell upon the bed and made unrestrained, drunken love.

~ **36** ~

It was a *rapprochement* of sorts, welcomed by Carolyne and thinly regretted by me. But we were not so tense with each other and it was easier for me to be with her. We were beginning to settle down into a more comfortable relationship, more relaxed, inertia more than anything else on my part keeping us together.

There arrived another letter from William, two pages of neat handwriting. He was so disappointed not to have received a reply from his old friend... I tore the letter to shreds without reading further.

It was at the end of January when Booth stepped into the passageway to greet me on my arrival at chambers one morning.

'A message for you, Mister Anthony. Mister Carlton would be very much obliged if you could call in at his office towards the end of the day. Say five o'clock?'

In his office, Simon was sitting at the far side of his desk. With her back to me sat a woman with almost straight hair, shaped in to just below the nape of her neck.

She turned in her chair and I saw the woman in the full-face photograph Arnold had passed over to me in the restaurant. I must have been wide-eyed and mouth agape in those first few seconds. She held my stare. Then, slowly, the set of her face relaxed. The woman rose from her chair and held out her hand to me.

Simon too rose. 'Allow me to, ahem, introduce you. Miss Cowper, Mister Ashley-Chetwyne. Miss Cowper has not long joined us in the Home Department.'

I took the woman's hand.

'Hello, Anthony. So nice to see you again.'

Sarah! Sarah Somebody-Else now, currently Mrs Sarah Ward, formerly Miss Sarah Hill, now Cowper today and, so far as I knew, still Miss K. But Sarah's fair skin was now lightly bronzed, the hair a light auburn, and something about the shape of the nose was different; it seemed thinner, longer.

Simon, I could see, was eager for an opinion: 'What do you, ahem, think, Anthony? Will she pass?'

I was amazed at the transformation, and said so.

Explanations followed. The Colonel had come round, as Simon had predicted. Things had changed, and there were more changes on the way both at home and in Czechoslovakia. There was political movement. Sir John and the Colonel had held further discussions and *this* – pointing to Sarah – was one result of their conflabs. Arnold Ward's gesture of goodwill in *voluntarily* offering up his tapes had appeased the Colonel, whose sense of propriety and of service to one's country had thereby been upheld. Also, as Simon put it to me in the simplest terms, 'there had been talks' – lifting his eyes upwards again.

As for Sarah's makeover, I had been the first real test, whether I would instantly recognise Sarah or not. Simon himself could not judge, since he had been present on the first occasion Sarah had been made up and so had seen the changes as they had taken place.

'Somehow he managed to get us into Shepperton, and one of their film make-up people there showed me how to get up like this. Then I had to learn to do all this for myself. It's taken hours of practice.'

Arnold would be the deciding test. When next he was in the country and went home to see the 'missus' he would find Miss Cowper waiting for him. All going well, and with the Colonel's final OK, Sarah would be sent out to join the Prague Embassy staff as a replacement assistant press officer. The changeover had been planned for next month.

I drew a finger around my face. Sarah Somebody – I did not believe the Cowper any more than any other of her names – took the mime of my question.

'The hair, well, obviously shaped and died, make-up to give me a darker skin tone, but I have to try not to laugh.'

'And why is that?'

'Spoil the effect.' At which she did laugh and I could see the change. The sides of her nose rose up, and lost its longer, thinner appearance. 'It's actually eye-shadow. Clever, isn't it?'

'Certainly had me fooled.'

'Fortunate we had Sarah to call on. Meets all the, ahem, basic physical requirements of height and body-shape and so on.'

Sarah smiled at Simon's embarrassed explanation. I took it as permission to look appraisingly at the woman before me. As to the numbers for the three vital measurements which had passed me by when Arnold had handed over his notes with the photographs, I could now see them for myself in the proportions that filled and took in the knee-length patterned blue dress (of several hues), belted and pulled in at the waist.

'Of course, I have a bit more weight to lose yet.'

I suppressed all contrary, gallant comment.

The discovery that 'with some, ahem, small adjustments' Sarah could pass for Arnold's StB lady-love was a bonus. It meant that 'we could keep the matter within the immediate family.'

When Simon was called away to another office, Sarah added to the explanation for her selection.

'Also it means that I can get away from here, which will be to the good. It's getting very difficult with' – she nodded her head to one side – 'you know, *him*.' Him, the greedy bastard MP, her former lover, reduced now to a second-person pronoun. Hesitatingly, she added: 'He's getting very demanding, spending too much time calling at too many offices. He's becoming noticeable again.'

'Probably on the hunt for something that will endear him once more to his StB masters and keep the money rolling in.'

Sarah looked at me, assessing me. There was something else she was on the edge of saying, considering whether to say, before deciding: 'And of course, knowing what only you know, this might be a way of, well, putting something right.'

Given what she had told me about the MP I could see the advantage of rendering another service to the service as recompense.

'What will become of Missus Sarah Ward?'

'Missus Sarah Ward has already handed in her notice here and within the next week or so will withdraw to Herefordshire to look after her ageing parents who will soon be not very well at all – ailing in fact, and needing her constant attention. Which, as a dutiful only child, she will give.' Sarah said this straight-faced.

Simon, re-entering the room, turned immediately to me.

'Sarah has told you, Anthony, that she will, ahem, soon be leaving us?'

There was more he needed to say to me. Arnold would be back again on a scheduled return in a few days. He might, as on another occasion, contact me before going 'home' to 'his wife.' I was about to ask how our meeting could have been known, but was forestalled by Sarah – 'He told me. Afterwards, after he'd spent the evening with you.'

On leaving I went to kiss Sarah on the cheek.

'No, no!' She raised a finger towards her face. 'The make-up.' She held out her hand to me. I turned it over, palm down, in my own hand. I lowered my head and lightly kissed the back of her hand.

'Milady.'

That was the last I saw of Sarah Somebody, Miss Hill, Mrs Ward, Miss Cowper, Miss K, for many years. Far too many years.

I did indeed meet up again with Arnold, complete with duffle bag, a few days later, but not before he had been 'home.'

'I gather you've seen the missus in her new rig?'

'I have. But it's what you think that matters.'

Arnold rubbed at the side of his face. 'Close. She's getting very near, perhaps just a little too rounded here' – he raised upturned palms, spread fingers, to his chest – 'though she tells me some strapping will make the difference.' He shook his head in gentle laughter. 'We've some work to do on the way she walks, and I've got to get her to light a cigarette and to hold it differently. That's a bit tough on Sarah, given that she doesn't smoke. But apart from that, I think she'll do very well. Except really close up, face to face, she's a pretty good copy.'

'Do you know what they have in mind?'

'Well, apart from the obvious, some sort of doubling, Sarah won't say. She did tell me one thing, though...' Arnold was laughing quietly and shaking his head. 'She tells me that before very much longer I shall have to fall in love with my wife all over again.'

'Meaning?'

'I don't know. And she won't tell.'

'Well,' I offered, 'your missus is a woman it would be very easy to fall in love with.'

'Unless you're already in love with someone else.' Arnold widened his eyes. 'Or if you are *not* now in love with someone else.'

We moved on to 'our' Indian restaurant – it's surprising how quickly one can appropriate a place as one's own – where we took up immediately the matter of the audiotapes. Arnold pushed his duffle bag towards me under the table.

'A present for you, Anthony. You have the tapes of two of my meetings with the fat bastard, now there's the recorder. You can have it when we've finished the evening. Been suggested to me the technical people might like to have the machine as well. Erase all doubt, you might say.'

"Wasn't Sarah by chance made the suggestion?'

'Actually no. A fellow journalist.'

'May I ask when you first told Sarah about our grasping MP?'

Arnold half-closed his eyes and rubbed the fingers of one hand across upper lip and chin. 'Must have been shortly after the first meeting with him. Felt pretty sure even then that he wanted to get up to something. Why do you ask?'

'Oh, just for the chronology of things, Arnold – so that I have the full narrative.'

'Anyway, you haven't told me the reaction to the tapes I handed on.'

I hesitated, wanting to form my words with care.

'The colonel was very gratified, very pleased to acknowledge your gesture. And the tapes themselves *are* strongly suggestive of an ulterior meaning and motive. As such, they add weight and support – but they are not, in themselves, conclusive. Sorry.'

Arnold was looking at me disparagingly.

'Certainly very helpful, though, no doubt of that, no doubt at all.'

'But they're still not enough, is what you are saying.' Arnold sat back on his chair. 'Which is why you need this.'

He held up a third reel of audiotape.

'I thought there were just the three meetings between you – the initial meeting and the two follow-up meetings which you taped – the ones already handed on.'

'There were just those two other additional meetings that I told you about.'

Arnold put the tape back into his pocket.

'Later, your place.'

We shifted the talk to some pleasantries, mostly to do with Arnold's planned changes to the property he had bought in Herefordshire.

'I gather your wife will be setting off to Herefordshire before long.'

'So I believe and, strangely enough, to the same house to look after her ancient parents who, I also believe, are going to be installed there before long. Whoever they will be. I just hope it all works. Personally I think it's a contrivance too far, but... I suppose our people know what they're doing. They must think it's possible the other lot might want to keep tabs on Sarah for a while until they're sure that she's no longer' – he waved a hand – 'active.'

'I wonder who they've found to play out that little charade. To be Sarah, I mean.'

Arnold shrugged and shook his head. 'Probably some little innocent they'll have prised away from her desk.'

He went on to surprise me with some news.

'By the by, I ran into an old friend of yours a couple of times when I was in Prague. Wishes to be remembered to you, told him I expected to see you.'

'Oh?'

'Looks the dandy, cuts the dash I must say – '

'William!'

'The same. William Walsh, must say he's made more than a bit of an impression in the short while he's been out there. Can't miss him, highly visible let's say, out and about a good deal, often seen at musical concerts – '

'Well, he *is* Honorary Cultural Attaché at the Embassy, so I believe.'

'So I've been told. But that man Dušan your people are so interested in seems to have formed a very strong cultural attachment of his own with your friend. A *close* attachment.'

'Really?'

'Your friend William and Dušan have been seen together at a good many venues. Could be pure chance, but tongues wag, and it's a dangerous place to have tongues wagging about you.' Arnold ran a forefinger around the rim of his glass. 'In that way. Two men together, and one of them calling attention to the fact of them being together' – he mimed a gesture, hand moving downwards in a parabola of flight, little finger outstretched – 'Whether or not they actually, you know...'

Whether or not. The phrase revolved like a merry-go-round in my head. Once there had been no doubt, as far as I was concerned. Then, following Carolyne's admission, there was no 'whether' about him, the undiscovered lothario of our Oxford years. Now, with this report from Arnold, William both was and was not what one had taken him for.

'Anyway your friend William asked me to be sure to let you know that he's sorry not to have heard from you and wonders if perhaps you haven't got the letters he sent you. Says you can contact him care of the Embassy.'

It was time for the whisky.

Arnold listened, wide-eyed at particular junctions of my account. It was the first time I had voiced the history of the three of us and my discovery of the affair between Carolyne and William, their earlier liaison at Oxford and then Switzerland the first time, more recently here as well as Switzerland again. In some strange way it felt disloyal to speak so openly of such an intimate, personal concern; yet at the same time the unburdening made vividly clear to me the deceptions practised upon me. When I had finished the narrative, there was a silence from Arnold before his first response, a drawn-out, sceptical 'No.' He downed the rest of his whisky and, without another word, signalled to one of the waiters for a refill of doubles for us both.

'Can't believe it. Are we talking about the same man? Tall, very tall, thin, dark, well almost black hair, black moustache and goatee beard, bow tie, silver-topped walking stick, black hat – '

I confirmed.

'But he's... I mean, everything about the man, the way he carries himself, those exaggerated little movements of his, that signet ring on his forefinger, a fop to his manicured nails. I hear he's good company, very droll sense of humour, and easy to be entertained by the man, but *not* a woman's man.'

Arnold was now as surprised as I had been shocked when disabused of my image of William.

'Obviously not seen that way by everyone, Arnold.'

I learned that William, whatever one's view of the man, in those few weeks since his posting there before Christmas had become a figure much in demand. He seemed to be on everyone's invitation list for those receptions and cultural events which were openly announced and officially licensed, as well as other unsanctioned entertainments which were condoned. William's lectures given at Charles University had been very popular and he was being pressed to do more. William attracted attention.

'You do have to say,' said Arnold, 'that there *is* something about the man – something distinctive.'

By the end of that whisky-liberated exchange with Arnold I knew that I would have to finish with Carolyne. And sooner rather than later.

We left the restaurant, Arnold's arm around my shoulders, a gesture of fellow-feeling.

'Sorry, Anthony, bad timing, given the way things are for you right now. But we still have a little business to attend to.'

We made our way to my place by taxi, arriving this time together.

'No need to hide away now – just two friends finishing off a boozy evening.'

Once whisky and water were on the coffee table in front of us, Arnold lifted the third spool of tape onto the recorder he took out from his duffel bag. He threaded the tape through the playback mechanism and wound it around the take-up reel.

'This one was quite a time later.'

'But why didn't you say?'

'Even *saying* would have invalidated my insurance. Told you I didn't trust them.'

'Yes but – '

'Listen.'

I did so in amazement. Arnold spun the tape on from one section of recording to another, stopping between excerpts and spinning on again against the numbers on the counter. The MP here talked openly about his 'revelations' to his StB handlers, what had been handed on, the naming of names, his attendance at various Czech Embassy receptions – where, of course, he was an honoured guest – his invitations to spend summer retreats in the Jizerské mountains, rivers, and lakes of rural Czechoslovakia; names of places, Prague, of course, Piestany – 'Do you know it?' – Bratislava; and this and that in some profusion.

'After the second bottle of claret again,' Arnold commented.

In short, here was a man of some self-professed importance. Sponsored by another state; one of Communist rule. The recording was breathtaking in its declarations – a *mea confessio*, unmistakable, unambiguous.

The end of the tape slapped gently against the take-up spool. 'But why?'

'Because he thought I was on his side. That we were both on the same side, working for the StB.'

It was Arnold, after all, who had made contact with the StB in the first place on behalf of the MP. The MP clearly had no inkling that Arnold had handed on the man's desire to the Colonel's service, nor any suspicion that this tape recorded him several times admitting to passing on particular items of information – 'With my contacts, I was able to tell them...' whatever it was, this, that, and something else. But among these particular items of information were some of the dummies, credible but untrue, first fed to him from the Colonel's operation.

'So, what do you think?'

'I think this could not be more conclusive'

'Good. Then you shall have it.' Arnold laid a hand upon my forearm.

'Don't let them let me down. Give me your word that you'll keep them to their word, Anthony.'

I could not promise that. I could promise only to try, should the need arise, but I was certain that they really did mean to act and... Arnold waved away the rest of the little speech I might have made.

'That will have to do.'

In the event, at the dinner I had booked at the same restaurant in Dean Street to which William had taken me, there was neither the bitterness nor recrimination I had expected from Carolyne.

'I knew, when you told me you had chosen this restaurant. It's where William brought me that time you had a drinking appointment with some man.'

'And William kindly offered to look after you. Again.'

Carolyne was drawn, but there were no tears.

'You're right, Anthony. You *are* right. I am so sorry, so very sorry. I have been unfair to you but there will always be William between us. I know that now.' Head a little to one side, she reached across to hold my hand. 'I *have* tried, Anthony, I really have tried, and I know that you have tried too, but it's just that, it's just...'

There was further confession as, strangely and unexpectedly, we relaxed with each other and a shared relief enabled us to talk freely with each other.

'I loved him, Anthony, ever since Oxford. I can not explain it, it is simply something which overwhelms me – wanting to be with him even through all those times when I could not be with him. I thought, when you and I got together again, that William would simply fade away, and I *had* got over him, I think, but then he turned up again. And...'

And the rest, as one says, was our recent history.

'Ever since...ever since this, really.' Carolyne opened her handbag and took from an inner sidepocket a small envelope. Carefully from that envelope she took out and unfolded a sheet of paper, laying before me the neat, black, handwritten lines:

> *Nulla potest mulier tantum se dicere amatam*
> *uere, quantam a me Carolyne amata mea est.*
> *Nulla fides ullo fuit umquam foedere tanta,*
> *Quanta in amore tuo ex parte reperta mea est.*

'And this was when?'

I knew. But desire for a small and tawdry revenge drove me to demand confession.

Carolyne lowered her head.

'Oxford.'

I had recognised the lines, of course; the Catullus which William had offered me as irresistible to women. I noted he had heeded his own advice, substituting Carolyne for the poet's Lesbia. I pushed the paper back towards Carolyne. She turned the paper over.

'And this.'

There, in the same formed hand was William's own rendering.

> *No woman can truly say*
> *She is more loved*
> *Than is Carolyne by me.*
> *No faith was ever kept*
> *So fully as the greatness*
> *Of my love for you.*

Beneath was the signature *William*. And despite all I had to admit the epigrammatic concision of William's version.

I was wounded; my man's pride had been bested by another man. Yet, even in that moment of defeat there was release, a certainty that a wrong course had been avoided. For both of us.

'And you?' I ran a finger across the last three of William's short lines.

Carolyne went very still. When she spoke, her words were a whisper.

'Yes. Always. Sorry.'

I held up a hand. 'Then I shall wish the two of you joy. And happiness.'

Oh the brave soldier that I was, magnanimous and heroic. And greatly relieved.

37

We broke our agreement to an engagement. The fact that our engagement had not actually taken place was thanks to mother's prolonged unavailability to attend the ('pretentious and wholly unnecessary') event at which Carolyne's mother had wanted the formal announcement to be made.

Carolyne's father asked to meet me a couple of weeks after she had informed her parents that our engagement would not go ahead.

'Is it some other woman?' he asked.

'No,' I said. 'It's another man.'

Mother's initial reaction to the same news betrayed her. The pleasure in her voice was unconcealed.

'I liked the girl,' she said. Pause, then predictably. 'The mother was insufferable, though.' Pause. 'Ah well, these things usually work out for the best. You shall soon find someone with a bit of background to her.'

The new year seemed to move swiftly. In April the chambers paid its regards to Philip with a champagne farewell. Booth himself made a witty speech and presented him, on behalf of chambers, with a carved English oak desk pipe-stand complete with integrated ceramic tobacco jar, silver tamper with blade, and a mounted silver lighter.

A Place for Everything: Everything in its Place had been carved into the stand.

I moved into Philip's vacated room, the smell of his pipe smoke and coffee his continuing presence. I got on with my career and set about making a name for myself. Booth encouraged me, putting a couple of important briefs my way and delaying me for a chat. I think he believed I missed Philip. I did. But so did he miss the man. Neither of us admitted the loss to the other.

Moving in to that chamber was an inheritance. It stiffened me to apply myself – not to let down two of its previous inhabitants, my mentor and his mentor.

In William's prolonged absence Carolyne and I still met on infrequent occasions. It seemed churlish not to do so, and we became good companions. In that word which evades any commitment I remained *fond* of the girl. She was suffering because William had made it clear that he could make no promise for the future. Even when he returned, whenever that might be, he would not be the man he had been. Carolyne looked distressed; none of this made any sense to her. I asked if she had heard from him.

'Not for ages. Those were his last words to me.'

Now the two of us had been rejected, in some strange way we each became a support for the other.

'I write to him every day.' It was a wan smile she turned upon me. 'And once a week I post to him one of the letters I've written.'

Simon Carlton had already explained why Carolyne had not heard from William. Nothing to do with 'our' lot, as he put it. William was now 'one of Sir John's boys'. But, he opined, it was possible that they – that impersonal third-person party again – wanted William to receive only that mail, sent by ordinary post rather than in a diplomatic bag, which they were happy to have intercepted 'at the other end' by the other party before being re-sealed and forwarded to the Embassy, then on to the addressee. Post which revealed things they did not want known about their man was intercepted 'at this end' and, therefore, would not be received by William himself. Given what William was out there to accomplish, it would not do to have it known that he had a female lover with expectations of marriage to him.

'Wrong, ahem, persona entirely.'

Simon and I had been meeting to go through the transcript of the third tape which Arnold had released. There, from his own mouth, was the proof positive needed to condemn our errant MP. Even though the MP had thought that he and Arnold 'were on the same side' one had to congratulate Arnold on the way in which he had subtly drawn on his man to declare all. We were confident of the case. It needed only the go-ahead.

That go-ahead would not be forthcoming until Sir John had secured the objective for which William had been seconded to him.

Weeks passed, the sunshine of spring lit up the spaces and courts of the Temple grounds. When I was working in chambers I took to a lunchtime stroll, savouring the freshness of air, the noise from nearby Fleet Street at most a subdued hum and its traffic fumes blocked. There had been a long period of waiting: waiting to learn what had happened, what would happen. Sarah-Somebody had not been mentioned by Simon, despite my asking. 'Nothing, ahem, to do with me.' After those torn up, unread letters from William, I had not heard again from him, and Carolyne still had not received anything. Arnold Ward, whom I had met once more on his most recent return to this country, had little more to add to the observations he had previously made of William. Except that he personally had seen the man only fleetingly on this tour, just a couple of times at the Hradčany press briefings. Arnold himself had limited time in which to linger in London. He had to spend as much time as possible 'with the missus and her parents at our place in Herefordshire. Needs a lot of doing up, you know – but at least we've made a start on it now.'

'The missus? Oh, I see, you mean the surrogate, your stand-in wife for your legally-unwed wife.'

'The same. Nice girl, moved in there with her newly-discovered parents. I call her Sarah.' Arnold laughed gently whilst poking his elbow into my ribs. '*And*, I must say, she does have a passing resemblance to Sarah. Except close up, of course.'

I shook my head in disbelief. It all seemed excessive. Deception too, I mused, breeds paranoia.

'Agree with you, Anthony. I do agree. But, so I'm told, until they can be sure that Sarah – the one I'm married to, well, *meant* to be married to – is no longer of interest to them *over there*' – a thumb pointing over his shoulder, supposedly towards Czechoslovakia – 'I have to be with *her*, the one who's standing in for her, when I'm back here.'

'And, of course, I suppose with Sarah – someone *as* Sarah – accounted for in Herefordshire, it means that they' – as soon said, that unattached 'they', as soon abandoned: 'I mean once it is established that Sarah is no longer at the Home Department, she can be sent out to Prague as Sarah Somebody-Else – '

'She's already there, been there months I gather. Met her last time I was there.'

I had not known. And was angered that I had not been told.

Arnold was pressing his lips together, suppressing something humorous which his eyes betrayed.

'What is it?'

He burst into laughter. 'That 'falling in love with my wife again' she warned me about? Well, I'm scheduled to do just that the next time I'm out there.'

Before I could put any of the questions which instantly occurred to me, Arnold threw up his hands above his head, palms upwards, a surrender. 'I have to do as I'm told.'

'And that is?'

'I am commanded to have an affair with the woman.'

'Sarah?'

Arnold stretched his neck, tipping his head fractionally from side to side, attempting to assume a superior look. 'No, no, no, Sarah is no more. She is Alyson. *Missus* Alyson Bath, if you don't mind.'

Arnold was playing out the line.

'Missus Alyson Bath, unlike Sarah, has different colour hair, not blonde, to here' – he tapped a hand to the back of his neck – 'rather more slender features, and looks altogether much more like Alžběta than the woman I'm supposedly married to.'

The woman's name, for the first time, proffered. Alžběta – there was a softness to the sound of her name. 'And?'

The fish had been hooked. And I was wriggling.

'Already we have been seen together, have made a point of being seen together. And obviously becoming close, as one says. So, they will not be surprised next time around when...'

Arnold's was a pause that asked one to ask what more there was. Perversity and foresight combined to restrain me.

'On my next trip I have been ordered by Missus Bath to spend some nights with her in my room at the *Jalta* Hotel. It seems that she has something in mind for me.' His eyes twinkled, his lips smiled widely. 'At a guess, I would say it seems she intends to be unfaithful to me. *With* me.'

As we parted on that occasion Arnold clasped my hand. 'Wish me luck. Next time I see you I hope things will have moved on. I'm fed up with all this waiting, all this play-acting.'

38

Of course! Pantomime-fashion I actually did slap my brow with the palm of a hand. I lifted down the volume from a shelf, flicked the pages. Yes! Chaucer's Wife of Bath was indeed named Alyson. Somebody had exercised his, or her, humour in the naming.

I wondered if Sarah had invented Mrs Alyson Bath, or whether she had been the invention of Simon Carlton. I thought Arnold might have the answer. In the early part of June we met up again. He was over-nighting in London before setting off the next day for Herefordshire, home, and second unlawful wife together with her unrelated elderly parents.

After the curries after the beers, I put the question.

'And did you? Did you do as directed?'

Arnold's half-closed eyes puckered at the corners.

'*Well?*'

'Well what?'

I made to throw the water from a glass at him. 'Alyson. Alyson Bath. Missus Sarah Ward-As-Was. Did you? as arranged...you know, your room at the *Jalta*.'

'Oh that!'

'Yes, *that!*'

In later years Arnold claimed he could see it in me, he said: loss, and hope – each feeds and feeds on the other. He knew the symptoms, a fellow sufferer, so desisted from tormenting me further.

'Not in any literal sense, Anthony, no. We did not. But she did have to hold a handkerchief over my mouth to stop me giving it away.'

I raised my eyebrows, but with just sufficient control to suppress another question.

'You have to remember that we were being watched – well, as far as the hotel – and then listened to. We'd set out to call attention to ourselves, and we knew, of course, that my room was bugged so, well, when it came to it we had to pretend we were *busy* with each other. All had to be done in dumb-show. So Sarah's pushing and pulling me around, getting me to shift about a bit, then a bit more so that we can get the bed springs going, and she's directing me, getting me to, well' – at which point he moved his hips forward – 'and trying to do all this without bursting out into laughter. I couldn't move for choking into my handkerchief so she sat astride my stomach, pumping the wind out of me, and bouncing up and down for the both of us. Must say, though, she was very good, *very* good' – Arnold gave then a pairing of little gasps – 'and so on. Bloody hilarious, the whole thing.'

'Wouldn't it have been simpler just to – ?'

'No, Anthony. Lovely girl and all that. But you're forgetting – she looked too much like someone else.'

Arnold's waiting, which he wanted so urgently to be done with, would not be over until the autumn, though he did not know that. Nor would he know that until he had been back to his Eastern Europe posting, via East Germany and Poland and into Czechoslovakia, on two more stretches of duty. Even then, also not known to him at the time, he would have to make an additional tour of his Eastern Europe journalistic territory be-fore his waiting would finally 'be over and done with.' I knew this before Arnold himself would know.

'Had to send the poor chap back again. The longer we could maintain the appearance of the *status quo*, the more we would appear to be in the clear.' Sir John added: 'Must say that I thought it a bit of a gamble, but getting the lady out was, as you predicted' – he looked from the Colonel to Simon and back again – 'that little bit of final pressure needed to get our own man on the move now, rather than later.'

Simon leaned in towards me. 'Dušan was also the girl's section head.'

'And given that his position was already being compromised for all to see, thanks to the, er, good offices of your William...' From Sir John a nod in my direction where Simon and I occupied the settee, Sir John and Colonel Jackson each in an armchair. Philip busied himself with a bottle of whisky, water jug, and glasses. Having poured out three good fingers of measure into each glass and offered the water jug around, he propped himself on the arm of the settee, raising a glass.

'First things first, Sir John, if I may. To a job well done.'

The Colonel held up a hand. 'To one job completed, and one on the way.'

'And a special toast for Sarah.' Philip raised his glass once more.

An early summer weekend of sunshine: a small self-congratulatory celebration. Simon had collected me Saturday morning following Philip's invitation to his place. Elizabeth Hathers had left us a buffet lunch while she, Jennifer, the Colonel's wife, and Geraldine, Sir John's wife, had 'left the men to it' – as they set off on a shopping trip together.

'Clothes. Got nothing to wear, you know.' The Colonel's opinion, offered with an upturning of his eyes.

'No, no, shoes. Always shoes for Geraldine.' Sir John's view.

In the absence, clearly pre-arranged, of the womenfolk, Sir John Holyoake and Colonel Vernon Jackson had decided it was a good opportunity 'to chew the fat'. That was how, if I may be excused a dreadful extension of the phrase, I got to know the bare bones of the matter.

Alžběta Jana Fiala, Arnold's StB lover, even as we spoke was being sympathetically and gently 'unburdened' (the Colonel's own vagrant word) of her 'presents' to the service; a luggage of information which she carried with her, and other items which she did not know she also lugged about.

'We all know more than we think we know.' Colonel Jackson had a way of suggesting a smile without actually mobilising his face to do so. 'And the good lady has no need of that surplus stuff now.'

The Colonel proceeded to assemble the skeleton of a narrative; to which, subsequently, I was able to put more flesh. Sarah had gone out to Prague, as planned, as Mrs Alyson Bath on her passport, her photograph bearing a strong resemblance to the woman I now knew of as Alžběta Jana Fiala – Arnold's StB lover. Outside the Embassy building, close to its entrance, there was a low door, behind which, as all the Embassy staff knew, the Czechoslovak StB state security police recorded arrivals and departures, staff and visitors alike. Additionally, they were particularly zealous in photographing any person not previously observed.

The Wife of Bath, arrived at her posting, made a point of being noticed. For her first few days she wore a wide-brimmed hat. Once established at the Embassy she would pause on her way in, hand to the brim of her hat, half-turn towards the hidden watchers and coquettishly dip at the knees, waving with her free hand. This 'signature' of herself actually diverted attention. The watchers would see the signs but not the person. Once established as 'known', she could vary her habit – after several days arriving sometimes with no hat, so that the colour and cut of her hair also identified her. The wave with the nearest arm, the pause, half-turn, and the beginnings of a curtsey then defined her.

On his later trips to Prague Arnold had met up again with Sarah What's-Her-Name-cum-Mrs Wife of Bath in Prague. On one of her assigned evenings, several weeks into the second of Arnold's postings, Alžběta Jana Fiala, in her StB officer rôle collected the key to Arnold's room at the *Jalta* hotel. On her way out she left the key with the same concierge at the desk. She then re-entered the hotel by a service exit she had blocked open so that, unobserved, she could go back up to Arnold's room, having left its door unlocked. There, she waited for the arrival of Arnold and Mrs Alyson Bath.

It was then up to the two women to dress for the deception, and for Mrs Bath, Sarah-As-Was, to rehearse Alžběta Jana in the 'signature' she must make on approaching the British Embassy. Sarah ensured that the Czech woman would wear an outfit she had worn frequently to work to make her even more recognisable.

Alžběta Jana went to work in Alyson Bath's stead the following morning at the Embassy. Sarah and Arnold stayed put in the hotel room – Arnold looking so pale (Sarah's dab hand at foundation) and coughing so badly that the maid who brought up food and drink for him did not linger. Sarah, therefore, had to spend only minutes in the bathroom before making her own escape from a service entrance dressed in Alžběta's favoured fawn coat and blue headscarf.

Long story short. The Czechoslovak authorities had been informed in advance that one female member of Embassy staff would be returning home that day at the end of her period of duty; and that another female member of staff would be returning home on compassionate leave – her elderly parents taken very ill. It was hoped it would be a short absence, two weeks at most; long enough to organise care for her parents. At mid-day a taxi arrived at the Embassy gates to take Alžběta Jana (who 'signed' herself to the StB duty officers), together with her Embassy staff minder to Ruzyně airport, the Embassy car and driver having left very early morning on one of their regular runs to buy essential provisions. Once at Ruzyně airport Miss Alžběta Jana Fiala, together with Her Britannic Majesty's passport and diplomatic credentials in the name and looks of Mrs Alyson Bath boarded a scheduled flight to London with her woman companion.

Sir John inclined his leonine head as he regarded each of us in that small company.

'And Sarah?' I had to ask.

'Ah yes, Sarah. No passport, no accreditation, *persona non grata*. Tricky.'

'Then how – '

Sir John, unsmilingly, hands upturned, gestured helplessness. I was about to speak –

'Well, if it comes to it, Anthony, we shall just have to have her returned as diplomatic baggage.'

The Colonel, Sir John, and Simon, all straight-faced, regarded me intently – my concern clearly evident to them.

'There was another way, Anthony.' Sir John relented with gentle laughter, joined by the other two. Those three in the know; Philip, by his look, also uninformed. 'I can say we have our own Ambassador in Prague to thank for her exit route – though he doesn't know it, and we're not going to tell him.' A smile of complicity. 'These diplomatic types don't want any contamination from us more combative souls.'

And? and? and? Despite my embarrassment, there were more silent questions.

'I am delighted to say that we have Sarah in safekeeping, but shall need to get her back into the country as soon as possible. We need her there, in her former rôle and as an accredited member of Embassy staff. Work still to be done.'

Congratulatory words all round.

'Ah, yes. But to get her back into Prague there is the matter of the good woman's identity to be resolved. Clearly she can not go back in as the Wife of Bath' – Sir John flicking that away with the fingers of a hand – 'which is why Simon has devised another stratagem for the Wife of Bath.'

Suddenly – how had I failed to make conscious conclusion before then? – it became clear that Simon was very much more than a Home Department legal advisor. He had been *placed* there. And at the reference to the Wife of Bath he raised a hand in acknowledgement – *his* naming of Sarah as Mrs Alyson Bath, then.

'Some days before Missus Alyson Bath left for Czechoslovakia those many weeks ago she, ahem, applied for a decree absolute, the *nisi* having been granted exactly six weeks and one day previously on the grounds of her husband's admitted adultery. The actual divorce then, ahem, most fortuitously came into affect just a few days before Missus Bath, Sarah, arrived back here. Notices were carried in both *The Times* and *The Telegraph*. Surprised you didn't, ahem, see them at the time.'

Simon had his own humour. I had seen where this fictive history was leading, however.

'I take it then that, following her divorce, Missus Alyson Bath will have had to apply for a new passport in her maiden name?'

Simon acknowledged. 'With a photograph of herself looking, ahem, a little more like herself.'

'And which self would that be?'

'Why, ahem, Miss Alyson Cowper, who else?'

Received with much amusement. Philip Hathers leant forward with a question:

'And your man Ward, Vernon? What did you decide about him?'

'We've left him out there for the remaining days of his current tour – by which time John's target will have been lifted over to us and be in our safe hands. I shall speak with Mister Ward when he gets back. He will want to see his Alžběta Jana. Which we shall arrange for him. Once he will have agreed to do the remaining Eastern Europe tours for his newspaper. To be sure.'

Colonel Jackson was not a man for negotiation, though his last words seemed to carry an implication which I did not understand. It was clear, however, that the right order of things had been re-established; he had the controlling hand again; Arnold Ward would do his bidding,

'Meanwhile' – Sir John, with serious tone, took up the narrative from the Colonel – 'we can have at most just two, possibly three days before the whistle blows. Can't think it will take them any longer than that to catch on.' At which point Sir John, putting together his large hands, as if in prayer, said: 'To business, gentlemen.'

He looked around each of us in turn, a chairman's gathering to order. 'Simon, Anthony' – a nod towards each of us – 'we need to fill you in so that you two understand what is wanted of you. First, the latest on Dušan.'

With evident pleasure Sir John announced that Dušan 'was known to be on his way, the long way round.' The long way round was a two-day journey by car from Prague into Hungary – 'we' had a sighting there – and from there, 'probably' into Romania, by car or train or both was not known, and finally to Bulgaria.

'Declined our help, gentlemen. Insisted that he would have to do it his way, a better chance for him to get through friendly countries for some arranged leave. There's a holiday camp of sorts in Bulgaria for Czech security officers, and our man has planned to take a few days' rest and recreation there. It's when he fails to turn up that the proverbial will go off.'

Sir John spread those large hands.

'However, we know our man to be resourceful. Once in Bulgaria he has the means to contact our American friends who will then help him into either Greece or Turkey for a flight to a USAF base here at Alconbury. We shall pick him up from Cambridgeshire and ensure that he gets comfortable lodgings. Supervised accommodation. Once he has handed over whatever baggage he's managed to bring with him – scraps rather than volumes of paper, I'm afraid – we shall want to ask him a few questions. Drill into his memory. After that, our American friends will have earned the right to ask him a few supplementary questions. So, when we shall have finished with him, it has been agreed we shall wave him goodbye and wish him *bon voyage* to the United States of America where, in due course, he will no doubt be eager to start a new life. In California perhaps. San Francisco might be to his taste.'

Sir John spoke without a trace of irony. He raised a hand in invitation to Colonel Jackson to take his turn.

'It has been agreed, gentlemen, that while our new friend enjoys our hospitality, Sir John's people will have first opportunity to discuss matters with him. We, when we take our turn, of course shall be most interested to hear what he has to tell us of our naughty Member of Parliament. And the others that we know about. With any unknown to us who have been tempted from the straight and narrow. What I would like you to do – '

What Simon and I were being invited to work on was to identify, from dossier and now transcripts of Arnold's three tape recordings, points where Dušan might be able to confirm or amend or, most critically, add to information already retrieved. The MP's hints and suggestions needed to be explored, supplemented.

'Am I allowed to know who, or perhaps it should be what, is Dušan?'

By an exchange of looks Colonel Jackson and Sir John Holyoake silently conferred.

'Of course.'

Sir John's brief explanation gave Dušan as a senior StB officer who had been on the British desk in Prague for the past six years. Prior to that he had done four years at the Czech Embassy in London, running agents who sought to recruit informers from among politicians, trades union officials, journalists, scientists and technicians who worked in sensitive defence organisations – anyone in fact who could provide useful information, either out of conviction to the principles of socialism or, quite simply, for money.

'And Dušan's motivation for wanting to, ahem, defect?'

Sir John raised a loud baritone of a laugh. 'Wanting to and *needing* to, Simon. For which we have Anthony's friend to thank for the final nudge.'

It seemed that Sir John's 'people on the ground there' knew of the man's disenchantment with the state as it had become: it was, in his view, falling faster and further away from his ideals, those principles which had made him, until two years ago, a loyal servant of that state. The freedom to make choices, to engage in the ordinary business of life, had been eroded and continued to be so. Corruption was widespread, many petty to high-ranking officials were amenable to bribery; there was mistrust everywhere and a good deal of fear. He had made an approach to Arnold, in the first instance. From an exchange of pleasantries they had moved to what appeared to be something more exploratory. Arnold had reported, as an irregular, to the service. Then, at the point where Dušan seemed to be considering his options, one of Sir John's people had arranged a number of clandestine meetings with him. For more than a year the possibility of Dušan's 'transfer of affections', as Sir John expressed the matter, had been explored and encouraged to grow; but on each occasion when Dušan came to the very edge of a resolution he had taken a pace or two back.

Being so close on so many occasions to getting their man, Sir John had finally agreed to authorise an alternative approach – 'provided the right man could be found.'

'And that was your William. Who fitted the bill perfectly, from what vetting could discover about him. What you and other friends confirmed about him.'

Had I but known then what I know now. The thought fluttered like a banner in the wind. The follies of ignorance, I thought. I know all the men would have been of one mind, but I did wonder what Carolyne would have said about William when that nice young man from one of the service's branches visited her. She must have concealed her own evidence of him?

The extensive profile of Dušan had identified, but only towards the end of his attachment to London, his 'alternative sexual preferences' through his covert attendance at two 'gentlemen's clubs.' Until that stage his deceptions had worked. As then, so on his return to Czechoslovakia, he appeared so often with a woman on his arm at receptions and concerts that he came to be seen as a lady's man. Some of the woman had been borrowed from his own service, others hired for the occasion. His hitherto secret obsession, the spur to his lust, it had been learned, was with what had been somewhat allusively described as 'the homosexual male popinjay.'

'You recall our original conversation, Anthony? About your friend?'

I remembered very well that exchange with the Colonel. But blown in on the same wind of this recollection were other thoughts: of the deceived, my playing and drinking chums from those Oxford days; and of the undeceived – all their then girl-friends. Including Carolyne. And the real William? A sort of co-lourful, dandified Rorschach test that gives back what one projects into it, so that one gratifyingly sees what one looks for? An exotic creature, to revert to an earlier description, to excite the taste buds of man and woman alike?

During Dušan's London years he had searched those select male clubs of the capital for the ideal he longed for; and had failed to find. So when a photograph of William was passed his way –

'Simon saw to it. Courtesy gesture – advance notice of a new appointment to the Embassy staff. A rather good photograph actually.'

There was a fractional glint in the corners of the Colonel's eyes.

'Not the one which your good lady arranged to borrow from you, Anthony. But it did give us the idea, the pose, the composi-tion. Got a similar one done after William had joined up with us. Same place, your old college, that archway. Must say, though, the man looks hardly any older in the one we had taken.'

'And that, apparently, did the, ahem, trick.'

Sir John pushed his large frame back against the cushion of his armchair. 'After that, Simon, we had to do very little really. Just allow things to run their course – with a little encouragement from William of that... what was your phrase, Vernon?'

'Cultivated and refined ostentation.'

'Indeed, just so. We simply bided our time, took notes, made observations – primed by William – and, finally, managed to get some appropriate, some might say highly inappropriate, additional photographs in which both men featured prominently.'

The rest unsaid, as one says. Into that unspoken cerebration Philip proposed we take a break and a walk through the nearby country park. We rose in agreement.

'Slippery creatures – love, lust, desire, the way they transform into each other. Whichever one you start off with, whatever we think or persuade ourselves it is, it's only later we discover its impure nature. By which time we are committed, or condemned, or know we have made a mistake.'

'A confession?'

'No, Anthony, just a judgement – speaking as one now legally authorised and sanctioned to make judgements.'

The bright sun of late afternoon splintered its light through the leaves of oak, chestnut, and beech as we strolled along a path beneath their branches. Simon and I had fallen behind the other three men, partly, I think, out of tacit deference to the fact of their long familiarity with each other. So we left them to lead us on.

'So in the end it is a simple case of blackmail that has tipped the balance?'

'It would seem so. But what was, ahem, tipped into the scale was very heavily weighted.'

A *Yes but*. 'I thought things were moving now, a more liberal attitude. There's been talk for years of legislation that would decriminalise – '

'Legislation for which, so I am given to believe, can be expected next year. But we are not, ahem, talking of *here*, Anthony. We are talking of over *there* and, even more particularly, we are talking of the Russian masters who may well decide to reassert their authority. We hear that they are getting, ahem, restless, as it is.'

I asked Simon if the Russian masters took a particularly hard line on –

'That custom of which the Marquis of Queensberry accused Oscar Wilde, ahem, of being a practitioner – a 'somdomite', to cite his famously mis-spelled nominative? Indeed, yes.' Simon, head down, slightly bent at the waist in his mode of walking, added: 'In Soviet Russia homosexuality is actually a crime against the, ahem, state, did you know that?'

According to the Russian state, courtesy of Stalin apparently, and, so I also learned, upon conviction carrying a sentence of up to five years hard labour. '*And*' – Simon completed his explanation – 'the offender of that act can be committed to a psychiatric institution because such a predisposition is officially, ahem, classed as a mental illness.'

Given the threat of being exposed as a practising homosexual – expressed in Simon's locutionary by-way from the incident of Queensberry's note left at the Albemarle club – and given the fact that when Alžběta Jana Fiala's disappearance would come to light he would be held responsible, one understood the irresistible force by which Sir John and the Colonel had engineered their grip on poor Dušan .

Returned to Philip's home just as a cooling, light wind had swayed the bushes at the edge of the parkland, I had one unanswered question. I think Sir John sensed what I wanted to ask, for he looked down to me, his smile large, a heavy hand resting on my shoulder and by its movement directing me to join him on the settee.

'William?' Sir John ran his thick fingers either side of his head, re-composing his mane of white hair disturbed in the breeze. 'Oh, William. We shall just leave him out there. He's not doing any harm, he does provide a distraction – that's useful in itself –

a diversion, you might say, while everyone is looking at the right hand, the left is the busy one.'

He glanced up at the Colonel, standing alongside Philip.

'Or do I mean the right is busy and the left is up to no good?'

There was a conspiracy of smiles all round.

'Anyway, your friend William does seem to be enjoying himself. Also seems to pick up all the tittle-tattle to hand on – some of it may even prove to have value.'

Philip was bringing round a 'warmer', as he called it – a whisky mac, the cooling breeze outside much colder, he insisted, than we had felt it to be. A preventative measure, therefore. We clinked glasses.

Sir John turned again to me.

'Do you know, Anthony, to begin with William was a puzzle to us. We were not at all certain how to *read* the man. After a time, however, we decided that there is something so overwhelmingly *obvious* about William that one simply could not take him for a man of subterfuge, of concealment.'

I withheld comment. Sir John was drumming fingers on the arm of the settee.

'I think, actually, he's having a thoroughly good time out there. Last month alone your friend William and his new Czech friend were at concerts which included works by Janacek, Tchaikovsky, Beethoven, Brahms, and, if memory serves correctly, Hindemith and Prokofiev. Privileged seats, naturally. And only last week he was at the Smetana Hall for the composer's *Má Vlast* – I think that's how it's said – *My Country*, to you and me.' Sir John paused, lips pressed together, then relaxing slowly into a rueful upturn, as he looked sideways at me. 'Now isn't that something to tickle the ironies, Anthony? *His,* Dušan's country, the one he is about to abandon, deceive, and betray?'

SEVEN

In and out of the box

London: *The Army and Navy*: Buckinghamshire

1966 – 1999

39

Eheu fugaces... Those lines from Horace's *Ode* again. The older one becomes, the more frequently echo these first words, tamping on the nerves, of the years passing. Alas.

They are lines which re-open thirty years of memory since that walk through parkland of oak, chestnut, and beech with Judge Hathers and his house guests. These now are the decades which refuse to queue in neat, sequential order. Drifting into that reverie of history I am interrupted. Seconds later I hold in my hand a large, thick brown envelope just signed for. In a blast of noise, his motorbike fumes still hanging in the air, a foul-smelling rising blue cloud, the courier speeds away from the Kensington mews houses.

I hold also several smaller envelopes from that morning's post, retrieved from the doormat before opening the front door to the black-leathered figure whose business with me, nothing more than my signature, was done in seconds.

I toss the package onto my desk. In the quiet of my study, in an atmosphere lightly carrying the waft of vanilla – a scent with which my housekeeper manages to permeate all the rooms – I look though the other envelopes. Bills and statements, except for one. The card inside is ornately (and expensively) produced: gold and silver, on embossed surfaces in the design of bells, hearts, ribbons, flowers. I read the inner leaf.

Sir William and Lady Carolyne Walsh

request

the presence of your company

at the marriage

of their daughter

Victoria Anne Carolyne

to

The Hon. Sebastian Hugh Tarquin Brett-Fenwick

I read no more, the *where* and *when* mere details to turn back to another time. I take off my reading glasses, the invitation splayed open in my other hand. It is signed both by William and by Carolyne.

Carolyne and Carolyne's mother (she of the plain Jane name) are to connect formally with a son of the minor nobility. My immediate response conjures up the picture of my old mother and the scorn with which she will greet this news. For her, now in her eighties, here is incontrovertible evidence that she had been right all along about 'that dreadful woman', Carolyne's mother.

As I am about to put down the invitation, a neatly folded sheet of paper pokes out from between the inner sheets and its endpaper. It is embossed letter-headed notepaper, as from the Principal of my old Oxford college, hand-written and underscored.

Dearest Anthony,

Do <u>please</u> *say you will. William and I would so* <u>love</u> *you to come. It is so long since last we saw you, and we do both miss you so. And Victoria has commanded me to be sure not to forget to ask Uncle Anthony to her special day. Sebastian is such a nice young man, you will like him I'm sure. William would particularly like you to come and see your old college again – and we could easily arrange some very comfortable accommodation, there are good hotels nearby, as you know.*

<u>Do</u> say you will come. I could not bear to think of you in that stuffy little place of yours on such a day.

Yours, with love,

Carolyne
PS And <u>I</u> should miss you <u>terribly</u>.

Carolyne's *post scriptum* is sincere in what she writes and entirely selfish in its motivation. She writes with the understanding, long-established, wordlessly, between the two of us that I shall resist this invitation, as others over the years, as a matter of principle. Also understood is the fact that Carolyne, as on previous occasions, will not willingly accept refusal. She will continue to undermine any reason or excuse offered until, worn into submission, I shall accede. *Dear Sir William and Lady Carolyne...*

On a shelf above my desk is a wooden box. Following the edges of its lid is a thin strip of inlaid ebony within which frame are set several other woods of varying colours and grains. The design of the marquetry displays the far side of a deep cleft of valley, trees clinging to its almost sheer sides, with a castle perched at its top. The castle is of an impossible construction, as well as location: towers topped with witches hats, pointed turrets, crennelations, a flagpole and the streamer of a pennant. The box, originally containing large and expensive cigars, belonged to Great-Uncle Ranulph and was passed on to me by my father. Apart from his enamelled coffee-pot handed on to me by Philip, this is the one possession of my Great-Uncle's that I own. It contains now a few scraps from a life. Mine.

I have a singular memory of those occasions when, as a young boy, I visited Great Uncle Ranulph. At some point in each visit he would open this cigar box and begin his own fumatory ritual. He would take up and crackle in turn between thumb and forefinger several of the cigars. To confirm his choice he crackled again the chosen cigar close to his ear, nodding in satisfaction at the auditory autograph of the chosen one. With great, unhurried concentration he would slice off the rounded end of the cigar with a silver guillotine concealing a razor-sharp blade in the cross-piece of its frame. The blunt end of the cigar would then be on the tip of his tongue and rotated until it was coated to his satisfaction in his own saliva. There would be a wafting of a match held in one hand at the end of the cigar held in the other hand. Only after this would the ceremony of actually lighting the cigar begin, until a satisfactory stormcloud of smoke had been created by a succession of short drawings in and puffings out. These rites were conducted always in total silence which, by some kind of sympathetic magic, was adhered to by all present. When, finally, the cigar was burning as desired, Great-Uncle Ranulph would settle back into his leather armchair, eyes closed with a smile of beaming pleasure, his free hand resting on the rounded rise of his stomach. It is that attitude, one of an old man entirely at peace with the world, contented with what his life has been, savouring its treasures in memory, which I later came to associate with the ritual of those cigars and the box which contained them.

The box had been given to him by, in that old-fashioned term, 'an admirer.' A female admirer, as finally admitted to me by mother. A lover. A married lover, even more distastefully divulged.

To be dealt with after a sufficient period of procrastination, into this box I put the latest arrival, the invitation to Victoria Anne Carolyne Walsh's wedding and sit again at my desk to scratch away at words of the past tense, beginning at the point where my reverie had taken me.

Two years after Alžběta Jana Fiala had arrived in England on Mrs Alyson Bath's passport, events in her home country took rapid turns. It was the year of 1968 which, in Czechoslovakia, had begun with great optimism for a 'democratisation' of its socialist systems, the lifting of censorship on books, newspapers, magazines, and, among other reforms, a greater freedom to travel. That same year of the 'Prague Spring' – as it became known in histories of the times – there took place those summer events which ended in the occupation of the city streets by Soviet tanks and troops. I followed the events with studied scrutiny, day by day reading the various despatches within the press here. On those occasions when I continued to meet with Simon or the Colonel I would ask if they had any 'locally-sourced' (as it was delicately phrased) information to add to or qualify these reports. I had a special concern. In as neutral a tone as I could simulate, I posed the concern as a question to the Colonel at one of these meetings.

'May one ask if Miss Cowper is still out there?'

'Who?' Colonel Jackson immediately covered his inadvertence. 'Oh, our Sarah. Yes, yes. Still a shortage of staff everywhere. Signed her over *pro tem* to continue at the Embassy. Needs must *et cetera*. Welcome her back with open arms as soon as conditions permit.'

'She has been there a long time now. More than two years.'

'Circumstances, Anthony. Circumstances.'

'Do you think – '

'Sorry, Anthony, but she's with Sir John's control now. Very busy times out there, as you know.'

Nothing further was volunteered.

I continued to watch events in Czechoslovakia and eastern Europe generally. There was turmoil and dissent throughout. It was to be more than another full year before, via Simon, the news was passed on to me that Miss Alyson Cowper-As-Was, formerly the Wife of Bath, was now 'home.' It took another twenty years after that homecoming before one could see that the Communist regime in Czechoslovakia, as in other countries within the Soviet bloc, was into its last gaspings. By then Carolyne's and William's daughter Vicky was a pert and precocious sixteen year-old, and my godson, Arnold's and Alžběta's son, who bore my name, was already a fine young man of twenty absolutely adored by his two younger sisters. It was also the year in which I proposed to Sarah and she refused me.

Within months of William's return from Czechoslovakia there took place his marriage to Carolyne. I have still the invitation to that wedding buried somewhere in Great-Uncle Ranulph's cigar box. It is ostentatious, over-designed and elaborate, promising a ceremony and its celebration which a mere glance at its contents would confirm to be costing a small fortune. The design, I do have to say, confirms my mother's judgement as to Jane Walker's pretensions to social advancement. I had to pull myself up short; for again I was bringing mother to mind and her social views.

Some months after Carolyne's and William's wedding Booth stopped me on my way into chambers one morning.

'Mister Anthony. I have taken calls both yesterday late on and early this morning from a gentleman by the name of Mister Walker. He wonders if you would be so kind as to afford him a few minutes of your time.'

'Mister *Peter* Walker?'

'Indeed yes, Mister Anthony. I fear, from the manner of this person's address – somewhat familiar – he would claim to be an acquaintance of yours. I fear also that there is an expectation that this consultation will be *gratis*. A grace and favour, one might say.'

Somehow, the thought not for the first time, I must contrive to get my mother and Booth together. They would surely get on like the proverbial consumption of a house by fire. Any division of class between them would crumble from the combined heat of their shared snobberies. My mother would have taken greatly to Booth for the added recommendation of his subservience – at least, his pretence thereof.

I did see Peter, as arranged reluctantly by Booth. Carolyne's father, by bearing and manner of address, was embarrassed. He was effusively cordial in greeting me, so sorry about the 'way things had turned out', but wished very much to re-establish my friendship with the family – 'Jane still has not got over losing you as our son-in-law.' *That* I did not believe for a moment, now that she had an Oxford academic in the family to boast about.

Finally, I brought him to the point. He wanted some advice. There was in the offing (a strange construction) the possibility that – unwittingly, of course – one of his companies may have – inadvertently, of course again – fallen foul of certain trading restrictions, according to authorities now pressing for 'some additional paperwork.' I noticed that Carolyne's father, in common with many clients observed in my career, presented himself as a victim of circumstance, not an agent of one's own will.

'You wouldn't believe, Anthony, the sheer volume of regulations you have to wade through.'

I listened on, knowing that I would say I could not be of help. Not my area, a very specialist area. Perhaps Booth could recommend...? I telephoned Booth, asking him to spare a few minutes with my guest.

Later, Booth ensured that I knew he had favoured both me and guest.

'I have recommended to your acquaintance a company of solicitors who would seem to be most suited to the gentleman's predicament.' Pause. 'They specialise in international trade and the sale of goods.' Pause. 'In Commercial Road, fittingly enough, given the gentleman's needs.'

And, unsaid by Booth but in the character of the man, well away from here, I thought.

Yet I liked Peter Walker. Following this encounter we continued to meet. Every few weeks we met for lunch or for an early evening drink; meetings which he concealed from his wife, but which he divulged to his daughter.

'She is still very fond of you, you know.'

On one occasion, head down, cradling his glass in both hands, he added: 'I just don't know what Carolyne sees in the man, that William.' Carolyne's father waved his arms in admission of helplessness. 'But my daughter dotes on him.'

Somehow or other Peter Walker had also convinced himself that it was through my good offices that the nature of his commercial sin, whatever it was, in the final outcome had been penalised by the imposition of substantial fines, rather than the more severe punishment he had feared. He wanted to express his gratitude. I told him that it was undeserved, that I had done nothing to assist. The more I protested, the more forcibly he pressed his gratitude upon me.

Peter Walker was, as one could see readily enough, an opportunist, whose rôle was to make money which Mrs Jane Walker could then spend in ways that enhanced their social status and position. For him the making of wealth was simply the by-product of the pleasure he derived from trading. He had become a very successful businessman, with several companies and offices in two capital cities. But as he had succeeded so had his wife's social ambitions found more stairs to climb. There must have been a tussle between mother and daughter over my invitation to the wedding.

Before the joy, finally, of her brief engagement to William, Carolyne had been made to suffer a prolonged absence from her new, or her old former lover – William having been kept on in Prague by Sir John for his unignorable visibility. When released from that posting, it was just prior to the events of the 'Prague Spring' that Carolyne and William actually married. By then I was far more concerned about Sarah-Otherwise-formerly Missus-Bath's continuing safety than their forthcoming nuptials.

I declined the invitation to Carolyne's wedding on a pretence, which Carolyne knew to be a pretence. She had managed to infiltrate into the envelope with the wedding invitation a narrow strip of paper in her own hand: *Do* please *say you will come, Anthony. Love, Carolyne XXX.* My attendance, I knew, would be taken gladly by her as another confirmatory gesture of forgiveness on my part for her duplicity in re-starting her affair with William when, as near as a visit to a jeweller's, she was engaged to be married to me. Somewhere in my box there remain examples of her rather girlish handwriting, her short letters always either just entreaties or ending with an entreaty. And, more evident to me as the years have passed; she has never stopped wanting me to miss her, the irreplaceable Carolyne.

As to the invitation to her daughter's wedding: even now, these decades further on, whilst she would not in fact miss me 'terribly' at her own daughter's wedding, as she claimed, I do know that my absence would create unease for her, a reminder that one's absence *et cetera...* Thus I enjoy for a minute or two playing with the thought of the uncertainties which Carolyne would suffer if I do not accept this latest invitation or, accepting, do not turn up. Then I think of Victoria (to her mother), Vicky (to everyone else – at her own insistence), her daughter, a lovely girl of whom I am very fond... and I know, as Carolyne also surely knows, that after due postponing I shall accept the invitation to her daughter's wedding. And shall attend. With Susan on my arm.

~ **40** ~

Upon his return to this country William soon took up his sine-cure as Visiting Fellow at our old college, as he also resumed his itinerant lecturing for the British Council. Carolyne resented greatly William's periods of time away on these duties, since having been returned to her, after all her waiting, she willed that he should be permanently available to her. I took it that he was still 'in service', and that he had been released from Sir John's left hand to return to the Colonel's right.

The years pass. There are other requests made of my presence from Carolyne; an invitation to share in the celebration of William's various stations on the way to eminence in the academic world. They include his installation as Principal of our old Oxford college and, some four years back, his knighthood. Now Charles University has awarded him an honorary doctorate for services to Czech literature – another of the garlands he has gathered over the decades. An invitation to the award ceremony, signed simply 'William', carried also a little note from Carolyne who wondered if I would like to join them in Prague for a few days. The usual plea: *Do* please *say yes*. I declined, I wanted very much to visit the city. But not with them.

Several weeks after Dušan, Alžběta Jana's former StB boss, had arrived safely in this country courtesy of the USAF, the embargo on letters to William was lifted. Carolyne had just received the first of William's replies to the first of her letters actually allowed through to him. By then she had been writing to him for many months. William, of course, could not have known of Carolyne's changed circumstances *vis-à-vis* me – and, consequently, his own altered standing *vis-à-vis* Carolyne.

She waved the letter at me.

'Well?'

At which question from me the tears started in Carolyne's eyes, the wetness welling in each underlid to a fullness that then overflowed. The drop of each tear slowly traced its course over her cheeks, to the side of her lips, and then met again to form a single droplet at the point of her chin. She forced out the words between sobs.

'He doesn't even *miss* me, Anthony!'

She thrust the letter into my hands.

William being William he had been making use of his extended stay in Prague to study the history of Czech literature and, from the tone of his letter, it appeared that he was quite content to stay there. The music concerts were wonderful.

Carolyne had not known that her open post letters to William had been intercepted here, since they would certainly have been opened by the StB at the other end. Thus William had not received any of her declarations to him. To Czechoslovakian eyes, those of Dušan especially, her feminine claims upon William would have been at odds with those other expectations of him that had been so carefully nurtured. Nothing could be chanced to diminish his effectiveness as an exotic lure for Dušan's rarefied tastes.

Not knowing any of this, to Carolyne everything was simple. William knew of her love for him, so he simply *must* love her in return. She was *his* now, free for him to be *hers*. He was simply ignoring her, this change in circumstance (no more *me* in the equation) which meant that they could now be openly together. So why..? Carolyne faltered, biting on her underlip that trembled in her distress.

'Is he refusing me, Anthony? Has he rejected me?'

Carolyne held on to my arm.

'How can he be happy there, Anthony, knowing I am here waiting for him? and not even knowing when he's likely to be back here?'

My reply was meditated.

'I am sure he continues to be of great service there, Carolyne. As he has been.'

Following the lifting of the embargo, months after Dušan's and Alžběta Jana's escape from Czechoslovakia, letters from William arrived weekly, though they remained guardedly bland.

'But what is he *doing* there? Apart from reading books. He just doesn't say, not really. I mean, he goes here and there for music concerts, but really he tells me nothing.'

Well, nothing of what you want to hear, I thought.

'He never says, no matter how often I write to ask him.'

What William was not saying was what Carolyne wanted of him now; a confirmation of his undying love for her, his dearest wish to be with her *at this very moment*. And in all the years to come. I could have written for William the perfect reply.

'He doesn't even tell me what he went there for in the first place.'

Nor did I say. Then or in all the years since. It was not difficult to keep silence in this instance. How could one tell his prospective wife why William had been chosen for that particular assignment? How could I tell her he had been sent there with the mission of seducing a man, in order to suborn him so that his position became impossible? And how could I say that it was my appraisal of the man which had clinched his selection for the task?

I could also have told Carolyne what William was doing now as a marker of the service's lack of involvement in Dušan's disappearance by asking for the man's whereabouts. And looking bereft at the man's disappearance; a ploy intended to suggest that Dušan had absconded for personal reasons – to escape his disgrace rather than that he had defected to the enemy. William was also a useful, and accurate, reporter of events through people he had become familiar with.

'I really don't know what to think, Anthony. I was so sure, and now...'

In this period of uncertainty during the time of William's pro-longed absence, Carolyne and I still entertained each other on occasion. She could not easily be with her parents, her mother especially, with whom there was constant battling; and she simply was no good at being alone. A confession. I relished the additional satisfaction I felt when, in that period awaiting William's return, we ended up in bed; a *quid pro quo* which was some kind of revenge upon William. Strangely, or perverse-ly, for reasons I can not explain, these were occasions when Carolyne abandoned herself, with no pretence of reserve, to the shifts and turns of love-making, those varied indulgences each of the other. She became a different lover. There was something newly avid, needy, grasping in her ways. We would clamp lips, breaking away from each other finally with ten-der flesh feeling bruised and breath coming in heaving gasps. Afterwards I would experience a sense of shame. Carolyne was so vulnerable in that long period of waiting for William that somehow, despite her willing participation – initiation of our love-making in fact – I felt that I had taken advantage of her. When the opportunity next presented itself, however, the sweetness of revenge short-circuited any reluctance one might have felt.

Somewhere in Great-Uncle Ranulph's box there is also a book of matches taken from the table of one of the restaurants where Carolyne and I had dinner during this period of waiting for William's return. On the inside cover Carolyne wrote: *Forgive me XXX.*

I do not know if William knows of this *interregnum*, the for-mer king reinstated in the new king's absence, the new king having abdicated. At times throughout the years since I have turned back to my *Anthology* to read *The Answer* to *A Question* of which of two lovers the Lady 'did love best'; the one from whom she took a garland of flowers or the one to whom she gave the garland. I have never been able to resolve the reasoning of *The Answer*. William and I – as I saw and see things – had our garlands swapped with Carolyne *by* Carolyne, give and take, taken from and given to, several times over. That being so, I never could make sense of the final couplet:

> ...*where She takes; She honours most; and where*
> *She doth most honour; She most love doth bear!*

The end of the matter was simpler than that: Carolyne had taken my crown away from me and given it to William; who still wore it to this day. The puzzle of the poem confirms for me why I gave up the study, the struggle, of literature. At least in my trade, however long-winded an answer may be, it is definitive – Guilty or Not Guilty.

Once the prohibition on her correspondence was lifted, William would have learned of his coronation as Carolyne's new king. The new king did also learn, however, that in his continuing absence in Prague before his return from Czechoslovakia I 'took care of' Carolyne. The economy of the phrase is hers. One of the two letters of William's I have retained thanks me for 'looking after' Carolyne and 'keeping up her spirits' during his absence.

The time for victory or revenge, however tawdry, is long past. I must look out that letter and destroy it. Something always distracts me from that good intention.

The second of William's letters cached among the memorabilia is longer, more extensive, the closest to a *mea culpa* the man ever arrived at or was capable of. I am not being fair. For William to be too ready to assume guilt for his actions, given the track of his life, given especially that he had for so long lived a solitary life, would have weakened the man. He had had to remain strong, resolute, hardened. Certainly, I admit, he is – and was – tougher than me. This letter, at the least, apologises for the way things turned out. There is the unstressed implication that particular events were not of his own making, though he was a contributor to some of them. There is no admission that what he did was wrong. And, apart from one's injured pride, in the longer run what he did turned out to have been the right thing. Nearly thirty years on he and Carolyne are still together and, by all the signs that one sees, still love each other. Carolyne and I would have parted somewhere into our future without William's intrusion. And *that*, in the first place, had been at my invitation – asking him to look after Carolyne while the men of our group sought the rowdy pleasures of post-match intoxication at Oxford. I shake my head in amused disbelief: that was before any of us knew about William. I mean, one assumed, from all appearances and so on... we *all* did, all of the deceived men in our group, we all entrusted our women to him. *Jollied every one of them.*

Fools! What young fools we were. Today I can smile at the thought, but for a long time after my discovery of the truth about William both anger and betrayal clung to the thought. Yet he freed me from what would have been a disastrous marriage to Carolyne. Thus, as the years slipped past, resentment became gratitude. One thought, however, abided. The men in our group at Oxford had been his procurers. Unwittingly we had provided his women for him by handing to him our own. We pimped for him; he did not have to bestir himself. We had fed our pet to satiated contentment.

Before William was returned home, there were letters from Arnold. And more invitations. Arnold Ward came back from his enforced additional eastern Europe tours several months after Alžběta Jana's safe reception here.

Within two days of his safe return Arnold bounced into my chamber, with Booth red-faced just a step or two behind him, and made for my desk. Reaching across, he lifted my arm and squeezed a very hearty handshake upon me.

Booth, panting, offended. 'I am very sorry, Mister Anthony, the gentleman gave me no – '

'It's alright, Booth. Let me introduce you.'

Only following a fulsome apology from Arnold did Booth allow himself to be placated.

'Most irregular, Mister Ward, most irregular – '

At which Arnold burst into laughter; and I joined in the un-witting joke. Booth looked wounded again.

'An irregular, in a manner of speaking, Booth, is precisely what Arnold is. Or was.'

Booth glowered, explanation mutely demanded.

'Coffee, everyone?'

I motioned to Booth and Arnold to seat themselves while I brewed up, in the pot bequeathed to me by Philip, a concoction of which he would have approved. Explanations went with the coffee, and Booth was suitably appeased and gratified.

'And I owe it to this man.' Arnold, hand outstretched towards me, spoke to Booth.

I tried to disabuse them both. It was through no act or speech of persuasion of mine that the absconding of Alžběta Jana had been agreed. Arnold simply refused to accept my denial.

'And so what changed their minds, Anthony? Whoever *they* are.'

'Circumstances, Arnold. Circumstances.'

To the present, Arnold has refused to believe this truth. I am garlanded in the lie he finds easier to accept. Soon after that day on the top floor of these chambers Arnold also enlisted Alžběta Jana to his belief. She converted instantly and unshakeably to the same falsehood; and no appeal by me to the accurately vague explanation I had offered was countenanced by either of them. Eventually I simply accepted their joint gratitude rather than begin again on another doomed repetition of the truth. As the years went by, and their gratitude was renewed with every correspondence and at every meeting, I simply accommodated myself to the fiction, losing all sense of embarrassment and almost beginning to believe it myself.

The year following Alžběta Jana's arrival in England – and the year before Carolyne married her William – Arnold Ward married Miss Fiala in a quiet Registry Office ceremony.

'Remind you of your first marriage, Arnold?'

Arnold merely grimaced.

'I wonder where Sarah is now. It would have been wonderful to have been able to ask her here. Alžběta and I owe her a great deal.'

I did not say that she was still out there, in Prague, with duties now assigned to her by Sir John's section, but for how much longer I had not been told.

Arnold and his new wife and I wondered for a good deal longer when she would return. They wanted her to know their gratitude; my motive was otherwise. My occasional inquiries met always with the same response from the Colonel as to the whereabouts of Miss Sarah or Alyson Cowper-by-Any-Other-Name. By the time I was allowed to know something, Alžběta Jana and Arnold had been long settled in their refurbished manse in Herefordshire and Alžběta Jana, following her speeded naturalisation approval, had become officially Elizabeth Jane. As Elizabeth Jane she had from the first been introduced by Arnold to his family, friends, and neighbours once she had been released to join him, following her lengthy series of extended 'conversations' with some of Sir John's people.

For the best part of a year following his delayed return from Prague, William had been trying to persuade me to meet up with him. There had been letters to my flat and to chambers. I had ignored them all. Two or three times I had been able to suppress even the smallest pique of curiosity and had been able to deposit them in the waste bin without even opening them. That gave me the greatest pleasure.

'But he really does want to speak with you. He knows he has been beastly to you – we both have. He wants you to know how sorry he is for the way... for how things turned out. And he does value you, you know, he still thinks of you as his dearest friend... *Please*, Anthony. For me as well as for William.'

Thus Carolyne, in one of many telephone calls to me following William's homecoming. What restrained me, and gave me the tenacity to refuse, was one luminous recognition: that this was something, however petty, that I *could* do. My refusals stood in the way of their peace of mind: of Carolyne's pre-eminently, but through her agitation, William's. He had to settle her, one knew this of Carolyne, and induce a poise of calmness if she were ever to be managed in partnership. Of course, as I recognised at the time, my repeated refusal of them was a mean and petty act. *But*... I wanted some kind of retribution. I wanted to inflict hurt.

Carolyne, following that long telephone conversation with me must have given William a good talking to. At least it is the only explanation I can offer for the second of William's letters. Its paper has slowly taken on over the years the faint remnant odour of Great-Uncle Ranulph's cigars that were for so many years past trapped in that box. The letter is marked by a complete change of tone. It is composed in simple sentences, not at all like William's characteristically elaborate compositions in subordinate clauses.

I did try very hard to ignore my feelings for Carolyne. I am truly sorry that I have hurt you. I do not excuse myself. But I do hope that some time you will be able to be magnanimous and agree

*to us meeting. I miss your company. I miss the one adult male
friendship I have known.*

There was more to the letter. But it was those last two short
sentences which undid my resolve. I wrote to say that I would
meet him. I chose the Gin Palace at Putney crossroads, Arnold's first meeting-place with me, for our venue. It would
be unfamiliar territory for William. It would discomfit him, I
thought.

In the event he confounded me. He arrived at the bar sans hat,
sans brightly-coloured cravat, sans ostentation altogether. He
was dressed casually: an open-necked shirt, blue check sports
jacket and light grey trousers. Only the black of his thick, long
hair, the black goatee beard and those dark eyes behind the steel
frames of his glasses remained of William. The fop had gone.
So too had the silver-topped walking-stick. And the limp.

He approached me, diffidently, uncertain whether to greet
me with a smile, but with hand outstretched, his eyes watching,
cautious, waiting for any minute gesture of mine that would
betray me.

'It is *so* good to see you again, Anthony.'

He had my hand gripped. I felt his sinewy strength.

'Hello, William.' I was not prepared to concede instantly.

He continued to hold my hand in his grip.

'It really has been such a long time, but – '

'But here we are.' I thought to finish for him, quite distinctly
now pulling at my hand to free it.

'At last.' With which he released my hand.

We continued to stand, close to each other, in uncomfortable
silence for some seconds.

'By the way, William' – I had no idea at the time what prompted this remark – 'I see that the entry in the *National Biography* for
your man William Walsh says that his writings are insignificant.'

William smacked a hand against his chest, head tilted back, savouring his own delight.

'Ah... the estimable Sir Adolphus William Ward, doubtless, the author of the piece. But I am gratified to see you have taken an interest in my man, the selfsame composer of 'trifles' – to use William Walsh's own word for his writings.'

'Answer the charge, William.'

'It would be gentler and kinder of us to refer to him as a light versifier, an *amuseur* might we not say? As for the verse, most of it was intended for the ladies, not for a severe and remote middle-aged male critic in centuries to come. What thinkest thou, my dear Anthony?'

All of a sudden we were back at Oxford, William in the pomp of his erudition, his instant recall, the intellectual badinage that dissolved my enmity.

'Then what do such slight things say about those ladies?'

For a second or two William's eyes caught the reflections from the suspended globe lights in the bar, so that they twinkled and seemed altogether to lose the darkness of their depths.

'Let us just say that *folies de jeunesse* may be perpetrated by either sex.'

'And not just by those whose youth excuses them.'

For the first time I had produced an unanswerable sally.

Perhaps I needed that small, mean victory in order to begin to release the magnanimity which William sought of me. The truth is that within minutes of meeting with him again I realised that I had missed William, that I enjoyed his company and wanted his company – of which I had somewhat perversely deprived myself since his return from Czechoslovakia.

We moved from the bar to a table. With an unremembered consumption of alcohol, having moved on to the whiskies, we became fully relaxed with each other; to the point that we could talk openly about the no-longer-to-be postponed subject we needed to talk through.

'I did try, Anthony, I tried so very hard to suppress my feelings for Carolyne.'

'I know. I know that now.' Those lines, poetry and prose, those excerpted words he had copied out in his own hand. 'The words of William Walsh *by* William Walsh.'

William grimaced. 'Alerts, my dear chap, warnings.'

'You hid behind another man's words.'

There was a small wincing of his eyes. 'I took another man's words into myself. In this sense they became my words too.'

'Thief!'

'Borrowed. And used for different ends. They were intended to serve and were deployed in the manner also of invitations.'

'Invitations?'

'To work things out. To intervene. To put a stop to something I knew I could not willingly put a stop to for myself.'

'But you cheated' – I sounded like a schoolboy; even so, I waved down whatever William was about to say – 'the one you entitled *Rivals,* in my edition is just called *Song.*'

William nodded admission.

'Six lines of which you changed. So, a joint composition by William Walsh *and* a pretender to his name of William Walsh.'

I allowed the silence to ride, watching William rehearsing his own lines of response, deciding which to offer.

'All to try to make things clearer. I thought you would comprehend.'

'Actually they're not a bad six lines. Now that I understand, they make sense. At the time, not knowing, they did not.'

William held up his hands, shoulder high, palms showing, his signal of defeat. He drained his whisky, signalled to me to do likewise, then took our empty glasses to the bar.

Returned, he did look genuinely distressed. 'Both friend and enemy,' as he had cast one of those spurious lines, he had had to choose either 'Lover or friend.' He had chosen lover, Carolyne.

'I shall understand, Anthony, if you feel you can not – '

'William, I must wish you and Carolyne all joy and happiness.' I held out my hand. We shook. Suddenly William unclasped my hand and in one continuous movement had pushed up from his seat, got to my side of the table and lifted me by my elbows in order to pull me to him and clasp me in his hug. Now on unsteady feet, I was too drunk to be embarrassed.

William Walsh's handwritten *Rivals* version of William Walsh's poem was discarded many years ago. On the morning of the marriage of Carolyne to William in Oxford I tore the paper into many tiny pieces. I let the confetti run through my fingers into the waste paper basket.

On the next meeting, following our rapprochement, I insisted that William and I meet at *The Spotted Horse*. I wanted to repeat what Arnold had done to me on my first visit. As we entered, to William I said out loud Klaus Fuchs's surname, in its anglicised version, actually a mock-London East End pronunciation. He was nonplussed. I was gratified. It was a little pleasure to explain the reference to the traitor. It was also the opening into the classic question which I wanted to put.

'Tell me' – as I held out to him his pint of ale I had just ordered – 'in your judgement – to pose the old question – is it more noble to betray one's country or one's friend? Or is one of them simply easier to forfeit? '

William put his glass down on the bar and nodded slowly to me in acknowledgement of the question.

'Friend I *have* betrayed, and I am sorry for it. I struggled not to do so, Anthony – and I think you do know that. Country, my adopted country, the country that gave refuge to my mother and to me as an infant... I have not betrayed. Indeed I have been of some small service to this country. And in so doing I have betrayed myself, and I shudder to think of' – a long silence as *William* struggled for words! – 'of the offence to my own nature. I can not...'

William bowed his head. At that instant I resolved never again to try to unsettle the man, to pursue any further attempts to avenge myself on him in this shabby fashion. I was ashamed of my own miserly spirit. I looked away, head down. But William laid a hand on my shoulder, made me look directly at him.

'I have had to be untrue to myself, Anthony, in order to serve this country. It is something for which I struggle to come to terms – and try not to despise myself for it. I plead the greater good in my defence to myself. In the scale of things, however – who knows? – what I did may be nothing, may lead to nothing. May *have* led to nothing. I must live with the uncertain hope that *something* has been achieved. It is how I reconcile myself to myself.'

William's eyes at that moment appeared even blacker, and certainly more doleful.

'*Th'expense of spirit in a waste of shame*, Anthony.'

There was a return I might have made. It was something I had known for months, and knowing it might very well have helped William come to terms with himself. William's part in deciding, or compelling, Dušan to leave his own country had indeed proved most profitable here. It was a coup. There had been a sense of great satisfaction that the plan hatched by Sir John and his folk had proved such an unqualified success. For Dušan had had much to say.

But it was not my place to say so. Instead of offering this confirmation to William, I bowed my head over my drink. Then, looking up at William, of the possible – and rejected – things to say in that silence, I was left with:

'Come on, drink up. I know this wonderful Indian restaurant in Fulham Road.'

41

Outside the box there are other memories which simply insist on themselves.

There was the telephone call which Booth transferred to me late in the year of Arnold's marriage to Elizabeth Jane. Booth informed me that Mister Simon Carlton of the Home Department wondered if he might have a word. Simon, on behalf of Colonel Jackson, wished to invite me to lunch; *The Army and Navy* his chosen venue.

'Don't make any, ahem, plans for the rest of the day, Anthony. I gather that this will be a sort of celebration. Colonel Jackson appeared to be very, ahem, chipper when I spoke with him.'

The day for lunch agreed on, my curiosity stirred.

'Does that mean we shall get the go-ahead for the trial?'

Simon would not be drawn. He simply did not know what the Colonel would have decided.

'But do you think, from the way he sounded to you – ?'

'I really could not say.'

The case of the MP on which so much time had been expended by so many had stalled. The exhaustive and prolonged 'interviewing' of Dušan had taken very much longer than anticipated. He had arrived with a far heavier freight of information than anticipated by his questioners, of whom I was one. Every item of information had to be checked, confirmed, and correlated, of course. And that meant extensive searches through archived files and the follow-up questioning and challenging of the prime testifier. The delay in forwarding Dušan was such that his next hosts, in America, became restless, then impatient, then demanding to see 'their' man (strange how both national services exerted their proprietorial ownership over the man).

Finally, following the man's transfer across the Atlantic Ocean for that additional unburdening, a good many more months had to be allowed to elapse for the brouhaha of his escape from Prague and the StB to die down and to allow time for him to be settled somewhere in the States with his new history and new name.

Despite Simon's restraint I felt sure that, with all this cleared away, we were about to hear that we could indeed proceed further with the charges of spying against the dis-Honourable MP. All was in place. The new evidence from Dušan, the tapes supplied by Arnold, supported and complemented by the portfolio evidences, would be convincing enough for a conviction. The direct testimony of Sarah Whoever-She-Was-Really could be dispensed with now. Her presence would be, in fact, a complication – and in any case she had not yet been returned from her Prague Embassy duties assigned to her by Sir John.

Inwardly I was gladdened. It was clear that she could now be spared the distress of a court appearance. She could also be reassured that the confession of her secret to me would remain secret. But she was not here to be reassured.

What was certain was that the trial of the MP, assuming it got the go-ahead, would make very big news to add to the numerous events of those Cold War years. Certainly William would not have been able to accuse me, by then, of being unknowledgeable about the previous twenty-plus post-war years. In my youth, and throughout my university days, the charge he had mounted was true. I had largely ignored the world of events which were outside the immediacy of my own narrow, privileged life, its needs and desires. Even I could not have failed to notice some particular events: the erection of the Berlin Wall; the stand-off between Kruschev and Kennedy over the Soviet shipment of missiles to Cuba, for example. One followed even that in the semi-detached fashion one views something a very long way off. One did not realise at the time of those days of political manoeuvrings just how close the world came to a nuclear confrontation. Or so was the assumed reality of the time; only in later years did we know of Kruschev's poker play and the lack of warheads in his hand of cards. The assassination of Kennedy just over a year later, however, did strike one with immediacy and a sense of involvement.

Even so, even in the instance of the death of an individual, world events were somewhere else. They were not a part of one's daily living. But then... the Cold War of the nineteen-sixties had entered my chambers in the tall, straight-backed form of Colonel Jackson. Since his entry into my life I had made myself familiar with the post-war spy trials conducted in this country. I had made numerous visits to the Colindale Newspaper Library in north London expressly for the purpose of reading up on Fuchs, Lonsdale, the Krogers, Blake, and the rest – as far as the public domain took one. I had also shared several conversations with Philip before his elevation to the judiciary. He had been happy enough to engage at length on these and other more recent histories. I received a few nudges from him in that reflective manner of his – not directly affirming anything, of course – which invited one to speculate on 'possibilities' not detailed in the public accounts.

'The end of a trial, my dear Anthony, does not end things.' Philip attempting still the task, for him impossible, of blowing smoke rings. 'Ramifications, matters to be followed up, things to be looked into.' An exhalation of small clouds. 'Things to be done.' Another cloud ascending. 'Things still being done, I wouldn't wonder.'

Every end is a beginning.

There is a reminder of Philip which I had put into my Great-Uncle Ranulph's cigar case. There had been occasions when I had suffered pangs of conscience, some of the *Yes buts* I had voiced, others unspoken. Though I was then only on the periphery of events taking place in the shadows, there were matters which troubled me. I had spoken with Philip more than once about such reservations. He had always been reassuring – the greater good as a moral imperative. One morning he strode into my chamber with long, loping paces, holding out to me a note-book-sized sheet of paper folded lengthwise.

'Thought this might help.'

Unfolding the paper, in Philip's own neat fountain-pen hand, I read:

> *To the rulers of the state then, if to any, it belongs of right to use falsehood, to deceive either enemies or their own citizens, for the good of the state: and no-one else may meddle with this privilege.*

'Plato.'

So saying, Philip turned on his heel and loped out of the room.

For many years I used this folded piece of paper as a book-mark. I was soon word perfect. Once I had put down the receiver following the telephone call from Simon inviting me to lunch with the Colonel, these words lifted from Plato and handed to me by Philip instantly came to mind.

The call itself, however, had stirred me. I was excited at the prospect that at last the Colonel was to give the signal for pro-ceedings to be set in motion against 'the greedy bastard MP' as he had become most frequently referred to among those of us aware of his doings. The trial itself, undoubtedly, would be a major occasion with maximum exposure. There would be much satisfaction in having been involved; together with some profes-sional recognition, which would not go amiss with me.

42

In the event the year-end lunch to which I had been invited by Simon on behalf of Colonel Jackson was memorable because, more than simply chipper, I saw the Colonel in the nearest to a playful mood one could conceive of the man. There was almost a bounce in his words.

'Apologies from Sir John, by the way. Can't make it today, hopes to do similar another time with you both. Still got his hands full following up various matters vouchsafed to us by our recent arrivals.'

Unsaid: Alžběta and Dušan, the recent arrivals.

As to Dušan, who had arrived in the country just days after Alžběta's reception, I knew that the StB man had been particularly helpful to Sir John's left hand of the service before being passed over to Colonel Jackson's other-hand operation. A new pupillage had begun for me then, directing questions to the StB man about our greedy fat bastard MP. And others. Around the time of that handover a telephone call from Sir John had just been transferred to me from Booth, a call from the great man visibly and vocally enhancing my status with our Clerk of Chambers.

'Wanted to thank you personally for your help, Anthony, in recent events. No names, but you will know who I'm talking about. Would like you to know how much we appreciate too the part played by your friend. It made all the difference. But without your say-so on the man I don't think we should have gone ahead with him.'

I was flattered. Such gratitude was undeserved – the result of a misunderstanding, my little contribution enlarged in the magnifying glass of a successful operation. Objections brushed aside, Sir John told me that 'our visitor' (as Dušan had now become) was very grateful for having been offered a refuge from what might have become, in his own words, 'a bit of a difficult situation for him.'

'Ironic, wouldn't you say?'

With some chuckling Sir John had ended the call and left me to work out the irony. There was one obvious irony: it was in the fact that the service to which Dušan was offering his gratitude was the same service which had put him into the very jeopardy from which he needed to escape.

Of the man himself, he was viewed as a valuable prize. Eventually, helpful also to our American colleagues, he disappeared into a homeland and habitat of his choosing. Of Alžbĕta, however, I knew a good deal from Arnold even before her arrival in England. On Arnold's own return from eastern Europe, following Alžbĕta's arrival here, I was charged with Colonel Jackson's order to persuade him to return to eastern Europe for those two additional postings. Not until his return from the second of those postings would he be permitted to see Alžbĕta. The Colonel had spoken.

'Afraid she's going to be rather busy rendering her own service to the service. Don't want any distractions.' So had the matter been put to me by Colonel Jackson in a very brief telephone call to my chambers.

Arnold resisted. He resisted forcefully to begin with, and he had my sympathies. I tried to reason with him the difference between unfair treatment and what was right as an outcome of the greatest good.

He had finally conceded only when the editor of his broadsheet announced in an editorial, without any consultation, that the paper would soon be losing the services of Mr Arnold Ward as a correspondent 'on the ground' whilst confirming that Arnold would soon begin his penultimate posting to eastern Europe in exactly one week from that day's date. I gather the terms of his leaving and the financial package that would go with it were conditional upon his completing those final obligations. At first

Arnold suspected my involvement in that pre-emptive action. For my own part I suspect 'a word' (in that most economical and undefined expression) from the Home Department to the editor of Arnold's newspaper. I suspected that the Home Department, in this instance, was Simon. I did not ask. I was not told.

'No, no, won't do. Can't let her go all the while we have her boss here. Very useful to be able to cross-check between them.' Colonel Jackson's interruption, in that same call, as I attempted a plea on Arnold's behalf.

Chipper, or playful, but certainly the most forthcoming I have known Colonel Jackson. He insisted on pre-lunch drinks in the lounge

'A good decision to get your journalist friend's lady to come and join us, Anthony. Very gratifying.'

I ventured a comment.

'But I thought you were not so keen to get her out.'

That hint of a smile; the slow lowering and raising of eye-lids. 'As things were then. Things change. Circumstances, circumstances.' The Colonel smoothed his moustache. 'And sometimes coincidence can make the finest of circumstances. The two of them getting out at the same time was most opportune.'

'One wanting to, the other, ahem, needing to.'

'Quite. Giving him no choice but to jump ship.' The Colonel's eyes crinkled. 'Sir John's way of putting the matter. Getting out of the bunker he'd dug himself into another way of putting it.'

Alžběta's defection, as things evolved, would have brought some closer attention upon Dušan as a senior officer responsible for the home English desk. Ultimately under his command, her disappearance would have added undoubtedly to the pressure upon the man. The disappearance of both of them, within two or three days of each other, would have spread more than a few grains of doubt. To doubt the agent is to doubt the intelligence he or she brings. Unsurprisingly, therefore, it did not take the StB long to begin the process of downgrading Dušan as a minor official of very little account. The propaganda experts had also allowed it to be 'assumed' (having themselves put the rumour into circulation) that Dušan and Alžběta had absconded together. It was 'an affair of the heart.'

'But without the, what shall one say? decisive contribution made by your friend William, Mister Dušan's disenchantment with things as they are there might have gone on for a very much longer time. It is surprising how long one can live with disenchantment.'

'As most of us do. Ahem, learn to.' Simon's surprising interjection. 'Of one kind or another.'

'Quite. However, Mister Dušan was, finally, persuaded that it was time for him to leave. We had cards we could play to trump him.'

Colonel Jackson indulged a small laugh.

After that, not much more was said. We scanned the luncheon menu in the dining room and engaged in small talk throughout the meal. There was a sense of something more important to follow.

After lunch the Colonel suggested we retire to the lounge for coffees and cognacs, the Colonel himself clearly not disposed to any further talking until they had been served to us. After a couple of sips of coffee, he lifted his glass of cognac to Simon and me. We reciprocated in the silent toast.

'Here's to our new friend Dušan – and the new information he has spilled out. Stuff we had not latched onto for ourselves. Now we know who we need to look at rather more closely. Theirs *and* ours.'

The Colonel's unaccustomed *bonhomie* emboldened me to put a long-suppressed question:

'Have you heard anything about Sarah, her whereabouts?'

'Still there, Anthony. So I, ahem, believe.'

The Colonel offered: 'Sir John tells me she's making herself very useful.'

I waited, anticipating further information. Instead, the Colonel took us into another subject.

'I expect you two would like to know about our other friend, given the amount of time you've both spent on him. What's been decided about our naughty MP.'

Simon and I both sat forward. The portfolio of evidence we had worked on had been fully corroborated by Dušan. Now, it seemed to me, the case against the MP would be irrefutable.

'We shall not proceed.'

Both Simon and I sat upright.

'Higher needs, I'm afraid.'

'Might it be because your people are rather, ahem, busy at present? – with other matters on their hands. I believe I caught a whisper somewhere.'

'Strictly on the QT, you understand.' The Colonel beckoned me forwards as he himself leaned towards the low table. 'Let us just say that the foreign Embassy in London with the largest staff contains also the largest number of intelligence officers.'

The Colonel leaned back, elbows propped on the arms of his chair, forearms steepling upwards to hands of interlocked fingers.

'Even with the additional good men and women we have been allowed, keeping tabs on them all...' Fingers unlocked, hands parted, in self-evident conclusion of the implications. 'Just too many of them, numbers going up every year.'

It was well over another year before I caught the relayed whisper of another whisper caught by Simon. Then there followed even more years of 'shilly-shallying' (the Colonel's phrase), or 'high-level diplomatic evaluation' (Simon's expression) before the political decision, long-agitated for by the Colonel, was finally taken. For then, more than four years after this lunch in the Colonel's club, one could read of the mass expulsion of Russian intelligence officers from the UK – scores of them, more than one hundred of them in all.

At a signal from the Colonel we took up our cognacs and sipped simultaneously, as if in colluded understanding. The Colonel's face assumed a look of benign satisfaction as he savoured the cognac.

Simon prodded. 'And so our, ahem, delinquent MP...?'

'In good time, Simon, in good time.'

There was a faintly mischievous look upon the Colonel's face. He was play-acting – suddenly I realised that he was enjoying holding up the narrative he had brought us here to relate.

'Back to our new friend. Mister Dušan has been remarkably helpful – much appreciated, Anthony, your help in lightening his load. Thanks to all who had questions for him, we now have a portfolio of suspects. Some we have had in mind for some time. Minor and major. Trades Union officials we knew about, fellow travellers among our politicians, local and national, political columnists – no surprises there – a lone technician working in one of our research establishments, suspected if not decisively known, a couple of civil servants we did not know about... *And*, gentlemen, the prize. Confirmation of serving and former government ministers of state. Of the serving we did have some prior scentings of one. Another one, though, *is* a surprise to us. A complete surprise.'

The Colonel sat back in his chair following what was, for him, an extended speech on an occasion that proved him to be almost loquacious.

'Bigger fish, gentlemen. We shall be casting our lures for some time yet.'

Yes, but –

'All a question of priorities.'

Yes but – 'What about the MP himself? Our man. Does he just get off scot-free?'

The Colonel faced me with that familiar hint of a suppressed smile, his greyish-blue eyes twinkling the giveaway.

'Ah yes, our little fry. Well, we certainly don't want to frighten off our important targets, especially the surprise package. And that is precisely what would happen if we went ahead with a trial now. It would be a very big splash for such a little fish. Newspapers, radio, television. Do you see?'

Colonel Jackson looked at Simon and me to see that we did indeed see.

'This way you can monitor the big fish, as it were, without, ahem, alarming them. And render them harmless. Even turn them to one's own, ahem, uses, perhaps?'

'Just so.'

But my *Yes but* was insistent. 'So nothing happens to our man?'

The Colonel, it was clear, was being deliberately provoking, and enjoying it. He raised an arm, a waiter attending him in seconds.

'More coffee, gentlemen?' He gestured loosely to our brandy glasses then held out forefinger and middle finger of one hand as if pointing a revolver.

Doubles of the cognac duly were served. Not until he had taken his first appreciative sip did Colonel Jackson take to the lectern again. He was in, as near as I ever saw him, self-congratulatory mode.

'I think you will find that there will be an announcement in tomorrow's newspapers. It will have been issued by our particular gentleman. You will read that he has resigned his seat in the House with immediate effect, citing health and family reasons. What you will not read is that he has been barred from holding political office, of any kind, national or local. For life.' The Colonel smoothed his moustache with the finger and thumb of each hand. One could see he was enjoying considerably his narration. 'Neither will you read that Her Majesty's Inspector of Taxes will be taking a special interest in the man's undeclared income. Ill-gotten gains over a number of years on which he will now be taxed at the highest possible rate. Perhaps, who knows? it may even be determined that his accumulation of dirty money will all be taxable within the current financial year.' There was that glint in his eyes again. 'Pure speculation on my part, of course. Oh' – as if an afterthought – 'but I do think it may be safely said that a substantial fine will also have to be imposed. For non-payment. Of selfsame taxes.' At which the Colonel actually winked. 'Oh yes, something else. His passport will be withdrawn until all of this process has been completed. And all the dues paid.'

Simon and I exchanged looks, both of us trying very hard to hold back our laughter.

'The dues also include, of course, a signed confession.' Colonel Jackson glanced at his wristwatch. 'Being dictated to him as we speak, I shouldn't doubt. We shall keep it on file – just to ensure that he stays on the straight and narrow we have marked out for him. Today's exercise will have sobered him up more than a little, no doubt.'

There was no doubt too that Colonel Jackson was enjoying himself. His eyes narrowed slightly as he delayed, taking a slow sip of cognac, playing our curiosity.

'Had the pleasure of dining with our little fish just yesterday evening. We had a long over-the-table conversation. He seemed very eager to please me. I do believe, to begin with, he thought he was being assessed for some important security post. Agreed with all the generalities I put forth.'

He stroked at his moustache.

'*Mirabelle's*, do you know it?'

Simon and I both shook our heads.

'Mayfair. A favourite of Winnie's, you know.' A glance was sufficient. 'Winston. Not the sole reason for choosing it, though I knew our man would know, of course. Splendid choice of some rather expensive wines. He almost leapt down the 'phone line when I invited him to join me there yesterday evening. 'Fraid I did rather give him the impression that I had something to say which would be to his advantage. 'Fraid I also allowed him to form the impression that this dinner was to be paid for by Her Majesty's Government. Started with some vintage bubbly stuff. Not really my tipple, but *he* seemed to enjoy it.'

Cognac was not really my tipple either, but one had to enjoy the Colonel's very evident enjoyment of the drink, his way of cradling the bulb of the glass in his hand, his swirling of the brandy in the glass, his inhalation of its fumes, nose against the rim, his way of taking a sip and allowing it simply to seep down his throat without any visible swallowing.

'Could see his beady eyes looking through the menu to pick the most expensive dishes. Went through the lot. Every course. A couple of very fine bottles of Burgundy. The works. Finished with coffees and some vintage champagne cognac, a Montifaud if that means anything, a leftover from the 'forties. Told the waiter to leave the bottle on the table. Waited 'til then to switch the subject of the conversation. He must have got through three or four glasses of brandy by the time I'd said my piece. Must have run up quite a bill.'

Simon and I, by our looks towards each other, anticipated at the same moment where the recounting was heading.

'Had to excuse myself to go to the cloakroom. Picked up my hat and coat and umbrella and walked out. Left the greedy little bastard to pick up the bill.'

Not until that point did Colonel Jackson allow himself unrestrained laughter. It was evident that this duping of the MP was his own additional punishment of the man; one in which he took great delight. Within our own laughter Simon and I offered our compliments.

'Cognacs and a top-up of coffee, gentlemen? By way of celebration.'

Simon demurred. I seconded.

'Gentlemen, gentlemen.' The Colonel assumed a hurt demeanour. 'I insist.' A pause while he looked hard at each of us in turn. 'Don't worry, gentlemen. On this occasion I *shall* be paying the bill.'

I felt both disappointed and relieved at Colonel Jackson's decision not to prosecute the MP. I think he must have registered the disappointment.

'Sorry about that, Anthony, Simon. I'm sure the two of you would have liked to see him squirm in the dock just as much as I would. But can't be helped. For the greater good. We move on. More important things to worry about now than that self-important little glutton.'

With that the Colonel made his apologies and left to 'put in a show' at the office.

Simon, I thought, took the news, as he seemed to take everything, with practised imperturbability. He turned to me as we were collecting our coats in the cloakroom.

'At least this way we avoid certain, ahem, embarrassments. There is your friend Arnold to consider, for instance.'

I nodded my assent to that.

'And in the larger scale of things – '

'Even so – '

'Not everything must, ahem, end in the flame and thunder of a firework display. Some things are simply quietly managed. No fuss, no noise.' His experience added: 'No fires to put out. And no smoke in which things may be made to disappear.'

At that point I still had to learn the wisdom and the arts of managing, with as little flame and noise as possible, a troublesome circumstance.

43

There were a good many other meetings over the years at the Colonel's club. One in particular, on the hinge of spring to early summer almost twenty years later, remains in the mind. Both Sir John and the Colonel had each retired four years previously and I think they were both glad of occasions to meet up and fill a blank in their respective diaries. Philip, after a long day on the bench, was also there, as was Simon. Over dinner Simon said he had something to tell us. But, just as had the Colonel all those years previously teased us by refusing to be hurried into his tale, so did Simon now refuse to be drawn. It was evident too that, whatever it was Simon was hugging to himself, Sir John was in the know, aiding and abetting Simon's show of diffidence.

After dinner as we relaxed in the leather armchairs of the members' lounge, and after the first of the single malts so beloved by Colonel Jackson and Judge Hathers, Simon was prevailed upon to divulge his news.

'Well?' The colonel turned his gaze upon Simon, who glanced at Sir John. Simon withdrew a folded sheet of paper from a side pocket.

'Simon thought you would all like to hear this.' Sir John raised his thick, white eyebrows. 'Unless, of course, you had a hand in it, Philip.'

'What is it?'

'It, Philip, is a masterly example of the language of legal prestidigitation. Which is why you are suspected.'

Now all were curious to know. Simon held up the scrap of paper he held in his hand.

'There has been much talk – as we all know – for some time, about putting the service on a more, ahem, secure footing – '

Sir John placed a large hand on Colonel Jackson's shoulder. At that moment it was clear that he was enjoying the privilege of knowing in advance what the Colonel was about to learn.

'Well, the decision has been made. The government has, ahem, determined that next year shall see the introduction of a Security Service Act. To place the service on a statutory basis.'

There was a sense of a communal question beginning to shape itself. It was put by Philip.

'And do you know, Simon, how the legislators intend to legislate for a service that does not and never did exist?'

'Ah, well. This is just a whisper you must understand. These may not be the final form of words, but... these are the words I wrote down, having heard the, ahem, whisper.' Simon unfolded the paper in his hand. '*There shall continue to be a Security Service under the authority of the Secretary of State.*'

Silence. Then, 'No more? Is that it?'

Philip had spoken for all of us.

'First, ahem, sentence of the proposed Act – so is the whisper.'

Suddenly Philip was laughing, almost braying, loudly.

'Masterly! And that, my dears, is how you announce that something which has never existed will continue to live.'

Philip insisted that we all swallow the news with a very large brandy.

'After all the talk it's finally going to happen, Vernon' – Sir John to the Colonel – 'Next year they're going to bring your lot out of the shadows and make you walk on the sunny side of the street. The boys and girls as were yours to command.'

Colonel Jackson stroked his moustache. 'Then we must hope they don't get sunstroke from too much exposure.'

'Changed times, Vernon, changed times.'

'And your lot, John? Yours as were?'

'Ah, well, I gather that they're going to leave the left hand alone. Not that I have done the Lambeth walk since leaving – hardly been south of the river at all – so I don't know what my former compatriots in the battle think. But Simon tells me there are no immediate plans. Perhaps the left hand is far too sinister to interfere with.'

It was clear by Sir John's chuckling that he was enjoying the special treatment, or special neglect, which his own former service had been allocated – though in point of fact it was just a few years later that the left hand also became subject to its own Act.

'There shall continue to be a Security Service under the authority of the Secretary of State.' Philip intoned the words to each of us in turn as he went the rounds with the brandy decanter he had somehow contrived to exfiltrate from the dining room.

In the autumn of the year following we met again at the same club, with Booth an added, special guest of the Colonel. Given that by this date Booth no longer had a chambers on which to keep a watchful eye, the Colonel had taken to asking him along on occasions as a former Army subordinate whom he held in high esteem and who had seen war service alongside him. We met not to toast the forthcoming Security Service Act due to pass into law in a later month of that year of 1989, but to wonder at the events that had so far occupied several years up to that point and taken observers (to include ourselves) of eastern Europe by surprise. We wondered what else was to happen before the year's end.

44

A different year comes to mind, an earlier year, a year stained with a lethal cloud of iodine-131, caesium-134 and -137. Blown by the changing winds a spreading cloud of radioactive materials reached across from eastern Europe in the Ukraine to western tracts and as far north as Norway and Finland, south to Spain and Portugal, and along the Mediterranean into Greece.

Chernobyl, April 1986.

For more than a year we had been accommodating ourselves to a new word: the *glasnost* of Mikhail Gorbachev's Russia. We waited to see where this new 'open-ness' would lead. And watched as events unfolded in the following years as they accumulated towards the summer onwards of 1989. Events, dear boy... as a British Prime Minister almost certainly did *not* say, events, dear boy, events. If the attribution is questionable, the events were real – and astonishing. We observed the changes, and the speed of those changes in eastern Europe which had moved on with accelerating pace.

Poland, Hungary, the Ukraine, Bulgaria, Czechoslovakia, East Germany... it was a year of political revolution in which, to the disbelief of many observers, the East German authorities declared the border open. In effect the Berlin Wall had been breached. Suddenly, as many tens of thousands did, it was possible to walk from East to West.

Into this swirl of change arrived the invitation from Philip and Elizabeth Havers to their pre-Christmas house-party. It was a gathering by far the most memorable.

Elizabeth greeted me on the steps to the front porch, just as Simon pulled up on the driveway. We went in together to shouted greetings from Philip who was busily assembling glasses in the dining-room.

No sooner had Elizabeth led us into the reception room than Colonel Jackson and his wife Jennifer arrived in a taxi from the local station, followed shortly afterwards by Sir John Holyoake and his wife. Drinks in hand, we 'chewed the fat'; animatedly discussing the events throughout eastern Europe.

After lunch, and after the obligatory brisk walk, in the late afternoon dusk we all re-settled. At some point Philip came to sit alongside me. He regarded me closely.

'I had hoped we would have been able to welcome another guest to our little gathering. Sir John did say he would try to work his charm.'

To my silent questioning he made no response. I pressed him to say.

'Later, Anthony, later. If it gets to the point where it's too late to expect – '

Just then Sir John raised a finger.

'Ah! Thought so.' There was the sound of tyres scrunching on the driveway. Sir John put down his drink and went with Philip to the front door.

There were subdued voices in the hallway. Elizabeth came out of the kitchen to join her husband there. The rest of us stilled our curiosity and tried to pick up our conversations. Philip appeared in the doorway, his arm holding back the door to allow someone to pass by him and enter the room.

45

Sarah? There was a likeness... There was a momentary doubting, the shock of her *being* there after all the years of absence.

It was.

It was indeed Sarah-Somebody, Sarah-By-Any-Other-Name. Sarah whom I had not seen for twenty-three years. Sarah last seen in Simon's office with light auburn hair, a darker complexion, a thinner nose, and about to be somebody else somewhere else. Undoubtedly Sarah, her body fuller, still shapely, the blonde of her hair faded to tinges of grey and white and cut shorter to frame her face – Sarah undoubtedly, Miss K, the light blue of her eyes unmistakeable.

She waved to me from the doorway.

After she had done the rounds to all present, she came up to me. She offered me her hand, her head turned a little downwards, her eyes looking up at me.

'Mister Anthony Ranulph Ashley-Chetwyne, I believe.'

I bowed from the waist, heels touching, my free hand behind my back, acknowledging her pleasantry.

'QC, as I also believe.'

I conceded with a nod of the head.

'How *are* you?' My question encompassed all the missing years, not just the current state of her health. Three words that wanted to know her history between last seeing her in Simon Carlton's room in Westminster and her presence here, at this time – all the wheres, hows, and whys.

'And *you*?'

Hers was the same tone. Of concerned curiosity.

We stepped closer into a fleeting embrace, apart again almost as soon as we touched. She took each of my hands in hers as we stepped apart, her eyes searching me for the answer.

'You haven't answered my question.'

'You first,' I said. 'I asked first.'

Sarah simply waved away my priority.

'Not here. Not now, Anthony.'

Not until after a long, sociable evening meal with our hosts and their other guests, could I at last contrive to sit alongside her.

'After all this time. It is so good to see you again, Sarah. Where have you been all these years?'

Biting lightly on her underlip, she turned to face me.

'Susan.'

I thought I detected the beginning of a smile. I was being teased.

'Pardon?'

'Susan.'

'And how long, pray, if one may ask, have you been Susan?'

Pertly, 'I have been Susan all my life.'

I shook my head. 'But never to me.'

'Susan is the name given to me by my parents. It is' – her look was designed to test my credulousness – 'my real name.'

'Then where did Sarah come from?'

Sarah laid a hand on my knee, a gesture that unhinged – for me – the years between this present and my last sighting of her.

'From me. From a young girl I always wanted to be Sarah, ever since I learned that Sarah meant 'princess.' So when it became convenient, as a name to be known by, I became Sarah.'

'And now?'

'And now that it no longer matters, I am Susan again.' There was sadness in her voice. 'I have been a princess to a man I loved very deeply, Anthony. I shall not be a princess again.'

There was such a sense of loss about Sarah – Susan as I had to learn to say – that it would have been impertinent to have pursued the matter.

We arranged to meet again within two days of the Hathers' house-party. I met her at King's Cross station, as she had insisted we should – and so that I would not know, I was convinced, where she lived. We went for lunch and, to begin with, skirted around the matters we really wanted to explore with each other.

'Is it really that long ago?'

'Nineteen sixty-six, Susan.'

The events of that day, our last sighting of each other, were clear to both of us.

'Did you hear what happened to your MP, the one who – ' I bit off the rest of the question but could not unsay the words. Susan offered me a slow, indulgent smile as I flushed my embarrassment.

'It's alright, Anthony. It was a long time ago now. But yes, I did hear.'

At which she rested a hand on my arm across the table.

'Sorry, Susan, just didn't think – '

'No, no, it's for me to *thank* you for not, you know... for somehow keeping me out of that business.'

I tried to explain: it was nothing of my doing, the actions took the turn they did – '

'Thank you anyway, Anthony.'

'Gratitude undeserved. But I know two people who really do want to thank *you.*' It was clear she did not make the connection. 'Arnold and Elizabeth Ward – Alžběta as was.'

Susan lifted the outspread fingers of each hand to the sides of her face. 'How *are* they?'

'They want to see you. They have waited a long time.'

I knew from Arnold that they had not seen Susan – Sarah as she still was to them also – since their last separate sightings of her in Czechoslovakia. Susan, I learned, had assumed that the Wards would have been placed out of the way and living under assumed names. So she had not asked questions on her return from duties in Czechoslovakia. She knew nothing of the pretences which had been organised in order that they could take up open residence in Herefordshire.

'And in any case, when I did get home I asked to resign. Of course I had to be debriefed and so on, and after all that I took up a sort of clerical-liaison post with the RAF, Cambridgeshire, operational base.' There was a hesitation. 'It worked out very well. I was happy there.'

Said in a decisive and somewhat clipped fashion, and clearly intended to put an end to the matter before it could be pursued. But I was an experienced QC by now, I knew about the tiny give-aways of speech and the betrayal of the words we use. To ask to resign is not to resign; nor, perhaps even more to the point, not to be given permission to resign. Besides, I knew of *two* operational airbases in Cambridgeshire which were not many miles apart; and only one of those was an RAF base. The other was operated by our transatlantic partners. And I knew that the latter base was concerned with photographic reconnaissance. There was also that word 'liaison' – a tricky word, even when qualified as 'sort of' it requires parties between whom one passes to and fro. I had to stop. My mind had raced off to its own invention, simply because I now knew the way some things worked. Defence I have none. A but, though: when you have traded with those whose profession trades in deceptions and lies, you begin to see evasion and dissembling everywhere, their possibility anyway, even where they might not exist. As in the smiling face of a still beautiful woman who sat by my side.

There is a coda. Many months after this exchange I sidled up again to the subject of her time in 'liaison'. Susan had an opportunity to reject the imputation I made. In the classic formula, she neither confirmed nor denied – 'Oh it was all so long ago,' said with a shake of the head.

On this occasion, though, despite my delay because of the flickerings of questions I might have put, I disciplined myself.

'When *did* you get back from Prague?'

Susan tilted her head a little, looking at me steadily, reluctant to respond, I thought. I was about to change the subject when she offered:

'Nineteen sixty-nine. Towards the end of the year, home just in time for Christmas.' A pause, an upward tilt of the head as if looking for the place to start. 'Things had always been difficult out there, but they were getting very much worse. There was fear and suspicion everywhere.'

Susan shook her head. I encouraged her to go on by waiting.

'Just everyday living was difficult. There was very little to be got in the shops, including food. Any Czech goods worth having were being dispatched to Russia. Fortunately our Ambassador had been sending his Czech driver over into west Germany to stock up with goods. Been doing it for years – regularly. Had he not done so, we would have gone hungry and unwashed.'

Susan was pensive, speaking quietly. 'Lovely man, that Petr, our Embassy driver, very loyal to us.'

She was drawing invisible shapes on the table with her forefinger.

'Do you know Weiden? No? A pretty town. That's where Petr would drive and I became the regular shopper with him so that the border guards got used to my comings and goings. I used to give them a wave so that they knew it was me.'

A smile from Susan. 'And?' from me.

'Of course, we had diplomatic plates on the car, but the cigarettes and goodies we dropped off on our way back through helped make things even easier with the Czech guards. They would go into a bit of a noisy huddle with Petr at the side of the car, while giving a cursory look-over the car. That's how Petr slipped them the cigarettes and so on. I might just as well not have been there, the invisible woman.'

Many, many residents in the country did not approve of its regime of the time and, given the privations of that period in its history, one could understand easily enough the temptations of a little bribery.

'Then, after we got Alžběta and me out via our separate ways, after due delay and a new passport I went back in to

Czechoslovakia. By the front door, just flew in. But I think you know all this.'

'And when you went back in?'

'I noticed the difference immediately – the StB had started to monitor us even more closely. Their Russian masters had clamped down on them since Dušan's disappearance, with the result that things got even more tricky. It was getting difficult for me to carry on.'

'With what?' Instantly rubbed out, my hand back and forth across my mouth as if wiping out the words on a blackboard.

Susan rebuked me with a smiling eyes-wide look of feigned horror that I should dare the question.

'So, more than three years after I'd gone back in I was brought home.'

She tapped me on the knee.

'Tell me about the Wards.'

Susan and I became close, as friends are close. We did not become lovers for more than a full year after the get-together at Judge Hathers's which had re-introduced us to each other. The impulse to intimacy was not imperative for either of us. To begin with, or to begin again with, we both needed to share our aloneness. We became a kind of compensation to each other.

In the event we did became lovers, or at least we became lovers at the time that we did through the good, though unintentional, offices of my mother. Mother had become resigned to the fact that her younger son would not be producing offspring to share the family name and add to the two grandchildren she had by my older brother. Beyond that disappointment there was a maternal concern; she worried about me.

'It is not good, Anthony, for a man to be alone.'

It was an irony, since father, I knew, had spent and still did spend much inventiveness and energy fabricating contrivances to be on his own or to spend time with his cronies away from mother. Her admonition of me, regretful, was intended also to make me do something about acquiring a permanent woman partner. Therefore, when in a telephone conversation, without thinking beyond the moment itself, I informed mother that I was 'seeing' a special woman, mother pounced.

'Are you *fond* of the woman, Anthony?'

My mother had a way of expressing a word that made it an inquisition in its own right of all of its latent and future possibilities. So there was prevarication at my end. And in that hesitation I heard from all those decades before the voice of Sarah-As-Was-Then asking me of Carolyne:

'Do you love the girl?' – and my response:

'Yes, I suppose I do.'

I thought of the long-ago rejoinder that Susan-As-Now had made to my reply when she had asked the same question as my mother:

'Then, Anthony, I suppose you do not.'

'*Well?*' Mother's voice recalled me to the present dragging a large suitcase of the past with me. It was time to unpack and discard.

'No, mother. I am not fond of the woman... I *love* her.'

There was the barest of pauses. 'And have you *told* the good woman so?'

My mother allowed me only a fractional silence before: 'Well you had better tell her so. Then you can bring her here one weekend so that we can all get to know one another.'

I did tell Susan that I loved her. She received my protestation very quietly, almost sadly. 'I do know that,' she said, 'but...' She took my hand between hers. 'It's not you, Anthony, it's...'

She did agree, however, to spend a weekend at my parents' place.

Mother met us at the front porch. She greeted Susan by clasping a hand on each of Susan's arms above the elbows and scrutinising her at close range.

'Yes,' said mother. And nothing more before leading Susan into the house to meet father.

After coffee: 'I've put you two in the back bedroom of the wing. You'll be very private there.'

I flushed. I had not told mother that Susan and I did not share a bed. Susan took the news calmly, with an outward calm anyway. But mother read the signs.

'Of course, we can always have a bed made up for you in your old room, Anthony. It's just that, well, in today's world when two people are in love, one assumes that... rather like the 'thirties' really.'

Father raised a quizzical eyebrow. Susan said simply: 'The arrangement is fine, Missus Ashley-Chetwyne.'

'Georgina. Georgie.'

Mother had taken to Susan.

Something of the same reluctance to cross borders that had held us back from physical love-making may be the reason why Susan turned down my proposal of marriage much after we shared the bed prepared for us by my mother.

'Oh Anthony, you are a good man.'

I demurred. There was a long wait. After several starts Susan broke into a longer, dislocated speech.

'It's not that... I mean I *do* love you... but so much has happened, and... you *must* know how things were, my time there... I do want us to be together, while you want to be with me, that is... and, yes, I do think it might have all been so different when we first met. I know for me it was... but that was so long ago, Anthony, so long ago... and now...'

History. Too much of the past. She looked at me with such a pained expression that I could not then persist with further questioning. I think that even now she never has truly forgiven herself for those years of young womanhood when – nothing said in so many words – she lent her body to the cause.

It was difficult for both of us, professional doubters in our different professions, immediately to suspend suspicion; to *trust*, unguardedly to offer and to receive without reserve. I thought with some irony of the service's motto: *Securitas Vigilantiae instantis premium* – security is the reward of constant vigilance – and thought how it might serve us both as a personal motto.

EIGHT

No more questions, Your Honour

Prague

1999

46

In a city of music of course we had to attend concerts whilst here. Susan surprised me with her first choice of venue and event. We went to an early evening concert of sacred music held in the baroque splendour and ornamentation of Saint Nicholas Church in the Old Town Square. The programme of choral music (copy retained somewhere in Great-Uncle Ranulph's cigar case), including works by Delibes, Mozart and Dvořák, was given by a Concert Choir of young people. There were beautiful, resonant tones which seemed to wash into the recesses of the building and lap themselves around one. Somewhere into a passage of a *Missa Brevis* I became aware of an uncommon stillness in the woman seated alongside me. For how long she had been immobile – even her breathing hardly moving her chest – I do not know. Hands laid palms up, one on the other in her lap, tears were falling down her cheeks from unblinking eyes. She made no move to reach for a handkerchief. She simply let the tears continue to fall, to follow the course of their predecessors. Her stillness, her silence unnerved me somewhat.

What confounded me later as we sat down to dinner, Susan all tidied again following a quick visit back to the hotel, was the brightness of her face. Cliché but true, she was radiant. Smiling, her light blue eyes bright despite their faded redness of earlier, she was especially tender. She took my hand in hers.

'Thank you.'

'For what, Susan?'

'For being a bully. For not taking No as an answer and making me be here.'

Somewhere within the accumulation of years a person may have preserved a *locum secretum* entered only, usually, when the owner is alone. Exceptionally, as on this occasion, someone else is present at the moment the person retreats into the shadows within that crypt of private memories.

Something changed in Susan. Or something between us ceased to hold the same power to keep us that little apart, as two negative poles of a magnet.

Before the first of our weekends with my parents Susan and I had continued to meet regularly. Once the early awkwardnesses between us dispersed and we had more or less stopped apologising to each other, she took my arm, then my hand, when we walked together. I learned, a little at a time, of her return to England from Czechoslovakia, her meeting with and, nine weeks later, marriage to a handsome young naval officer introduced to her by Sir John.

'By way of liaison between the services, you know.' By way of explanation. Everyone learns to live with his or her own secrets. It is living with someone else's secrets which one finds truly testing. It is, I might add, even more of a trial for one whose very profession is grounded on the asking of questions.

Susan spoke to me, reluctantly, of their wholly fulfilling fourteen years together, then her husband's contraction of cancer. She nursed him through his final twelve or so months. A sad, sad story, these the mere ciphers of an inadequate summary gleaned, always with some unwillingness, from Miss K.

'You are a heartless inquisitor, Anthony. You have spent too many of your years in court challenging and cross-questioning.'

In a larger sense than she knew Susan was right. For decades at that point I had no longer taken things for granted. Doubting, *learning* to doubt had made me a more persistent and incisive questioner. I learned how to articulate all my *Yes buts*. It was the change in me, in my constitution, that made me a better barrister, a more formidable opponent. I had Carolyne and William to thank for that and for their dissembling and deceptions. I suppose I also had them to thank for the distinguished, as the word is, achievement which my career later became.

Some doubting is akin to fear. Susan was in Prague during threatening times. I remember the conversations with Simon Carlton in which he handed on to me what news came his way in the Home Department. It was a breach of trust for which I was very grateful. Simon accused me of being in love with her, which I denied, and which denial he did not believe.

The stirrings of discontent in Czechoslovakia had come to a head in the same year, 1968, in which William married my once almost-fiancée Carolyne: Russian troops on Czechoslovak soil and their tanks in Prague and other cities. It is all history now. So, yes, I feared for Sarah during those dangerous times.

After that early evening concert, after whatever it was that happened, Susan and I were released to talk freely and openly. At dinner I knew that I could ask questions long suppressed and that, by some kind of shift in her disposition, Susan would even welcome the relief of answers. Our long-held vow of silence was broken.

Susan talked of two Pragues.

'You know, Anthony, seeing the city as it is now, this beautiful city, it begins to feel unreal to think of it as it was all those years ago.'

I busied myself pouring out wine.

'There was such suspicion everywhere. Nobody trusted anybody. They were dark days. Everyone was being watched – even the watchers were being watched. You could sense the fear everywhere you went. People here knew that anyone might be reported to the authorities on any trumped-up charge. It all had a dreadful *clamping* effect on life. One had to be so careful. Yet now...'

Susan offered a thin smile. When she took up her own thought it followed an unexpected trajectory.

'Now we can be free to be *ourselves*, can't we? In those days we *all* traded in lies and deceptions – practising to deceive.' Her brow furrowed. 'We made a profession of it.'

Susan held me in a gaze which was some kind of apology –
for not trusting me, at least not trusting me sooner. Somehow her
look prompted a question I had wanted to ask for some while.

'The other night, at dinner...' I hesitated. 'You asked me about
William, and I've been wondering why.'

Susan leant back, half-closed her eyes.

'You know I saw a lot of him when he was out here, don't you?'

'Well, you were both based at the Embassy. Which is why I
could not understand his reaction to you when we did actually
meet up.'

'*Finally* meet up. After you had delayed and prevaricated and had
kept us away from William and his Carolyne for months on end.'

Palms up, admission of the charge.

'I have never said this to you...'

'Go on.'

'There were two objectives to the initial mission I was giv-
en here.' She paused to look directly to me. 'What I said earlier,
about not trusting anyone... well, William was the first reason
why I was sent out here.'

'Really?' That *was* unexpected. I had believed that Susan was
here, in the first instance, to ease Arnold's Alžběta Jana out of
the country.

'I was to gain his confidence, to support him, to try to monitor his dealings with our StB target. Dušan.' A small hesitation,
then: 'To keep a beady eye on him. And, whenever possible, keep
an eye on the two of them together. And then' – Susan bit on her
lower lip – 'if I could secure anything in any way compromising
we would have a stronger hold on him.'

The curiosity of the cat was aroused. 'But why? I mean William had full clearance, he'd been thoroughly vetted, properly
trained presumably – well, as much as he needed to be – fully
briefed and specially selected for the task.'

Susan narrowed her eyes. 'Because he was never fully
trusted.'

'Do you mean by the powers that be?'

'The same.'

'But he was *their* idea in the first place.'

Susan simply raised her eyebrows, then sipped at her wine. I persisted.

'I mean, *they* sent him here. They *chose* him because – '

'On *your* say-so, don't forget.' Susan gave me an indulgent smile. There was another hesitation. 'I know he is your friend' – Susan reached across the table, rested a hand on the back of mine – 'and Carolyne clearly still *dotes* on him...'

There was a *but* hanging in the air. I waited.

'But in a way it's almost as if when you speak with William you are talking to the dummy, not the one who's pulling the strings and making the dummy speak.'

Susan smoothed her hand over my fingers.

'I'm still not sure why it was felt necessary to, to *spy* on William.'

'Because, my dear Counsel for the defence, what William was out here to achieve was far too important to allow any change of mind, any hesitation or backsliding on his part.' Susan paused, on the cusp of deciding whether to speak the addendum on her mind. 'Hence the value of' – a brief glance – 'photographs. Compromising photographs. Don't forget there was always the possibility that William would warn the target.' I was shaking my head. 'And we needed to know that William himself would not be turned – point one. Point two: that nothing William did would change Dušan's mind about coming over to our side.'

Involuntarily, something which William had said to me in that long confession of his true history – that night in the Soho restaurant – claimed a sharper attention. 'I have betrayed myself', he had said.

'Or, more to the point of your point two: that what William *did* would actually jeopardise Dušan and force him to escape from his country. Leave him no choice.'

'Exactly. Once we had that evidence we could intervene.'

'*We?*'

Susan smiled. 'No, not me, Anthony. I was William's *friend* while we were both here.'

'Then it makes even less sense that he should treat you with such disregard when we did meet him and Carolyne.'

Susan leant forward, elbows on the table, chin resting in the cupped fingers of her hands. She held the silence, a slight sideways to and fro of her head somehow inviting me to think again.

Lifting her head a little, slowly and quietly, almost as if to a slow-witted learner, Susan said: 'I said I *was* William's friend. For the duration.'

'Yes, and *I* said – '

'Must I spell it out for you? you, the great inquisitor?'

'I think you must. I simply do not understand why he treated you so distantly when we did first get together.'

'Very well, Anthony Ranulph Ashley-Chetwyne QC.' Susan sat upright, assuming a serious face. Between thumb and forefinger of each hand she held onto the collar of her blouse, and, as if addressing the jury (of one) proceeded.

'Let us assume that the said William Walsh either came to know, or very strongly suspected – it matters not which of these was the true cause – that the full nature of his engagement with Dušan was known to an Embassy colleague he knew as Missus Alyson Bath. The moot point is that William *believed* this to be so.'

Susan dropped her hands. She took up her glass of wine, took a small sip, then leaned in to me. Almost in a whisper she spoke: 'That made me the guardian of *his* secret. Hence his embarrassment in my company.'

I suppressed my Philippian 'Aahh, yes': just as I had been the guardian of Susan's secret as Sarah. Our looks confirmed the shared thought.

'And that, Anthony, makes one vulnerable to the keeper of one's secret.'

47

There were other questions.

'You said there were *two* objectives to your mission that sent you out here. What was the second?'

'That you know already, my dear sir. Alžběta.'

'Getting her out of here.'

'No, that would be the outcome – all being well and if everything tested out. But the first and prime objective was to make quite sure that it would be safe to bring her out.'

'Test the defences, as it were.'

Susan pulled a face that somehow rebuked my innocence. Her words of explanation were laid out as cards in a game of patience.

'Let me put it this way. All we knew of Alžběta was what we had been told by a man who claimed to be in love with her and who was attempting to blackmail the service. Now, though love may not be blind it can most certainly be blinkered. After all, we only had Arnold's say-so that she was in earnest, that she wanted to defect in order to be with him – as his wife; that there was no other ulterior motive; and that she would be willing to betray whatever she knew for our help in getting her away.'

Susan crinkled her eyes in that characteristic way of hers to confirm that I had followed and understood.

'There was always the possibility that Arnold had been caught in a honey-trap planted by the StB to snare him and that Alžběta might have been what the Russian KGB masters referred to as a 'swallow'. And when you think about *that,* if the StB *had* managed to turn him he could have become a very useful asset – east Europe correspondent for a national broadsheet, regular landings in London, well-known to a good few in Her Majesty's Foreign Department and their off-the-record briefings... and so on. Perhaps even gaining an entrée into our own service. All to win the lady. For all we knew he might already have been playing the game. We knew only what he had told me and, later, what he reported to you.'

Admission. 'I have to say that the thought never occurred to me at the time that Arnold could be anything other than completely honest. I thought him a man of integrity. I believed him.'

At this Susan sat back in her chair. Smiling, she raised her glass of wine. We chinked glasses together, their rims singing as she said to me:

'Think about it.'

Which I did. And with very little prompting from Susan and in very little space of time, I could see an alternative scheme of possible events. Suppose Arnold was already playing the game, then he was playing me. Providing evidence to bring our greedy fat bastard MP to justice would rid the StB of a man who had become an embarrassment to them and, at the same time, ingratiate Arnold both with his new masters *and* with our own service. Too late, I was beginning to see the possibilities which had exercised the Colonel's extreme caution.

'I can see there *could* well be a different interpretation put upon things.'

Susan simply laughed. Then clamped a hand to her mouth as other diners turned in our direction.

'What *is* different is your way of thinking and the way the Colonel's girls and boys had to think. You are an advocate. You take sides – defence or prosecution, and you settle the matter of guilt or innocence of the accused.'

'Agreed, but there is, of course, much more to it than that. There is – '

Even as I said that, I heard my own pomposity and stopped. Certainly Susan did not miss the tone.

'Spoken like a lawyer, my dear. But for us, evidence was a two-sided coin, and every coin had to line up heads or tails with all the other coins. The facts of a matter might not be facts at all.

So in the case of Alžběta I had to be sure, to put it simply, that she was genuine.'

There was a *how* forming to be asked.

'I had to get to know her. Because I did not have much time I had to take the first opportunity I could to have a meeting between just the two of us. And don't forget that I was relying on Arnold – someone we were not at that stage wholly convinced by – as go-between to set up that first meeting. Which is also, by the way, the real reason why the Colonel insisted that Arnold did those additional tours even after we had got Alžběta safely away.' Susan saw my slowness. 'To see if there was a reception committee to meet him on his return. If not, then –'

'Then he was *not* one of theirs. And you took that chance.'

I now had a very different reason for the Colonel's resolve to send Arnold back here after Alžběta had been safely got to England.

'I simply had to take the chance, Anthony, that I wasn't being set up myself. Then I had to contrive times and places for more meetings. And there was very little back-up to call on – other than a couple of times when I was able to arrange a watcher or two to see where Alžběta went and what she did immediately after leaving me.'

'But in the end she convinced you.'

'Yes. Though I did get some insurance from her – StB operational stuff, fairly low-grade, which would be useful as a bit of a hold, and helpful to our people back home as a check on what she would say to them. Once we got her there. Her real use to us was that her disappearance would add more pressure upon Dušan to defect. He was the ultimate target.'

At this I could not suppress the Philippian Aahh: 'So both William and Alžběta were in fact just the pincers to squeeze Dušan, put pressure upon him until his discomfort became so great – '

Susan half-stood, leaned across to kiss me lightly on the lips. 'Bravo, *mon brave*.'

The implicit accord we had lived by, not to speak to each other of our service to the service, had been rent to shreds and tatters. When we returned to our hotel room that night we lay alongside each other with all defences down, in a new accord, finally having learned that each of us, despite the service, had found someone we *could* trust. Without shame or rebuke.

In the remaining two days of our visit we were released to indulge in the delights of the city, visiting tourist spots, stopping for coffees or a beer, a snack perhaps, before a long and leisurely dinner.

'Why did you stay on so long in Czechoslovakia, Susan?'

'I was asked to.'

'By Sir John?'

'By Sir John.'

'But why? The business you'd been sent out here for, ensuring no back-tracking from Dušan and getting Arnold's lady out of the country, was done.'

Susan pursed her lips, gently shaking her head from side to side.

'There was a good deal of other business to attend to, Anthony.'

A question by way of raised eyebrows.

'There were others to keep an eye on, others who might be persuaded to drop a word or two.'

Susan stared intently at me, measuring I suppose just how much I could make of this by implication. I shrugged too quickly.

'And I did manage to get close to a couple of officers in those years.'

Said as an uncompromising assertion so that it sounded as a challenge which, by Susan's narrowed eyes, I could see that it was. Ahhh! that moment of understanding. *That* close. Close enough to share whispered indiscretions in the dark of a shared bedroom.

'Take it as a compliment, Anthony: I no longer have to guard against the guardian of *my* secret.'

Serving and servicing: to service in order to serve the service.

No more questions, Your Honour.

The afternoon of our last day in Prague. We were sitting on a bench by the Vltava river embankment, a spot from which we could take in Charles Bridge and Hradčany Castle on the opposite bank. Below us swans pedalled their sedate progress while a light breeze cooled the afternoon warmth of sun.

'Susan...'

'This sounds like another question about to come.'

'My last question, Susan.'

'I thought you had done.'

'No, no, this is a different kind of question.'

'You have had all your birthday indulgences, Mister Anthony Ashley-Chetwyne, QC. And more. ' Susan assumed a frigid air, head tilted back.

'It's one I've wondered about. And Sir John was absolutely no help to me in getting an answer when I asked him how you would get out of this country – '

Susan suddenly subsided, leant her weight against me, trying to stifle the start of her giggles, then turned sideways and pecked a kiss upon my cheek.

'You mean when he told you that, failing all else, they would get me out as diplomatic baggage?'

'Well, yes.'

'He shared that with me too some years after I'd returned. Though in a way I suppose you *could* call me diplomatic baggage.'

Now I was being teased, just as I had been teased by the Colonel.

'Susan.' One word, clipped, demanding. 'Your passport and accreditation in the name of Missus Bath had been used up by Alžběta –'

'Which meant I had to use the side door.'

'Susan,' with some exasperation, 'I know how you were able to get back *in* here – Simon explained all that, looking more like yourself, new passport, pseudo divorce, change of name, all of that. But I still don't understand how you got *out* in order to get back in.'

'Anthony Ashley-Chetwyne, QC' – the tone was of affected resignation – 'I have already told you. Had you been listening you would know everything you need to work it out.' She gave me a sideways look, clearly amused, her frustrating of me adding to her enjoyment.

'Now let's go for a beer. The one you seem to be so enamoured with.'

That last night in Prague we exorcised the final remnants of the past. We left the past behind by going further into the past, to the time before the troubling past.

I talked of my first meeting with her, the impression she had made on me.

'And do you know, Sarah – '

'Susan.'

'Sorry, a slip of the tongue. But you were Sarah then – '

'But hardly a princess now.'

'To me you are a princess still, Sarah.'

'Flatterer.'

Eyes wide, hands lifted above the table, palms upwards, I simulated the innocent man falsely accused.

Susan chuckled. Then, her smile subsiding, she looked hard at me. After a small hesitation:

'And you, Anthony? What about you? You've questioned *me*. Remorselessly, until there's no more to say. But you haven't said, you haven't told me anything much of *your* story – just the bare bones – even after we have been all these years together – what *exactly* happened with Carolyne and you? why did you not marry *your* princess?'

She let me take her hand.

'I lost my garland to a rival.'

'Do tell,' she said.

ACKNOWLEDGEMENTS

My largest debt is to Edward Lee who read the first completed draft of this fiction, recording his reader responses as he went through the typescript. His notes – once deciphered – allowed me to know his contemporaneous reactions, good or ill, at times page-by-page, to each section of the story. I thank him for his responses from which I, and subsequent drafts of the story, profited greatly.

It is a pleasure also to record my gratitude to James Gordon, Classics scholar, whose reading of a much later draft drew attention to two errors in my Latin. One of these inadvertences provided us with much humour and had something to do with onions – though neither of us can now recall with confidence how they made their appearance in the text of that time.

I am also grateful to Ron Smith for his reading of one of the earlier drafts and for his pertinent and perceptive appraisal. Apart from some references to writers with whom I did not know I shared some stylistic likenesses, he – as an experienced former publisher – provided invaluable criticism, advice, and encouragement.

I owe an apology to Janet Ferguson for a small deception in allowing her to think that one of the earlier drafts of the novel which she read was by another hand. The objectivity of her criticism, however, resulted in an initial change whose influence carried to other sections of text.

Finally I must acknowledge my debt to Colonel Jackson who, in person though not in that name, made his appearance in my office more than a decade later than the setting of the central events of this story. 'On behalf of the Home Office' his business, 'strictly on the QT, you understand', was something to do with the attenuations of security. Questions, questions, so many questions.

ECG

ELM VILLAGE ARTS PUBLICATIONS

is pleased to announce the forthcoming collection of stories by E.C.Gardiner scheduled for publication in Autumn 2019.

A young girl finds a Buddha and asks her father, 'Daddy, you know when you and Mummy made me?'... a young man who is unaware of the mixed nature of ambition fulfilled ... the sister who loses her lover and the younger sister who experiences the tremendum of that war-time loss ... a young man who fears his night-time visitors are intent on killing him ...an elderly woman celebrating the last meal with her husband as he dies his planned death ... a middle-aged man celebrating in song the one passionate love of his life...

These are some of the stories, from the humorous to the tragic, each told through a uniquely different voice. Some tellers of their tales are female, some male, their ages ranging from childhood to old age. Characteristically, beneath the surface words of their narrations are the hidden meanings and motivations of the tales they tell or hints of other stories which remain untold.

Several of these stories are planned for recording by experienced readers and performers and will be made available through Elm Village Arts.

To learn of the range of other productions in print and in music from Elm Village Arts please visit **www.elmvillagearts.co.uk**. To contact the author of *Follies, Fools, and Garlands* write to **elmvillageartspublications@gmail.com**

E.C.Gardiner has worked for various organisations in countries of continental Europe, and has held a senior academic post in an English university. Under an adoptive name given in childhood has published and edited non-fiction books and essays and articles in books and journals. Academic work was recognised in the English Association award of a Founding Fellowship.

Photograph of the author
by Youri Aleksandrov